Eve's Apples

Also by Lena Kennedy

Maggie
Autumn Alley
Nelly Kelly
Lizzie
Lady Penelope
Susan
Lily, My Lovely
Down Our Street
The Dandelion Seed
The Inn on the Marsh
Owen Oliver
Kate of Clyve Shore
Ivy of the Angel
Queenie's Castle

About the author

Lena Kennedy lived all her life in the East End of London and wrote with great energy about the people and times she knew there. She was 67 before her first novel, *Maggie*, was accepted for publication. Since then her bestselling novels have shown her to be among the finest and best loved of contemporary novelists. Lena Kennedy died in 1986.

LENA KENNEDY

Eve's Apples

HODDER

First published in Great Britain in 1989 by Macdonald & Co
(Publishers) Ltd

This edition published in 2013 by Hodder & Stoughton
An Hachette UK company

1

A CIP catalogue record for this title is available
from the British Library

Paperback ISBN 978 1 444 76739 1
Ebook ISBN 978 1 444 76740 7

Printed and bound by Clays Ltd, St Ives plc

Hodder & Stoughton policy is to use papers that are natural, renewable
and recyclable products and made from wood grown in sustainable
forests. The logging and manufacturing processes are expected to
conform to the environmental regulations of the country of origin.

Hodder & Stoughton Ltd
338 Euston Road
London NW1 3BH

www.hodder.co.uk

BOOK ONE

BOOK ONE

I

The Streets of London

Little Daisy Smith skipped down the street with the wind blowing her stiffly starched pinafore. Her thick black stockings were baggy and fell in wrinkles around her legs, but Daisy did not care. She was quite careless of her looks for her main concern at that moment was the position of her skipping rope.

'Salt, mustard and pepper,' she said with a flat intonation to her voice. 'Oh bovver!' she cried as the rope twisted about her ankles. 'I means vinegar, salt, mustard and pepper.' She laughed and twirled the rope triumphantly as she got the timing precisely right at last.

If anyone asked Daisy who she was she would be very open. 'I'm Daisy Smith,' she would say, 'I lives in Beffnal Green. This is our street, Willow Walk, and that's me muvver's shop, right over there on the corner.' At twelve years old Daisy had quite a lot to say for herself.

Willow Walk was one of those long, winding slum streets in Bethnal Green running towards Gardener's Corner in the Aldgate. These streets were made up of long lines of small houses, occasionally brightened by a few painted stalls and coster barrows. Even narrower lanes ran off the streets, each with several pubs and the inevitable corner shop selling everything from half a pound of cheese to a packet of hair pins. Almost anything could be purchased at the corner shop, and most of it 'on tick'.

Into those small houses were crammed big families, for it was the custom for couples in those days to have ten or twelve children, or even more.

Life was hard during those years in the 1860s. One cold tap served several families, as did the privy, which was just a hole in the ground with a rough wooden seat built around it. London was a grim place for the poor to live in and there were numerous homeless people who would huddle in deep doorways at night, wrapped up in newspapers or sacks to protect themselves from the bitter, inhospitable cold.

But in spite of the poverty, the public houses did a roaring trade and were open all day. It seemed that there was always money to be found for an alcoholic beverage.

To little Daisy Smith, so engrossed in her skipping in the street, the plight of the people worse off than she was not a worry. She lived above the corner shop which was run by her big sister Harriet nowadays, since their mother had become so crippled by rheumatism and had to spend her days in an invalid chair.

Daisy's black stockings did not get darned and her scuffed old boots were never laced up quite correctly but she was clean and free of vermin and, most important of all, she never went hungry. Yes, Daisy was a happy little girl.

Just as Daisy had completed another skipping routine she noticed a thin ragged boy walk slowly past the shop and swiftly pinch a carrot as he went. Watching him shove the carrot into the pocket of his pants, Daisy was incensed. 'Hey, you!' she yelled, dropping her skipping rope and advancing towards him. 'Put that carrot back!'

The freckled-faced boy was startled by her shout and after a moment's hesitation turned to run. But Daisy was having none of it. She grabbed his bony arm and yanked it. 'Put that back at once!' she ordered.

The boy winced. 'Let me keep it,' he whined. 'I'm just so hungry.'

Daisy was taken aback. 'Hungry?' she said. 'Ain't yer had no breakfast?'

The boy shook his head pathetically. 'None, and no dinner yesterday, either,' he whispered.

Daisy scrutinized him for a few moments with her big brown eyes. 'All right, then,' she finally said, 'yer can eat it. I won't tell nobody.'

The boy pulled the carrot from his trouser pocket and started to gnaw on it with frantic bites. He was obviously starving. And as he walked away, Daisy picked up her skipping rope and began to skip along beside him. 'Yer don't go to our school,' she stated.

'No, oi don't go to school at all,' the boy muttered.

As she heard the lilt in his voice, Daisy raised her eyebrows suspiciously. 'Are yer Irish?' she demanded.

'Oi am that,' the boy replied quietly, glancing at her sideways.

Daisy sniffed. 'I'm not supposed ter speak wiff the Irish,' she said loftily.

'Well now, you can plaise y'self about that,' the boy replied. He had finished the carrot and was beginning to quicken his pace.

Daisy was not going to be brushed off so lightly. She quickened her own pace and crept up closer. 'Wot's yer name?' she asked.

'Oi'm Jackie Murphy,' the boy said with a note of pride. 'Oi came o'er from Oirland tree weeks since and oi lives in me ould Granny's house down the road.'

Daisy's eyes widened. 'Coo!' she cried. 'Not at number nine? That dirty old 'ouse wiff all them kids innit?'

The boy suddenly looked deflated.

'Sure, that's the place,' he replied, dropping his head. 'We've just come o'er and we're terrible poor. I'm going t'get me a job down the market, so I am. Well, at laist I'll have a try,' he added with some uncertainty.

'Ow old are yer, then?' asked Daisy.

'Oi'm twelve, nearly tirteen,' Jackie replied.

'Same age as me,' said Daisy, spinning around on her toes. 'Let's be pals, and I'll pinch yer a carrot ev'ry day from my muvver's shop.'

So on this promise began the life-long friendship between Daisy Smith and Jackie Murphy, a friendship that was to travel from the wretched back streets of London to a new land thousands of miles away and back again.

In those mid-Victorian days, the summer evenings

seemed endless. The children played out in the street until well after the sun had gone down and the pavements had cooled after the heat of the day. These urchins never wore shoes or stockings. The girls were mostly clad in long ragged cotton dresses while the boys made do with just a pair of well-patched pants. But they did not care what they wore. They laughed and screamed at each other, played ball, skipped and swung round the lamp posts, or simply sat on the doorstep of each other's houses chatting and arguing. In one street alone there were probably fifty children so it was not surprising that when the weather was fine almost everything went on outside in the street.

While the children played outside, the corner pub was usually packed with their parents, the beer-swilling residents who occasionally fought each other after time. When the pub closed, there were always a few belligerent characters who had had too much to drink and who would provide further entertainment for the youngsters with their swearing and fighting until the police arrived to break up the disturbance.

Overall, life was not so bad, and Daisy Smith certainly had no complaints, especially now that she had her special new pal, Jackie Murphy. He was her secret. Every day she filled her pockets with his favourite treat, brandy balls, and then, as she nipped outside the shop where the boxes of vegetables had been laid out by her sister Harriet, Daisy would steal a nice big juicy carrot. Then, a few minutes later, Jackie would appear sidling stealthily past the shop in the knowledge that Daisy was waiting just around the corner ready to present him with her booty.

The children would then sit on the wall and talk, during which time Jackie munched noisily on the carrot like an old donkey. He was very appreciative of the food. After he had eaten a few brandy balls, he carefully placed the remaining ones in his ragged pants pocket. 'I won't eat 'em all,' he would say. 'Oi'll save a few for our kids – they never gets any sweets.'

'Why is it you are so poor and don't gerr' enough to eat?' Daisy demanded one day with avid interest.

'Because of the famine that's been going on since before I was born,' Jackie informed her.

'But what's a famine?' Daisy's sharp little face studied his quizzically.

'The potatoes won't grow,' replied Jackie.

'Well, then, why don't you all eat somefink else?' suggested Daisy.

Jackie looked sad. 'We can't live as we want,' he said. ''Tis not our land any more.'

Daisy was losing interest. She was sucking on a big sweet and now she took it from her mouth to have a look at it. 'Oh, come on,' she said. 'Let's go and play wiff the ovver kids. They're playing pork and beans.'

Jackie smiled. 'It's called what?' he asked.

'Pork and beans,' repeated Daisy.

'It goes like this.' She began to chant in a very loud voice: 'There was an old man from Botany Bay, What'd 'e 'ave for dinner today? Then you reply, "Pork and beans." '

The expression on Jackie's face became gloomier and his freckles seemed to stand out against his pale skin. 'I'll never play that,' he said, shaking his head. There was a strange defiance in his voice. 'I don't think you know anythin',' he shouted at Daisy. 'You're a very silly gel.'

'No, I'm not!' Daisy stamped her foot in temper. She was quite alarmed by Jackie's outburst.

'Don't you know where Botany Bay is? That's the place they sent me father.'

'Whatever for?' Daisy asked, lowering her voice and looking at him seriously.

'It's a penal colony in Australia,' said Jackie, climbing down from his perch. 'And one day I'm goin' to find him. But now I must go. I haven't the time to play with you anymore because tomorrow I start work.' He looked around as he told her. 'I'm goin' to be a barrow boy and save up me money to go and see me father.'

At this announcement Daisy's lip quivered and dropped but she wasn't going to let Jackie see how she felt. 'Right then,' she said as cheerfully as she could. 'I won't have ter pinch yer any more carrots then.'

Jackie shrugged. 'I'll see you around, Daisy,' he said lightly and sauntered off down the street.

After that day, Daisy often saw Jackie working the streets and pushing a coster barrow loaded with goods. It was clearly an effort and his thin legs seemed to bend under him as he went. She would see him in the early morning and sometimes very late in the evening but generally Jackie ceased to feature in Daisy's world of skipping and street games, and she quickly forgot how close they had been in those early days.

While Daisy played, Jackie slaved to help feed his large family. Living in his grandmother's house in addition to the horde of brothers and sisters, there were also two little cousins called Julie and Abbey. Their mother, Aunt Jane Kennedy, was in a mental institution. She had been sent there after she had tried to kill her last baby, when her husband had been tried, convicted and hanged in Ireland. So it was that these two flaxen-haired girls were now the responsibility of Jackie's mother, Rita.

Rita Murphy was made of tough stuff. Years of hardship and poverty had never once weakened her extraordinary capacity for loving and protecting her family. When Rita's own husband had recently been imprisoned and deported, she had fled to London with her family, determined to survive the famine. She was tall and dark and, while no raging beauty, she had fine dark eyes and walked those bleak streets of London with her head held high as a queen. A black shawl was pulled tightly around her thin shoulders and she took little notice of the indigenous residents of Willow Walk. They were all very suspicious of the Irish since they had been condemned as troublemakers by the illustrious young Queen Victoria.

And how Rita worked hard! Every day she would walk for miles to the big houses to scrub floors, peel potatoes and do any menial tasks that might bring in a little money to feed her own five children and her nieces. Now at last Jackie was earning some money, with Mick not far behind him, so there was a little bit more to survive on and perhaps life would brighten up a little after this terrible period of gloom.

2

Barrow Boy

In London's East End stood Spitalfields Market, an imposing place in the dock area which had served Londoners since medieval times. Early in the morning, before the city was awake, huge wagons rolled in having made their way up from the countryside loaded with fresh fruit and vegetables grown in the fertile fields and orchards of rural Kent. From Essex, in the other direction, lumbered the big hay wagons and carts loaded with sacks of potatoes or grain, all of which was deposited at the huge market at Spitalfields.

A little later the traders arrived to inspect and buy the produce, which they would then sell in the small streets all around the town. The air was filled with noise from the carts rolling down the cobbled streets, the shouts of the buyers and the young barrow boys as they sped swiftly to and fro, pushing their overloaded coster barrows out of the market to their various places of business.

A feudal system still existed in this busy fruit and vegetable market. The barrows were owned by various wholesalers who employed the barrow boys. These boys were all under age and on a bonus system paid only for the amount of work done and each barrow-load brought its own reward depending on its weight and the time it took to deliver.

These ragged and mostly homeless little boys often slept under the stalls at night in order to get an early start in the morning. For there was as much competition between the boys as there was between the barrow owners themselves. Rushing frantically here and there, the boys swore and fought each other all day long and everywhere in the market coster barrows whizzed dangerously by as one lad or other determined to beat a colleague.

To this cut-throat and busy life came poor undernourished Jackie Murphy, not yet thirteen. Big Ed Sullivan looked down over his vast protruding belly at little Jackie who had come timidly asking for a job. Ed scrutinized the pale, freckled face under the shock of dark curls, flattened by a brown felt cap. 'You don't look strong enough, laddie,' he said, shaking his head and walking away.

As Ed walked off, Jackie ran up to him and pulled at his jacket. 'Please, sir,' he begged. 'Oi'm strong, so I am, just look at me muscles.' He held out his thin arms, clenching his fists.

At the sight of Jackie flexing his little biceps, big Ed roared with laughter. Turning around, he looked at Jackie with a little more interest and bent down towards him. 'Just come over, 'ave yer, boyo?'

Tears filled Jackie's eyes as he looked reproachfully back at big Ed. 'Six weeks ago,' he whispered.

Big Ed glanced around and then held out his arm. 'Come lad,' he said. 'I bet you could murder a meat pie.' He led Jackie into a nearby tavern which was filled with men, noise and smoke. Edging their way through the crowd, Ed ordered a meat pie and two pints of ale.

'There, lad,' he said, banging down the glasses and pie on to a nearby table. 'Just get that inside yer, then we'll have a chat.'

Jackie munched the pie and gulped the ale thirstily, taking just enough time to draw his breath.

'Don't go away,' said Ed, downing his beer in one go and then joining a crowd of men with whom he drank pint after pint. Between drinks his loud voice bellowed out across the tavern to all and sundry.

Jackie sat at the table waiting patiently until the bar was almost empty. The pie had filled his empty belly and the alé had gone to his head, giving him a most pleasant sensation. At last Ed came back. He was very drunk and patted Jackie roughly on the head. 'Now, son, tell me 'ow's tings are in the ould countree?'

''Tis pretty bad,' replied Jackie and smiled. 'I didn't know that ye were Irish, Mr Sullivan,' he whispered.

'Ah well, laddie, we don't advertise it since the last trouble but, me boyo, 'tis where me ould heart is. Oi've been in this stinkin' town twenty years or more now.'

The two left the tavern and walked along together, big drunken Ed and thin little Jackie who related the story of his family's flight from Ireland after his father had been sent to Botany Bay and his uncle had died in a military prison.

'Ah, 'tis sad times,' sighed Ed, shaking his big tousled head like a shaggy dog. 'Now, 'tis to me own house you will come where we'll have a dish of tay. We starts early in the morn' down the market, and I've taken one too many and must get some rest.'

Jackie followed Ed through a maze of alleys until they reached a tumble-down place which looked no better than a shack. The yard outside was littered with parts of old barrows and piles of smelly socks. Inside the house it was dark and musty.

'Oi'll take me rest now,' said Ed. 'You can wet me a pot o' tay when oi wakes up.' He lay down on a rickety old bed of dark mouldy blankets and he was asleep and snoring within seconds.

Like an alert, faithful terrier, Jackie sat beside the open fire warming his bare feet and watching the large iron kettle come to the boil. He looked around him with interest. Books and papers littered the table and floor. There were two rickety old armchairs, a wooden shelf with a few crocks on it, and some fruit and a loaf of bread on the table. For a man in his position, Ed lived very poorly, and not cleanly either, decided Jackie, noting the grime on the table, but he stuck loyally to his post by the fire and felt strangely contented.

When the evening time came and Ed finally awoke, Jackie was there with a steaming mug of hot tea.

'Well, oi'll be damned!' exclaimed Ed. 'Tis the best mug o' tay oi've had in years.' He swung his huge feet to the floor and appreciatively sipped at the hot brew. 'Take one yerself, laddie, there's plenty tay and sugar,' he said invitingly.

'Well,' Ed said later as he lit up his smelly old clay pipe, 'it seems ye are a lad after me own heart and from Cork, did ye say? Well now, come tomorrer and oi'll give ye a start. 'Tis hard work and them devils will plague ye, being Irish, but chin up, me lad, no one treads the shamrock in the sod.'

So Jackie had his first real job in England. As far as Ed was concerned, Jackie was the blue-eyed boy. He got the pick of the work and often the lightest of loads.

The other lads raced him and yelled, 'Go home, Irish bastard!' as they rushed past, but at the end of the first week he got ten shillings in tips. Jackie Murphy felt like a millionaire.

It was extremely hard work from early morning to late at night but the more he worked the stronger Jackie became. He could now afford to buy a meat pie and a pint. He also gave eight shillings to his mother to help to feed the family for he was the grown-up man of the house. He saved to buy secondhand boots to wear to Mass on Sundays though bare feet served the best purpose when he was running swiftly through the streets with a loaded barrow.

Come Sunday, with his trousers well pressed, a clean shirt on and wearing his newly acquired boots, Jackie was lord of all he surveyed. He liked Ed and he loved working in the market. But most of all, he was proud to be able to look after his family, as was expected of him.

One day when Jackie was almost sixteen, he swaggered into Mrs Smith's corner shop to buy two ounces of brandy balls as a little treat for the other kids.

Behind the counter in that dimly lighted shop was

Daisy. Her hair was piled up neatly on top of her head and she was wearing a neat shirt blouse with a high neck. At first she did not seem to know him. She demanded what he would like and began to put the brandy balls in the paper bag without a word. Then she looked and squinted at him. 'Ain't you that Irish boy, Jackie Murphy, from down the road?' she said.

Jackie grinned cheekily. 'The same fella,' he replied with a laugh.

'Blimey, you've come up in the world!' Daisy remarked casually. 'I remembers when yer used to pinch our carrots.'

Jackie frowned and looked offended. 'That was years ago,' he said rather defensively. 'I work now. Oi've a good position down the market.'

'Good for you,' said Daisy with a cheeky grin, putting extra brandy balls into the bag. 'And I've got this shop now since our Harriet got married.'

Jackie was interested and lingered a while. 'I always come by this way on Friday nights,' he said, hoping that Daisy would pick up the hint.

She did. 'Come in, then,' she said with her wide cheerful smile. Jackie noticed that where her mouth curved up, two dimples appeared. Her wide brown eyes were full of humour.

'So I will,' he said, and he always kept his word.

During the next six months Jackie went regularly to chat to Daisy on his way home on Friday nights. With his wages in his pocket, he always felt rather full of himself and he was always pleased to see Daisy and impress her.

Sometimes when the shop closed the two of them stood chatting outside under the lamplight. Jackie could not help noticing how Daisy's nice shirt blouse grew tighter as she matured and grew more shapely. His blue eyes glowed as he looked at the little high bosoms which stuck out so provocatively. One night he gave her a swift kiss on the lips.

Daisy yelped and aimed a quick blow at him. 'You stop that, Jackie Murphy!' she yelled. 'Don't be so cheeky!'

Jackie glanced at her sideways and smiled. 'Come for a walk on Saturday night?'

Daisy nodded gleefully, her outrage forgotten. 'Yeh! I'll meet you round the corner.'

And so their young love affair began. Every Saturday night Daisy quietly shut up the shop and called out to her mother: 'Won't be long, Muvver, just goin' for a walk.'

Her poor mother, confined to a wheelchair, could only fuss and bluster about not staying out late. Then Jackie and Daisy would walk hand in hand down to the quiet area where the factories were all closed and silent for the weekend. It was here they learned and shared the secrets of life as Jackie fondled her high bosoms and pressed her close to him, while Daisy's lips parted in passion. It was a long hot summer and their love was young and very sweet. Neither could have wanted anything or anyone else, Daisy was Jackie's girl, and the one he would love for almost all of his life.

Daisy's mother was not pleased and she grumbled

at Daisy. 'Now you stay away from that Irish lad,' she would warn. 'Bloomin' trouble, they is. An' wot time did yer get in last night? Slept in me chair, I did. Didn't have nobody ter 'help me inter me bed.'

'Sorry, Muvver,' mumbled Daisy. She felt uncomfortable because she was already full of guilt because of the sex complications between her and Jackie. It wasn't as heavenly as she had hoped, but no one was ever going to turn her against him.

When sister Harriet came visiting one day with her new Sunday School teacher husband, she was concerned to hear what was going on. 'Daisy,' she said, 'that boy Jackie is a Roman Catholic and they are the worst. They says prayers to idols, they does.'

'Oh, shut yer big mouff!' sniffed Daisy. 'I'm old 'nuff to know me own mind.'

'You'll get in the family way and then whose goin' to mind the shop and take care of Muvver?' demanded Harriet.

'That's your worry,' replied Daisy. 'Anyway, I'm getting married as soon as I'm eighteen.'

'Yer can't,' jeered Harriet. 'Got to wait till yer twenty-one.'

'Well, I won't *see*,' said Daisy. 'I'll run away.'

This familiar squabble began every time the two sisters saw each other but Jackie and Daisy ignored Harriet and continued to grow very close.

Daisy was now a head taller than Jackie and her body big and muscular. Her skin was white and her hair a deep shining auburn. At seventeen she was a real beauty and many men looked in her direction. But

Daisy Smith had eyes for no one but her successful barrow boy, lively little Jackie Murphy.

Jackie was now Ed's right-hand man. He had taken charge of the barrows, checked the loads and paid out the wages. Ed had become obese in the past few years; he sat outside the tavern, his beer jug beside him, his old nose quite red and bulbous. He wore a greasy leather waistcoat and a hard square-topped hat. Around his fat neck he always wore a bright green kerchief.

By the end of each day, chock-full of ale, Ed would start to sing rebel Irish songs such as 'The Fenian Boys' or 'Foggy Foggy Dew' which then resulted in him being pelted with bad oranges by rival barrow boys. Whenever this happened, Jackie would be there to defend his mentor, indulging in fisticuffs and delivering black eyes left, right and centre.

'Jackie, me boyo, yer me champion,' Big Ed would say as the boy escorted him home. 'And anything I got is yours when I leave this rotten world.'

That winter Ed was confined to his bed. Jackie's mother, Rita Murphy, went down to care for him and clean his house. As Ed sat up in his bed gasping for his breath, he would watch Rita's tall graceful shape doing the chores.

''Tis a foine woman, ye are,' he said. 'And a real good laddie is Jackie. There's money hid in the chimney stack. Use it to send me home to the auld country to be buried and the rest is yours. I already told Jackie that the business will be his.' Ed wheezed as he struggled to hold on to life.

'Whisht now,' snapped Rita. 'Don't ye be talking nonsense. Ye'll be foine when the spring comes round.'

Ed seemed to know that his time had come and would not hear otherwise. Then one morning, Rita arrived to find Ed's pipe cold in his stiff mouth.

Jackie wept for his old pal and benefactor. He was heart-broken to lose Big Ed but now also excited to be his own boss.

Rita pulled down a brown paper parcel from the chimney breast. Opening it up she found three hundred pounds. 'Dear God!' she exclaimed, as she finished counting. 'What shall we do with it?'

''Tis yours, if Ed said so,' said Jackie. 'He had no kin. He just wanted us to send him home to be buried in Ireland.'

Rita looked at that sooty bundle of notes. 'We'll arrange that for him,' she said quietly. She paused in thought. 'And then we will all go to find Da in Australia, for now we can really afford it.'

Jackie's freckled brow crossed in worried lines as he heard his mother's decision. His own thoughts were on his lovely happy-go-lucky Daisy. He was not at all sure that he could leave her behind. She was as yet too young to be married. But he did not say a thing to his mother whose eyes were shining brightly at the thought that she might be reunited with her beloved husband.

That night on the park bench Jackie and Daisy huddled close. Daisy held out her hand to admire the small diamond engagement ring which Jackie had just bought her.

'We will save up to get married,' she said, 'and move out of this nasty district to someplace a bit posher.'

Jackie stroked her fair arm and looked sad. 'Me ma

is bent on goin' to Australia to find me Da. I don't think she will go without me.'

'She's goin' ter Australia?' cried Daisy, suddenly very disturbed. 'You can't go and leave me, Jackie, I'll die if you do.'

'It's not easy to die,' said Jackie, rather defensively. 'Anyway, you can follow on once I've established meself out there.'

'Oh, but Jackie!' Daisy threw her strong arms around him. 'You can't go, I won't let you go,' she cried.

'Now, now,' Jackie soothed her. 'Don't be upsetting yerself, nothing's settled yet.'

They went to lie down in the tall green grass out of sight of the road. Daisy's long curvy body pressed close to him. 'Do it proper this time, Jackie,' she whispered. 'Then I'll get a baby and you won't ever leave me.'

'No, no, sweetheart,' cried Jackie as he shivered with passion. 'We must still be careful, I don't want to leave you with a child and I must go with my mother because I promised years ago that I would.'

Daisy's hips quivered as tears pricked her eyes. How cruel fate was to do this to her just when the course of her life had seemed so sure and clear! She turned her head towards Jackie and sobbed quietly into his chest.

3

Refugees

It was a cold and dreary evening in the dockside town of Bremerhaven. A deep cold biting wind swept and howled over the harbour. It seemed an uninviting place yet it was a true haven for the Jewish families huddled together in those wretched wooden huts, perched high up on the windy hill facing the cold grey North Sea. For here were gathered the refugees at the end of their flight from Russian persecution. After the long trek through the deep snows to Poland, camping out in primitive lodgings, and the dark nights of terrible fear, they came over the border to Germany to this safe harbour. There, one could, if there were sufficient funds, get on a ship to America, the land of milk and honey, where a Jew had the freedom to live, work and practise his religious beliefs without persecution and where it was said that all men were equal.

Such had been the fate of the Feldamanski family. Now on this cold December night they all huddled around a small wood fire, coughing as the acrid smoke filled the room because there was no proper outlet for it, and the door and window were stuffed with old papers and sacks to keep out the frost.

In one large room with beds in every corner and a

central stove, Rebecca Feldamanski sat nursing her youngest child, a babe of just two years, born on that long hazardous flight from Russia. Rebecca's face was grey and haggard as she thought of that terrible night when she had seen her own friends butchered by the mounted Cossacks who were trampling the small children into the dust with their huge black mounts and wielding sabres as they rode into the crowds of escaping Jews. Rebecca had seen her own mother lying in the snow dying but there had been no time for compassion. Her husband Jacob had whipped his horses and driven madly on, out into the night away from this scene of carnage. His two sons clung to the back of the dray while Rebecca and the girls crouched in the back of the cart under the blood-stained straw. The straw was blood-stained because Jacob was a butcher by trade and this was the cart in which he had transported his meat. In the heat of the moment, as they had to flee for their lives, he had no time to think about changing the straw. He had watched the Cossacks raid and burn his shop and kill his mother-in-law, but he had managed to grab hold of his family and flee. He had left behind all his possessions, but that did not matter. What was important was the fact that he had his precious family with him now.

Through the dark night while fires raged all around them, they sped over the border into Poland, yet even there they were not safe, so on and on the long trek continued into Germany. Cold and hungry, but determined, they pressed on after the birth of the child.

The little child on Rebecca's lap wailed continuously.

There was yellow pus in her eyes and her button nose was raw with cold. Rebecca stared at the smoky flames and listened to her husband and sons who were sitting at the rough wooden table holding a discussion.

Rebecca's eldest daughter, tall dark Rosa, served the men onion soup in wooden bowls while the smaller fair Ruth stood at the other end of the table hacking off bits of rye bread with a large knife.

'Be careful, Ruth,' warned her mother. 'Don't cut your hand with that knife, and see that there is a piece for everyone.'

Ruth's golden hair hung over her eyes. Occasionally she wiped the dewdrop from her nose with the back of her hand.

'Blow your nose or it will drip in the food,' ordered Rosa, throwing a napkin at her.

Still the baby on Rebecca's lap cried, and still Jacob and his two sons sat talking in hushed voices. Maxi was eighteen and Yossel fifteen. They all looked extremely tired, having worked at the dockside all day unloading salt and carrying sacks of grain. They were discussing money and how much they had to earn and save to enable them to get to America.

'We give the agent the last payment tomorrow,' said Jacob. 'Then we must leave immediately, for that agent is a rogue and will in no time confiscate our money if he can. We must be very careful. The Walochoskis and the Kolaskis are booked on the *Columbus* which is sailing next week. I will try to get us aboard her tomorrow. It will not be easy and there is the added problem of the babe.'

The baby had no proper name or papers because she had been born while the family had been on the move from Russia. She was a true refugee. She was a sickly child and since her birth the Rabbi had mumbled the burial service over her several times but on each occasion, as if by a miracle, the child survived.

Since this child was female, she was not considered important to the already struggling Jewish family but Rebecca loved her poor little sickly babe and sat for many hours nursing her. She was a very pretty little thing with bright red hair and blue eyes but her tongue frequently lolled out of her mouth and she was subject to terrible tantrums of screaming. To this poor family couped up in one room in a wooden hut in a refugee camp, such a baby was a true burden.

Everyone had to work hard for very little pay. They rose with the dawn, the girls set out for the fields and to do housework, and the men went to the dockside. Every penny that anyone made was saved for their future journey to the Americas.

The Feldamanskis had been working and saving for a long time. This was the second year they had waited at Bremerhaven and in that time had seen many ships loaded with immigrants sail away for the New World.

Still the Jews fled from the pogroms and crowded into the refugee camp to live in dire poverty. The only way they could tolerate the disgusting conditions was to live with one goal in mind: to sail to America.

The Germans in Bremerhaven were hostile and did not want them there. There was no place left to hide for the exodus of Jews from Europe was beyond belief.

In that smoky hut, the child quietened and the men mumbled. Ruth and Rosa came to sit around the fire, knitting warm stockings. In that cold climate they were much needed.

''Tis the baby who worries me,' said Jacob.

Maxi nodded.

'I heard only yesterday,' he said, 'how a family had to stay behind because one of them did not pass the medical examination.'

Jacob shook his big shaggy head. Bits of the onion soup clung to his thick beard. 'I heard that also.'

Rebecca stared anxiously at them. 'The babe will be all right in a day or so. It is just the measles, she is recovering.'

'We can't wait that long, mother,' replied Maxi.

Little Yossel looked very sad and the men began to whisper once more. 'Tomorrow I will make arrangements with the captain and the German authorities. We cannot afford to miss the *Columbus*. She is a good ship and is going to England first. Then we get across the Atlantic from a place called Liverpool.'

'We will have to leave you off with Uncle Harry in London, Maxi,' said Jacob. 'He wishes to take you into his business, so we must not miss such an opportunity.'

'I will not like to let you go on alone,' said Maxi, 'but as you say, it is kind of Uncle Harry to take me in. He has a good business and has no children. I promise that as soon as I am able I will join you in New York. I have heard that it is the city of real opportunities.'

Rebecca heaved a deep sigh and laid the baby down in its crib to sleep. She did not want to split her family and she longed for her old home in that pleasant town near the Russian border. But that had gone forever now so she must face this long journey over the sea. Thank goodness they were able to leave this camp at last! She mumbled her prayers and lay down on her rough bed to sleep hoping that the child would not wake so that they could all have a peaceful night. But the poor little baby had a terrible fit and the camp doctor was called in.

'This child is very sick,' he said. 'Nothing can be done for her now. She is not long for this world,' he informed them.

Rebecca cried and moaned and sat up until the early hours beside the baby's crib. Jacob decided that he had to act.

'Rebecca,' he said sternly, 'we have all worked hard and saved our money. If we miss the passage on this ship that crook might run away with our money. Something must be done. The child will not be passed fit to travel tomorrow.'

'Oh, what can I do?' wept Rebecca in despair. 'You go, then, I'll stay with my sick child. I must. I am her mother.'

But this was not the answer that Jacob wanted to hear. He and Rebecca argued until dawn when Rebecca sat down with a bent head and slept the deep sleep of exhaustion unable to keep her eyes open any longer.

When she awoke five hours later, the baby's crib

was empty. The children were all dressed and what few belongings they had already packed into bags and boxes. They stood around her with gloomy dejected faces.

'Where is the babe?' Rebecca cried.

'Momma, she died in the night,' whispered Rosa. 'There was nothing we could do and we wanted you to have your sleep. She has been buried by the camp doctor and we are to be on our way today.' Her voice was cracked and faint. 'It wasn't possible to give her a Jewish burial,' she added sadly.

'Oiy! Oiy!' wailed Rebecca, rocking backwards and forwards with her hands over her face. 'My baby, my darling,' she cried. 'I don't believe you,' her voice sounded urgent. 'Tell me, Ruth, tell me, Rosa, *please*, little Yos, you tell your Momma the truth.'

Firmly the children picked Rebecca up and guided her out of that depressing hut to join the queue of refugees waiting to pass through emigration. They were all very glum but little Yos was the saddest one of all. Tears stained his cheeks as he looked at his mother for it had been his task to take the baby from her crib and creep through the night to deposit her in the snow outside the door of a Catholic Convent in the town. Now, hours later, he could still feel the warm little bundle in his arms and hear her screams as he had put her down in the cold snow and run away from her. He would remember that for the rest of his life.

It was six o'clock as the Feldamanski family sat huddled on the harbour along with hundreds of other Jewish families waiting for the emigration office to open. They could hear the bells from the convent ringing across town.

As the angelus rang out at the Ursuline Convent, a long line of black-clad nuns quietly walked down the path to pray at the church. Behind them followed the novices dressed in white. As the leaders entered the church, they noticed a little bundle on the steps. It seemed to move and a little whimper came from it. One of the sisters stopped the long line with a wave of her hand and bent down to unwrap the bundle.

'Oh, dear God, 'tis a child!' she cried. The baby was quite blue and stiff with the cold. The sister lifted it up in her arms crying, 'Make way, sisters, it scarcely breathes. I will take it quickly to the hospital.'

The little hospital was situated in the lovely grounds of this Ursuline Convent. There the nuns worked to give back life to this poor emaciated child whose body was covered with a rash and whose skin was dry and scaly.

''Tis a girl of a year or two,' said the sister. 'But she is so badly undernourished that she looks like a baby.'

'Oh, poor child,' they cried, petting and fussing her.

'She has complications from the measles,' said the Mother Superior, 'but from now on she is our child. She was brought to us on the Feast of Joseph and it is God's blessing that she will live.'

So this tiny unwanted Jewish girl was named Ursula after the convent order and Joseph because of the time of the year when the nuns celebrated the feast of the foster Father of our Lord. While her real parents were far out in the Atlantic in hellish conditions below deck as they sailed to a new life, their baby daughter was being loved and cared for by this band of nuns to grow up a strong, healthy and beautiful singing star. But now she was a little Jewish girl in a German Catholic Convent.

4

The Immigrants

The narrow muddy track which wound its way over the mountain was known to the local people as the old bog road. This track cut through the blue misty hills of Cork County to reach the valleys and lakes of Killarney's green lush country. Beside it a long shining stream ran down the mountain side to reach the wide flowing river where the silver salmon came from across the Atlantic, back to their own native waters to spawn, just as the Irishman who lives abroad comes back to find his roots in the country of his ancestors who had been dug out from that moist soil by poverty and aggression.

It was 1865 and the early morning dew was sparkling like diamonds on the hedgerows. Clad in clumsy homemade shoes, Eli Lehane's thin legs plodded up the old bog road. She moved very quietly and every now and then she glanced around her furtively. Over one bony arm she carried a basket covered with a red-and-white checked cloth. She cut a delicate figure with her woollen shawl over her shoulders and a long plaid skirt. Her hair was nut brown, her features and figure were small and neat. She certainly did not look her fifteen years.

Eli lived with her grandparents in a small farm outside the village at the foot of the mountain. Her mother had died giving birth to Eli, and her father, a foreign soldier, had gone away back to his own land once the Troubles were over. Eli had been happy enough living with Grandpa and Grandma Foley and all her grown-up cousins, until the recent fighting in the hills, prompted by the Irishmen rebelling against their English landlords, had sent her cousins into hiding. Eli felt quite lonely now as her relatives camped up in the mountain. They had spent the whole of that long hard winter in caverns, defending Ireland's soul.

As she walked on now, the sad strains of the Gaelic minstrel wafted across the air. This was the signal that the way was clear for Eli and that she could proceed.

As Eli rounded the bend in the road, she saw a small figure sitting hunched up under a bush holding a long flute in his hands. Whenever he placed it on his lips, the long pure notes reached far out up into the mountain peak. The man looked like a little leprechaun dressed in ragged green pants and perched there with his legs crossed. As Eli passed, he gave her a welcome grin. Eli smiled a sweet smile in return and he pointed upwards above him to where another figure was coming over the thick purple heather towards her. It was a young lad with red-gold hair which shone like burnished gold in the early morning sun. He was tall with wide shoulders and strong-looking arms. Otherwise, there was little flesh on him. He too was dressed in rags and wore no shoes on his feet.

This was sixteen-year-old David Kennedy. All his life he had known little else but hunger and terror. His own folk had been separated by fate now for four years. His beloved father had been shot and David himself was now on the run. While the rest of the family had gone to America, David's home had been with Grandma Foley, that is, until the troubles at the farm. After that, he had lived up in the mountain with the Foley boys all through that long lean winter.

Eli was now climbing the old bog road to bring sustenance to the patriots there, while down in the valley British soldiers were camping out in wait for the spring. They planned to flush out these last remaining rebels who had survived that last great fight for freedom.

David took Eli's hand and led her carefully through the rough heather over the rocks and crags to the hide-out. In a smoky cavern there lived at least a dozen men who sat around, guns at the ready, while armed look-outs stood high on the rocks above. They were taking no chances and even Eli was only allowed to go as far as the end of the old bog road.

The girl's eyes were moist with tears as she handed over the heavily laden basket. It was full of food. But its most treasured items were the letters to the men from their loved ones down in the village.

As David and Eli sat down beside a big rock, David stared hungrily at the basket.

'It's all right,' said Eli. 'Eat! I put in an extra piece of cake for you.'

They sat very silently and close, aware of the still

mountain air all around them. Suddenly there was heard a shrill whistle from above.

'The way is clear now, Eli,' said David, 'I'll see you tomorrow.'

Slowly, the girl started down the path, passing the minstrel boy who still played his sad song: 'Forced from your home, Here I was born, To roam the world. Helpless and forlorn. Eric Mavournem, *alan leat go brah.*'

Once past, Eli pulled her shawl tight about her shoulders and hurried on back home.

As she came in sight of the farm she started. She knew that something terrible was happening. Trembling uncontrollably, she hid behind a rock and watched the urgent activity of the soldiers down in the valley. Suddenly a shot rang out and then a cry of terror. Neither sound was new to her. Controlling her panic, she raced back up the mountain path and gasped breathlessly to the minstrel boy: 'They are attacking our farm!'

The minstrel leaped up and gave three blasts on his flute. Turning to Eli, he pointed to where she was standing. 'Stay here,' he said.

Eli ignored him. Turning around, she began to run quickly down that steep mountain road, down to Grandpa and Grandma, whom she could see being brutally manhandled by the soldiers. Grandma was on her knees by the farmhouse door begging the soldiers to be merciful.

As Eli drew near, she could hear what was being said.

'Get up, old woman!' the sergeant ordered, pushing her with his boot. 'The lease on this farm has expired. Your sons are rebels and the landlord will not renew the lease.'

'Oh dear God, where will we go?' cried Grandma.

'That's not my business,' sneered the sergeant. 'Out!' He gave the frail old woman an extra kick in the side and sent her sprawling on the ground.

With a little cry of rage, Eli suddenly came rushing in, attacking the sergeant with her teeth and nails, grabbing at his long hair and screeching like a banshee.

The man spun round in one quick movement and crashed the butt of his gun into the girl's face. Eli dropped like a stone and lay unconscious on the blood-spattered floor.

The sergeant then kicked Eli and her grandmother aside and proceeded to wreck the farm, smashing furniture, letting the animals loose and setting fire to the barn.

When Eli finally regained consciousness, she was in a farm cart driven by a neighbour. Alongside poor Grandma lay weeping and Grandpa sat with his grizzly head in hands. The little farm had been the work of a lifetime and now it was wrecked. There was nothing left.

The neighbour took them to a poor little shack in the village and placed them in the care of a kind couple who bathed Eli's face and gently tended Grandma. The village priest came to pray with them but a feeling of hopelessness prevailed. The Foleys were honoured folk in the area. They had provided food for all the villagers during the famine and did not deserve to be treated in such a way, beaten up and deprived of their beloved home.

As they lay on the rough earth floor of the shack that night, the sound of gun fire cracked through the night air. The priest suddenly appeared and whispered in Grandpa's ear. Quickly they were all hustled out into the night and bundled back into the farm cart. The cart then rumbled on through the night down dark winding lanes until they reached the city of Cork and Mary Wood's house on the coal quay.

Mary Wood was Grandma's and Grandpa's eldest daughter, so they knew they were safe in this neat but impoverished home.

Mary was very welcoming and matter-of-fact. 'We must all stick together in these troubled times,' she said.

But Grandma was feeling the strain and her control was breaking down. 'But the boys, my dear boys. What happened to them?' she wept.

'Now, stop this worryin',' Mary replied kindly. 'We will soon get news of them. Someone will soon get news of them. Someone will let us know.'

That night Eli slept with her cousin Bluebell in a soft clean bed. Although she was comfortable, she tossed and turned as her thoughts returned over and over again to David Kennedy up there on the cold mountainside. She prayed many times that he was safe.

'I am so worried about David Kennedy,' she

confided to Bluebell. 'Do you know, I think I'm in love with him,' she added with a blush.

Bluebell sniffed. She was even more matter-of-fact than her mother. 'Well, you are silly enough to be,' she grunted, and turned on her side to sleep.

Mary Wood was a widow. She sold vinegar and coals from the back door of her small house behind the quay and rented a fair bit of land further down the road where she kept pigs. Mary was the astute businesswoman of the family. Her husband, Tom, had gone off to be an English soldier and got himself killed in India, so Mary's loyalties were somewhat divided. Her heart was here with her family but her head was with the local authorities who issued permits for trading. They regarded Mary as a loyal Anglo-Irish widow but there was more in Mary than met the eye. It was in her house that the Fenian boys gathered to drink her poteen, plots were hatched, news transmitted. But often, when there was a curfew and the armed soldiers patrolled the street, Mary would put her curly head out of the top of the window and smile at them.

'Put in your bloody head or I'll shoot it off,' a soldier would holler.

'Well now,' Mary would say sweetly, 'then 'tis unable ye are to drink a nice cup of tay I've made for ye.' And no one would suspect her of anything.

A week later came news of the troubles out in Bantree. Apparently the boys had come down from the mountain during the night and attacked the soldiers' camp. There had been a lot of bloodshed and several of the boys had been killed. Miraculously, however, the Foley brothers, Dave and Dan, had managed to escape with Mylo Dowdy who had been wounded. Most of the others, including David Kennedy, were now prisoners in Dublin Gaol.

That night, in response to the news, friends and relations of the Foleys gathered in Mary Wood's house to sup her home-made poteen. They were all relieved to hear that Dave and Dan had survived and escaped. David Kennedy, although a prisoner, was not harmed. Eli had said prayers of thanks more than once for this very fact.

The conversation turned, as always, to the future. ''Tis becoming a very hard contree to live in,' said Mary. 'If it were not for me small business I got here, I'd go to me sister Lily out in America, so I would.'

Grandpa looked throughtfully at Eli whose pale face was still badly bruised. ''Tis a great thought,' he said. 'Sure, this is no place for the young folk. Ireland doesn't belong to the Irish no more.'

So that night the seeds were sown for the entire family to emigrate to a new land.

As the year went by, more and more refugees gathered down at the quayside waiting for passage to America. They slept out in the streets and in the fields, holding on to their few possessions with them, making the most of their little store of money so as to be able to pay their way to America once their fare was paid.

Mary scrounged flour and yeast from the military camp and made homemade bread which she sold cheaply to the hungry wayfarers, while Eli was put to good use, going with her cousins, Bluebell and Marion, to feed the pigs every day. Each time they passed the British soldiers on guard, they did not dare to look in their direction, for these were lonely boys far away from home and this trio of Irish colleens were more than good to look at.

It was a strictly observed rule that there should be no fraternising with the foreign soldiers. Ireland was once more under the hated English military yoke and 'Freedom for old Ireland' was the cry of the oppressed people.

Thousands, they were, those queuing up for passages to foreign parts, huge families to be packed into coffin ships – so called because they were old hulks that could not cope with the stormy Atlantic or the overcrowding. Many people died on them, never to reach that other land. Disease and starvation were rife. Yet still the emigration went on as the Irish were forced to flee their emerald isle.

Eli's family was now waiting for news of Dave and Dan Foley who, it was reported, had sailed to Liverpool and were now on their way to New York. This had been great news for Grandpa and cheered him up no end. He had got himself a job in the coal quay carrying huge sacks up the gangways of cargo boats. He was sixty years old and not as strong as he used to be but hope and faith kept him going and every penny he earned was put away for this grand new life of theirs in America.

It was New Year's Eve at Mary Wood's house. Behind the coal quay in Cork city, voices were lowered to a hushed whisper as Mary closed the shutters and bolted the door. Family and friends were all gathered to hear Grandpa Foley read out the contents of a letter with a foreign stamp on it. It had stood all day perched high on the old mantelpiece amid the tea caddies and the holy pictures, for all to view, waiting for Grandpa to come home from work, which he did punctually at six o'clock every evening. The air was electric with excitement. The young girls had stared up at this letter throughout the day. Eli's hazel eyes had been serious but her cousins' blue eyes had sparkled with merriment. 'You know,' giggled Marion, 'they say no one ever comes back home once they go out there.'

'That's because 'tis a far better land to live in,' replied Eli. 'There's plenty of space to live and work, men live in peace and all are equal regardless of race or class.'

Her cousins stopped laughing and stared back at Eli in awe. Wasn't she always the wise one, little Eli?

At last they heard Grandpa trudging down the lane. He looked very tired and with bowed shoulders he paused to put his head under the pump in the back yard and to wash his hands. Then the tall figure bent his grey head to enter the low portals of Mary's house and come into that welcoming room with its huge fireplace and shining crocks on the dresser.

'Whisht,' said Mary with authority. 'I'll tell him.'

Grandma Foley stirred in the one and only easy chair. She put down her rosary beads which nowadays she constantly clutched in her heavily veined hands and looked gravely at Grandpa as Mary stepped forward, a beaming smile on her face. She handed him the envelope.

'Oh, thank the dear God!' cried Grandpa as he took hold of the letter. A smile lighted up his grey face.

'Well now,' he said, 'all be seated and I will try to read it out to you.' He felt in his waistcoat pocket for his old pair of steel-rimmed spectacles. 'Well now, me ould eyes are not what they were, nor is me readin' for that matter, but sure I will do me best.'

He sat down at the table and cleared his throat. Mary rushed to move the kettle off the hob so as not to have any disturbance from that old iron kettle which bubbled and boiled all through the day.

At last there was complete silence. All eyes were focussed on Grandpa as he slowly and ponderously read out the letter in his rich Irish brogue.

Dear Mama and Papa,

We, your loving sons Dan and Dave send you greetings and pray that you are well. We have at last reached New York. It was not an easy voyage, so we say to you, make sure that you get a good ship if you want to come over.

We are going out west to work on the new railroad but Mylo Dowdy who came over with us is staying in New York where he is working in a bar. He will wait for you and help you through the immigration, that is also not easy.

We pray each night that you are safe and well and away from the trouble out in the hills. Please God we

will all meet again. This is a good country, and a man
can make a good living.

    God bless Ireland, and God keep you safe.
    Your loving sons,
    Dave and Dan.

Tears coursed down Grandpa's wrinkled face and
his voice choked as he read the last line. Grandma
began to sob.

'Be Jasus,' cried Mary, springing to her feet. ''Tis
not a wake, now. The boys are safe so let's have a drink
and celebrate.'

Bluebell got out the glasses and the poteen for the
older folk and the elderberry wine for the girls, and
they toasted the health of the boys.

'This is a very great day,' said Grandpa. 'And by the
springtime we will all be off to the grand new
country.'

Eli's eyes filled with tears. She did not want to leave
Ireland in spite of all its troubles. And she was broken-
hearted at the thought of leaving poor David Kennedy
moping in Dublin Gaol. After all, she might never see
him again and that seemed too hard to bear.

In early spring, the celebrations on St Patrick's Day
were loaded with emotion as Mary's house was filled
with guests and boys on the run popped in for a quick
drink. Over and over again Grandma, Grandpa and
Eli said goodbye to the old friends and associates of a
lifetime.

When spring was in its glory and the moist green

fields were sprinkled with shamrocks, the old folk wept as they said a final goodbye to their homeland.

Awaiting at the docks were so many sad families saying farewell to each other and praying for the blood of Ireland. In this way, week after week, the youth of this unhappy country slowly poured away, all bound for a new land.

Eli was also there with her grandparents. Like everyone else, they clutched their bundles of possessions to them as they said goodbye to Mary and her daughters. Even Aunt Mary's face was clouded with tears this morning, while Bluebell and Marion hung around Eli's neck crying: 'You will write to us, won't you, Eli?'

Little Eli's pale face was screwed up with emotion as she blinked back tears. 'Yes,' she whispered. 'I will when I am able.'

The queue was slowly moving up on the gangplank of the old cargo ship that would soon battle its way around the stormy coast and take them up to Liverpool where the big immigrant ship would be waiting.

On the cargo ship, everyone was packed in very tight. Eli and her grandparents stood on deck and watched the fading shapes of Mary and her daughters on the quayside. Eli's cousins wept into their handkerchiefs while their mother waved frantically. Thinking that this was to be the last picture of her homeland, Eli kept it in her mind constantly. The sun was dropping and the harbour began to glow pink.

'We will stay above on deck,' said Grandpa. 'Then it

will not be so bad when the rest of them start to get sick. The salt wind will refresh us.'

So the three of them huddled in a corner out of the wind. Grandpa held Grandma, who was wrapped in a shawl and still fingering her rosary beads, and Grandma hugged Eli beside her.

The trip was rough and stormy and by the time they arrived in Liverpool they were extremely cold, wet and tired.

After more hours of waiting they boarded the big ship *Columbus* which travelled between New York and Liverpool carrying hordes of passengers from Ireland and Europe. Along with the Irish, there were many Jews from the continent, escaping Russian and German persecution. But regardless of where they came from, they were all bound for New York in the New World where it was rumoured that the streets were paved with gold.

Everyone aboard this great ship had to take their place in steerage, below decks. Each family was herded into its own spot, everyone was talking in every known language, crying and complaining or just sitting dumbly staring into space.

Marked on the ship's passenger list of the *Columbus* were the names of John Foley, aged sixty-two, Jane Foley aged sixty and Eli Lehane, aged seventeen. They were just one more family booked on their way to America, the land of hopes and dreams.

Eli stared in wide-eyed wonder at the other passengers coming on board ship. Many looked so very different to the thin scraggy Irish women. The men were heavily bearded and wore odd round-brimmed hats while the women were mostly dressed in black and had calm pale faces. They all seemed to gesture excitedly and gabble in a strange language. They were loaded on the ship with bundles and parcels and many of them had crowds of children travelling with them as well. They all looked tired and some were very sad.

''Tis the Jewish folk coming aboard,' said Grandpa from his view on the lower deck. 'God knows how they will get them all in, there's so many of them, poor devils.'

Eli watched these people as they trailed slowly in to their own part of the lower deck and sank wearily down on their allocated bunks. Some muttered and prayed while others wept and wailed. How strange they seemed to Eli, who was so inexperienced about the world.

''Tis like a lot of cattle, we are,' muttered Grandpa, 'but 'tis the best we could afford.' He lifted Eli up onto the top bunk. 'Stay there,' he said, 'or you might lose yer place. The powers that be will no doubt overcrowd the ship.'

Once the passengers were all packed like sardines, with a squeak and rattle of chains, the big ship started its engines. For this was a sailing ship with one of those new-fangled steam engines, and Grandpa was not at all sure that this would be such an improvement.

''Tis the law of the winds that must carry a ship over the sea,' he informed them.

But the *Columbus* carried a full sail and had the assisted drive of steam engines which broke down frequently on that long voyage. The ship would lie becalmed at times when the heat was oppressive and the drinking water was short. Then the steerage passengers would complain about the posh passengers in First Class who had good food and plenty to drink.

Conditions were awful. Only a few passengers at a time were allowed up on deck each day for exercise. The rest of the time they were all confined below decks, either cooped up in their bunks or sitting in groups. Many got seasick, some had diarrhoea and the smell below decks, emanating from the bucket latrines, was disgusting.

To pass the time, the men played cards and the women knitted. Family squabbles broke out constantly, and there was always shouting and yelling going on.

Grandpa was a man used to keeping busy and he offered his help to the galley cook, and in this way he got extra food for Grandma and Eli.

Sadly, it was these first long weeks that saw Grandma fall ill and begin to fade. Eli took care of her and seldom left her side. The only time she felt she could take a break was when Grandpa took her place. Then Eli would go up on deck for a short time.

One day as she stood by the rail breathing in the clean air, a young Jewish girl came and stood beside her. Eli had noticed her before. She was tall and sturdy with long black hair. The girl's mother was not old but was markedly small and frail, a sad contrast to her daughter. She sat huddled in one corner with a shawl over her head. Whenever Eli saw her she seemed to be weeping.

The daughter now came up to Eli. 'Hallo, I am Rosa Feldamanski,' she said with a friendly smile. Her English was comprehensible although she had a thick German accent.

Eli was only about half the size of this husky young Jewish girl. 'Hello,' she said, 'I'm Eli.'

''Ow ees you Grandmutter?' asked Rosa.

'Not very good,' replied Eli shaking her head. 'I am truly worried about her.'

'My mother sits and mopes. She will not pull out of her doldrums,' said Rosa.

'Yes, I see how she weeps so often.'

'Ve lose our baba se night before ve leave Germany. Zat ees vy she mourns.'

'Ah! I'm truly sorry,' replied Eli.

'Not much goot ees it?' said Rosa. 'Ve are just animals. Ve got to get on living not like zose up zere, born vit all.' She raised her eyes to the upper deck where women walked at their leisure, dressed immaculately in their bonnets and crinolines and holding their children on leather reins to prevent them falling overboard.

'Yes, it must be nice to be rich, right enough,' ventured Eli.

'Oh, I do not vant to be rich,' replied Rosa. 'I vant to be a human being equal vit mein fellowman. I tell to you, ven I get to the new land I make some of that lot pay.'

'Oh dear,' sighed Eli, 'are you a rebel?'

'No, just tired vit being kicked about,' said Rosa, and Eli laughed.

So began the girls' friendship. They met each day for exercise and as the voyage progressed they became very close.

'I am supposed to keep to myself,' Rosa confided to Eli, 'but I do like you, Eli, and I hope ve vill always be friends.'

Through the long hazardous voyage the girls shared any little pleasures they happened to come by, whether it was some fresh fruit which Grandpa had been given by a first-class passenger or a hunk of dried fish that Rosa had come by. The food on the ship was neither sufficient nor nutritious, so hunger was prevalent and they eagerly devoured anything they came across. And Rosa was certainly never concerned about whether it was Kosher or not!

Eli soon learned that Rosa had a younger sister called Ruth and a brother called Yossel. She had another brother who had stayed in England with their uncle. Rosa told Eli that they were not allowed to mix with the rest of the passengers. While Ruth and Yossel obeyed their parents, Rosa did what she liked and roamed free.

'Ve left our older brother Maxi in Liverpool. He is going to London to Whitechapel where we haff an oncle vit a good business. Momma moans and groans over heem too. I just hope she gets vell ven ve get to New York.'

'It is this terrible long voyage and the heat,' said Eli. 'I'm sure she will be all right, Rosa. I can't say as much for me Grandma. I know she is slowly fading, and she does not eat a morsel of food.'

That night Eli sat watching Grandma, as she usually did. Grandma's lips were dry and cracked and her tongue discoloured. 'Water,' she whispered. But water was on ration. Only one dipperful was allowed daily, and salt water was doled out for washing. Eli felt quite desperate and was sure that Grandma would die if she did not do something.

Late that night, she crept down to the place where the large barrels of drinking water were kept. 'I'll just dip in me hanky just enough to wet me Grandma's lips. Sure no one will know,' she told herself.

Bravely she crept along the dark companionway to the barrels. Standing on tip-toe she carefully lifted the heavy lid of the water butt and was about to dip in her handkerchief when a loud voice yelled out. The broad bearded face of the sailor on guard loomed over her. 'Hey!' he said. 'Pinching water, eh? I'll take you to the Captain.'

Eli cringed back but the sailor grabbed her arm and pushed his vile face near to her. 'Now', he said, 'suppose I lets yer orf. Wot treat yer gonner give me, eh?'

Wide-eyed and speechless with fright, Eli started to shake like a startled rabbit. She was incapable of moving.

'Come on, wot abaht a kiss to start wiff?' The sailor put down his rifle and pushed his sweaty body against hers. Then he thrust his face so close that Eli could smell the rum on his breath.

Suddenly, the sailor groaned and crashed sideways as a galvanised bucket descended on his head and sent him spinning. Eli heard Rosa's voice, 'Run, Eli, run!'

Eli did not wait to be told a second time, but fled like a soul possessed.

Rosa paused only long enough to dip the bucket into the barrel and was lucky enough to get at least half a bucketful of water. Then she ran down the companionway to join Eli.

'Oh, I was only going to dip me hanky in the water,' wept Eli. 'It was just to ease the dryness of Grandma's lips.'

'Now you can give her a good drink,' grinned Rosa, putting the dipper into the bucket and handing it to Eli.

So, dear Grandma was given a nice cool drink and, as Eli held her head, she whispered: 'Don't worry so, my pet. I will live to see the new land, of that I am sure.'

The following day the Captain came down to the immigrants' deck to give them a lecture. He told them that the water barrel must not be tampered with again. If it was, he said, then the guard would shoot to kill. He said he would overlook what might have been a childish prank this time but whoever it was, woman or child, they would be severely punished if it ever happened again.

Eli sat in her bunk with her head bowed. She felt thoroughly ashamed of her misdeed. Looking defiant and rather proud Rosa gave Eli a big smile and a wink of encouragement.

The Captain ended his speech by giving them the good news that they were entering a colder zone and the need for fresh water would not be so urgent.

As the days passed the weather worsened but the air was cooler and the closer they got to America the colder it became. When at last land was sighted people gathered at the port holes and up on the decks to cheer, amazed that in spite of the deaths aboard and the general hazards, they had indeed reached the promised land.

A week later they sailed up the Hudson. Manhattan was in sight and the real troubles were about to begin.

The *Columbus* sailed in and anchored off Ellis Island in Upper New York Bay. Once an arsenal and a fort, this island had recently become the chief immigration station of the United States. It was here that the *Columbus* disgorged her immigrants and then sailed on across the harbour to land her first-class passengers.

Feeling more than a little dazed and very light-hearted, the lines of immigrants stepped ashore. They were exhausted and travel-weary but full of hope until they caught sight of that grim island with its huddle of government buildings and long rows of wooden huts. It reminded them immediately of the refugee camp at Bremerhaven, the place the frightened Jewish fold had only just left. The big stone fort full of armed soldiers frightened them and since few of them spoke any English, they were not at all sure about what was going to happen to them.

Old Grandpa Foley explained the situation to Rosa, so that she could reassure her folk. ''Tis only a temporary stay,' he said. 'This is where they sort us all out and make sure we are fit enough to work. After all, no country wants a lot of invalids. So there is nothing to worry about, colleen.'

Each little family was bedded down in a wooden hut. It was miserably cold and the place seemed filled with dejected people strolling around aimlessly searching among the new arrivals for others from their own land. There were poor unfortunates who did not have enough money to pay the landing fee and so had to wait for their American sponsors who had not yet turned up.

"Tis a dreary place, all right,' said Grandpa, 'but it's only a day or so. Mylo Dowdy will be here to welcome us, of that I am sure, and I have sufficient money to enter the country, I made sure of that too. So as long as we all pass the medical there is little to worry over, Eli.'

'But Grandpa,' whispered Eli, 'what about Grandma? Will she pass?'

'That's all right, 'tis just old age, it's nothing contagious. We will be taken care of, don't you worry.'

Rosa arrived with an uncharacteristically gloomy face. 'Oh, zey are all a weeping and wailing,' she said. 'It seems if you can't get into the State zey ship you back home and they are refugees an' haff no place to go.'

The food eaten at the community hut was disgusting and on a small hill there were little lines of crosses in memory of those who got so far and no further. The place was undoubtedly very depressing. The next day the new arrivals all stood in long queues waiting their turn at the immigration offices where their papers were examined and most of their money taken. They were then sent on for a medical which turned out to be a most degrading experience. Men were sent off on one side and women on the other, and all were stripped naked while rough grubby hands poked and pawed at them. If some unfortunate was diagnosed as having a contagious disease, there would be a loud and distressing scene as he or she was packed off to the cleansing station inside the compound.

Grandpa was correct about Grandma. She passed the medical without any problem. And at last they reached the iron gates that separated them from the new land and stood looking through the bars like a herd of cattle as they waited for someone on the other side to recognize them. Then there were tremendous scenes of rejoicing as sponsors came forward to claim those they were responsible for and many tears of happiness were wept as families were reunited.

Eli had never seen such emotions expressed, not even in her own homeland. Wide-eyed with wonder, the seventeen-year-old girl stood beside her tall, white-haired grandfather. She looked like a child.

Excited by these momentous final steps, Grandma seemed to be in better health and good spirits. She spotted their contact in no time. 'There he is!' she cried. 'That's Mylo Dowdy!' She pointed to a large and red-faced Irishman who was coming towards them. He wore a tight-fitting suit in the latest fashion and a little felt hat perched precariously on his very large head. His great voice boomed a deep welcome and then his lips formed a large grin as the gates opened to allow the Foley family out into the new land.

''Tis a foine lass, ye are,' cried Mylo, swinging Eli up in the air like a small child. She felt quite embarrassed. 'Now come with me,' continued Mylo. 'I've a foine carriage awaiting. 'Tis a real treat so, to see ye lookin' so well,' he hollered in Grandma's ear.

'I'm not deaf, Mylo,' replied Grandma, drawing away, 'only very tired, so I am.'

Eli looked back to catch sight of Rosa and her family but she could not see her. In that crowd with that level of excitement it was not surprising.

In Mylo's grand buggy, they rode through the streets of New York. As they passed, Mylo proudly pointed to the East side of town where he now had his own bar. He had done well for himself, particularly since he had always been regarded as the village idiot back home in Ireland.

Although he was big and awkward and slow to learn, Mylo was a born gambler and had come to a thriving place to make money in big poker games. The liberal attitudes of the new world suited him to perfection.

The rooms above Mylo's bar were all prepared for the grand welcome of John and Jane Foley and their granddaughter Eli. Many of the recently arrived Irish families such as the Callahans and the Kellys came to greet them, and they all toasted each other. By the end of the evening they were drunk with beer and happiness. They could hardly believe that they were here, on the same soil as their beloved sons. They did not know where Dan and Dave were exactly but they knew that they would all meet up again soon.

Utterly exhausted by the ten-week journey, Eli was soon curled up in an armchair and sleeping more peacefully than she had done for months.

5

Down Under

It was nearly morning as the big ship *Rajah* sailed out of Gravesend. Dawn had risen over the Kentish Downs leaving a rosy hue across the sky, and a pale winter sun rose slowly over the Thames estuary. Jackie Murphy stood on deck leaning against the rail as he stared sadly back towards the shore. Underneath his cloth cap, held on with one hand, his pale freckled face looked troubled. The disappearing shoreline meant only one thing to him: that he had said goodbye to his beloved Daisy. In his mind's eye he could still see her, as he had left her, with the tears coursing down her tip-tilted nose and rolling over her rosy cheeks. For Daisy had wept unashamedly on the dock at the departure of her little barrow boy for foreign lands.

Jackie had tried to reassure her as much as possible. 'I'll send for you, Daisy, when I settle,' he had told her. 'You will be eighteen next year, and it will be the right age for you to get out there. Then we will be married, my love,' Jackie promised, holding her tight.

But poor Daisy could only think of the immediate present. Australia was a very long way off and next year a life-time. With loud sobs, she hung desperately round Jackie's neck and cried her heart out.

Jackie's mother, Rita, tall and imposing as ever, waited for this goodbye to be over. She had discarded her shabby shawl and was wearing a neat navy blue dress with a small bustle and had a tricorn hat perched on top of her thick black hair which was piled neatly into a bun.

Rita nudged Jackie impatiently as Daisy continued to prolong the farewell. 'Now get a move on,' she said, 'we are sailing soon.' With a proud step she walked up the gang plank with her trail of children behind her – five of her own and her two nieces.

Bound for Sydney, Australia, she had been able to ensure that they travelled fairly comfortably on the upper deck where they had booked two cabins. Ever since her husband had been sent to Botany Bay as punishment for his crime of trying to protect their home against the British military regime in Ireland, Rita had sworn she would go out to him. At last, five years later, she was on her way, strong, brave and determined, and her large brood travelling with her.

She walked across the deck with her head held high to let all know that she was a fee-paying passenger and not an immigrant travelling at the government's expense. The windfall from Jackie's friend Ed Sullivan had seen to that.

Now on deck with the coastline rapidly disappearing, Jackie felt forlorn and miserable as his mind went back over the passionate farewells with his Daisy the night before. His brow creased with anxiety. He had tried to be careful but he sincerely hoped that he had not left her in trouble.

The majestic vessel battled its way out to sea, shuddering and rolling as they sailed westward towards the north coast of Spain. Then the weather became hot and sunny. Adults lay in the sun and the children played on deck and laughed at the flying fish and porpoises. Jackie sat reading his books about Australia. He loved to read tales about gold digging and the great Outback of Australia.

Below decks, the steerage passengers were not quite so comfortable. Rita rather enjoyed this fact. 'Ah money, boyo,' she said to Jackie, 'it speaks many languages. I've been without but never again will I wallow in the gutters. They say there are great opportunities in this new land. I think the world owes us that much.'

'But, Mother, you have already made a big hole in the money by travelling second-class,' said Jackie. 'It will not last long if we don't settle.'

'Leave that to me, son,' said Rita. 'I've got a few ideas up me sleeve and old Mac the Captain knows a few people out there. He has been back and forth for ten years, so I am not worried.' Rita had become very friendly with the old captain and often had a drink with him locked in his cabin.

But Jackie was worried. He did not share his mother's carefree attitude, he was a born worrier and in all his eighteen years, life had not been easy for him.

Four months later a very travel-weary *Rajah* sailed into Sydney Harbour and her passengers were delighted to step ashore onto the new land which they thought was theirs to conquer.

The harbour was very crowded. There were hundreds of ships being loaded and unloaded and people and animals were everywhere. Their cries filled the air.

Crowds of men were waiting at the harbour entrance all watching the new arrivals being disgorged in the fervent hope that they might see someone they knew. Many were rough-looking men in wide hats and sporting long beards.

Jackie stared into their faces looking for one he might know. Could one of these grim-looking faces be that of his Da, who had been sent out to serve seven years penal servitude, and having done four years, then set out for the Outback and the gold fields?

Rita had always been highly confident that as soon as they stepped ashore she would find her husband. But Jackie knew different. This was an immense empty country and the chances of finding the one person they knew were very slim indeed.

Decked out in her best gown, Rita gave the captain an affectionate farewell, and then, with her crocodile line of children, she stepped ashore. Jackie trailed behind loaded with baggage and looking quite miserable.

They rode up-hill in a bullock cart on wide dirt roads. Shabby wooden shacks stood on either side but as they approached the town, the condition of the houses was much better, being tall and imposing and built of real timber. There were a few stores and numerous bars which were very full and noisy.

In her seat in the bullock cart, Rita sat like a statue, undaunted and as upright as a queen. Her children were all tired and they squabbled among themselves. For once Rita was not annoyed by the children. ''Tis that good-looking old Captain Mac who has recommended me to some foine ladies. So hold your whisht, children, for we will soon be there.'

At last they arrived at a long wooden shack surrounded by smaller ones. Their hostess was a Mrs Miller, a sun-burned little woman who welcomed them warmly.

''Tis from the ould countree, ye are, and very welcome,' she said with a smile.

Mrs Miller was from Ireland but her husband, a tall glum man who ran a big sawmill and was known as Dusty, came from Yorkshire.

The Murphy family were all fed and bathed and given the use of one of the smaller shacks.

'Call me Tess,' Mrs Miller said as she fussed over the children. 'With not one chick nor child of our own, it will be nice to hear children around the place.'

Jackie would always remember with fondness that first taste of Australia, with its friendly folk and the lovely clean mountain air.

They rested for a week but then they had to start earning some money. Jackie and his brother Mick were all set to work in the sawmills, and Rita walked into town to get a domestic job. 'Just until we get enough moeny for a place of our own,' she assured everyone.

But it was not easy to get a domestic job in the town. For some reason the really wealthy settlers did not like the Irish, but Rita soon got around that problem. 'I am from Wales,' she told them.

After a series of small jobs Rita was offered a position in the Town House, a big dwelling situated on the harbour road. It was a daily domestic job, cleaning, cooking and being generally useful. The pay was very good and Rita was rightly pleased with herself.

Mrs Miller's face dropped when Rita told her about the job. 'Dear God, Rita! That is known as a bad house, you can't work there!'

'Why not?' asked Rita. 'Shall I let me children starve because someone else lives a bad life? No, I'll go where I can get good money. I intend to buy land once I find me husband so I must save all I can.'

'Well, me dear,' replied Mrs Miller, 'all I can say is the children will be safe with me. The girls can go to the Dame school and the younger boys can work on the land. We will be grateful for the extra help, to be sure, but take care, Rita, because it's a wild town to be sure.'

Rita shrugged her shoulders. 'I've lived in wilder ones,' she said.

Rita braided her thick black hair, put on a big white apron and went each day to wash, cook and clean at the Town House in Sydney. It was indeed an odd place and known for its mysterious comings and goings, and its partially dressed young ladies who often lounged in the sun on the second-floor balcony facing the harbour. Carriages drove up late at night and scented ladies tiptoed upstairs with drunken simpering gentlemen behind them.

The owner of the Town House was a woman known as Pearly Ladell, an over-weight, flamboyant and

attractive creature, originally from the East End. She
had a big mouth which very often let out bad words in
anger if someone upset her but she was also always the
first to forgive and forget.

Pearly loved money, having earned her pile in the
gold town and now invested it in this huge hotel
brothel so conveniently overlooking Sydney Harbour.
When this tall attractive Irish woman, who insisted
she was Welsh, had applied for the domestic post she
had advertised, Pearly's deep-set sparking eyes scrutinized her. 'You're not one of them there Bible
punchers are yer?'

'No,' replied Rita. 'What's religion got to do with it?
I work to feed my family. Me husband's gone missing
since his release from Botany Bay.'

Pearly chewed her nail and said. 'Up at the gold
diggings, that's where you'll find him. They all end up
there and that way they end up in the Outback. There's
not much for a woman and kids up there.'

'Well, do I get the position?' asked Rita. She looked
at Pearly boldly in the eyes.

'Don't see why not. Yer look like the type to keep yer
trap shut. What about twenty dollars a month?'

To Rita this was a fortune untold. 'Right!' she said,
with a broad smile. 'I'll start now.'

The two women got on tremendously well. The rest
of the staff were mostly native girls, Aborigines, who
were sweet and gentle women with little to say but who
worked very willingly.

The bedrooms were always occupied but the guests
had always mysteriously departed before daylight.

What went on made no difference to Rita who cleaned, cooked and supervised the coloured staff with her usual cheerfulness.

In no time Pearly Ladell was dependent on her and delighted to have taken her on. 'Rita's a bleedin' Godsend,' she would tell anyone who would listen.

Pearly did not rise before noon and liked breakfast in bed. Rita always saw that it was cooked and served nicely. At midday, Pearly would get up and then she would walk around the town with a little dog on a lead collecting customers for the evening's entertainment.

Once her work was done, Rita would trudge wearily home to her family. Jackie and Mick would come in from the sawmill, and the girls back from school, while her youngest, Shaun, would come to greet her. Shaun was now the turkey boy for Mrs Miller. He fed the chickens and chased the turkeys back home. When Rita sat down at last, Shaun would come and sit on her lap, and Rita would feel content with her family in their first little home in Australia, a wooden shack in the outskirts of Sydney.

Every week Jackie wrote letters to various officials and once even went up to the barracks to try to find out news of his father. But so far he had had no luck. He also wrote long letters to Daisy, telling her about their life there and reminding her that once they had settled in a place of their own he would ask her to join him. Strangely and sadly, in all that time, he never received any replies from her, and he could not understand her silence but finally concluded, and accepted with some bitterness, that she had met someone else and forgotten him. With a long face, he slaved away every day at the sawmill saving up his money, determined to travel to the gold diggings as soon as he had a fair stake.

There were times now when Rita looked very tired. But she was happy, particularly when she would sit around the fire at night with her family. In her big white apron would be tidbits and sweets for the children and occasionally a cigar for Jackie, but mostly her pockets bulged with the coins she had got as tips. Every night she counted them out and put them into a big earthenware tea caddy. 'That's our stake to buy our own farm,' she would say, 'when we find Dadda. And I know we will.'

Come the spring Jackie packed his bag and prepared to leave. 'I'm sad to be going, Mother,' he said, 'but I must. When I'm gone, Mick will take care of you, I'm off to make me fortune. I'll travel the gold fields and maybe I'll come across Da.'

Rita kissed him fondly. 'I know you must go, lad. This is a great country and I wish you well. You know I'll be here when you return.'

So Jackie left his family in the care of the kind Tess Miller and her husband and set off to seek his fortune. He was excited at the thought of the adventures ahead of him but deep in his heart there was a dull ache at the thought of his beloved Daisy who had forgotten him. He felt like the loneliest man in the world.

Back in London, Daisy's mother held a letter in her crippled fingers. Twisting up her face in a sneer, she viciously screwed up the letter and threw it on the fire. 'That's another one of them there letters from that Irish boy. It came yesterday, and the fire's the only place for it.'

'Coo! You wouldn't 'alf cop it if Daisy finds out,' said Harriet, her daughter, who watched the paper curl up and burn.

'I'm bleedin' fed up wiff 'er mopin' abaht,' replied her mother. 'It's time she forgot abaht 'im, she's behaving very peculiarly lately. In fact, I don't see much of 'er.' She thought for a moment and cackled: 'I expects she's got a new bloke.'

In fact, her daughter Daisy was at that moment feeling very sad and sorry for herself as she strolled through Middlesex Street. It was Sunday morning and Petticoat Lane Market was in full swing. The traders shouted loudly at the crowds of shoppers walking up and down looking out for a bargain. Daisy was looking pretty with a long full skirt and a little bonnet with a feather stuck in it perched on her head. She went over to a stall with a pile of skirts on it. A young Jewish lad was serving. ''Ere, how about this one?' he said, picking up one of the skirts. 'That is good material, a tailor made these.'

Daisy gazed at him with dull eyes, and barely seemed to focus on his steel-rimmed spectacles balanced on the bridge of his nose. 'I want a big skirt,' she said. 'One with a large placket.'

'Oh,' he eyed her sideways. 'Got a belly full, eh?'

'Don't be so bloody cheeky!' snapped Daisy, ''ow much this one?'

'Want me to measure you?' he asked. 'If this don't fit, I'll make you one. I made these up myself.'

'No, I don't want you to measure me,' Daisy replied decisively. 'This one will do.'

The lad put the skirt in a bag and handed it to Daisy. Solemnly she went on her way.

The noisy, lively market usually interested her but today she felt quite down-hearted and barely noticed all the activity around her. Harriet had looked at her so oddly this morning, as had her mother, and Daisy was sure that they suspected her secret.

Inside her tight corset, the child kicked in protest at being so restricted. 'Now I've got a bigger skirt, perhaps they won't notice so much,' she muttered to herself hopefully.

In all these months there had been not one letter from her beloved Jackie. What on earth was she going to do? She could write to him herself but she had no address to send it to. Jackie had said that he would tell her where she could write the moment he got there. She wondered if he had ever got there and if he was all right. It was all so worrying. He had been away for six months now and his baby was growing big inside her. What would her mother or Harriet do if they found out? She felt so helpless and so hopeless. Whom could she tell? What could she do?

Daisy was lost in her daydreams as she walked through the Sunday crowds when a sudden tap on the shoulder startled her. With a little cry, she spun around to see behind the breathless bespectacled stallholder.

'You forgot to take your change,' he said, thrusting

the money into her hand. With a quick smile, he turned and ran off.

Daisy's face brightened with a smile. How kind that was, she thought. It was an unusual gesture and she appreciated it. The lad seemed nice, she thought. She reminded herself to thank him the next time she saw him.

Daisy walked all the way back to Bethnal Green to the corner shop in Willow Walk without stopping. She was dreading coming home. Every time she saw her mother or Harriet she was sure that they would notice the change in her shape.

Harriet was just visiting that morning and was cooking the Sunday lunch. Hot and sweaty, Daisy came into the room. She suddenly felt very light-headed and taking one look at Harriet who was basting a big beef joint at the open range, Daisy opened her open mouth to speak and sank to the ground in a deep faint.

When she came round the family doctor was there examining her extended belly.

'It must be nearly seven months,' he said to Harriet. 'How did she keep it a secret for so long?'

Harriet was very upset and red-eyed with weeping. 'Oh dear,' she wailed, 'this will kill my mother!'

But to the astonishment of both Daisy and Harriet, their mother took the news stoically. 'Oh well,' she said. 'One more mouth to feed won't make much difference. The poor little sod didn't ask to come 'ere, did it?'

'Well, Muvver, I'll help with the baby if you let

Daisy keep it. I'll pretend it is mine,' Harriet said eagerly.

'Right!' said Ma, 'that's wot we'll do.'

Daisy listened to this conversation sadly. It was as if Jackie's baby was being taken away from her already and she had no say in the matter.

From that day Daisy was kept a virtual prisoner in order to prevent the neighbours knowing. Harriet put a cushion up her skirt and told the customers who popped into the shop that she was pregnant and very excited about it too.

When Daisy had her baby, a lovely little girl, the nurse who delivered it in the parlour was sworn to secrecy. Sitting in her wheelchair, Daisy's mother held the babe in her thin arthritic arms and said, 'Why, she is the living spit of my Daisy when she was born. What you going to call 'er?'

Daisy sat up in bed and looked at her newborn babe. The sight of the wrinkled face and squashed features caused tears to pour down her cheeks as she thought of Jackie. 'I'll call her Petal,' she said quietly, 'because she is part of me.'

So the baby was called Petal and she was brought up in that close-knit unit of women. Harriet's husband Bill was so quiet and unobtrusive that most people forgot that he was there at all.

Mrs Smith made it quite plain that she intended to be in charge. 'Now, Daisy, you behave your bleedin' self and we will look after Petal. Remember now,' she said, 'she is Harriet's baby, not yours,' she added faithfully.

Daisy's brown eyes hardened. 'Please your bleedin' self,' she said. 'I don't care.'

But Daisy did care. She cared and she never showed it. But night after night she cried herself to sleep curled up in a little ball and hugging herself. If only she could escape to Australia and find her little barrow boy! But even if she had enough money for the journey, where would she find him? How could she find out about these things?

Every day she was kept in the shop and at weekends shut in the family house. She was like a caged bird frantically beating its wings against the bars. She seemed oblivious to her growing beauty, or at least not to care. The only time her serious brown eyes sparkled or a smile crossed her face was when she looked down at Petal who thrived and grew bonnier as each day passed.

6

Daisy

In that long hot summer of 1869 Londoners spent many hours out of doors. On Sundays they would put on their best and then *en famille* would take long walks in the late afternoon, some to church or chapel, and others just to stroll leisurely along the high road, pausing to watch the Salvation Army Band march by, to meet other friends and neighbours. Chatting in groups, they would stand on the street corners while their large groups of children played around them. The roads were quiet without traffic on Sundays, with just the occasional hackney cab passing by, and all the shops were shut. It was indeed a peaceful city then.

Every Sunday, Daisy was now forced to take her mother out for an airing pushing her in her heavy wheelchair all the way to Gardiner's Corner, round the pump at Aldgate and home again. Often she had to stop and wait while her mother talked with an old neighbour. Daisy could never do this without a sulky expression on her face and often she had to go and sit on a bench until Ma had stopped nattering.

Then one Sunday evening in Aldgate, a young man stopped and politely raised his hat to her. He was slim and dark and wore steel-rimmed spectacles on his long nose. 'Good evening,' he said. 'How did the skirt fit?'

Suddenly Daisy remembered, it was the young stall holder. She smiled back at him. 'I don't need it now,' she said, 'it's too big.'

He smiled gently and glanced down at her hand to see that she wore no wedding ring.

Daisy knew what he was thinking and self-consciously moved her left hand behind her back. 'Thanks for giving me my change,' she said coyly.

'It was a pleasure,' he said, and stood laughing with her.

'Daisy!' yelled Mrs Smith. 'What are you up to?'

Daisy said goodnight to the young man and went over to push her mother's wheelchair on its way.

'What were yer talkin' to that Jew boy for?' nagged her mother. 'This place is lousy wiff 'em round 'ere.'

But Daisy ignored her mother's remark. Deep inside her, she felt a warm glow. Someone had noticed her! And she had been so lonely since Jackie had left. She hoped that she would see him again.

She did. A few days later, Daisy was out window shopping in Whitechapel, staring with a smile at the pretty dresses and wishing that she could afford one, when he came out of a shop nearby.

'Hallo!' he said. 'Nice model in the window. They've got one your size in the shop.'

'Oh, you seem to crop up in a lot of different places,' said Daisy.

'Well, this is where I work,' he replied. 'Upstairs, I'm learning to be a cutter. What's your name?' he asked.

They were standing very close as Daisy answered and he touched her arm gently. 'That's a very nice name,' he said. 'Mine's Maxi. Now, if you would like to come in I'll show you some very fashionable dresses . . .'

Daisy hesitated for a moment and then tossed her head defiantly. 'Why not?' she said, more to herself than anyone else.

Beads of perspiration were running down Maxi's brow and his hands seemed to be trembling as he closed the door. Daisy stared down at him in surprise. This strange boy needed her, of that she was quite sure. 'Well,' she said briskly, 'come on then, where's all these nice frocks?' With a provocative gesture, she stuck out her firm young breasts.

'Over there,' said Maxi, putting his arms all the way around her, 'but be nice to me, please.'

So being Daisy she was as nice as she could possibly be. In fact, Maxi was so nervous that he would have made a hash of the whole incident but for her. They leaned against a bale of cloth and it was over very quickly.

Afterwards Daisy concentrated on what she wanted. She let Maxi fondle her fair body while she tried on the dress. 'That's all, Maxi, you've had your ration.' Ten minutes later she left, proudly carrying the dress in a bag. 'See you again, Maxi,' she called.

On the way home Daisy suddenly wondered about the wisdom of her behaviour. She should not really have done it, and she had enjoyed it! As she ticked herself off, she peered in the bag at her new blue dress.

Ah well, not to worry, she thought. No one else was to know about it.

But Daisy's trips to Whitechapel became more frequent and she began to look forward to her meetings with Maxi. On the days when he minded the shop, they would go upstairs, lie under the cutting room table and make love. Then afterwards there was always a nice little gift for Daisy to go home with. This way Daisy built up her wardrobe and became very smart, but her new clothes did not pass unnoticed by Harriet.

'Where'd yer get all these nice clothes?' she asked one day.

'Wiff me pocket money,' declared Daisy. 'Anyway, you can mind yer own business.'

'Don't you bring any more troubles 'ome 'ere, Daisy,' cried Harriet, who had moved back home to look after Petal.

'Shut up!' said Daisy, 'yer 'ave got me baby from me, wot more d'yer want?'

Daisy complained about her family to Maxi. 'I'm bloody fed up with 'em all,' she said. 'I'd like to run away from 'ome. Me life's not me own in that crummy shop, I'd sooner go out to work.'

'Come and work here, Daisy,' urged Maxi. 'Uncle Harry will give you a job and teach you all about the dressmaking. It's a good game, it is.'

'Would he really?' asked Daisy.

'Yes, I'll ask for you. I came here from Russia to work with 'im. It will be my own business later on. My folks have all gone to America.'

'I'd like to go to Australia,' said Daisy.

'Whatever for?' demanded Maxi, looking surprised and a little hurt.

'None of your business,' reported Daisy.

Maxi chose not to pursue the matter.

'You know what,' he said, 'you could pack in with me. I've only got an attic but you and I go together like nobody's business.'

Daisy thought this was a good idea. Her warm little body had got quite used to Maxi's love now and she no longer thought quite so often of Jackie. So, why not? She had nothing to lose.

So in an open act of defiance, Daisy packed up all her nice clothes. 'I am leaving home,' she announced, 'and I'm going into lodgings.'

Her mother's screams and Harriet's insults fell on deaf ears as Daisy proceeded to move out. She kissed and hugged the baby. 'Goodbye, little Petal,' she whispered. 'Don't forget me.' Then with a cold, hard expression on her face, she turned to Harriet and said: 'And you can shut yer face or I'll tell everyone that Petal's not yer baby.'

Harriet's face paled and she shrank away at the idea, while her mother shook her head meanly.

'You'll come to a bad end, Daisy,' Mrs Smith said.

'Good job,' snapped back Daisy as she swept out carrying her bags. She did not look back once.

So Daisy moved into Maxi's tiny attic in Whitechapel. Situated at the top of a big house on a corner, it had a view from the dormer window right across to the city. The smoky chimneys set against the light of the stars soon held their own kind of charm to Daisy.

Maxi only had a single bed but he managed to find a large feather mattress which they placed on the floor beside it. They lived on fish and chips and salt beef sandwiches, and made love frequently.

While Daisy was happy with Maxi, she did not give her heart to him. 'I don't love you Maxi, but I do like you,' she would say.

'Well, that's something to be thankful for,' said Maxi ruefully.

Daisy told him of Jackie and Maxi told her of his family's flight from Russia, for the baby that they had to abandon, and of the parting of his Momma and Poppa who were now in New York.

Daisy listened sympathetically. 'And how come you talk such good English?' she asked.

'Well, my sister Rosa and I went to a good school but then they banned the Jews from the university.'

Daisy was very puzzled by this. 'Why don't people like Jews?' she asked. 'You seem all right to me.'

Maxi sighed. 'Jews are the scapegoats of the world,' he said.

Daisy was not sure what that meant but she nodded sagely all the same.

Daisy soon had a job in Uncle Harry's factory which was in a big yard at the back of the shop. At first she cut off the cotton but soon progressed to being an ironer, flattening the seams with a heavy hot iron. She was very skilful and became very good at it.

'Is zat yer voman, Maxi?' Uncle Harry would holler. He was as fat as a barrel and very genial.

'Yes, that is the girl I love,' Maxi would reply, putting a protective arm about Daisy.

'Vocha yer want a shicksa for?' demanded Uncle Harry one day, 'vit all the nice Yiddisher girls about here?'

But Maxi laughed and replied that he had to have someone to practise on as all the Yiddisher girls were virgins.

This sent Uncle Harry off into peels of laughter but it meant nothing to Daisy as the two men conversed in Yiddish which she did not understand at all.

The three months Daisy lived with Maxi were happy and contented ones. She had pretty clothes to wear, lots of friends, and plenty of love. Now she was eighteen years old and fully matured. Her cheeks were rosy, her nut brown hair very glossy and her figure perfect. Her only worry was that she might get into trouble again.

Maxi was blasé about it. 'Stop worrying,' he said. 'I'm not even sure that I can make a baby. I never did yet and I've been having sex since I had me Barmitzva.'

So Daisy relaxed and stopped worrying about it. Life was good for Daisy, until the return of Greta Martin from Paris.

Greta was a very important figure, for not only was she Uncle Harry's second wife, but she was also designer to the most fashionably dressed of the day. Before the commercial use of a sewing machine, dresses were all made to measure and a lot of work went into them. Wealthy ladies liked to get their fashions from Paris, the heart of the rag trade. Greta, who had been born Martha Cohen, popped back and forth to the French salons to get her ideas. She was tall, very skinny and always dressed very flamboyantly. Her hair was dyed and in spite of all its false pieces never out of place. Thirty years younger than Uncle Harry, she treated her husband with obvious contempt but she was extremely partial to his little nephew Maxi.

This fact filled Daisy with intense jealousy.

Maxi's attitude did not help much either. 'Don't let Greta know about us,' he whispered as he went through the workroom.

They could both hear Greta's shrill voice echoing around the workshop. Suddenly, she appeared with a tape measure around her neck. Wearing a wide flowered smock and a pink mob cap on her head, she set about creating new ideas, beckoning Maxi to follow her wherever she went.

So while Daisy sweated over the big steam iron, her hair straggly and falling over her face, her blouse undone to help her cool off, there was her Maxi following the smart glamorous woman around like some lap dog. It was just too much to bear.

One night Daisy sat wearily upstairs with their supper in a bag. She was waiting for Maxi who was usually delayed by Greta these days. When he came in at last, Daisy burst into tears and accused her lover of neglecting her.

'Oh no, Daisy,' protested Maxi. 'I love you, I promise you, but I've got to get on in the world. I want my own business, you see, so I can look after you properly.

Then we will find a nice place to live and you need not go to work any more.'

Daisy was momentarily quietened but it was her love of dressing-up which brought her up against Greta in a dangerous way.

Sometimes when she and Maxi went up West to a show, Maxi would give her a new dress for the occasion. 'Pop one of these samples on, Daisy,' he would say. 'Who's going to know? We got to look the part, and we can put it back tomorrow.'

So wearing one of these smart little gowns and with a feathered hat perched on top of her curls, Daisy would swagger down the road in the latest creation. Sometimes, dressed in long trailing skirts with glamorous stripes and a bustle at the back, she would feel like a queen. She would strut along in a stately manner being careful not to drop the train, have a ball of an evening, be admired by everyone, and then replace the dress in the cabinet early the next morning.

One particular Saturday afternoon business was very quiet. Maxi had gone with his Uncle Harry and Greta to the synagogue while Daisy finished a few outstanding orders. Then when she had finished she went to the dress cabinet to look at the latest ensemble which Greta had created – a mass of pale blue frills, lace and organdie. It was in the very latest style with a frilled bustle at the back and skirt hitched high in the front. There was a dear little bonnet of the same material, and blue kid boots. There was also a parasol made in the same way, with frills and lace everywhere.

'Oh,' sighed Daisy. 'It's lovely, I wonder if I could . . .

I'll just borrow it for this afternoon to try out. They're all at church so there won't be anyone to see me,' she told herself.

With her heart beating with excitement, Daisy climbed into the outfit and then paraded in front of the mirror. 'I'll just walk down to the high road,' she told herself. She tripped lightly failed her. She stopped for a moment and then gave a little laugh. Drawing in a deep breath she held herself upright and with the little parasol held lightly in her hands she set off down Whitechapel Street.

Suddenly, out of the blue appeared a skinny figure who rushed at her screaming hysterically. 'My model! My Paris model! Get that gown off!' she screeched. 'This girl is wearing my sample!'

But Daisy had no intention of being shown up on the street and stood her ground. Giving Greta a good poke in the stomach with the parasol she marched on.

Greta doubled up and fell into the road, screaming in hysterics. Other women who had emerged with her from the synagogue rushed to her aid.

Now Daisy knew she was in trouble. Taking a back route, she hurried back to the attic, undressed and packed up the outfit very carefully. Then she waited.

Sure enough, half an hour later, Maxi dashed up the six flights of stairs, white and breathless.

'Oh, Daisy,' he cried. 'You really have gorn and done it now. Greta is raving mad. She has gone bloody berserk. Where is the model?'

With a sulky gesture Daisy indicated towards the box on the bed. 'It's all there,' she said. 'But I don't know what all the bleedin' fuss is abaht.'

'But you pinched her new Paris model what's goin' into the exhibition. And not only that, but you attacked her too!' declared Maxi.

'I never did!' said Daisy stubbornly. 'I just gave her a poke. I wasn't goin' to be shown up by her in the street wiff all them women lookin' on!'

Maxi wiped the sweat from his brow, and picked up the box. 'I'll take it back, Daisy, and do what I can to smooth Greta over. You'd better wish me luck. She can be a bloody bitch and you've really annoyed her.'

'Good job,' said Daisy, flouncing down on the bed. 'Who's she tink she is, anyway?'

Maxi picked up the box and disappeared.

He did not come back that night or the next morning. It was Sunday and Daisy lay in bed weeping most of the day. Finally, she got up and went down the road to have a bowl of jellied eels.

It was here that Maxi found her, standing forlornly by the jellied eel stall with the oil lamps lighting up her tear-stained face.

He walked her home with his arm around her waist, and he seemed very gloomy. 'I did what I could, Daisy,' he said, 'but you've lost your job and Greta won't give you a reference. It won't be easy for you to get another job now, so perhaps you had better go home,' said Maxi.

'Go 'ome?' cried Daisy in astonishment. 'Wot the 'ell are yer talking abaht, Maxi? I'm going to live 'ere wiff you till we gets married.'

Maxi sighed and looked at the floor. 'It's like this,' he said, 'we won't be getting married, now or ever. I am a Jew. So it's not possible. I love you, Daisy, I really do, and no one will ever take your place, but I have my own future to think about and it's not easy for a penniless Jew like me. I am so dependent on my relatives.'

Daisy's eyes filled with tears. 'Oh, Maxi, why didn't you say so?'

'I wanted us to be happy,' Maxi replied, 'and we were, you know that, but it's all over. I've got to do what is expected of me. I've got to go to Paris with Greta. She is going to open a dress salon there and she is the one with enough money. So what can I do?' He looked at her plaintively.

'Well!' said Daisy defiantly. 'One thing I do know, is that I won't go home.'

'All right,' said Maxi. 'you can keep this dump if you want it. I'll get a loan from old Harry and give you enough to keep you going until you get another job.'

'No fank you!' cried Daisy. 'Yer can stick yer money up yer arse, I don't want it.'

'Oh, Daisy,' Maxi cried as he tried to kiss her.

'Oppit!' said Daisy. 'Go now while yer 'ave the mind ter go wiff that scraggy old bitch, I'll get by on me own.'

Maxi put his bits and pieces in a bag and walked out.

Once he had gone, Daisy really began to cry. She wept her heart out for the loved ones she had lost – Jackie, Petal and now Maxi. For yes, deep down she had to admit that she had come to love him a lot.

For three weeks, Daisy clung on to that gloomy attic. But it was cold and lonely without Maxi and it just reminded her of happier times. The main problem on her mind however was where to get another job. Every day she applied to different factories for a job.

'Have you any references?' The question was always asked and always Daisy would have to shake her head glumly and go on her way. Work was scarce for the unskilled.

Three weeks after Maxi had left came that awful night when Daisy opened her purse to find it empty. She didn't have a penny and the rent was overdue. Daisy was terrified of the landlord anyway and recently he had begun to eye her suspiciously every time she passed his open door on the first floor. After all, the weekly rent of three shillings had not been paid.

Late that night, Daisy packed her bag with all her beautiful dresses and outfits and crept quietly down the smelly stairs and out into the dimly lit street. All she could do now was go home to Willow Walk and put herself at the mercy of her mother and Harriet. Much as she dreaded it, this was her only alternative.

Not many respectable women walked alone through the back streets of the East End in those days and certainly not after midnight. For vice was everywhere. Rowdy sailors from the ships sought out the noisy bars, while women prostitutes paraded the main highway and hid in the dark alleys whenever the peelers came looking for them.

A cleaning-up campaign of the East End streets had begun recently and any woman hanging about after midnight was arrested on suspicion of being a whore and would eventually end up at the police station.

As Daisy headed for home, unaware of any dangers the night might hold and thinking only of her own problems, a rough hand suddenly grabbed her by the shoulder.

She swung around with a gasp and saw the policeman with his cape and high hat, wielding a big stick.

'Ah, got yer! I knows yer kind. I seed her often on me beat. Now yer come wiff me dahn ter the cop shop.'

Daisy swore at him and lashed out angrily but the peeler blue his whistle and within seconds two more had raced to his aid. Then poor Daisy was literally frog-marched down to the police station and thrown into jail with the rest of the night's catch. This included some very drunk women stinking of vomit and urine, and two highly perfumed prostitutes who shouted and jeered at their jailers.

Daisy was very confused and could not understand what was happening to her.

'Tell us your name?' the policemen ordered. 'Have you a permanent residence?'

But Daisy shut her mouth tightly and refused to say a word. Nothing would make her tell them her name, not if they tortured her.

The whores passed a bottle of gin around and offered it to Daisy. 'Have a drink,' one said. 'You're new on the game, ain't yer?'

Daisy still would not reply.

'Potty,' sniffed the other.

'No, she's stuck up,' the first one said.

After that they left Daisy alone and she sat on the

filthy floor dozing fitfully until the morning and worrying about what had happened to her bag with all her precious clothes in it.

When she finally awoke properly in the morning, the sun barely penetrated the prison cell window. Daisy was by now feeling numb with terror. However did she manage to end up in this place, she wondered, over and over again. She was stripped and then scrubbed down with lysol soap, and pushed and prodded until she felt thoroughly humiliated. She was then dressed up in an old striped gown with a hat to match.

'She's clean,' announced the medic, 'but probably suffering from some kind of shock.'

Two more policemen marched Daisy off to a long room full of women all dressed in the same kind of garment. They were sitting at a long table in total silence.

Daisy sat down and then someone said grace. After that bowls of grey porridge were passed down the table.

Daisy sat in despair trying to swallow the sticky porridge. Lumps of it stuck in her throat. Never had she felt so alone! Big tears rolled down her cheeks, as she wondered if she should have let her family know where she was.

She had been charged with soliciting, found guilty in court and the penalty was two months or ten pounds. She had no money so it was two months inside after which she would be set free. Stubborn pride forbade her to ask for help from anyone. She would stick it out, they could not kill her pride.

'Keep yer eye on that one,' said the husky female warden to her colleague. 'She might be a mental case. Since she won't talk, we don't know how she will react yet.'

Daisy was given a bucket, soap and scrubbing brush and set to scrub the long concrete corridors. At first she was very diligent, believing that she would somehow get rewarded for working until the skin was rubbed off her knuckles and her hands were raw from the carbolic soap. But she soon learned.

A thin girl came and knelt beside her.

'Don't work so hard,' she whispered to Daisy. 'Only use the scrubbing brush when someone is looking. These floors don't need it. They bleedin' well get scrubbed every day.' She paused and grinned. 'Cheer yerself up, love, it's not forever,' she added.

Daisy soon learned that her new friend was called Sally. She was in her late twenties and she had a mop of curly hair and dark eyes. She seemed tough and very hard-bitten but she had a charming smile.

''Ow comes yer was on the game?' Sally asked. 'Don't seem the type, somehow.' She had a strange way of speaking. She slurred her words and rarely finished off a sentence. 'I've done a year in here,' she informed Daisy. 'Knifed a bloke, I did. He was a bastard to me, so I grabbed a knife and let 'im 'ave it. Coo! wot a mess! Smothered in blood, I was.' She smiled sweetly.

Daisy stared at her in horror but realized that Sally would not harm her. Quietly she told Sally her tale of woe.

Much to her surprise, Sally burst out in hysterical laughter. 'Oh, gor blimey, Daisy!' she cried. 'Wot a bleedin mug!' And suddenly Daisy could see the funny side to her situation.

As they knelt together on the cold stone floors or slept next to each other in that gloomy cell, a close bond developed between them.

Take me advice, Daisy,' Sally would say, 'stick it out, love, but keep yer nose clean. If they asks yer to go into the reformatory, don't say no, 'cos it's kind of cushy in there, they try to reform yer so as ter keep yer orf the streets. Never did me no good, mind you, I've bin on the game ten years now, on and orf like,' she giggled.

To Daisy, Sally was like a breath of sunshine in that appalling prison. But her story was a grim one. Spawned in a back alley, father unknown, raped at twelve and a prostitute at fourteen, that was Sally's life and she did not care who knew it. A spell in the nick was quite a treat for Sally; it was the only time she ever got regular food and regular work.

Daisy was now almost at the end of her sentence. She stood before the prison welfare board with her head held high. There was a line of stern faces before her, all bearded men and pofaced women.

'We are here to help you, Daisy,' the chairman said. 'You are a clean girl and very industrious. We are pleased with you. However, since you have consistently refused to tell us anything about your background or yourself, we hesitate to send you out there back to the streets of shame.'

Daisy hung her head in a penitent manner as Sally had instructed her to do.

'We feel that a spell in our home will benefit you,' he continued. 'You will be taught to live in society and get a good position when you leave here.'

'No, thank you,' Daisy muttered.

'But, my dear,' said one lady with a posh voice. 'We might even send you out to Australia. They need young women out there and you might find a nice husband.'

Daisy looked up quickly, her eyes alert. 'Australia?' she repeated.

'If you want to, dear,' cajoled the benevolent lady.

'Oh yes!' cried Daisy. 'I'd like that very much.'

When Sally heard Daisy's news she was intrigued. 'Why are yer so keen ter get to Australia?' she asked.

'To find my Jackie,' replied Daisy with shining eyes.

'Well,' said Sally. 'Perhaps I should try me luck out there too. I know there are plenty men out there, which means plenty cash. I'll go wiff yer, if I can,' she said decisively.

So it was that Daisy and Sally went on to the Arbour Lodge, a big house in the East End's Arbour Square, run by a regular benevolent society. The purpose of the Arbour Lodge was to take young girls off the streets and make new lives for them. In fact, it was not much different from the prison, being cold and clinical, and a real institution. Inmates rose at dawn and worked all day before going early to bed. They were taught to sew, cook and clean, and absolutely everything was done with a prayer for their better life, which still did not deter Sally from sneaking out to the local bar some nights.

After six months of Arbour Lodge, Daisy and Sally were given neat new outfits and each presented with a Bible. They were also given a hat box containing a spare outfit, and tickets for their passage aboard a ship bound for Sydney, Australia.

Two other girls from the Lodge were to travel with them. One had got religion and the other was a poor soul who suffered with nerves and muttered and mumbled constantly to herself.

'Oh dear,' said Sally, when she realized that they were headed for the same place, 'who do they think's goin' to fancy them?'

'We are going to a good position to work for a missionary family,' the devout one said sniffily and once aboard the ship they both stayed well away from Daisy and Sally, who were sharing a second-class cabin.

The old captain was a tough hard-drinking seafarer called Ben Morgan. 'How about a little snorter,' he would offer the girls once the ship got underway.

Daisy always declined but Sally made good use of Captain Morgan to brighten the voyage. She not only obliged him but also the mate and occasionally a passenger or two. Afterwards, she would take the coins from inside her blouse and wrap them in a handkerchief. This she would hide in a special purse. 'Well, if I don't like it out there, at least I've got me fare 'ome,' she would comment.

Daisy was amazed by Sally's behaviour. 'I don't know how you can do that,' she said one time.

'It's easy when yer knows how,' grinned Sally. 'Yer a fool, Daisy. Men 'ave used yer and always will. They gives us nothin' in return, so no one gets me unless they pays.'

'I'll wait for my Jackie,' replied Daisy dreamily.

'You'll be bloody lucky! It's a big country, so they says, so I doubt if you'll ever find him.'

7

Pearly

After four months of terrible storms, Daisy's ship eventually sailed into Sydney harbour. Daisy stood on deck at the rail and stared at the blue misty mountain.

'Here I am, Jackie,' she murmured.

Once the ship had anchored and the cargo unloaded, the missionary folk came on board to take off their protégées. The old captain rubbed his hands in glee. 'You are in luck, girls,' he said. 'A very old friend of mine has spoken for you. As a matter of fact, I'm going to take you down into Sydney myself. She has a big house right in the centre of the town.' He brushed his jacket and put on his neat cap.

Sally narrowed her eyes. 'I wonder what the crafty old sod is up to,' she said.

But soon they were in a hansom cab driving up the hill. The wide dirt road was full of people, mostly men, and the bars were noisy and very busy. Some of the houses by the roadside were quite prosperous looking.

The cab turned up the drive of a big white house with a balcony built all the way round it. It had a magnificent view of the harbour but the blinds were drawn. Behind them came the sounds of much activity within.

'Ah, here we are,' said Captain Morgan. 'This is the home of my friend Pearly Ladell. You will be all right here, girls. Pearly seems to be having a party so we will go in the back way.'

As the captain whistled for the young black boy who came to help with their baggage, Daisy gazed in wide-eyed wonder at the vast house with its splendid garden. There were big red roses blooming so late in the year, and scarlet geraniums in all the window boxes.

Inside, they sat at a big well-scrubbed table in the kitchen and waited for Pearly to appear.

With an apologetic enough cough Captain Morgan said, 'I'll go and find myself a drink, I'm sure Pearly won't be long. Well, good luck, girls,' he added and walked out.

Sally looked about her. 'There's something fishy about this place,' she said.

'It's very nice and clean,' Daisy said.

'No, it stinks,' said Sally wrinkling her pretty nose, 'and I don't trust that old Morgan.'

With a waft of heavy perfume, Pearly came at last to greet her new arrivals. She was big and wide and dressed in some bright pink material with sequins all over her large bosom. A pink feather quivered in her hair. 'Oh dear, you poor darlings,' she said. 'You must be so travel-weary. Now, I suggest you go up to your rooms and I'll send up some supper. You should have a good early night and we will attend to details tomorrow.'

'Sounds all right to me,' drawled Sally, a little insolently.

Pearly's piggy eyes shot Sally a shrewd glance. 'How old are you?' she asked.

'Old enough,' grinned Sally.

'Well, you look your age,' replied Pearly drily. She turned to survey Daisy, who was pale and silent and looking a trifle bewildered. 'So, you are Daisy,' she said. 'What a lovely girl! And such a strong figure!' Pearly came forward and kissed Daisy on the cheek.

Daisy was quite taken aback and tried to draw away. But Pearly's lips were set tight, then she clicked her fingers and the same small black boy came forward. 'Take the ladies up to the last room at the back. Everything's ready and I'll get some supper sent up.' She turned and, with a half smile, said: 'Good-night, girls. I'll see you in the morning.' With that, Pearly waddled out of the kitchen leaving a heady smell of perfume behind her.

Upstairs they were shown into a very pretty room. There were two beds and a frilly draped dressing table, red velvet curtains and shaded lights.

'Blimey!' exclaimed Sally. 'This is a bit posh for a couple of skivvies. I'm convinced that I know what's going on, and it's something dodgy.'

Daisy looked at that nice inviting bed with its snow-white sheets and immediately fell on it. 'Oh, shut up, Sally,' she said. 'I'm dead beat and starving hungry. Stop going on about your suspicions and let's make ourselves comfortable.'

The supper was delicious – chicken, bread rolls and wine, followed by sweet cakes.

'Well,' said Sally tucking in, 'if this is Australian life, I ain't goin' ter mind.'

Downstairs the noise of music went on all night and carriages rattled in and out of the drive till dawn. But Daisy hardly noticed. After her good supper, she got into the comfortable bed and dozed off with hardly a care in the world.

Sally, however, had already noticed the bars on the windows behind the drawn curtains. Peering through the keyhole, she saw enough to confirm what was going on. 'Cor blimey!' she said, 'if we ain't landed up in a brothel!'

Daisy did not hear her. She was already miles away, dreaming that she was in the arms of her Jackie.

Late that night Sally heard someone turn the key in the door from the outside. She knew that they were now locked in. 'Oh well,' she muttered philosophically. 'It might be more comfortable than the nick.'

The next morning, breakfast was brought up to them by a young black girl who did not answer when they spoke to her but pointed to the bathroom. The bathroom turned out to be very luxurious!

Daisy and Sally bathed and dressed themselves and then sat waiting for Pearly to arrive. But eventually, the black girl came to collect them and took them to her room to see her.

Pearly was in a very wide bed with lots of frilly covers on it. She wore a green turban over her crackers, big knobs of hair bound up in strips of cloth, and her eyes were baggy. Her mouth had a sullen droop to it. She looked like a very different woman to the glamorous one of the previous evening. Now she sat up in bed with her huge bosom exposed. 'I never get up before the afternoon,' she explained, 'but you girls can take it easy today and help me entertain tonight. I have a lot of important people coming to visit me and sometimes I need a bit of help. Got a pretty dress, have you?'

'No,' said Sally, 'only these ones the Society gave us.'

Pearly stared in horror at their long shapeless print dresses. 'Oh dear,' she muttered. 'I'll get you fixed up and then perhaps we can go shopping once you have settled down.'

Daisy and Sally lounged about on the balcony looking out over the view. The harbour was a grand sight! The air was perfectly clear and the sun shone on the sparkling water as the ships sailed in and out. The town of Sydney was built on a hill. There were long lines of little shacks and here and there large stores built of wood. Main Street was very crowded with people but from this great height they looked like dwarfs to the two girls from England.

'It's very pretty,' said Daisy, 'but I'd like to go out there and see the places.'

'You'll be lucky,' said Sally. 'Pearly owns us now. I bet you she paid good money to the old captain for us.'

Daisy stared at her quizzically. 'I don't know what you mean,' she said.

'Well, you'll 'ave to find out tonight,' said Sally ominously.

The servants who polished and cleaned all the day were black and spoke no English and although there was a tall white woman, who officiated in the kitchen, she made no contact with Daisy and Sally at all. So it was impossible to ask anymore what the set-up was.

Early in the evening Pearly arrived beaming brightly and she handed them both bundles. 'There you are, my little darlings,' she said 'Now dress yourselves up and make yourselves pretty. Tonight we will be having a party.'

Daisy's dress was emerald green. It was obviously second-hand but it fitted her well. Daisy rather liked it although she was worried a little about the low neckline.

Sally's garment turned out to be a little red satin gown which fitted neatly over her thin shape. It had a fluted trailing skirt which ended in a small train. 'Where'd she get these, I wonder,' she cried. ''Owzat!' She paraded up and down before Daisy.

'Oh dear, you do look like some actress,' declared Daisy. 'I fink I'll put somefink in the neck of mine, it's very low.'

But Sally only giggled. 'Daisy, my love,' she said, 'in this game it's show most, take all.'

'What game?' asked Daisy irritably. 'Pearly has been so nice to us, I don't know what you are grumbling at. We could have been scrubbing the floors but all she wants is for us to be her companions. I think we have struck it lucky.'

'Oh, you will find out,' cackled Sally, winding her dark hair up and pinning it on top of her head.

Daisy just brushed her curly locks and allowed them to hang free and natural.

The black girl arrived and led them down to the sitting-room where Pearly was ready and waiting for them.

Daisy and Sally entered a wide room full of white-and-gold chairs. In the corners were two big *chaise-longues* covered with white velvet. There was a big bar filled with bottles of drink and a piano which played itself, rattling out martial music and popular songs at quite a pace. Everywhere there were men sitting around talking loudly. They were all sorts – young and old, fat and thin, tall and short. Some were very red faced and full of booze. Daisy stood in the doorway staring in wonder.

Pearly cleared her throat. 'Let me introduce my new ladies,' she said loudly. Silence fell. 'This is Daisy and this is Sally, and they are both just over from England.'

Within seconds a crowd of men had gathered around Daisy and Sally. They handed the girls drinks, and fussed over them. Sally seemed to love it but Daisy found it confusing. She just sat on the edge of a chair next to a young red-coated army officer who had buck teeth and very sandy hair, playing with her drink. She felt quite light-headed. The noise and the heat and the fact that Sally was sitting on the lap of a big fat man, all rather overwhelmed her.

'Well, Daisy, you are a lovely girl,' the officer said, stroking her knee and looking down at her breasts.

Daisy wanted to protest, especially when he started to kiss her in a most familiar way, even putting his tongue into her mouth. But at the same time she felt warm, comfortable and almost carefree.

People came in and out, many men accompanied by women and there was a spirit of gaiety everywhere. At one point, Pearly sat at the piano and pretended to play while she sang old London songs in a flat, tone-less voice.

The young officer had become even more familiar and Daisy saw that Sally had disappeared.

'Better go up to bed, Daisy,' said Pearly. 'You've had too much to drink.' Pearly put a finger to her lips as the young man protested. 'I will take her up,' he said.

'It's ten dollars,' said Pearly. 'You can go up in a minute.'

What happened after that, Daisy was not quite sure. But she certainly had a terrible headache the next morning and she woke up in another room to her own. Although she was on her own, she had the distinct feeling that someone else had slept there too. Her body felt a little sore and bruised, she thought. Holding her throbbing head in her hands, she sat on the side of the bed feeling very confused.

Some time later, there was a knock on the door and Pearly came in with a breakfast tray. Daisy was surprised to see her up so early. 'Don't get up yet,' said Pearly. 'Have a lay-in. You were such a good girl last night, you know,' she said. 'You did enjoy yourself, didn't you?' Pearly raised her eyebrows suggestively.

Daisy felt very confused through the haze of her

headache. She nodded vaguely as Pearly set down the tray on her bed.

'I'll leave you be then, dear,' said Pearly. She winked as she backed out of the room.

Daisy took a sip of tea but soon went back to sleep. She was having trouble concentrating and there was still a swimming feeling in her head and a sickly feeling in her stomach.

She awoke an hour later to find Sally standing beside the bed all dressed up in a new outfit. Daisy thought that she looked very sheepish. ''Ow are we, mate?' Sally asked.

'I think I'm all right,' said Daisy, sitting up. 'What happened to me?'

'She doped you, that's what,' said Sally. 'She knew you were new to it. I told you we had ended up in a bleedin' brothel, didn't I? But who cares? I had me two blokes last night and Pearly gave me five dollars this morning,' Sally laughed softly. 'Not to worry, kid, you'll soon get used to it and make plenty of money.'

Daisy's jaw dropped as she heard Sally's words. Pulling back the bedclothes, she jumped to her feet. 'Oh! Oh!' she screeched and pulled at her hair. 'Oh my God!' she wailed. 'So that was what it was! Oh, Sally, how could you?'

'Well, I warned you, didn't I? I told her you was new. That's why she gave you a bit of dope.'

Daisy screwed up her face in horror.

'Oh my God! How degrading can you get Sally? To take money from men for that? It might be your way of life, but it'll never be mine. I'm getting out of here.

Oh, my dear God!' she wailed. 'I must wash myself. I feel disgusting. I feel unclean.'

But Sally shrugged her shoulders again. 'Pearly won't let you go, Daisy, at least not until you have earned them the money she paid for you. It's a racket they work, her and the captain. After their stint in this joint, the women are sent on up to the gold towns where women are in short supply and there are lots of hungry men. I can't help you, Daisy, but if you want to run away, do it. As for myself, I am quite content here.' Then, and without a backward glance, Sally left the room and shut the door. But, contrary to Pearly's instructions, she did not lock it.

Daisy hurriedly scrubbed herself all over and then got dressed in her old print dress. Even then, she still felt dirty, defiled and very humiliated. Picking up her box she quietly opened the door and began to creep downstairs.

When Daisy was halfway down the stairs the woman from the kitchen suddenly appeared, carrying a tray for Pearly, who was still in her room resting. When she saw Daisy creeping downstairs, the woman stopped. 'Where are you off to?' she asked. 'You can't get out the front door, you know. It's locked, and the back door is, too.'

Daisy stood on the stairs with tears filling her eyes as she looked down at the woman with a pleading and desperate look. Suddenly she realized who the woman was. How extraordinary. She was Jackie's mother, Rita, but she looked much older than when Daisy had last seen her, very thin and tired-looking.

At the very same moment, Rita recognized Daisy. 'Dear God!' she cried in astonishment. ''Tis Jackie's girl.'

Daisy smiled with relief but her moment of hope passed as Rita decisively placed the tray on the stairs and shouted: 'Pearly, one of them gels is gettin' away!' Then she grabbed Daisy's arm and held it in a vicious grip.

Daisy squealed in panic and tried to pull away. 'Oh please, Rita,' she begged, 'help me get out of here! Please tell me where my Jackie is.'

Rita's face twisted up with hatred. 'He didn't miss no bargain in you,' she hissed. 'Pearly!' she called again. Turning back to Daisy, she said 'You've ended up where you belong, me gel.'

Suddenly Pearly appeared at the top of the stairs. Grabbing Daisy from behind she began to beat her hard with hefty blows. As Pearly's fists rained down on her, Daisy sank down against the banister, holding one arm up to protect herself. She could not fight back. Together Pearly and Rita pushed and pulled Daisy back into her room.

'Wicked girl!' screamed Pearly. 'I paid bleedin' good money for yer and I'll sees yer earn it afore yer gets outa here!'

The two strong women bundled Daisy into her room and pushed her to the floor. 'Lock her in, Rita,' Pearly screeched. 'Let her stop there till she comes to her senses.' With that she swept out of the room.

With her body stunned by the blows and her mouth bleeding, Daisy looked up at Rita with a pleading expression on her face.

Rita's face remained hard. 'Well,' she said, 'I never thought to see you in a place like this, but Pearly picked you whores up in the Sydney harbour area. If that's where you were, then you deserve it.'

'But I'm not a whore, I'm not,' wept Daisy. 'I only just came on the boat. I came all the way here to find Jackie. Oh please tell me where he is.'

But Rita snarled and gave her another thump.

From outside the room Pearly called out. 'Lock her in now Rita, and don't give her nothing to eat. She'll soon learn what's good for her.'

Rita stomped out and locked the door, leaving Daisy lying full-length on the floor and crying as if her heart would break. What an irony, she thought, that she should be looking for Jackie and then find his mother in this terrible place. Oh, how she could die! Well, they could beat her, bully her and starve her, but she would never be a whore.

That evening Daisy heard Sally whispering to her through the keyhole. 'Are you all right, Daisy?' she called softly.

'No, I'm not,' returned Daisy. 'Let me out.'

'I can't love, Pearly won't let me.'

'Oh please! I'll kill myself, I'll never stay here,' wailed Daisy.

'Sorry love,' said Sally. Her voice sounded chilled and guilty as she crept away.

That was indeed a very long night for Daisy. She was too afraid to sleep as she listened to the revelry downstairs, so terrified was she that some man would come charging into the room and rape her.

She had not eaten or drunk anything all day. Her lips were dry and her head ached. Sitting curled up on the bed, she watched the dawn come up over the harbour and listened to the sirens of the boats. Soon she could see the ferry going back and forth to the other shore early in the morning. 'Oh, please, God, don't desert me now,' she wept. 'I'm sorry I have been so wicked.'

Early in the morning, once Pearly had retired to her boudoir, Rita unlocked the door. 'Do you want the lavatory?' she asked. 'It's vacant.'

But Daisy just sat with her head hanging down.

'I'll get you a cup o' tay,' continued Rita. 'If I were you I'd give in to Pearly and do as she says. She's not bad really and might let you go if you pay the money back. She's very fond of money, is Pearly.'

'I haven't got any money,' said Daisy mournfully. 'How can I pay her back? I was sent over by the Missionary Society and they told me I was going to get a good position.'

Rita shut the door and came over to the bed. 'So you ain't one of those whores from Sydney harbour,' she asked in a softer voice.

'No,' replied Daisy. 'I came to be with Jackie. We had a baby after he left. She's back home with me sister.'

Rita's dark eyes suddenly filled with tears, creeping back to the door, she locked it from the inside. Then she went and sat on the bed next to Daisy. 'But your friend is a whore,' she said. 'How come you was with her?'

'I travelled over with her,' explained Daisy. 'We were in a home for fallen women but, honestly Rita, I was never on the game. I ran away from home and the peelers got me and took me to jail.'

Rita did not need any more convincing. She nodded. 'I'll see what I can do,' she muttered after she had listened to Daisy's tale of woe. Then her hard-lined face lit up. 'So, I'm a Grandma,' she said. 'That is fine news to me.'

Daisy smiled at the thought of her baby. 'Her name is Petal,' she said quietly.

'Well, I will say that Jackie thought the world of you,' said Rita. 'But I'm afraid that I don't know where he is meself. He went out to the diggings last year and I never heard from him since. I never found me husband, so I'm trapped here with all the children. That's why I work for Pearly. She is generous and I need the money.' She paused and then added, 'Don't get me wrong, I only do the domestic chores here, but at times it's a very unrewarding job when I see the poor girls who go through here.'

'Oh, please help me, Rita,' pleaded Daisy.

'Look now, drink your tay and relax,' said Rita. 'I can't jeopardize me own job because I need the money. But if I were you, I'd tell Pearly that you're sorry for trying to escape and then make out you feel ill. Say it's your time of the month, or something like that. She will leave you alone for a few days and that will give me time to think of something.'

It was very hot and dry that summer in Sydney. The bars stayed open all night and the gold hunters who had struck it rich came into town to live it up. The harbour thronged with ships and small boats, more and more immigrants arrived each day. So far the wars out East had not affected the Australians and apart from a few troubles with the Aborigines, it was a peaceful country.

But the discovery of gold was changing everything fast. Fortune-hunters came in from all over the world – the roamers and the riff-raff – all hoping to find that hidden gold mine.

Being the first city in the colony, Sydney was first a rip-roaring town full of vice and drunkenness, crooks and con-men with the hardened women who accompanied them. They all came with large families and settled in shacks and tin huts, any place they could find. And the hillside in Sydney was a maze of tents and roughly built dwellings. Most of these people moved on, trekking into the bush or out to the western deserts and on to the huge mountain ranges. Many died in this virgin country but always some would survive, the strong and the brave, the most adventurous or the most unholy.

In this great heatwave, Daisy Smith was locked up in Pearly Ladell's brothel with the blinds drawn over the barred window. She sat on the bed in her nightdress and wept tears of mortification.

Several times a day Rita arrived to bring her some food or escort her to the lavatory down the corridor. She had become Daisy's sole confidante.

'Darlin' girl,' said Rita in her rich brogue. 'I am genuinely sorry for you but I have me own self to think about and Pearly's a very hard case if you goes agin her.'

'Oh, please Rita,' begged Daisy. 'For the sake of Jackie and little Petal, let me out of here. I promise I'll try to get back home.'

'I'll do what I can,' said Rita, 'but in the meantime you will have to go along with Pearly. She is determined not to lose money on you, but she will let you go if someone buys you out. Daisy, who will be able to do that if you don't go down to find someone?'

'No!' cried Daisy, horrified at the very thought. 'Pearly can kill me, but I'll never do that for money.'

'Please yourself,' said Rita going out and locking the door behind her.

That evening the black girl came up to help Daisy bathe. She brought some new clothes up with her. 'Ma'am says you are to get ready to go down tonight,' she informed Daisy.

As she sat in the hip bath, Daisy felt so grateful for the hot scented water poured over her back that she did not argue.

Not long afterwards in bustled Pearly, all smiles. 'Well, dear,' she said, 'and how are you feeling? Better, I hope.' Her fat cheeks puffed out as she gave Daisy another big smile. But her dark eyes remained hard and unsmiling. 'There now, put this nice dress on. Look, there's a yellow satin petticoat to match it,' she crowed. 'Why, I just bought these today, this gown is the very latest fashion.'

Daisy gazed wearily at the yellow dress trimmed with pink feathers, the little boots and the amazing headdress that was a combination of bows, balls and feathers. 'Make yourself look pretty,' continued Pearly, 'there's a good girl. A very nice young man's asked for you. He's going to give me good money, so you will earn a nice bit out of it. Be a good girl, then, you don't want to ruin Pearly's business, do you?'

Daisy just scowled. All she could think was that once she got downstairs perhaps she could find a way out.

After Pearly had gone, Daisy allowed the black girl to paint her face and frizz out her hair. 'I look like a bleedin' clown,' said Daisy as she scowled at her reflection in the mirror. But the young girl pretended not to understand her.

Eventually Daisy, all dressed up, was sitting among the other dressed and scented girls on the fur-covered divan. Sally, looking very pleased with herself, sat opposite.

Balanced on her high heels with much of her bosom exposed, fat Pearly paraded up and down before them all. 'Now, girls, behave yourselves. I keep a respectable house and I'll have no rowdiness. And I won't overwork you. Daisy, dear, you look simply lovely. There's a very nice young man who usually comes here just to drink and gamble. He does not need women but tonight he has asked for an English girl. In fact, he insisted on you, so do be a good girl and oblige him nicely.'

Daisy just sat stiff and upright and glared at her. Pearly smiled faintly and her fat shoulders quivered as she gave a deep sigh and went out to greet her first guest.

Soon the old piano was rattling away and the men were at the bar swallowing drinks or off up and down the stairs with the girls.

Still Daisy sat staring frigidly about her and did not move. But a pair of dark eyes were scrutinizing her with amusement as a very drunk man came from the gambling room straight towards her.

'Well, Daisy,' he said, 'you sure look a hum-dinger. I never thought you would be so pretty.'

Daisy stared steadily up at him unsmiling. She was very conscious of the atrocious headdress of feathers on top of her hair.

'You're a finely built Sheila,' he said with familiarity and fondled her thigh.

Daisy pushed him off.

'Hey!' he shouted so that everyone heard him, 'Knock it off! I paid fifty dollars for you, honeybun, and I want my money's worth. Otherwise there's gonner be trouble.' Daisy stared at him with cold hatred, ignoring Pearly's appealing glances at her.

'Right,' Daisy said finally getting up to her full height and looking down at him with disgust. 'Come and get your money's worth and get it over with.'

The man's eyes gleamed with delight as he put an arm about her shoulders. Pretending to be drunker than he was, he slowly walked her upstairs.

As soon as they reached Daisy's room, the man seemed to change totally. Suddenly he was sober. 'Now Daisy move it,' he said. 'You want to get out of this place, don't you? Then pick up your bits and pieces and let's go.'

Daisy was astonished but she was not going to wait to find out what was going on. She grabbed her little bag that still contained the ten dollars that Pearly had put there and indicated that she was ready.

The man held her wrist with a strong rough hand. 'Don't make a sound,' he said, 'and take off them bloody feathers.'

Daisy smiled. She pulled off the headdress and threw it on the bed. Breathlessly she allowed him to guide her down the corridor into a small pantry next to a lavatory. Above the big linen shelf, there was a small window. With a sharp pen knife the man prised it open. 'I'll go first,' he said. 'Reckon you can make it? I'll catch you down below. Good luck.' He stopped for a moment, and flashed her a big smile. 'By the way, my name's Dukey.' Within seconds, he had disappeared.

Daisy looked at the small opening she was to disappear through. She had no choice. Hoisting herself up onto the shelf, she squeezed herself out of the window. It was a tight fit and she had no idea what was down below until she landed on top of Dukey, almost flattening him, they rolled over and over on the grass.

'Christ!' exclaimed Dukey. 'I didn't realise you was such a big girl. But pick up your skirts now and run like hell. I'll lead the way.'

So running as fast as she could, Daisy followed the long-legged young man, across the dark lawns, through a clump of trees, and out into a long lane that led towards the harbour. At full tilt they went down the hill without a word uttered. When they reached the bottom Dukey threw himself over a low brick wall and lay on the ground laughing. A very red-faced and breathless Daisy sank down beside him.

'It's all clear,' said Dukey. 'Pearly won't miss us until the morning now. I booked you up for the night.'

'But why?' Daisy stared at him. 'Why did you save me?'

Dukey lit a long black cigar and puffed at it. 'Rita told me about you,' he said. 'We are old friends, she and I. I have often had to make a quick exit from Pearly's so I knew how to get you out.'

'Oh, thank you,' gasped Daisy and dropped her head on his shoulder.

'Not to worry,' said Dukey giving her a pat on the back. 'I didn't want you anyway. I never sleep with whores.'

Daisy looked up at him quickly. 'But I'm not a whore!' she wept.

'So you tell me, but I don't really care. As far as I am concerned, I did it for Rita because she has done many a favour for me. Mind you, it cost me fifty dollars, which leaves me skint.'

'I've got ten dollars in me handbag,' volunteered Daisy woefully.

'You have money?' Dukey looked delighted. 'Well, that's great. I might get a game going. Old Bluey's tramp steamer is off down the river any moment. Come on,' he said, pulling Daisy to her feet. 'You might as well travel with me. She might start looking around the town in the morning and she can turn bloody nasty, can old Pearly!'

As they walked along by the river, there were blue flashes of light in the sky heralding a storm which suddenly burst. Now huge rain drops drenched Daisy to the skin, causing her yellow dress to hang wet and sticky, and the yellow feather trimming to become pathetically bedraggled.

Daisy did not care what she looked like, she was so happy to be free. She took off her shoes to help her keep pace with Dukey as he strode along.

When they reached the harbour wall, Dukey jumped on top and called out, 'Ahoy, there, Bluey! Can I come aboard?'

A light flashed and a voice called out in answer: 'That you, Dukey? Yes, you can if you got a stake.'

'Give us that ten dollars,' whispered Dukey to Daisy.

She handed over the crumpled bill.

'Got a lady with me,' cried Dukey.

'Okay,' yelled the voice. 'Come aboard.'

They waded waist-deep out into the river and climbed the ladder to board the old tramp steamer. In the light of a hurricane lamp they entered a small cabin where two villainous-looking men sat playing cards. Behind them there was a warm glowing stove and an old bunk full of dirty looking blankets.

'Right!' cried Dukey, rubbing his hands together, 'let's get weaving. Here you are, Daisy, get under them blankets. The fire will dry you out quick enough.' He pointed her towards the bunk.

Wet, cold and miserable but glad to be safe, Daisy

crept under the smelly blankets. Totally exhausted, she soon dropped off to sleep with the sound of voices as the men played cards fading away into the distance. She had no idea of where she was or what was going to happen next.

8

The Promised City

New York in 1865 was a very confusing city to the unsophisticated eyes of her new residents, who were pouring in by the thousands. Built by the new rich of the period, hotels and big stores lined Seventh Avenue and Broadway, a maze of bars, peep shows and gambling joints. Fifth Avenue was a mass of carriages and hansom cabs, wagons and carts and even barrows. The ladies paraded the main streets to display their finery and the newcomers walked along in a daze, overawed at the splendour of this new city.

Some were not impressed. 'The Lord will seek vengeance on this wicked city,' muttered Grandma Foley every now and then.

Eli held on to Grandma's frail arm as she guided her along to St Patrick's Cathedral for mass every day. She agreed that it was indeed a frightening place. There were so many loud voices all speaking in different tongues, and the yellow fog that crept off the river every evening dimmed the street lamps and made her cough. The wonderful promised land that she had so much looked forward to had failed to impress her.

It was now four years since they had left Ireland and still they lived over Mylo Dowdy's bar on Fifth Avenue, and still Grandpa worked as a pot man in the bar.

Soon after the family had arrived in New York a terrible war had broken out between the northern and southern states. Dan and Dave Foley who were still out West working on the rail-road had found themselves conscripted into the Yankee Army and had never been heard of since. Every day Grandma would go to pray for them at St Patrick's Cathedral and every day her footsteps became slower as she leaned more heavily on Eli's frail shoulders.

Mylo had been very good to them all but he also persistently pestered Eli to marry him. Every now and then he would present her with a bouquet, a coy smile on his ugly features. Eli always backed away, fearful of the leer on his face and his disgusting beery breath.

Eli found it impossible to keep her feelings to herself but her complaints fell on deaf ears. ''Tis not a bad thing,' Grandpa would say. 'Grandma and I can't live forever and we worry about leaving you alone in this Godforsaken city.'

'Oh, please, Grandpa,' wept Eli. 'You know that I would do anything in the world for you, I love you both so, but don't ask me to marry Mylo Dowdy.'

It was therefore with a sense of relief that Eli heard the news that Mylo had got himself recruited into the army one night when he had been very drunk.

'I'll have no man call me a coward,' roared Mylo. 'This may not be my country but by God I'll fight for it.'

Eli may have been saved from marrying Mylo but his impulsive decision meant that the whole family was suddenly made homeless as Mylo sold his bar and the dwellings above. So it was that Grandpa had to find them new lodgings. He eventually found them an apartment over on the East Side. It had once been fairly prosperous but the original owners, having made their piles of riches, had moved on and the neighbourhood had become wholly working class, embracing all types of people, of all colours and creeds.

Eli and her grandparents moved into lodgings right at the top of the building. There was one large living room with a sloping ceiling and two small bedrooms. Lavatories and water taps were a communal affair housed on the lower floor and shared by all the inhabitants of this large house.

Grandpa, still very hale and hearty, made short work of the six flights of stairs but for Grandma they were too much. Soon after they moved in, Grandma took to her bed and did not go outside any more.

It was a very noisy building to live in but they were different noises to what Eli was used to. It was not the sound of raucous voices from the drunken men down in the bar but the sound of children playing in the courtyard and women shouting gossip to each other as they strung up their lines of washing from the fire escapes.

On Saturday night, when it was warm, the families all held drinking parties and sat outside till all hours on the iron steps of the fire escapes. Eli loved to sit outside and listen to the chatter going on between all these very different people. There were Italians, Greeks and Jews all living side by side, making do with the terrible conditions with uncomplaining cheerfulness. Then Eli would tell her bedridden Grandma everything that had been going on in an attempt to cheer up her dreary life confined to bed, clutching her rosary beads.

One of the worst aspects of the living arrangements was having to share the water supply. Eli frequently had to wait for ages for the lavatory to become free and then the smell was usually disgusting. That was as hard to put up with as the long wait for her turn at the water tap.

One morning Eli was sitting on the stairs with her big water jug waiting for her turn at the tap when a tall girl pushed her way past. 'Hurry up, you lot,' she said. 'I'll be late for work.'

Eli immediately looked up; there was a familiar ring to that voice, which was confirmed when an old lady in the queue said: 'No, Rosa, you just wait your turn.'

Eli's jaw dropped with surprise as she stared into the dark merry eyes of Rosa Feldamanski, her companion on the long voyage from the old country. The buxom Rosa clasped Eli in her arms, nearly knocking the breath out of her.

'Eli Lehane! What are you doing here?'

'I live here,' said Eli. 'Upstairs. We have been here just a week.'

'Oh, it's great news,' cried Rosa. 'I'm off to work now and mustn't be late. Tonight I'll come and get you to have supper with us. We are on the second floor.' She smiled excitedly. 'What a lovely surprise! I just can't believe my luck.' She turned to the onlookers. 'This is Eli, my little Irish friend who came over on the boat with me,' she informed them. 'Isn't that great?'

That evening Eli went to supper with Rosa's Momma and Poppa. She met her sister Ruth who had grown into a very pretty girl and her brother Yossel who was quite a nice young man but who put on airs and graces in an attempt to impress Eli. At seventeen Yossel was doing his utmost to get Americanized but his accent was bad and every now and then a tell-tale Hebrew word would creep into his speech.

Rosa's Momma looked very smart in a black dress and her hair rolled ito a bun held in position with a comb. And her Poppa was as big and bearded as ever, slow to speak and still very genial.

At dinner there was delicious beetroot soup which was ladled out with a big scoop, followed by potatoes and a kind of pancake for dessert.

It had been a long time since Eli had tasted such a nourishing meal. At her home money was running short and to give Grandma the nourishment she needed, Eli and Grandpa often went without.

Rosa was as much a chatterbox as ever. 'We all go out to work, you know, Eli, and we give Momma our wages so we can all eat well. Ruth and I work in the factory making army uniforms and Yossel is working in a big store. Even Poppa got a part-time job at the butcher in the market, so we are not doing bad.'

It was heartening for Eli to see how the family had all settled down and that Momma no longer pined for her lost baby. How happy she was just keeping busy looking after her big family here in New York!

'How is your Grandma?' Rosa's Momma asked Eli.

'Not very well,' replied Eli. 'She is confined to her bed nowadays.'

'Tomorrow I will visit her and make a nice egg custard to take,' Mrs Feldman said. (Their name had been simplified by the immigration officers, Rosa explained.)

Eli's grandparents were not so delighted to hear that Eli had met up with Rosa again. Grandma considered Jews to be heathens and even easy-going Grandpa seemed concerned.

Eli frowned. 'I am very happy to be with Rosa and her family,' she said with some indignation. 'It does not matter what religion people are. We all get the same chance and there is only one heaven.'

'Tut! Tut!' said Grandpa shaking his head. 'Who has been filling your head with such nonsense?'

'Rosa tells me that when the war is won women will be on the same level as men and get the same wages because women will demand it.'

'I never heard such rubbish,' said Grandpa.

Grandma in her melancholy way joined in from her bed. 'A whistling woman and a crowing hen is neither fit for God nor men,' she recited.

Eli laughed carelessly. She did not mind what they thought, she was sure of her friendship.

'Come to the factory with us, Eli,' said Rosa a few days later. 'Your Grandpa can look after your Grandma now that he does not work.'

Indeed, Grandpa had been unable to get a job since the move and he had been getting worried about money. So he was very relieved when little Eli landed a job in a sweatshop. It was in a back street in a vast and draughty warehouse down by the river. The wartime emergency had turned uniform making into mass production, a new approach to tailoring. The sewing machine was in its infancy and most of the work was still done by hand by girls huddled together in poor light stitching away at the badly made uniforms. These uniforms were made for men to die in and as the war between the states became bloodier and bloodier the girls sang patriotic songs as they stitched, wrapped in old sacks for protection against the cold draughts that came from the river.

The girls worked from eight in the morning until seven o'clock in the evening with a midday meal of sandwiches, eaten on the spot where they worked. Their total wages were a mere two dollars a week. Eli sat with Ruth and they stitched on endless buttons while Rosa, who was big and strong, packed up the finished uniforms, labelled them and sent them on their way.

All through the cold winter of 1865 Eli worked. She was not unhappy because her friend kept her cheerful but it was not long before the frail little girl got a bad cough because of the conditions. Mrs Feldman made her a special cough syrup with onions and sugar. Rosa was in charge of the bottle and she would hand it to her as soon as Eli's cough became troublesome. When the foreman said: 'My life, Eli, you got on the booze so soon already,' they all laughed.

The money that Eli earned was useful. It fed her and her grandparents and paid the rent. Grandpa looked after Grandma while Eli worked but Grandma was growing more feeble every day. One evening she sighed gently and closed her eyes. 'Send for the priest,' she said. 'My time has come.'

Eli sat beside her bed while Grandpa went to the church to find the priest. 'You will be all right, Grandma,' Eli said, trying to sound reassuring. But inside she was afraid.

Wearily Grandma shook her head. Her breathing was getting bad and life seemed to be draining out of her. 'I'm going home, Eli,' she whispered. 'It's all there, the old bog road and the farm. The hills are getting misty and I can hear my parents calling me.'

'Oh, Grandma,' sighed Eli. 'I know you are not happy. I'll save up my money and take you home, I promise, next year.'

But Grandma grasped her hand. 'No, Eli, your destiny is here,' she said. Then she paused for breath and closed her eyes. 'He is coming to you, the one you love. I have been home and they tell me David is coming.'

Eli put her head down on the bed and wept at the thought of her beloved David.

'Take care of Grandpa,' Grandma said. These were her last words. She shut her eyes and never opened them again.

The priest arrived soon afterwards to give Grandma the last rites, and a few days later she was buried in St Patrick's Catholic cemetery. They all knew that her heart was at home in Ireland.

Grandpa was very sad at the death of his beloved

wife and Eli did not like to leave him alone. She made him go walking in Central Park with Rosa and Yossel on Sunday mornings or go to supper with Momma and Poppa Feldman. He was so grateful for the company, he managed to forget that this large friendly family was not Catholic.

Eli wrote to Mary Wood to tell her of Grandma's death. The reply took a long time to get back to her. When it did, it was written by Marion, Eli's cousin. Marion added that she had wanted to go to Dublin to study law but they had not the time for women in that profession. But she was not beaten, she wrote. She was a good enough scholar and might even try her luck in England.

> *Dear Eli,*
> *All is as well as to be expected. There are still*
> *troubles in Ireland and they are not getting better.*

She also stated that Mary had taken a bigger house outside Cork overlooking the harbour and that they were catering for English lodgers, which did not please Marion at all.

There was a postscript:

> *I don't know if you are interested, but David Kennedy*
> *got released from prison and is working his way over*
> *to America on a cargo ship.*

Eli's heart thumped wildly in her chest as she read and reread that postscript. David was coming over!

She could not believe what she saw! So Grandma had not been dreaming, she had seen that very clearly.

Thinking of the thin, red-headed lad, standing next to her on the mountainside that morning so long ago, Eli hugged the letter to her. Although she had been heavy-hearted with Grandma gone, now she had something to look forward to. She was very content to wait for David's arrival in this big city.

9

David Arrives

There was no doubt that Rosa Feldman had a very proud spirit. Independent and obstinate, she also radiated good will and affection for all her fellow workers. She also stood up for herself and others and spoke her mind. This was unusual amongst most Jewish immigrants, who were used to the yoke of oppression. They rarely voiced their own opinions but instead worked hard and saved hard as they dug their roots deeply into this new land. So big loud-voiced Rosa was an exceptional asset to this newly formed community. Frequently she went voluntarily to the boat ferry to help talk with Jewish families who were stranded either from the lack of money or the inability to understand the laws of New York. With her good command of English, Russian and German in addition to Yiddish, she was a great help to many a forlorn immigrant. She was then involved with the setting up of a benevolent society among the new settlers to aid their poorer friends. As well as all this, Rosa worked extremely hard in the factory making army uniforms with her sister Ruth and little Eli Lehane.

Once she had recovered from her cough, the good food and extra money soon helped Eli to blossom. She was still gentle but had lost the pallor in her cheeks, which were now rosy, and her merry hazel eyes smiled at people from a pixie-like face surrounded by soft wavy hair.

Rosa's sister Ruth was a strange girl. She was very beautiful, with long golden curls and cornflower blue eyes that were as cold as the snows of Russia where she had been born. She still found the American way of life difficult and she spoke the language slowly with an attractive accent. With striking features and a fine figure, she was overall very good-looking.

Rosa was very protective of her younger sister and worried a lot about the attentions of the bully boys who worked with them.

The huge unheated warehouse accommodated a hundred workers at a time. The noises of the river were terrible but neither they nor the cold mist from the water could deter any of the girls. This was their way of life. It was the only way to survive. Many reasoned that at least they had their freedom after all the horrors of persecution they had left behind. Here they were able to live as Jews, and that was all they asked.

So the girls did not complain but wrapped sacking around their legs and protected themselves against the cold by wearing their outdoor clothes as they sat for twelve hours a day stitching, ironing and packing. The war seemed endless and the profiteers must make their millions. And in spite of all these bad conditions, the women grew tough and desirable.

When Barney Cohen, the big boss, began to take notice of Ruth Feldman, Rosa became extremely angry. He would stand and watch Ruth as her dainty hands threaded the needle and her white teeth bit off the ends of the cotton. The buttons were attached to the trousers manually, sewn on with waxed thread that cut through the girls' hands, making them sore and cracked.

Barney found an excuse to sit Ruth closer to him. He was a big-bellied man in his fifties, and his breath smelled of the pickled herrings which he always seemed to be scoffing.

'We'll put Ruth on a lighter job,' he said. 'She can do passing, or something. Her hands are very sore.'

'So are twenty others!' exclaimed Rosa. 'Why move just Ruthie? Besides, she likes to be near me.'

'Shut your big mouth Rosa!' cried the foreman. 'That's Barney and he's the boss. What he says goes.'

'Who cares?' snorted Rosa. 'He's making plenty of money out of this war and us, ain't he?'

Despite Rosa's remarks, Ruth was moved up into the booking office and soon little presents were coming her way from Barney.

'Ruthie!' cried Rosa, 'don't let that fat old profiteer get around you or I'll tell Momma,' she threatened.

Then the sisters began to quarrel. 'Mind your own business,' snapped Ruth.

Little Eli tried to keep the peace between the girls but one weekend Ruth went off to stay in Barney's posh apartment and was away two nights.

Momma, Poppa and little Yossel were informed of this escapade and all hell broke loose when Ruth came home. They were all shouting and crying and the whole tenement was out listening to the Feldman family quarrel. And all the while Eli sat out on the steps worrying about the outcome of this dreadful brawl.

Ruth was now absolutely forbidden to go to the factory.

'I'm very tempted to tell that slob I'm leaving,' Rosa sniffed.

Momma frowned. 'Hush! Don't be hasty, Rosa,' she said. 'We need the money.'

The next morning, Eli and Rosa went back to the factory without Ruth. As they walked along the cold deserted streets early in the morning, Rosa came out with her thoughts. 'Eli, what are we? Just bloody cogs in a big wheel that goes round and round. Once a man gets hold of you, you are finished. I'll never marry, I swear!' she vowed vehemently.

Eli smiled sweetly. 'I will, if my David gets here safely,' she said.

'Oh, you are a hopeless dreamer,' Rosa said. 'Life's not the way you dream about it, not one bit.'

With the aid of the Rabbi, and a little pressure from the Feldman's, Ruth's problems were solved. Barney was a single man and well respected by the Jewish community. He happily offered Ruth marriage.

Momma and Poppa were delighted, for Barney was a very rich man. But cold, far-sighted Ruth had little to say on the subject. Once they were betrothed, she was allowed to court Barney in the orthodox manner while a big wedding was arranged.

Rosa disliked and distrusted Barney, and said that she would not attend the wedding. In deference to her friend, Eli would also not go but in the event they both stood outside the synagogue to watch Ruth go by dressed in her lovely white dress – a wide crinoline with a great headdress.

Rosa was dressed in her old working togs as she sat on the stairs, chewing gum, as she told Eli about Victor Hugo who wrote all about the French Revolution. 'That's what will happen here,' she commented. 'Everyone is getting too greedy, I tell you. Down Battery Park hundreds are practically starving to death because they have no money to get into the country. They are waiting to be sent back to where they came from and can't even afford that! It is a nasty world we live in, Eli.'

Eli sat dreamily thinking of Ruth in her lovely white dress and the flowers she carried. Perhaps one day soon it would be her turn. One day there would be tall David Kennedy with his red-gold hair and beside him Eli in a white dress walking down the aisle of St Patrick's Cathedral.

Meanwhile there was Grandpa to take care of and lots of hard work. The war was almost over and Rosa began to predict that the factory would soon close down, when Barney decided to cash in his war profits. Eli was not sure that he would really do that but she did think that she and Rosa should think of some other way to get a living.

'I might get a regular job with the Jewish Benevolent Society,' Rosa said. 'We've set it up to help the poorest immigrants, and they will all begin to come over again now that the war is nearly finished. I am truly glad that the North won. If the South had won we Jews would all be made slaves just like the black folk.'

'Oh, I don't think so,' said Eli. 'Why, this is a free country. That's why we came here.'

'Well, let's hope it remains so,' replied Rosa gloomily.

After Ruth's wedding, Rosa and Eli became even closer friends. At weekends they spent all their time together, often walking around Central Park. Rosa would spout off.

'What are we?' Rosa would demand. 'Everywhere woman is the underdog, the hardest worker and the poorest paid. The only escape is marriage and then it's work and kids. There is nothing else.'

Little Eli would glance at her friend with a puzzled look on her face. 'But surely, Rosa,' she would say in an effort to understand, 'it must be nice to belong to someone and have their children.'

'Not for me,' declared Rosa shaking her head. 'I'll get out of this ghetto, I will, one way or another. That I swear.'

Now a married woman, Ruth would visit her parents regularly, all dressed up in her finery. She now lived uptown in a brand new house and demanded that Momma and Poppa leave their tenement building and go to live in her house.

But neither Poppa nor Momma would agree to that. 'This is our home, Ruthie, and here we will stay.'

Ruth showered them with huge gifts, such as a big ornate clock and a candelabra.

'My life,' said Momma, 'we will have to move to

make room for the presents she brings. Ruthie is a very good daughter to us.'

'Not I,' growled Poppa. 'Let her live her own life and I will make the best of mine.'

Rosa still did not speak with her sister and refused to visit her. Eli was a little sad about this as Ruth did so want to show off her grand house and Eli felt she had to be loyal to Rosa.

As Rosa had predicted, Barney Cohen did decide to close down his factory. He gave all his workers extra wages and stated that he was leaving the rag trade for good and going into property development.

From that day on Rosa really hated Barney. On the day Barney announced his plans, she gathered her workmates about her and made an impassioned speech on the evils of war profiteering, but it did not do any good. They were all out of work now.

As soon as peace was properly restored, the immigrants from Europe began to arrive as never before and Rosa got a regular position as a welfare worker and interpreter to the Jewish folk down at Battery Park. With the new job Rosa came into her own. She was very happy and extremely busy. With a bright yellow badge on her lapel and a portfolio under her arm, she would wait to escort the poorest immigrants to prevent them being robbed and exploited by evil predators. Rosa was one of many; a movement started in a small way soon reached great proportions.

Literature was printed and money poured in from many sources. Every day big husky Rosa stood down at the immigrant dock of New York Harbour handing out leaflets which explained to the newcomers in Hebrew, German or Russian the qualities and hazards of this new land.

Eli missed Rosa a lot during the day but then she got herself a position as a housemaid in the house of the local priests. This move pleased Grandpa enormously, particularly since he had become very devout since he had lost Grandma, spending most of his days now praying at St Patrick's.

The work at the priests' house was tedious but Eli was glad to have any job at all. She had written to her cousins in Ireland to ask the name of the ship that David Kennedy was travelling on but the reply, which was unbearably long in coming, told Eli that they did not know.

During that bad winter, many old boats carrying the immigrants in overcrowded conditions across the sea to America had foundered and gone down into the Atlantic.

Every time this happened Eli felt disheartened, convinced that David had died and that now there was no point in anything any more. She watched Grandpa fade and could tell that he was not happy either. 'Let's return home to Ireland,' she said to him one day.

But Grandpa shook his white head. 'Nay,' he said. 'Not until the boys come home from the war will I make a move anywhere.'

But there had been no news from the Foley boys or from Mylo Dowdy for months. Everyone assumed (but did not like to say it) that they had gone down in that bloody war.

Those were difficult days but suddenly everything changed on the day that Rosa rushed breathlessly up to the priests' house and banged on the window for Eli to come out. Eli peered timidly out of the window.

'Eli!' gasped Rosa. 'Come with me at once. I've got a good idea that your David has arrived. His name *is* Kennedy, isn't it?'

'Oh yes!' cried Eli. 'Wait a minute.' Tearing off her cap and apron she dashed outside and ran off with Rosa, ignoring the angry glare from the housekeeper.

'Come on with me,' Rosa held Eli's hand tightly. 'He is at the immigration offices. Tall with red hair, right? It seems he can't come in because some guy pinched all his money.'

'Oh!' sighed Eli. 'Poor David, what can we do?'

'Well, let's confirm that he is your man first,' said Rosa. 'I told him to stand at the gates and I will bring you over on the ferry.'

An hour later the heavy ferry neared Ellis Island. As the big gates came into view, Eli suddenly felt faint. There he was, her loved one, David, with his bright red hair blazing in the midday sun. He looked pale and thin but was still so very tall.

Soon Eli and Rosa had fought their way off the ferry and through the milling crowd. David gripped the bars of the gate so hard that his knuckles turned white. 'Oh, little Eli!' he cried when he saw her. 'How foine it is to see you looking so pretty!'

Eli pressed her face close to his as tears flooded down her cheeks. 'Oh, David, I have waited so long for this moment.'

A dry cough behind her reminded Eli of Rosa's presence.

'Now cut the romance,' Rosa said briskly. 'Ask him how much he needs to get through the immigration office and if his papers are in order.'

For several minutes there was a whispered talk between Eli and David and their tears intermingled as he told her of the shipwreck and the money he had lost, and his fear that he would be shipped home again in several days unless she had enough money as a sponsor to get him ashore.

'I'll come back soon,' said Eli as their lips met again through the bars of the gate.

'Well?' asked Rosa, 'You found your man, little Eli, but how are you going to bail him out?'

'I don't know,' Eli said sadly, shaking her head forlornly.

'I do!' stated Rosa. 'He will need fifty dollars and your Grandpa and the old priest to sponsor him. Then they will let him go.'

'But what about the money?' asked Eli. 'How will we raise that?'

'There's only one place I know and that is my sister Ruth. She's rich enough with Barney's immoral profits. I'll not go, Eli, but *you* must. In the meantime I'll start negotiations with the Port Authorities. Off you go, now.'

Ruth was looking very motherly with her new baby in her arms and she seemed very pleased to see Eli. 'Rosa is not with you?' she asked rather sadly. Her English had never been very good and since she had

been living in a Jewish neighbourhood, it had deterio-
rated from lack of practice.

'Rosa is so busy,' said Eli, 'but she sends her love to
you and the baby.'

Momma Feldman was staying with Ruth and she
came downstairs to greet Eli. Later she poured tea
from a big samovar and arranged little spicy cakes on
a tray. The large airy living room was full of strange
objects, a couple of gilt-edged mirrors, a whole host of
large pictures and china ornaments, and soft carpets
and pots of ferns everywhere.

Eli was a little nervous but she asked Momma to
explain to Ruth why she was there.

As Momma rattled away in Yiddish and told Ruth
of Eli's problem, Ruth's big eyes opened wide with
pleasure. Sweeping Eli against her now ample bosom,
she cried, 'Eli, eet iz so goot! Just like real fairee story.
You want monee? You have all you need. I vill see zat
Barnee giffs 'im vork too.'

'Oh, thank you,' wept Eli, too happy for words.

Within hours Eli's problems were solved; David
was freed from that terrible island and admitted into
America, the land of opportunity. Eli felt that she
would be indebted to Ruth forever and even Rosa
grudgingly agreed that her sister had behaved
admirably.

David seemed quite shy and a little awkward, after
his recent experiences. After all, he had served a long
prison sentence in Dublin, and then been shipwrecked and had his money stolen. He may have
looked like a raw youth but underneath, there was a

very self-possessed young man determined to make good in his new country.

Grandpa was highly delighted to see this youth from his old homeland. He spent many evenings asking about the old village and all the folk he used to know. It made him feel less homesick, which pleased Eli.

Eli was ecstatic to have her David with her at last. Everyone agreed that they made a perfect couple and soon the priest was talking about putting up the banns.

But David had other ideas. 'I have kin in Boston,' he said. 'I'd like to go and meet them before I settle down. But indeed I love Eli and I intend to marry her as soon as I am able to support her.'

Eli sat demurely with her hands clasped in her lap. When she heard David say this, tears filled her downcast eyes. In her mind's eye she watched her lovely dream of a white wedding at St Patrick's fade away. She choked back a sob and smiled at her beloved. After all it did not matter. David was here and *that* was what was important.

The couple often walked hand in hand around the neighbourhood talking of home and those left behind. David was a shy lover but he gave her the occasional kiss. Eli was grateful even for that but her warm little heart yearned for so much more.

'I love you, Eli,' said David. 'I always have, but I'll not marry you till I have made a good living and repaid Ruth the money she lent me. I cannot stay in this overcrowded town. I need space and fresh air. I will make a good home for you somewhere, and pretty soon, I hope,' he added.

'I am sure if you stayed in New York,' said Eli, 'that Barney Cohen would set you up in a good position.'

David shook his head.

'I don't need that kind of help, Eli,' he said. 'And not from a Jew,' he added rather haughtily.

Eli was hurt by his words and did not truly understand what he meant. Her friends were mostly Jewish and she was fond of them all.

'They have all been very good friends to Grandpa and me,' she said quietly.

David lifted her chin up with his hand and then pressed his lips down on to hers. 'I swear by all that's holy, Eli, that you are the woman I want, no other. But try to understand that a man has his pride. I must make it on my own.'

Eli snuggled up close. 'I'll try, David,' she said, 'but it will not be easy to part from you.'

'Oh, Eli Lehane,' exclaimed David. 'You are the bravest little girl I've ever known. When I have enough money we will travel out west and get ourselves some land. I shall be a rich farmer and you will be my wife.'

A week later, David, looking much fitter, packed a small shoulder bag and set off for Boston where his family, which had left Ireland some years back, had settled.

Eli returned to the priests' house to dust and polish and try to appease the frosty-faced housekeeper, while Grandpa sat outside the tenement building staring dreamily towards the west, as he waited and waited for Dan and Dave Foley to come home from the war.

Two years passed in this way. Grandpa was now

seventy years old but still fit and hardy, while Eli lived
only for the letters from David who was working up
in Boston on a big bridge-building project with some
Kennedy cousins and saving hard to make a home
for them.

Meanwhile her friend Rosa had gone to university,
having passed all the entrance exams. Her fees were
paid for by the Jewish-German Society, and she was in
her element – a true blue stocking!

With Rosa studying, Eli hardly ever saw her and so
she spent most of her spare time in church, praying for
her David to return to her soon.

10

The Call of the West

As the days passed Eli waited patiently for letters from David. They were few and far between, the mail was very expensive and it took many weeks to arrive. Letters either rattled over the mountainous roads on a stage coach – in danger of attack from Indians and outlaws – or travelled in slow, ponderous, man-rowed boats down the wide rivers. But one day Eli received news of David's imminent return to New York. Ruth came to visit Eli and told her that David had just repaid the loan she had given him. She was now giving all this money to Eli. 'Put it in your hope chest,' she said. 'It will be needed ven the babies come.'

Not long after, on a fine spring day, David arrived at the door of the apartment. He had grown so big and broad that Eli hardly recognised him. He swept her up in his arms and gave her a resounding kiss on the lips, not caring that Grandpa was a witness to it. At twenty-four David had developed into a fine man. The muscles had built up on that big-boned body. The hard work and the bad conditions involved in building the bridge across Boston's Charles River had hardened him. His hair was still bright red and flopped over his face in an unruly mop but his rippling muscles showed through his old faded shirt.

Eli was excited by his presence and could not take her eyes off him as he sat after supper, telling Grandpa what a fine city Boston was.

'Many Irishmen live there,' he said, 'but it has a bitter winter. Now I would like to go to California where they say it is summer all the year.'

Grandpa puffed his pipe thoughtfully but he had one eye on Eli, watching her expression as David talked of moving on again. 'Well now,' said Grandpa. 'I am all for a man trying to get the best for his family. I'm not sure that I would like to have summer all year round. I'd miss the seasons but they do say there are great opportunities out west. Now there is talk of a big railroad being built out there.'

David nodded. 'Yes. They plan to open up the west with their railroad but I am for getting some land of my own and farming it. I was born on a farm and that's how I'd like to live.'

'Good,' said Grandpa, 'and since Eli is from farm folk too, you should work well together.'

Now for the first time David glanced at Eli. He smiled as he saw how shy and coy she was. He put an arm around her. 'Have we your permission to marry, Grandpa Foley?' he asked.

Grandpa nodded. 'Aye, you have, indeed you have, laddie,' he cried, Grandpa grasping David's hand and pumping it up and down.

Despite her dream of a big wedding, in the event it was a very quiet affair because David wanted it so. 'I can't afford to hang around in New York or the money I have saved will dwindle,' he told her. 'We will be married quickly and then start for California immediately.'

Eli stared at him, wide-eyed with fear. 'But how will we travel?' she asked. 'And what about Grandpa?'

'Well, I have decided to ask him to come with us,' replied David. 'I know you won't leave him here alone.'

'But he is too old to travel,' cried Eli in dismay. 'And I have heard that there are Indians out west and other dangers. I don't think I want to go.'

David's normally pleasant face hardened and his lips clamped in a thin hard line. 'Eli Lehane,' he said sternly. 'I love you as I always have. But if it is necessary, I'll go out west alone. I am determined to get away from these crowded cities to start a new life, I have worked hard and saved my earnings so it's now or never. Just give me an answer.'

Eli wept but nodded weakly. 'All right, David, if Grandpa will come, I'll give in.'

David held her tight to his chest. 'Little Eli, trust me. I'll take good care of you and your Grandpa, I have learned the hard way.'

The Feldmans wept as they watched Eli leave with David and Grandpa Foley. Eli was a bride of just two weeks looking so pretty in her neat grey dress and pink bonnet, but so vulnerable too.

Grandpa had agreed to travel with them without any hesitation. 'It don't matter where I die,' he said. 'I've had a good life and I can risk a little more excitement before it's over.'

So the apartment was given up and the furniture sold. They were to start anew, leaving New York by the overland stage to meet Mick O'Shea, a cousin of David who was to join them all on this pioneering adventure out to the golden west.

Eli was more than a little forlorn at leaving her home but looked with lovelight in her eyes at her magnificent David who was so full of plans. 'First we get to where my cousin Mick is settled,' he said. 'He has been working at the railhead but now wants to move out west. He has several wagons already and all the equipment. We made all these plans when he came to Boston last Christmas to visit his wife's family. We estimated that it could take six months to get to California but in the end it will be worth it.'

Eli listened to David and tried to suppress her fears of this long journey. There were so many possible dangers on the way. How could they possibly survive?

Much to Eli's surprise, Grandpa braved that long stage trip very well. He enjoyed it, too, and always insisted on riding up front with the driver most of the way. 'They will not like the smell of me old pipe in there,' he said, and he was probably right.

After many bone-rattling weeks, the stage pulled into Omaha, where they were to find David's cousin Mick. Omaha was a big sprawling town full of wooden shacks built higgledy-piggledy along a wide muddy river.

This was the railhead and a very busy place it was too. Logs came down the river and were then hauled up to the sawmills by bullock trains of seven or eight big oxen.

As the railroad progressed, the huge engine, puffing steam, carried hundreds of cheering men in over-loaded railcars, moved further along the track and out into the Nevada Desert where they worked tirelessly in the blinding heat. There was a great deal of pressure for them to work harder and harder, for a rival railroad company, the Central Pacific Railroad, was also racing to reach the midway mark first, so the competition was intense.

Eli did not understand that but she was appalled by the noise and dirt of Omaha, as well as the taverns full of men and brazen women.

''Tis a rough ould place,' commented Grandpa.

David nodded. 'Well, what can you expect? These people come here from all over America because there is money and work here. Those things bring the rest with it. But I've no intention of staying here. We're off to the wide open spaces, that's the life for me.'

They found David's cousin, Mick O'Shea, without too much difficulty. He worked on the bullock trains unloading the supplies for the army of workers out on the prairie. He and his wife lived in a cabin beside the railroad track. Mick's wife was a thin miserable woman and very religious. Because of the conditions in Omaha, they had left their baby son back in Boston with her parents and she fretted and pined for him a lot. And she was no keener than Eli to go into this unknown land of wild Indians and bad men.

Eli liked her and quickly made friends with Kitty

O'Shea. The two women looked after the old cabin and enjoyed each other's company.

Most of the time they all ate outside the cabin, having cooked the meals on wood stoves outside the back door. Inside the cabin it was so cramped that Grandpa and David liked to sleep out in the open beside a camp fire. At first this worried Eli but there was no need. The nights were mild and warm and stars shone down brilliantly and benevolently on their sleeping bodies.

David spent most of his days preparing for the rest of the trip, laying in supplies and planning. And Grandpa would help him where he could.

One day as Grandpa sat outside the main store waiting for David, who was buying some supplies, a large, bulky figure of a man rolled down the dusty street. He wore a broad-rimmed hat and wore a gun on each hip. When he saw Grandpa, he let out a great roar.

'Well, I'll be blowed! Is it you, old Grandpa Foley? Or is it a ghost?' It was Mylo Dowdy. He dashed and grabbed Grandpa in his arms. ''Tis the greatest day of me loife!' he cried, wiping away the tears from his eyes.

When David came out of the store a few moments later, he was wild with delight at the sight of Mylo, whom he had not seen since Mylo left Ireland many years before.

It seemed that Mylo had been working out on the trail and had just been paid off. He had arrived in Omaha to spend some of his money. 'And wait till the boys find out,' he cried.

Old Grandpa's face creased up with emotion. 'My boys Dave and Dan? How did they fare in the war?' he asked.

'They are here as large as loife,' replied Mylo with a laugh. 'Why, I left them only two days ago. They ride with the General, and foine soldier boys they were, too.'

Grandpa wanted to hear everything about what his boys had been up to.

'After the war we got stranded down in the south,' Mylo continued. 'But then we joined the General. Nowadays we ride along the trail to protect the survey-ors of the railway from the Indians.'

David nodded knowingly. He had heard of these unofficial soldiers and the good work they did protect-ing the railway workers and their families.

'And Dan is now married out at Fremont.' Mylo smiled. 'You be expecting a grandchild any day now.'

This unexpected news proved to be too much for poor Grandpa. Tears poured down his cheeks and he did not know what he was crying for. All he knew was that he felt happier than he had done in years and he had never expected to feel this happy again.

A week later when the Foley boys rode in, there was a grand reunion. These were Eli's uncles, the men she remembered as the wild rebels in Ireland. Now they were big, bearded men, and gun-slingers of the west.

Together, they all rode out to Fremont, to the little homestead nestling in the green valley. Dan's wife was an Irish girl whose folk had been killed by the Indians. She was fair and lovely, and heavily pregnant.

All the family, including Eli, begged David Kennedy to stay in Fremont and work with them on the new railroad. But David had his plans and he wanted to stick to them. He was typical of the kin who had descended from the ancient Irish King of Munster Boru.

'You can stay if you wish, Eli,' he said, 'but I must push on.'

With much heart-searching, Eli gave in to her man and left her beloved Grandpa behind. For Grandpa had decided that he had had enough travelling. He wanted to stay in Fremont and await the birth of his new grandchild, and then to spend his last years with his long lost sons.

So on a bright and sunny day, dressed in a white sun bonnet and a print dress, Eli sat high up on the wagon seat beside her big strong men, red-haired David Kennedy and Mick O'Shea. Inside the wagon sat Kitty.

They left the green beauty of the riverside of Fremont and travelled out to the hot dry desert of the west, headed towards the high-peaked mountains in the distance, standing so shadowy and solemn in the shimmery heat.

Still terrified of the unknown dangers that lay ahead of them Eli now felt a sense of inner courage. Around her neck was Grandma Foley's mother-of-pearl rosary and in moments of danger she held that little crucifix in her hands. Her faith was still very strong and she often gave courage to the other settlers who travelled with them in the other wagons.

Into the strange unknown prairie land they went,

where freak storms rose up suddenly and high winds ripped the canvas from the wagons. There were deep rivers to ford, treacherous tracks to negotiate and intense heat to bear with. It was hard for everyone but David was a born leader of men and encouraged them all with great strength and courage. He gradually assumed the role of leader and was on the constant look-out for hostile Indians whose small war parties still attacked the wagon trains. The buffalo trail was littered with small crosses marking the graves of those who did not finish the journey.

Following Dan Foley's advice, the wagons took the animal trail, walked by the buffalo and the elk, who had travelled this area for centuries. By doing this, they found the easier route over the mountains for animals have an instinct for survival – and survival was all important to any living creature out there – even humans.

Happy-go-lucky David rarely listened to any chatter about Indians. He sat up on the wagon seat with his red hair shining like burnished gold in the sun, and singing old rebel ditties from his homeland.

When they had been two months out on the trail Eli discovered she was pregnant. Although she felt poorly she was thrilled, but David was concerned.

'I wish we had reached our destination,' he said. 'It will be hard for you now, especially since winter is now on the way.'

'Oh, I trust in my Maker,' said Eli. 'He will protect me, and each night I pray to Our Lady to take care of us.'

David smiled and cuddled her close. 'Nevertheless,' he said, 'I will talk with the rest about the idea of going into winter quarters. It will be bitterly cold up in the mountains.'

The wagon train was headed for that hard trail where the frosts came even on the prairie land and snow lay deep on the mountain paths. With the shortage of food and fresh water, the travellers grew thin and gaunt. The climate played havoc with what was left of the women's beauty. Their clothes and shoes got old and ragged and the menfolk became irritable and unshaven. As the weather worsened, David Kennedy finally convinced the other men that it would be kinder to the women and children to rest up until the spring, rather than risking going through the mountain pass where they were likely to get snowed up.

The wagon train soon pulled into Ogden, Utah, a sprawling railroad town of the Union Pacific Railroad. Everywhere there were lines of shacks and piles of equipment, and beer tents, gambling booths and other dens of vice to accommodate all the rowdy immigrants crowding in away from the bitter winds and snow of the trail.

There were many wagons wintering in this sheltered spot and Chinese and Irish worked together to clear the forest in preparation for the railway that was to be brought over the high Sierra mountains in the spring.

There was plenty of food and plenty of drink in Ogden but money was running out for David and he was restless. Good fortune had it around that time that the boss from the rival railroad company rode into town to recruit labour, and it was not long before his eye rested on big strong David Kennedy.

'Hallo, so you are a Kennedy,' he said to David. 'I knew your folk in the old country. How would you like a job on the railway?'

'No,' David shook his head. 'I'm heading west in the spring. I am a farmer and I intend to claim some good farming land out in Oregon.'

Charlie Crocker eyed David speculatively. 'Well,' he said. 'I need some good strong Irishmen. These Chinese are good workers but they don't come up to the Irish lads. If you can get a gang together, the pay will be good. We have to bring the railroad over the mountain by the spring, and time is getting short.'

'I have my wife with me and she is expecting,' David said. 'But I must admit that the money would be useful.'

'Well, lad, set about it,' Charlie Crocker slapped him on the back. 'I'll not let you down. The women can have a couple of nice warm cabooses in the meantime, and I'll release you in the spring. I am desperate. Those poor bloody yellow buggers are dropping like flies up there on the mountain. I need tough men now,' he said.

So David, Mike O'Shea and six other Irishmen signed up to work on the railroad for Charlie Crocker.

Eli was quite upset at the prospect of David going off to work in the mountains. She was afraid for them both.

'Don't leave me, David,' she wept.

But, as always, David's mind was made up. 'You will be all right with Kitty,' he tried to reassure her. 'You can draw money from the railway paymaster and I'll be back in the spring in time for our baby to be born. It's better this way, Eli. I shall be earning good money and you will be well protected by the railroad men and safe from the dangers of the trail.'

Eli knew that she had to give in. With a glum face, she watched David ride off in a big wagon drawn by six oxen. Some of the men were already drunk, shouting and singing amongst their load of picks and shovels in the big truck. Left behind, their weeping women bade them farewell.

It was a very long and cold winter in those high Sierra mountains where David and his team slaved to tunnel through the granite rock and carve a way through for the railroad.

Down in the valley, Eli shared a wooden shack with Kitty O'Shea. Every night she would kneel beside the rough wooden bed to pray for her David and for her little child within her womb. Never once did her faith fail her. In her mind's eye she could see the lovely homestead that David would build for her when they finally reached warmth and sunshine in the land where it was always summer. Never would they experience such bitter conditions again.

The snow piled high and weighed down the roof but the shack was well-built and sturdy, so there was nothing to be afraid of. Then, at the end of February, Eli gave birth to her first baby. Two of the Irishwomen helped her through the ordeal.

'That Eli is a little angel if ever there was one,' remarked Kitty O'Shea, impressed by Eli's courage.

After fifteen painful hours, Eli gave birth to a lovely little girl with deep violet eyes and a tuft of bright red hair.

'She is beautiful,' crooned Kitty O'Shea. 'Now, what about a name? Perhaps a good Irish name like Bernadette.'

'No,' said Eli. 'I will call her Violet because she reminds me of a little flower and the cool moss violets in the fields back home.'

'Bedad, 'tis not a Catholic name,' Kitty clucked. 'It sounds *heathen*.' But in her way, Eli was as stubborn as David. The baby girl was baptized by the priest and named Violet. And although David had missed their darling baby's birth, Eli was blissfully happy.

The rough conditions and the poverty of their surroundings did not matter any more as she lay dreaming and waiting for her David to return.

At last the snows began to melt and the sun to shine but it was Eastertide before David appeared once more. As big and husky as ever, he dashed in to see Eli and the new baby. Overcome with joy his whiskery face came close to hers and he whispered. 'Oh, Eli, I missed you so, my darling, and our little one is beautiful. Soon we will be on our way to the bright sunshine and then we will make a fine home and raise a big family.'

Eli sighed. All her life she had given in to someone else. She supposed she always would but in her heart that long wagon trip into the beyond was not something she looked forward to.

Charlie Crocker rode down to try to get David and his team of men to stay on. He was way behind schedule and these strong Irishmen had been a great asset during that hard winter. But David Kennedy was his own man in all things. As he had planned, he began the preparations for the final push west and up to Oregon, where David had heard that there was good land waiting to be settled in. But it was almost summer before they started out once more. Eli's baby, Violet, was now plump and bonny with red gold curls and a big toothless smile for everyone. With her bonny nature, she was the pet of the wagoners. Eli adored her and spent hours embroidering violets on to her garments.

With the old wagon repainted and a spirited new team of horses, the Kennedys were at last ready to go. As their many friends came to wish them a good trip, there were several warnings about Indians. 'They don't like the new railroad,' said one old-timer. 'They say it frightens away the buffalo, so some says the tribes are gathering for war.'

David always ignored such gloomy warnings. He believed that life was full of risks and that one had to take them. He was ready to lead the wagon train again; six wagons this time, including the O'Sheas and some Swedish travellers who had recently joined them and who were heading for the northern part of California.

The wagon train planned to by-pass Salt Lake City and continue all the time along the old buffalo trail until they reached a small range of mountains. Once they passed this, then they were on the doorstep of this land of milk and honey.

The way was impenetrable for the wagons until the army of workmen for the railroad had cut down large numbers of trees, and the cries of 'timber!' resounded through the daylight hours as the heavy teams of ox wagons laboured up the high mountain path. The drivers with large bull whips belaboured the poor beasts, apparently without mercy. This Eli hated to see and many times she hid her head on David's shoulder to avoid having to see this cruelty.

They left the railroad and went across the hot dry desert heading for the next mountain range. Sometimes before the day got too hot, causing the air to shimmer, Eli would walk along beside the wagon, her baby strapped to her back. But in the heat of the day, it was almost unbearable and anyone who could sought the shaded protection of the wagons. In the evenings, the temperature would drop a little and the wagoners then set up camp. Around their fires the women sat gossiping and the men smoking, swapping tales of their homeland, while the children played around them.

As they neared the range of sombre black mountains, Eli felt quite apprehensive. She could not say why but she would sit in the back of the wagon with Grandma Foley's beads in her hands, her lips moving in prayer.

One afternoon a scouting party of cavalry had appeared to warn them of dangers in front of them. A terrible sense of foreboding enveloped Eli.

'It's a tricky pass ahead,' the captain said, 'with

plenty of hostile Indians. I suggest you wait until we can send out a proper military party to escort you through before you enter the pass.'

David was very blasé. Producing his old pistol, he said defiantly, 'We are prepared for any trouble.'

The captain raised his eyebrows. 'You'll need more than that if you get ambushed up there,' he said, pointing up the pass. He looked at the gun. 'That looks a bit old, to me. And do you know how to use it?' he asked patronizingly.

David bristled at the implied insult. 'I am quite used to guns,' he said sharply. 'I had plenty of use in the old country.'

The captain saw that there was no point in trying to persuade this young man to change his plans. 'Well,' he said, 'we won't be so far ahead. Send someone on if you get into trouble. Don't try to run. It is very rocky country and there are plenty of Redskins.'

The scouting party rode on, and Eli, who had been listening from the back of the wagon, placed her rosary beads around the baby's neck whispering, 'Holy Virgin, protect my child.' She felt nothing but dread.

David signalled for the wagon train to roll ahead just as the huge orange sun set over the dark mountain in a blaze of glory.

'We will go through tonight,' David announced. 'On the other side is the fresh green country we have all been waiting for. It's only a few hours away.'

Clutching her baby, Eli crept up to sit beside David at the front of the wagon. From there she gazed fearfully out at the gathering mist.

Towering rocks inside the canyon cut out the light as the dusty trail twisted and turned along the pass. For a while an eerie silence hung in the air until suddenly there was a terrifying wail, then more shouts as the heads of the Indians began to appear behind the rocks. An arrow whizzed by with a hiss and then the small party of Indians attacked, negotiating the rocks on their nimble pinto ponies, shouting and hollering as they came.

Eli was terrified and tried to clutch David's arm but David stood up and whipped the horses into a gallop. The Indians had rifles as well as arrows and now began to fire. Several men fell from their wagons and women screamed as the horses gathered speed. The Indians were gaining on them and as David's wagon reached a sharp bend, it tilted sideways, throwing Eli out onto the ground. The Indians were galloping past. The last she saw of her sweet Violet was the evil face of the Indian who had snatched the baby and ridden away.

The travellers gathered up their wounded and back-tracked out of the dark canyon to make camp on the plain outside. As quickly as they had come, the Indians disappeared, when the cavalry, hearing the shots being fired, came to the aid of the wagon train.

They found little Eli unconscious. She was bruised and shaken but fortunately no bones were broken. While the women cared for her, David rode out with the soldiers to look for his baby. But by then it was too late. Darkness had descended and the Indians had fled.

The next day, the wagon train returned to the fort where the military doctor attended the wounded and to Eli, who wept constantly for her child.

'It's better you tell her that the baby is dead and buried,' the doctor advised David, 'and she will cease to fret. She is a good religious girl and will soon find peace of mind that way.'

Listening to Eli cry out in her delirium for her baby, David knew that he had to make his decision quickly. 'They do not always kill stolen children,' one old timer told him, 'but God knows if she will e'er be found when you get this far off the track. It would be almost impossible to find anyone in the prairie.'

So David made his decision and told Eli that the baby had died in the fight and that she had been buried out on the plain.

'For that I thank God,' said Eli quietly. She looked shattered by her ordeal. 'Her soul has gone to Heaven. Did you take Grandma's rosary from around her neck?'

'No, darlin',' David shook his head sadly. 'I thought you would like her to keep it.'

Eli smiled wanly and began to sob into her shawl, lost in her sorrow. Eli improved slowly but she was pale, thin and listless.

When the other wagoners announced that they were leaving to continue their journey, David discussed it with Eli. 'What do you want to do, darlin'?' he asked.

She looked at him sadly with tears in her eyes. 'Take me home, David,' she whispered.

'Back East, to New York?' David asked in surprise.

'No, my love, home to Ireland,' she said. 'I hate this terrible country.'

David wiped away her tears and put his hand over his eyes so that she would not see the disappointment in his face.

'Then we will, darlin',' he said. 'Just as you wish, I'll have to find some way to get us back home and by God, I will.'

11

The Call of Ireland

That autumn David and Eli left the fort and, escorted by a military party, they returned to Ogden. By now the Union Pacific railway had made great headway. It was over the mountain and down on the plain.

'That's it, Eli,' said David. 'I will take you home, darlin', as I said, and the only way I know how is by the sweat of my brow. It is back to the railroad for me and when it's finished you shall travel back in the latest style. But it will take a little time so just be patient for a while.'

Charlie Crocker was very pleased to have this strong Irishman back with him. David was made a ganger and head plate-layer. He and Eli settled in a little caboose beside the track which moved on with the railway as it progressed.

Eli was still affected by her experience. She had become quite remote and unable to cope with life properly, especially in this rip-roaring railhead, but David took good care of her, cherishing his sad little wife, and she received much sympathy from the other wives when the story of the loss of her beautiful baby was told.

David worked with great energy and became a

master at his trade. With his big healthy body stripped to the waist, all day he would swing that heavy hammer and ram the heavy sleepers into place on the track as it slowly proceeded eastward to meet its rival, the Central Pacific railroad. David seemed to grow bigger and browner each day. There was no doubt that the hard work and fresh air suited him.

As the railroad moved on, the little caboose was hooked up to the train and Eli and her belongings went with it into another rough railhead where men and women from all over the world had gathered. Easy money was to be had and loose women were attracted from the big towns, bringing with them gamblers, murderers and every kind of vice. In no time the small railhead was transformed into a big shanty town with bars and shops and gambling dens.

Eli was not happy with their circumstances and she prayed fervently to the Lord her God to help her live a good life in these wicked places. She kept herself occupied by doing washing for the rail workers and helping with their children. Mobs of youngsters, born to parents who were always on the move, ran abut wild, but Eli loved children and she cared for them all. It seemed that there was always some little orphan needing loving care and attention and living in her caboose.

Slowly the hurt of losing her baby began to heal and David returned to the matrimonial bed once more. They were united again as a couple.

Time came when the railroad was almost finished. The boss travelled up and down the track rallying the men and insisting that they must not let the other side win. The race had become very serious indeed. Charlie Crocker had boasted that his men could lay the last piece of track in record time and a vast amount of money was bet on it. Excitement was running high and Charlie was determined to win. He picked out eight of the strongest Irishmen, appointed David as their leader and set them to work on shifts day and night, swinging the huge hammers, the sweat pouring from their strong bodies. At the end of each shift they would fall down and sleep until it was time to begin again the next day, toiling with massive strength to complete the railroad before the specified time. It was a super-human effort which was to go down in the annals of railroad history. The Irish Giants, they called these men. At last the track came to an end and the railroads met at Promontory Point, Utah.

The opening ceremony of the railway was a magnificent occasion. Officials came to Utah from across the country and the steam engines were covered in bunting flapping in the breeze. There were railway officials everywhere and the people roared as big David Kennedy rammed in the final pin of the railroad. Throughout this memorable day the Irish drank and fought, their two ways of celebrating and having a good time.

It was all over. Most of the men were paid off and those who no longer had jobs, packed up their kit and moved on. Some, like David, were to be retained to do the final clearing-up.

David was very drunk for several days. Now he cuddled close to Eli and kissed her. 'Darlin',' he said, 'would you like to go up to Canada? They are going to start a new railroad up there and I've had a good offer for my gang.'

Abruptly Eli sat up in bed and stared at him in horror. 'David Kennedy!' she said sternly. 'May God forgive you for asking me to go through all this again! I lost my lovely baby, I've lived in these hell towns waiting to leave and now it's time. I want to go home.'

'All right, darlin', don't cry.' David smiled as he petted her, stroking Eli's long brown tresses. 'We will go East back to New York and you will travel in style on this grand railroad.'

'Indeed I will not!' declared Eli. 'I will go back to Ireland where I belong, I hate this terrible country.'

'Well, if you say so,' sighed David, 'but there is very little left for us back home. It would be better to stay here in America.'

'No! I will not!' wept Eli. 'I'll not have another child in this God-forsaken place.'

David stared at her for a moment and then jubilantly he swept her into his strong arms. 'Oh, Eli, me darlin',' he declared, 'tell me 'tis true.'

She smiled gently. 'Yes,' she said, 'so we will take our baby back home. I'd like him to be born in the ould country.'

'We will try to make it, Eli, but there is much to do here before we leave. Also, we should go to Fremont to ask Grandpa if he wants to come home with us. How would you like that?'

'Oh, dear God, it sounds wonderful,' said Eli. 'Sure I'm the happiest woman in the world.'

The cleaning up of the railroad and the maintenance took quite a while but at last David was paid off. He and Eli travelled to Fremont to visit Grandpa, Dan and Dave and their families.

Eli was astonished to see the changes that had taken place along the banks of the wide river since they had left. The railroad shacks and piles of equipment had gone and in their place were smart wooden houses with wide balconies and front gardens that had replaced them. It was cool and lush beside the river which occasionally brought in the big paddle steamer from back east. Fremont now had the makings of a very prosperous little town. It had a well-attended wooden church with a spire, a bank and a big saloon where Mylo Dowdy spent most of his day and part of the night. He had become a kind of hero as sheriff, having helped to clean up the town of the no-gooders and bad men. He now lived on the notoriety of his past deeds.

Dan and Dave now had several children and were happy men. Poor Grandpa had lost his sight but sat happily enough on the balcony in a rocking chair while his grandchildren played about him.

Everyone was delighted to see Eli and David and there were weeks of parties and picnics.

Those three months at Fremont with her family did Eli a lot of good. She put on weight and was very content as her pregnancy continued.

Dan and the rest of the family pestered David to settle there. ''Tis no good in the ould countree now.

There is still plenty of trouble.' They persisted, 'and you have been in trouble, David. You would be much better off here.'

''Tis Eli,' David said, shaking his head. 'She is determined to have this baby in Ireland and I won't cross her. Next week we'll take the train east and book our passages back home.'

Grandpa decided not to leave. His once keen eyes were now sunk deep and unseeing in his wrinkled face. Through his long beard he sat clucking away as he sang the Irish airs. He still had a fine strong voice. 'Go home, girl, if that is your wish, and God go with you,' he said.

With farewells and many blessings David and Eli set out one winter's day to travel back east. Well wrapped in a nice fur cape and bonnet and seven months pregnant Eli was happily going home to her beloved green Isle. It was what she had always dreamed of.

It was not so easy to get a ship home, especially as the winter gales had taken a heavy toll of the immigrant ships and many lives had been lost. David was a little weary of waiting for a good reliable ship, eventually booking passage on a small tramp steamer called *Erin II* on the condition that he worked with the crew.

The Dutch captain was pleased to take him on. 'We can make good use of a big strong fellow like you. Your wife will be all right. My own wife is aboard and she will care for her.'

Eli's time was getting short and she prayed that they would be home in time before the birth. David assured

her that it would take four weeks at the most, weather
being fine for them, to arrive back in Cork Harbour.

The little ship battled bravely with the Atlantic
gales. Eli was very sick and spent most of her time in
the cabin. The days passed by and they were still only
half-way across the great ocean when Eli's labour
pains began. David held Eli's hand tight as the captain's
wife helped to deliver a fine red-headed boy, a real
Kennedy. They named him after the captain and the
ship. Cornelius Erin Kennedy.

At last, on a calm day, the *Erin II* sailed into Cork
Harbour. As Eli came down the gangway beside David
and with her baby son tucked up in her arms, she saw
Mary, Marion and Bluebell Wood there to fête their
relations' return with one hundred thousand Irish
welcomes.

Eli felt quite faint. 'Thank God,' she whispered, as
her feet touched the shore. 'Oh, lovely Ireland, I'll
never leave you again, no matter what you do to me.'

Aunt Mary's strong warm arms were held out to the
baby and, with David's tall shape towering over them,
they all went home to Mary's little house behind the
coal quay.

Settled in the tiny rooms with a big coal fire glowing
in the grate, Eli felt as though she had hardly been
away. It was more than six years and yet very little had
changed.

She looked up at her David with a sweet smile.
'How foine it is to come home, David,' she said quietly,
and kissed Cornelius' little head.

12

The Gold Trek

The relationship between Daisy and Dukey was flourishing. It had not taken long for Daisy to discover that Dukey was a wild colonial boy, but with her tough East End savvy, he presented no problem!

They sailed downriver in the old barge and put ashore at Port Hobson, a small thriving port full of sailing ships, rough wooden shacks and many immigrants hoping to find a foothold in this newly discovered land.

Port Hobson had been bought from the Aborigines for about two hundred pounds' worth of goods, and had quickly become a hive of industry with a harbour that looked like a forest of tall-masted sailing ships. The population, mostly male, hung about the harbour where bales of wool were being loaded and produce and livestock were being unloaded.

Daisy was feeling distinctly ill-attired when she came ashore still dressed in her tight hobble-skirted gown which did not make it easy to move in an agile manner. She was suddenly very conscious of the strange looks the men around were giving her. The yellow dress had shrunk and the feathers hung limply, as did her hair in long damp untidy strands. Annoyed by the giggles, she stopped in her tracks.

'Wot sort of place is this, Dukey? Everyone is laugh-ing at us,' she cried.

Dukey turned around to look at her and suddenly saw her as others did. With his hands on his hips, he burst out laughing too.

Daisy paused like a small child and swung her bag at him.

'Pax!' Dukey cried holding up both hands. 'But you do look funny, Daisy, and they ain't seen no one dressed that way since they hit this town.'

'What am I to do?' Daisy glanced down at herself and started to cry. 'Oh, I do look ridiculous, but all I own is what I stand up in. Oh dear, I wish I was dead!' she cried dramatically.

'Not to worry, cobber,' said Dukey. 'There's a shack up on that hill that belongs to a friend of mine. She is an old pal and I'm sure she will fix us up.'

They walked up the steep slope and arrived at a long line of shacks which sported big notices: 'Bed and Breakfast' – 'Hair cuts' – 'Hot baths'.

Dukey's friend Mary Kelly was out in the yard hanging out some washing. A fresh-faced woman, she was as wide as she was tall and wore an enor-mous check dress with a very full skirt covered by a big white apron. She laughed with delight at the sight of Dukey and held out her fat arms in welcome. 'Well, ye bloody oun gossoon,' she said, 'yer back agin I sees.' Her accent was unusual, part Irish and part-Australian.

''Owdo, Mary!' said Dukey, giving her a slap on her large bottom.

'You mind yer manners, Dukey! I don't want none o' that hanky-panky from Sydney out here, eh!' She stared past him at Daisy. Her expression was not friendly. 'Wot yer brought that baggage up 'ere for? Take 'er back where she belongs.'

Poor Daisy, white-faced and miserable, looked forlornly down at the ground. But Dukey whispered something in Mary's ear and rattled the loose change in his pocket.

'All right then,' grumbled Mary, 'she can get a room and a bath. But you keep downstairs, Dukey. Your bath-house is around the corner.' Then, in a more kindly tone, she said to Daisy: 'Come on, gel, I'll fix yer up.'

Cold, dismal and feeling very hungry by now, Daisy followed Mary into the big shack. It was pleasantly cosy inside, and smelled welcoming as Mary led Daisy upstairs to a small room with a single bed covered with crisp clean linen.

'Pull out the hip bath from under the bed and me gal will bring up some hot water,' said Mary. 'I'll get yer some togs later on when I am not so busy.'

Off she swept, her large frame wobbling. But although she was so big and fat, she seemed quite light-footed. She reminded Daisy of a river barge in full sail, full of vigorous energy.

Daisy sat nervously waiting on the bed. A black girl came in with two big jugs, one with hot water and the other with cold. She also brought a clean fluffy towel and a large bar of soap. Daisy discarded her damp clothes, bathed in the hot water and then sat on the bed feeling more than a little bewildered, wondering what was about to happen next. Moments later, a shadow crossed the room, as Dukey now looking well-shaven and spruced up in a clean shirt and trousers hopped in at the window. Glancing around furtively, he held his finger to his lips.

'Shush!' he hissed. 'Don't let Mary hear me. She's a nice old biddy but so damned old-fashioned. I told her you was my cousin who got shipwrecked further down the river. The story worked, so don't say anything about Sydney. She's dead set against that town.'

Daisy held the big towel tight around her. 'Well, I can't move till I get some clothes,' she whispered. 'That lot is filthy.'

'She will be back,' whispered Duke. 'Anyway, try and get on with her. I tell yer, she's all right. I'll wait downstairs and we will get a good supper. See yer!' He cocked his long leg over the window sill and disappeared.

After a while Mary came bustling in with some clothes. 'These are the best I could get. I don't have none of that fancy stuff here. This is a working town, not like that fancy God-forsaken place they calls Sydney.'

Daisy did not reply but her jaw dropped in horror at the sight of a long pair of red flannel drawers, a shapeless white camisole, a checked blouse and a flowing navy serge skirt. In addition there was a large pair of stays.

'These should fit yer,' Mary said. 'You're a big gel. I

used not to be so fat but they ain't no good to me any more. Get dressed, love, and I've got steak-and-kidney pudding downstairs. See yer later.' And off she went as though time was very precious. She was not one to waste words in gossip.

Daisy pulled on the red flannel drawers which had a big split between the legs, then the stays and the camisole which dangled very loosely however she tried to tighten it. There were no stockings but Mary had provided a big pair of leather boots. The skirt felt very odd; there was yards and yards of it! There was no mirror, so Daisy tried to see her shape in the window glass but the sun was shining so brightly she could not.

'Oh dear,' she said out aloud. 'What do I look like?' But the rumbling in her belly told her that it did not matter. She had to eat and the thought of that steak-and-kidney pudding was very tempting.

She let her newly washed hair hang down free, and buttoned up the check blouse. Then she went timidly down the stairs.

In the big dining-room there was a long table. All the seats were occupied by men who shouted at each other as they gobbled up their food.

Dukey was sitting at the far end of the table and he beckoned Daisy to come and sit near him.

Immediately all went quiet, though there were the occasional polite murmurs of 'Evening, ma'am.'

The sight of a lovely young woman was most unusual in this predominantly male port.

Feeling very nervous, Daisy stared down and made

herself smile at the assembled company. Her cheeks were rosy and her chestnut hair, which was streaming down her back, was turned to autumn glints by shafts of sunshine. All was silent. Daisy had a captive audience staring at her.

At last Mary appeared from the kitchen and served Daisy with a big plate of delicious-smelling pudding, lots of boiled potatoes and bright green peas. It was succulent and satisfying, a splendid meal finished off with apple pie and washed down with plenty of beer for the men but only tea for Daisy. Mary, a strict teetotaller, expected other women to be the same.

After dinner, the men began to move out to get on with their jobs as wagoners and cowhands. Daisy felt much more relaxed. In spite of their rough appearance, these men were all very friendly and kind. She was beginning to feel more at home in Australia at last.

After the meal had been cleared away by the coloured girls, Mary came over to Dukey and Daisy and sat down with her elbows on the table. Beads of sweat still gathered on her brow and her face was fiery from the heat of the stove. 'Now that the men have gone, you got to tell me what this is all about, Dukey. You're not in more bloody trouble, I hope . . .' She looked genuinely concerned.

'No, darlin',' replied Dukey with a laugh. 'I just came down here with me cousin. Her husband's out in the diggings and I am going to take her up there.'

'Good,' said Mary. She looked satisfied. 'But you mind yourself,' she added, looking at Daisy. 'He's a real rogue, is Dukey. Now get a good night's kip.' She turned to Dukey. 'It's out to the bunk-house for you, me lad,' she said, lifting her heavy body off the stool with a sigh. 'Now I got to get on and see about the breakfast for the early risers. See you in the morning.' As she passed Dukey, she leaned over and whispered in his ear: 'She's a fine-looking gel. You just behave yourself.'

In the morning, when Daisy came downstairs, Mary greeted her. 'Sleep well?' she asked. 'Yer a bit late for the bacon but there's porridge and eggs and a bit of toast if yer want it. Dukey's out,' she added as she bustled off. 'He said he'd be back in about two hours.'

'Can I help you?' asked Daisy.

'Yes, lass, got some more travellers just coming. Fill up that big pot with tea and give the porridge a stir.'

So, having eaten her fill, Daisy poured out tea into big tin mugs and spread butter on toast for the rest of the guests until Dukey returned.

At last Dukey arrived back. He was wearing a wide bush hat which he took off and clamped on Daisy's head. 'Now you look a real digger,' he said. 'Come on, gal, we are moving out.'

Mary let out a great laugh. 'Well, she's a good gel, Dukey, she's bin helping all morning in the kitchen. Now you take good care of her.'

Outside was tethered a small donkey on whose back was loaded all sorts of gear. 'That's Henry,' said Dukey. 'Now don't start yelling, or yer might spook him. I had a bloody job loading him.' He turned to Mary. 'So long,' he said. 'Thanks for everything. See you one day soon. Now get those big boots moving, Daisy, 'cause 'ere we go.'

Daisy and Dukey trudged along together, with Dukey leading Henry the donkey through the dirt roads of the town and out into the open country-side. Soon they were climbing up a steep mountain road, and Daisy's feet slipped uncomfortably in the overlarge leather boots. Dukey whistled a tune and talked endearments to Henry. He seemed to ignore Daisy as if he had forgotten she was there. When the sun came out high in the sky and began to to beat down on them, Daisy's hat felt very heavy so she took it off.

'Keep the lid on, Daisy,' Dukey yelled. 'Yer don't want to get sunstroke, do yer?'

The road was far from lonely as there were many other travellers on it, all travelling in the same direction. Some sat resting by the side of the road, while others had made rough camps and sat drinking from tin mugs watching their billy cans hung over the smoky fires.

'I got to get ahead of this lot,' said Dukey surveying the scene. 'There's news of a big strike, which is why they are heading this way.'

Daisy was hardly listening. 'I am tired,' she grizzled. 'I want a cup of tea.'

'All in good time,' replied Dukey. 'Daisy, you are a big girl and this is tough country. You just can't afford to give in.'

Feeling disgruntled and very depressed, Daisy trudged on, wondering what she was doing in the

Outback and where on earth she was going. Certainly there seemed to be no immediate answer!

The sun was going down and they were now over the mountain and out in a plain that was cool and green beside a river.

'Right,' said Dukey. 'Now we'll make camp. Get going, girlie, and unpack the gear while I light a fire.'

Soon the billy can was hanging over the fire and Daisy had collapsed, exhausted, on a blanket. At least it was wonderfully cool and quiet in this valley. It seemed that they had left most of the other travellers behind, as Dukey had planned.

'Ah, this is the life,' said Dukey, lying down beside her. 'How goes it, Daisy?'

Daisy sighed wearily. 'I am so tired,' she complained.

'You'll be much more beat tomorrow,' Dukey said with a laugh. 'We got to climb up that big one.' He pointed to the massive mountain in the distance. 'Think you can make it?'

Daisy nodded feebly. 'Well, I ain't goin' to walk all that way back now,' she said.

'That's it, cobber,' grinned Dukey. 'Keep going.' He rolled her over and kissed her a smack on the lips. For a moment she resisted but then relaxed. Dukey's lips were hot, dry and passionate. Daisy's head swam as she felt all sorts of stirrings in her body. These were not the sweet timid kisses of Jackie nor the hot slobbery ones of Maxi. They seemed very different and truly sensual.

Then her sense of propriety got the better of her. She suddenly pushed him away. 'You got a bloody cheek,' she said, trying to sound indignant.

'That's just for starters,' said Dukey, getting up to put the tea in the billy which was boiling rapidly.

For their supper, they ate hard bread and dry beef, swilled down with lots of tea. Then, as night fell, Dukey rigged up a rough canvas shelter and laid the blanket on the ground. 'There,' he said, 'let's get some kip.'

Daisy stood hesitantly next to the blanket. Dukey lifted her serge skirt and grinned with amusement at the red flannel drawers underneath. 'Get them passion-killers off first,' he said. 'Or I'll take them off yer.'

'Oh, no you won't,' said Daisy. She tried not to smile and felt very confused about what she should do.

Dukey grabbed at her and she danced away. For a while the two of them larked about as Dukey tried to remove the offending garment but quite suddenly, as he held Daisy tight and kissed her passionately, she let him slide the red flannel drawers down her slim legs. Then she lay down as he stroked her smooth skin.

Dukey kissed her ear lobes and whispered: 'Come on, Daisy, you know you want to, don't resist.'

And Daisy knew that she could not resist at all.

She let out a little gasp as he entered her, his hard rough body so unfamiliar, but it felt good. Abandoning herself to pleasure, she put her arms around his neck and responded as best she could to Dukey's skilful lovemaking.

The sun had nearly risen over the high mountain range and the snows gleamed with rainbow colours as Daisy awoke the next morning. The ground felt hard beneath her, but a warm glow burned within her. Slowly she raised her head and looked towards Dukey who was up and staring dreamily at the camp fire. The billy can was steaming as it swung on some sticks and an aroma of coffee hit the morning air.

'What's that smell?' Daisy asked, sitting up.

'It's not me,' grinned Dukey. 'That's coffee. I scrounged some beans off Mary. Yer don't get much coffee out here so I thought we'd give ourselves a treat.'

'I'd sooner 'ave a cup of tea,' sniffed Daisy, staring at him in a melancholy way.

Dukey came over and squatted beside her, gently stroking her hair back from her forehead.

'Sorry about last night, Daisy,' he said. 'I got a bit carried away. It's a long time since I made love to such a beautiful woman.'

Daisy hung her head with a coy smile. Dimples began to appear in her cheeks. 'It's all right,' she whispered.

'Must have been those red flannel drawers,' grinned Dukey, pulling up a handful of grass and throwing it at her. Then his tone suddenly changed. 'Now,' he yelled, 'get yer arse outta that blanket, Daisy! We got a long day ahead of us. You look to the coffee, I'm off to take a swim.'

Daisy got up, put the blanket around her and sat by the fire waiting for the coffee to boil. She felt oddly happy and content. What a strange life she was leading at the moment.

Dukey came dashing back naked as the day he was

born and stood by the fire shivering. Daisy laughed as she gave him the blanket and helped him wrap it around himself. As she handed him a mug of coffee, Dukey's wet lips found hers.

'Thank you for last night, Daisy,' he whispered. 'Now, when you've drunk yer coffee, yer better get down and have a wash up. There's a little pool down there. Don't get into the river. It's running very high and fast. There's the soap and a little hand towel in the kitbag. As for me, I like to dry in the sun.' Then he stretched out beside the fire, his fine suntanned body exposed for all to view.

Daisy tripped off to the pool and put her feet into the silvery water. It felt chilly but very refreshing. She dressed herself, and plaited her hair, putting it up under the bush hat. By now the sun was truly risen and the warmth came out of the earth. Birds in the tangle of trees uttered strange shrill cries which wafted across the still air. It was certainly a peaceful and lovely spot. To a young girl who had spent all her life in a mean back street this was like the Garden of Eden.

When she returned, Dukey had already broken camp and was breathless from having to catch Henry who had chewed through the rope that had tethered him and run away. As Dukey loaded the gear on Henry's back, Daisy suddenly looked at him in a new light. Fully dressed with those leather-bound breeches and high riding boots, Dukey looked quite dapper and neat. In spite of his rough manner, there was a look of the gentleman about Dukey.

'Got to move quickly, Daisy,' he said, 'otherwise

them gold-chasing bastards will get ahead. You can see 'em moving off up the trail already.' He pointed to a long line of shapes wending its way over the mountain. It looked like a line of insects. 'Don't worry, Daisy,' he said, giving Henry a good whack. 'I know the way. And I got a few tricks up my sleeve.'

Not understanding much of what Dukey was up to, Daisy did not reply. She just plodded patiently behind Dukey and his loaded donkey. Oh, the heat of that long day! She was to remember it for a long time afterwards for it made the steep mountain path they had to climb seem endless.

'I'm hungry,' grumbled Daisy, after they had been walking for several hours.

'Later, my doxy,' said Dukey. 'A full stomach in this light air will only give you the cramps. Here have a chew.' He broke a strange-looking root stick in two and handed her half. 'Molasses,' he said, 'it gives you energy.'

The root was sweet and bitter but also soothing. So Daisy grimly dug those large boots into the uneven path and trudged on chewing slowly on her molasses. She often had to squeeze past huge bundles of under-growth until they passed the treeline and came to the snowy trail at the top of the mountain.

'Won't be long now, Daisy,' said Dukey. 'We had to take a short cut.'

It got colder and soon the track was a maze of foot-prints in that white snow.

'We'll be going down soon, Daisy,' Dukey told her. 'We have met the main trail at last. See the footprints?'

Daisy's head swam giddily as she gazed down from that great height to where the trees looked like pins and the moving stream of men still going on and down into another green valley looked like an army of ants.

At least they seemed to be making progress so, after a few more hours, they had gone down the side of the mountain and found a spot to make camp. They were not alone this time. Other travellers rested in this green valley after their hectic mountain trek. Billies were boiling, fires were blazing, snatches of songs and conversation broke the silence.

'Oh, crikey!' exclaimed Daisy, sinking down onto the grass. 'Ain't it nice to be back in civilisation!'

Dukey grinned as he tended the fire. 'You are a real towny, Daisy. Come on over here and I'll show you how to make dumpers.'

'What are dumpers?' she asked.

So Dukey showed her the art of mixing flour and water and baking the pancake on a flat stone.

'Not bad,' said Daisy later, munching the hot, sticky dumpers. 'Oh, it's nice not to be so hungry anymore. I felt as though I could eat a horse. I'm still pretty peckish, though,' she added.

'We will have a slap-up meal later on,' Dukey promised. 'So keep the fire going. I'll try to get a couple of rabbits or a wild fowl.'

'Can't cook on that fire,' declared Daisy. 'I need an oven.'

'Don't worry, I'll teach you how to cook on an open fire and survive. It's a necessity in this country. It may be a rough way to live but I'd never change it for all the castles in England.'

'Did you come from England, Dukey?' asked Daisy.

'Sort of,' said Dukey enigmatically. 'One day I'll tell you my story, but not yet. Now, mind the fire and I'll dig us up some grub. Watch out and take no notice of the travellers. There's a big cosh there if anyone gets fresh. I know that you'll use it if you have to,' he added with a grin.

So Dukey went off hunting, leaving Daisy alone for a couple of hours.

When Dukey came back he looked triumphant with a large wild turkey slung over his shoulder and a big bundle under his arm. 'Right, there's the grub,' he said 'and there is a nice big tent. I did a deal with a chap I know. I got a card game fixed for the day after tomorrow when we should arrive at the diggings, but in the meantime, Daisy, pluck those feathers and we'll roast this bird over the fire.'

'Do what?' cried Daisy in alarm. 'Pluck that thing? No fanks.'

But Dukey thrust it at her firmly. 'Pluck it and clean it or we won't eat,' he said. And she knew he meant it.

The poor bird was still warm. Daisy looked mournfully at it. Then, gritting her teeth, she began to pull out its feathers.

When she had finished, Dukey threw a knife to her. 'There now, finish the job. We can't eat with the guts in.'

Daisy closed her eyes and plunged the knife into the bird's back end. But her courage gave way. She began to weep as the blood oozed.

Dukey sighed and got to his feet. 'Christ, Daisy, where were you brought up? You mean to say you ain't cleaned a fowl before?'

'No,' wept Daisy, shaking her head pathetically. 'Me sister Harriet used to do it.'

'Right then, cobber, watch me 'cause next time the job is yours. Yer gotta pull yer weight, Daisy, and the women out here really look after their men.'

Dukey briskly disembowelled the fowl, and then took it down to the river to wash it.

Later they sat around the big blazing fire watching the turkey cook. Daisy leaned her head on Dukey's shoulder and said: 'I am sorry that I'm not much use to you, Dukey.'

'Oh, but you are, darling,' he replied, kissing her. He winked. 'And just look at the nice big tent! No nosey bugger is going to look at us tonight.'

That night, after they had finished making love, they lay close together in the warm tent. Daisy curled up cosily beside Dukey, almost purring like a contented cat. The effect his love-making had on her was quite a new experience. She felt as though they belonged beside each other and that she had known him a very long time. 'You are a real woman,' he whispered. 'And I should know,' he added.

Daisy pouted her full red lips. 'That's not fair, Dukey,' she said. 'You shouldn't talk about other women when you are in bed with me.'

Dukey's strong brown hands roved over her long body. Bringing his hand over her face, with his little finger he gently touched the freckles of her nose. 'Well, you can't say that you were such a pure young miss when you met me,' he said with a laugh. It sounded rather brutal.

Daisy turned away. 'Oh, Dukey, don't be so hard on me. I never wanted to get landed up in that brothel and no one got anything from me.'

'No,' Dukey agreed. 'I feel sure about that. Poor old Pearly got a bad bargain in you.'

'I know, I left my little girl behind in London but I really came to find my Jackie, who is her father.'

'So,' said Dukey, 'you *are* just using me to find your lover,' he said, putting on a mock-injured voice.

'Yes,' replied Daisy. 'But you have always known that. One day I hope to find him.'

Dukey grimaced. Taking his long knife from out of his boot, he slashed the air viciously. 'When that happens, I'll have the pleasure of cutting his ears off,' he said, grimly.

Daisy laughed nervously, not quite sure how serious Dukey was being. 'You are a real brute,' she said quietly. She was relieved to see him smile and leaned affectionately towards him.

Early the next morning they continued the long trek over the mountain and by midday they had caught up with some other travellers who hailed Dukey in a friendly manner and made remarks about Daisy.

'Who's the Sheila, Dukey?' one asked.

'Don't tell me you got hitched, matey,' said another.

They set up camp that evening on the steep mountainside. There were others who had pitched their tents nearby and Daisy found the lull of voices and the lights of the fires quite comforting. She had made a good meal, a stew made up with the remains of the turkey and some wild herbs Dukey had collected. It was aromatic and appetizing.

After dinner Dukey looked very restless. 'There's a big game being organized over there,' he said. 'I'm going to join them. You will be all right, Daisy. Just call out if you need me. I'll hear you, but don't forget about the cosh.' He pointed to a thick stick with a nobbly head. 'You never know who might be prowling around. Yer gets all kinds out here.'

'Oh, I'm all right,' said Daisy. She was thinking that she would heat up some water in the large billy and give herself a nice wash in the privacy of the tent.

Dukey had been gone for some time and Daisy was now sitting in the tent with a blanket around her. Otherwise, she was naked. In the weird light of the hurricane lamp she had given herself a good wash all over and then washed her underwear. Her red flannel drawers now swung in the breeze on a make-shift washing line between the trees.

It was warm inside the tent and the hurricane lamp cast distorted shadows against the canvas. She was thinking of London and of her little girl Petal who would probably be walking by now. When they reached their destination, she would write a letter home, she decided. She was beginning to feel very homesick.

Suddenly a noise made her start. There was a rustling and then the crack of a twig. She listened some more but there was silence. It must have been an animal stealing what was left of the food.

She pulled the blanket tighter around her and stepped out into the dark night.

'One move and you are dead,' hissed a voice. Something sharp was pushed against her ribs and a hand was placed on her shoulder. Daisy spun round and sank teeth into the sweaty hand. Her assailant released his grip with a growl but he dealt her a blow on the side of her head that sent her spinning.

At last she found her breath. 'Dukey! Dukey!' she screamed very loudly.

The man grabbed her with both hands and flung her to the ground, yanking the blanket from her body. As she lay naked on the grass, he straddled her and stuffed something into her mouth to stop her shouting more.

Squealing and whimpering, Daisy tried to twist away but he held her down and slobbered on her face. He was immensely strong. He had removed his trousers and was now trying to prise her legs apart. Panic gave her strength. With a quick movement, she brought up her knees and pushed them up into his groin. The man yelled in pain but he did not let go. Then she remembered the cosh. It was close by. Stretching out her arm, she grabbed it and swung it down on the man's head as hard as she could. He went limp and lay heavily on top of her.

Pushing him off her, Daisy pulled the foul-tasting cloth from her mouth. 'Dukey! Dukey!' she yelled. 'Help! Help!'

Within minutes Dukey rushed up quite out of breath just as Daisy had picked up the blanket to cover herself.

Other men now arrived at the scene and stood staring down at the unconscious shape of the man on the ground. Then they began to laugh. 'My, he's out cold. Who done that? Your woman, Dukey?'

'She did,' said Dukey, proudly putting an arm about the trembling Daisy.

'Some woman,' the men said, very impressed.

The unconscious man was dragged off by the legs in a very unceremonious manner. 'We'll take care of him when he comes round,' they said.

Daisy had suddenly felt quite weak as the shock of what had happened set in. She felt quite overwhelmed.

'You all right, cobber?' asked Dukey. 'He didn't hurt you, did he?'

'No, he bloody didn't.' replied Daisy. 'But he would have if that cosh hadn't been handy. I had just had a wash.'

'He was probably spying on you. You have to be very careful, because there is a shortage of women out here,' he told her. He suddenly noticed the washing line between the trees and burst out laughing. 'Oh, Daisy!' he laughed. 'There's them red drawers flying in the wind like a signal. No wonder he came after you!'

Daisy snatched in the offending garment. 'Oh, Dukey,' she said 'why do you make a joke of everything?'

'Laugh and the world laughs with you,' he returned. 'And now, my little wonder woman, let's go to bed.'

★   ★   ★

The sun was going down behind the mountain in a glorious array of colours when Daisy and Dukey finally reached their next destination. The little town of Ballarat was just a maze of shacks built on the side of the mountain. The short main street had a big wooden bar, a barber's shop and a store. The roads were little more than dusty paths and everywhere there were noises of donkeys braying, horses trotting and the rattle of ox carts coming to and fro. It was a hive of industry. All around were the miners wearing bush hats, a few toffs sporting high hats, some women in sombre dress and several dolled up in feathers and lace with big bustles and high-heeled boots.

Daisy gazed about her in amazement, and suddenly became quite aware of her own sorry state, for she was still clad in that big checked shirt, wide hat and badly stained skirt.

'Will you look at that, Dukey, those women are real smart,' she cried.

'Whores mostly,' said Dukey flatly as he offered a bucket of oats to a very jaded-looking Henry.

'There was a big gold strike here some years ago,' he told her. 'But it panned out and some of the girls settled down here. We are going on, Daisy, up that big hill. We will stay here tonight, and if you want to, I'll try to get a place in the hotel. I won't be staying though. I got business to attend to.'

Daisy gazed open-mouthed at him. 'I can't go in a hotel looking like this,' she said.

'It's all right, Daisy, they are used to us diggers out here. So long as they get their money, they don't care.

That's all they are after, I'll book you in overnight. We'll give Henry a rest and find a card game and maybe in the morning I'll buy you some nice new togs.'

'But Dukey, why do you have to gamble?' Daisy complained.

'Don't be a fool! How would we eat if I didn't?' he asked sharply.

'So if you don't win we don't eat?' Daisy was shocked.

'That's right,' he replied. 'Now, get your arse inside that hotel and I'll pick you up in the morning.'

As Dukey had predicted, no questions were asked when Daisy signed in at the hotel. A lad showed her to a shabby room and told her that breakfast started at eight o'clock in the morning. Daisy took one look at the wide bed and climbed straight into it. Then she slept until daybreak.

When she came downstairs Dukey was already in the dining room tucking into eggs and bacon. 'Tuck in, cobber,' he said. 'Had a good night, I did.'

Daisy sniffed. 'It don't look like you got much sleep,' she said.

'Don't need it,' Dukey remarked, slyly producing a bag of money. 'There's sovereigns there and two gold nuggets,' he whispered. 'You are my lucky little lady. We got a good stake now, I'll stoke up with stores and we will be off to find that gold mine.'

In the store Dukey bought Daisy the best dress there. It was not new but it was beautiful, made of grey silk with a taffeta-trimmed braid. Daisy stroked the shiny material, thrilled at its touch. Then Dukey produced a bonnet to match.

'There we are, Daisy, that's for Sunday best, so you won't keep on complaining.'

She nudged him. 'What about some bloomers?' she asked with a smile.

'Oh no,' Dukey said. 'We can't do away with them lucky red drawers. There's plenty of wear in them yet.'

With a loud chuckle he loaded up Henry and off they went once more over the mountain to Jacob's Gully where it was rumoured a big gold strike had begun.

Jacob's Gully was a desolate place. Along a river which ran down the mountainside, there were wooden shacks, canvas shelters, and a whole caboodle of inhabitants. Men huddled by the riverside working the gold pans while from a large ridge tent a big fellow sold booze. This tent was crammed with men guzzling huge jugs of beer and the noise was horrible, with singing, shouting, swearing and fighting.

'Oh crikey!' said Daisy. 'What a dump!'

'Well, it's here we stay until things brighten up,' said Dukey. 'Then one day we might get a home of our own, depending on how my luck holds out.'

Feeling a little low, Daisy helped to pitch the tent on a wet muddy patch. Then she lit the fire and put the billy on to boil.

Using a bit of old mirror and cold water, Dukey shaved his chin with his big cut-throat razor. 'I'm going out, Daisy,' he said, 'but watch for yourself with this rough lot. I'll find someone with a woman to be company for you, but I got to scout around a bit first.'

Before he left, Daisy looked at him with her large brown eyes. 'Give me half that money to hold for you, Dukey,' she said. 'Otherwise we will be broke again tomorrow.'

Dukey looked at her rather defiantly for a moment, but then he pulled her towards him. 'Okay, Daisy,' he said. 'We were good partners from the beginning, and I need you now as much as you need me.' He handed her the two gold nuggets and half the sovereigns. 'If you take off and leave me at least you won't be destitute,' he said with a laugh.

'Why should I do that, Dukey?' Daisy was shocked at the very suggestion.

Dukey smiled at her wide-eyed innocence. 'What have I done to deserve you, Daisy?' he asked, kissing her affectionately.

Daisy dropped the money into her old bag which contained her only photographs of Petal, then tacked down the side of the tent, made the beds comfy and put away the stores. She was in a strange mood. Life could not have held fewer comforts for her beside that muddy river, surrounded by this low-class population but Daisy was not unhappy. She was singing inside and she did not know why.

Still Dukey's luck held. Each night he halved his winnings and handed them to Daisy. She would count it and then put them all away.

This went on for some weeks until one night Dukey said 'How much we got in the kitty, Daisy?'

She looked at him annoyed. 'No, Dukey, that stays where it is,' she said, shaking her head.

'Well, I was thinking that we might settle in Jacob's Gully. The climate's good and one day this will be a big town.'

'Wot!' exclaimed Daisy. 'Spend our lives in a tent?'

'No,' replied Dukey. 'I know a fellow called Sullivan who is pulling out. He has got a missus and two kids. She wants to go back to Sydney. They have got a nice little home up over the other side of the hill. I could get it for a low price if we want it. Will you come and see it?'

A wide smile brightened Daisy's face. 'Well,' she said with a laugh. 'I feel extraordinarily fit and well here in spite of the mud and the muck. So it would be nice to have a real home.

The next Sunday, Daisy put on her new grey dress and bonnet. Dukey was shaved, trim and neat, as he always was, and arm in arm they walked sedately over the mountain track to another part of Jacob's Gully where there were neat little homesteads built well apart. In reality, they were still only wooden shacks but with windows and balconies, set on individual patches of land.

The Sullivans were a pleasant couple with two charming children. They invited Daisy and Dukey to drink tea in their cosy little parlour. The house seemed poorly furnished but pleasantly homely.

'I want to go back to Sydney,' said Mrs Sullivan. 'My folk are there and they have never seen their grandchildren.'

The Sullivans were very happy to sell their house to Dukey. A deal was soon agreed for fifty gold sovereigns and the price included most of the furniture as well.

Daisy and Dukey moved in the following week. The same day that they arrived at Rose Cottage, a starry-eyed Daisy announced that she was pregnant.

'Well, if that don't beat it all!' declared Dukey. 'It looks like I'll have to get a regular job, then.' He was delighted at the prospect of becoming a father.

'Yes,' said Daisy, 'and I will dig up the garden and plant food and grow lovely flowers. But first we must get married and you can put Henry out to grass, because we ain't going anywhere for quite a while.'

Daisy and Dukey were married one Sunday morning outside the beer tent by a travelling preacher who had had rather too many beers himself. Dukey and his friends celebrated in true Australian style. An old fellow played a fiddle and the square dancing went on late into the night. But by that time Dukey and Daisy were tucked up in bed in their small homestead, and the rest of the world did not matter any more.

Dukey kept his word and got a labouring job out at the big company-owned mine. He still gambled and Daisy continued to be stern with him, demanding her share of his earnings and continuing to save it.

'Do what you like with the rest,' she said. 'But that's my half and we need it to live.'

Theirs was a reasonably happy relationship. Daisy did not drink and had no intentions of doing so, as her strict Protestant upbringing still held sway over her conscience. She learned to bake bread, to make preserves, candles and soap and any other essentials for their everyday life. She also learned how to cut up a young pig and use every bit of its body for their consumption. Her larder was never empty.

Most of her recipes came from the older pioneer women who liked Daisy and came to talk of their homelands. Some were English, some were Scottish. There were even Norwegians and German women among her friends. They told of the very hard early days of living in a penal colony and then trekking out to the bush with their reprieved husbands.

Daisy admired their courage and learned their skills. Soon she had become one of the best-loved and the hardest workers in the settlement.

When Dukey leased another stretch of land, Daisy was out in all weathers raking the ground and burning the scrub almost to the last day that her baby was due. It was all idyllic and their life seemed quite perfect. Occasionally, however, Dukey would look anxiously out at the muddy creek which flowed past the back door. 'That worries me,' he would say. 'Suppose you was took bad and that creek was in flood. We would not be able to cross it. I ought to build a boat if I get the time.'

But there was never time for Dukey. He was too fond of the good things in life. After work, drinking and gambling took up most of his leisure time.

As Daisy's time grew nearer, she became big with rosy cheeks and bright eyes. The winter came and with it a healthy ten-pound boy, delivered in Rose Cottage by an ancient coloured woman. The whole community celebrated the arrival of Charlie. Another true Australian had been born.

13

Calpeady

Daisy was still content in her little homestead in Jacob's Gully. She worked hard on the land, on which she grew many vegetables. They bought a cow and Daisy learned to make cheese and butter which she sold to the travellers who wandered through on their endless trek for gold.

Dukey quit the mine and bought some sheep which he now took out on the range. He spent most of his day out in the open like a gipsy, as Daisy said, but the fresh free life suited him. He seemed content and settled.

The following year Daisy gave birth to another lusty boy, whom they called Frederick. Child-bearing seemed to bring few problems for Daisy; strong and healthy, she was happy with just an old native woman to assist her. She would be up and smiling the next day with no fuss and no bother. To her it was just a natural event.

After the hot dry summer came a long cold winter and Dukey began to get restless.

'Let's pull up stakes and move on,' he said one day.

Daisy was shocked. 'But Dukey, I thought you were happy here,' she said.

'Well, I am, but I want my sons to grow up wild and free and afraid of no man. This place is changing and not for the better. Too many settlers are coming in and vice will come with them.'

'Where could we go?' asked Daisy. 'Back to Sydney?'

'Not on your nelly, old gal! No, we will head into the bush, to the unknown lands where there is still gold to be found and every man is for himself.'

Dukey's mind was made up and Daisy found that there was no changing it however hard she argued. So that spring, very reluctantly, she left Jacob's Gully in a big ox wagon. One baby was balanced on her knees and the other lay in a homemade crib. All their wordly possessions were piled up in the wagon with them.

Dukey seemed as carefree as ever. He cracked the long whip, shouted a farewell to the neighbours and off they rolled out into the wild bushland, heading west to as yet undiscovered territory. The scenery grew wilder, the mountains higher, the sun hotter and all around there seemed to be great stretches of open plains without any vegetation apart from a few scrubby trees here and there.

Dukey and Daisy ate and slept in the shade beside the wagon; the weather was very hot. One day they arrived in a small dried-up town. It was made up of a line of shacks and dusty road but some civilisation existed there. Men lolled about outside the tavern and women walked children along the dusty street. It seemed that they had come all this way seeking for gold but found only opals. Now the men dug deep into the mountain to find opals.

When Daisy and Dukey arrived it was in the cool of the evening. The sun set, looking like a great orange ball behind a big red mountain. There was not a blade of green grass to be seen anywhere in this little town of Calpeady.

Daisy sighed. Were they going to live in yet another makeshift home on the rocky mountain? It was not a great prospect to look forward to. But she did not say anything.

The next morning she took her children down the main street to get supplies, while Dukey went off to see if he could get some work at the mine.

Daisy walked into the big ramshackle store on the main street. It was dark inside and the floor was piled up with sacks of supplies. The light was so dim that Daisy could hardly see the proprietor, who proved to be a thin scraggy woman with a marked Cockney accent. Daisy suddenly felt that she could have been walking down the Mile End Road any day of the week. In no time, they were in conversation. Daisy learned that this lady had been out in Australia for twenty years. She had recently lost her husband and she wanted nothing more than to go back home.

'It's not so bad out here if you can stand the heat,' she told Daisy, 'but now I just want to get this store off me hands and go back to London.'

'You mean sell it?' asked Daisy.

'Yes, if I can find someone to buy it. Most of them left to go up the mountain but it's handy and it's the only store.'

Daisy looked around with interest at the dusty shelves loaded with tins, boxes and jars. 'How much are yer asking?'

'Well, if you are interested you can buy it lock, stock and barrel for a hundred quid. That's enough to pay me fare back home.'

That evening Daisy discussed the idea with Dukey. He was not impressed. 'I'd rather we pushed on to the coast,' he said.

'How far is that?' asked Daisy.

'I am not sure, perhaps a thousand miles.'

That was quite enough for Daisy. She turned to him with an uncharacteristically stubborn look on her face. 'Well, we will stay put. We are not budging another inch. I am not going to risk my children's health in that hot desert. Furthermore, I hold the money, so I will make the decision.'

Dukey stared at her in amazement. 'Why? How much savings have you got, Daisy?'

'I've got one hundred and twenty pounds plus the two gold nuggets you gave me,' she replied very disagreeably. 'And I'll not part with them.'

'Well, I'll be buggered!' cried Dukey. 'How did you get hold of all that dough?'

'I worked for it,' she said. 'I sold my cheese and butter to the settlers and saved the money. Now I'd like to buy that store because it has great possibilities. It seems that it is the only place outside of the town that sells the commodities we all need to live.'

Dukey listened to her and was swayed by her argument. 'You might be right, Daisy,' he said. 'It's an up-and-coming place and they reckon these opals might be as popular as diamonds in time to come.'

'Well, whoever works up there has got to eat,' said Daisy, 'so tomorrow we will go and get that store signed over to us. I am just fed up with wandering, I want to stay put,' she added.

Within two weeks the old woman was on her way back home to the East End of London and Daisy was working hard to clean up the shop and its little shack to make another cosy nest for her family.

There was always plenty of business with the settlers who came to renew their provisions as well as the long trail of immigrants who came down the main street on their way out to the bush again in their quest to conquer this unknown land.

Daisy sold general goods but expanded the business to sell cold beers and delicious home-baked bread. These she served to the diggers when they came into town to water their horses. Refreshed and fed by Daisy, they would then go on their way.

Dukey swapped his team of oxen for some good strong saddle horses and went up to the mine for a few days at a time, taking with him fresh bread, milk and potatoes. He usually stayed to play cards with the miners who lived in a deep tunnel under the mountain, the heat outside being too much to bear.

As resilient as ever, Daisy looked after her babies and sweated and toiled to bake her bread and cakes and serve cold drinks. She no longer worried if Dukey did not return for a while because she knew he would in the end. One evening as dusk fell a group of Aborigines appeared at the back door. They carried spears with them but pointed to their mouths to indicate that they were hungry. Daisy had just taken a fresh batch of bread out of the big brick oven and was very frightened. Taking one look at their dark faces, she yelped and jumped back. Picking up two steaming loaves of bread, she threw them at the men. 'Now sod off!' she yelled, slamming the door and bolting it quickly. She was astonished when she peered out of the window to see them loping off into the bush carrying her loaves with them.

Dukey thought this incident was funny but he was also concerned. 'In future lock the back door, Daisy,' he said. 'You can't trust these fellas. Fortunately they don't come out of the bush very often. It must have been the smell of your bread that did it.'

The store began to prosper as Dukey and Daisy established themselves in this little community.

By the time their third son, John, was born, they were very much part of the town of Calpeady and in spite of the heat and hazards, Daisy rarely thought of returning home to England. But sometimes when she looked at her three thriving little boys she recalled, with a lump in her throat, the sweet little girl she had left behind. Petal was her first born, and she could always see in her mind's eye Petal's dark hair and her vivid blue eyes and remember the way her tiny soft hand had clung to Daisy's fingers as she kissed her goodbye.

'Why so pensive, Daisy?' asked Dukey one evening.

He was in one of his good moods as he lounged around the blazing log fire watching her nurse his son.

'I was thinking of my first baby,' replied Daisy. 'She will be a little girl by now.'

'Don't look back, Daisy,' Dukey warned. 'You just take each day as it comes. All I care about is living the best way I can. Come on now, cobber,' he cajoled her. 'Chin up! No complaints!'

Daisy smiled gently back at him. 'Oh no, Dukey, I have no regrets because I know in the end we will make it rich.'

'Well, there is no reason why we shouldn't, if we pull together you and I. This is an expanding place. Opals are producing good business. There's a new company out at the mine and bringing in new ideas, so plenty of people will come to this place. We might as well dig in our roots for the sake of our sons.'

Daisy laughed. 'Never heard you say that before, Dukey. You normally want to move on all the time.'

'Oh well, it's just a feeling I got,' said Dukey.

'I thought I might write to my sister Harriet and ask about Petal, now that I am a respectable wife,' said Daisy.

'Please yourself,' Dukey replied. 'But why worry about one child? We can have plenty you and I.'

Daisy sighed. 'Sometimes I do get a little homesick,' she said. 'It's my roots, I suppose, I think they always stay. You remember where you born, and I think of London.'

Dukey shook his head. 'I'll never believe that, Daisy,'

he said. 'I dug up my roots and planted them here in Australia.'

'I don't even know where you came from,' said Daisy.

'No,' said Dukey. 'I've never discussed my past with you. Perhaps it's the right time now.'

Daisy laid John in his wooden crib and sat beside Dukey, resting her head on his knee. The logs in the fire crackled, providing the only noise in the silent black night. Dukey stroked Daisy's russet hair which hung in thick tresses down to her waist.

'I'm a Guernsey man,' he announced.

'Now,' replied Daisy dreamily. 'What's that?'

Dukey smiled. 'That, my little chum, is an island in the English Channel. It's partly French. My family went there to escape the Revolution in France.'

'Now, don't lark about, Dukey,' Daisy said with a laugh. 'Please just tell me the truth.'

'It's true, Daisy. Guernsey is a grand rocky island surrounded by stormy seas. Every man there is a seaman. Roses bloom all the year round and wild flowers grow in the rocks. I grew up there in my grandfather's house. His name was Charles de Jean Duquin Beauclair.'

Daisy sat up straight. 'Cor, what a mouthful!' She laughed. 'So, I am not Mrs Dukes!' she exclaimed. 'That makes me very pleased.'

'I got the name Dukey aboard the ship I came over on,' continued Dukey. 'It was a tall-masted sailing ship. I worked my passage over because I was in dead trouble and the law was after me.'

Daisy looked at him, waiting to hear the bad news.

'I can't help gambling. It's a compulsive habit. I got in a fight over a bet with a soldier in Guernsey. I stowed away and came over here. I have never looked back since. As far as I am concerned I'm just Charlie Dukes and my sons are all true blue Aussies.'

'I don't care what you did,' said Daisy. 'We have all got something in our past lives. And out here we get a chance to start afresh. That's the best part of this country. No one cares what you did or who you were before you came here.'

'Well-spoken, cobber,' grinned Dukey. 'But one day when we make it rich, I'll take you on a holiday to that sweet island. Sometimes I can feel the fresh breeze of that wild, free island on my face and hear the sea breaking over the rocks at Black Rock. But Australia is my land now and there's no going back. I spent ten years back and forth on the gold trail and I will not give in, now that I have my sons and you, my love, for you are the best thing that ever happened to me.'

From that day on they never talked again about the past and only looked ahead. They built up the store, improved it, sold beer and made a cool shady place under the trees where the thirsty miners could sit and enjoy cold drinks.

Dukey bought a wagon and a team of mules and transported goods to and from the distant town and provided transport for the miners going downriver on the boat to Sydney.

As their profits increased Dukey had a smart bar built and into this the miners crowded on Saturday nights to drink, chat and gamble. Their hostess was, of course, the buxom Daisy. Bright and elegant, smiling but standing no nonsense, Daisy's one concern was to get the money flowing into the big wooden drawer which was her cash box. She still saved very carefully, for Dukey still could not control his gambling. Daisy was very strict with him and made sure that he got no extra money from her to gamble away. She had never got used to it and was still dead against it. She also did not like women who drank; not one was ever allowed in Daisy's bar. Drinking and gambling were for the men. Ladies were welcome to enjoy a soft drink in Daisy's parlour but never in the bar.

The tough sprawling settlement was inhabited by the poorest of the settlers. They were a rough lot, men far from home and very few women. In such places there were always women adventurers coming looking for the spoils, but Daisy never associated with or encouraged these ladies of the town.

Each Saturday night Daisy ran the bar, serving drinks in rapid succession. Those two gold nuggets that Dukey had given her swung from her ears, and she wore a high-necked black dress with her famous hair piled high and held in place by a comb that Dukey had bought for her when Frederick had been born.

Her customers all admired her, for Daisy was a good sight for these dreary men who spent most of their lives in a dark tunnel. They also respected her and her tough man Dukey who was always beside her.

In that rapidly growing settlement Daisy and Dukey became most important to the community. The Aborigines came to ask for employment in their house and when their children were sick they sought Daisy's aid.

One day Dukey came back from the big city in high spirits, looking very pleased with himself. With plenty of money in his pockets, he had bought himself a modern rifle and now he was behaving like a child with a new toy.

'Don't wave that thing around,' scolded Daisy. 'It bothers me.'

Although Dukey's old shotgun was really no good, he thought they ought to keep it around. 'In an emergency we might need it to protect ourselves. I have heard there is a lot of trouble brewing at the moment.'

'What? With the natives?' asked Daisy. 'Oh, they are no trouble. Frighten them off with a loaf of bread, I can,' she laughed.

Dukey laughed too, but added in a more serious tone, 'It's going to take more than a loaf of bread to settle these fellas. It's to do with the mine. A company is due to take it over and modernize it and there are a lot of old-timers up there who will not be easily moved. I also think that this place is changing, Daisy, and not for the best, I hate to say.'

Daisy shrugged. 'Oh well, we are doing quite nicely here,' she said. 'Don't talk to me about moving on. I'll face trouble when it comes. Anyway, I welcome new faces. We could do with some more life here. With all those damned shacks and all the gambling that goes on, it's time there was some law and order.'

Dukey sat polishing up his new rifle. 'Better to be safe than sorry, Daisy,' he said.

In Daisy's experience, the Aborigines were very friendly. The women who came to work for her in her house were kind and gentle, and they quickly learned the domestic routine. In spite of the language difficulty, Daisy was well able to communicate with them, using a combination of pidgin English and sign language. They seemed to be very fond of English baby clothes and she often rewarded them with little gifts of cast-off baby garments, such as white woolly shawls or knitted vests.

During this time their chief link with civilisation was news brought in by travellers, or the trips Dukey made to Port Harbour. With his big wagon and a strong team of horses Dukey took out supplies and brought the necessary commodities in to Calpeady. World news and such like did not bother Daisy who was nowadays completely wrapped up in running the store and taking care of her family. She grew big, buxom and more domineering, as far as men were concerned. Women friends bothered her very little and it was only to the native women that she was kind and considerate. She had not time at all for the frivolities of her own sex, but what she did like was jewellery. The gold nuggets Dukey had given her still swung from her ears, and on her bosom she wore a big opal brooch.

Her fingers were heavy with rings. All were presents that Dukey had given her when times were good.

'Can't lose lately,' he had said, 'not now that I have my lucky lady.'

Daisy crossed her fingers. 'Hush, Dukey,' she whispered. 'Don't let him hear you.'

'Who's bloody listening?' roared Dukey.

'The devil,' she whispered back.

'Oh, don't get involved in all that native superstition, Daisy,' Dukey sniffed. 'Life is what you yourself make it.'

'I am not so sure,' said Daisy. 'The Aborigines are a strange lot but I'm inclined to believe some of their ideas.'

Dukey still often disappeared for days out on the range to seek new territory and often stayed on the mountainside among the poor settlers who lived in rough shacks and tents. This was a drifting population that would pull up stakes overnight and move on, and Dukey would come home tired and unshaven but strangely relaxed, as if he had physically needed time among the hard-drinking gambling roughnecks.

When he returned, Daisy would look at him and sigh but she knew better than to start an argument with him. All the same, she often worried that he would get into trouble amongst that low-class community.

One day, Dukey seemed more animated than usual on his return. 'I met a couple of great guys up at the mine,' he said. 'A father and son. The father is a real old timer. They're spuddies. Old spud and young spud, come over from Ireland. They are doing quite well up there, but they will be pulling up stakes soon and going back to Sydney. I'd like to ask them to supper and have a game. They play a good game of rummy,' he added.

'All right,' replied Daisy. 'Just tell me when you want to invite them.' She rarely took much notice of Dukey's gambling pals.

One night in the bar, a wizened old man came in. He had a long red beard and wore a wide big bush hat. He spoke in a loud drawling voice and she could hardly understand what he said.

Suddenly Dukey rushed over to this man and slapped him hard on the back. 'Welcome, old timer,' he exclaimed. 'Meet me cobber, our Daisy.'

Daisy gave the man a charming smile but her gaze rested on the smaller dapper figure standing behind him.

'Young spud and old spud,' Dukey introduced them. 'These are me pals from up in the mine.'

The man behind was neatly dressed in a well-pressed khaki drill suit, and he sported a small black moustache. But it was his brilliant deep-blue eyes which caught Daisy's attention and made her start. Only one person in all the world possessed such eyes, as far as she was concerned. Her heart leaped in her breast. How like her Jackie he was! But he was so much older and so mature, surely it was not possible . . . But when she looked at him once more she knew for certain that it was he. Jackie himself had recognized her, she was sure, and his bright eyes smiled a silent greeting.

While Dukey escorted his guests off to a far corner to play cards, Daisy continued to serve the noisy customers in her own efficient style. But her mind was in a turmoil. So the old man was Jackie's father, who had been in the penal colony and then had gone off to seek gold. Jackie obviously searched the gold trail as he had planned and found him.

Daisy's breath came in quick gasps of excitement. Did Dukey know the connection? Was he trying to trick her? Should she tell him? about this? She looked over at the men but they were all playing cards, and drinking their beer steadily. She could get no sense of whether Dukey knew or not. It just seemed like such an extraordinary coincidence, surely it could not have just happened.

Later that evening when the bar was closed, Daisy, Dukey and their guests sat around the supper table, which was set with a clean white cloth and all the best cutlery and glassware. Daisy, the hostess, sat at one end with a faraway expression in her eyes waiting for something to happen, for someone to say something. But there were no surprises. There was just the usual chat and after supper the big sing-song when they were all full of good food and whiskey. They caroused and then sang that sentimental ditty 'The Song of the Thrush' and then raised their glasses high in a toast to 'our Daisy'. Yet throughout those deep-blue eyes avoided hers and gave no obvious sign of recognition.

It was in the early hours when Daisy excused herself and retired to bed. There in her room she shed tears of anguish for the first time in years. For she now had a fair idea of what had happened. There was a connection between the two men: Rita, Jackie's mother who had worked in Pearly's brothel back in Sydney. She was friends with Dukey. It was she who had asked Dukey to help Daisy escape. Had Rita also told Jackie of her presence in the brothel? Was that why he really had avoided her gaze at supper? Was she disgraced in his view?

Suddenly her world seemed to be collapsing about her and panic seized her. Please, God, don't let this ruin what happiness I have, she prayed, and she blotted out her fears in a deep sleep.

Dukey had been too drunk to get to bed so, early the next morning, Daisy roused him with her foot from under the table. The guests, it seemed, had gone, back into the dark tunnel of the mine where they slaved away to build a prosperous future.

It was another day before Dukey was completely sober again. He put an arm about her and said: 'Well, cobber, what do you think of my nice Irish pals?'

Tears flooded Daisy's sincere brown eyes. 'Dukey,' she said. 'I don't know what you are playing at but you know that that was Jackie Murphy, the father of my little girl.' As she said it, she knew that he knew.

Indeed, Dukey looked guilty. 'I'm sorry, Daisy,' he said. 'But I had to be sure. That's why I asked them to supper.'

'But why didn't Jackie give me any sign of recognition? Have I grown so fat and ugly?' she demanded. Her voice quavered.

'No! No! darlin',' Dukey comforted her. 'But I made him promise not to before he came.'

'But why? I don't understand!' she cried.

'Well, I was afraid I would lose you,' he confessed.

'Oh, gor blimey!' yelled Daisy. The strength had returned to her voice. 'I am the mother of your three sons. Whatever made you think I'd change my mind now?'

'I'm madly jealous of you, that's why, and I really love you. But he's a straight sort of bloke and he understood. Anyway, they are on their way home next week and I am taking them into Port Harbour. I'll let you say goodbye to him, if that's what you want.'

'Don't bother,' snapped Daisy. 'I don't want to see that little barrow boy any more.' Salty tears rolled down her cheeks.

'Don't cry,' begged Dukey, crushing her in his arms, 'I am your man and I'll show you I am the very best. Come on cobber, let's go to bed.'

Daisy did see Jackie and his father again, on the day they came in for a farewell beer. Dukey had loaded his wagon outside. Old man Murphy was looking a lot cleaner than he had before and he drawled away, beer dripping from his beard. 'I tank yer for yer hospitality, madam,' he said. 'My son and I whisht to give yer a little gift, with your husband's kind permission.'

Jackie came over, gave her a quick but deep stare and then handed her a little parcel. Then he turned and, without a word, walked out of the door.

With much shouting, hustle and bustle, the big wagon rolled off down the dry sandy road to the town a hundred miles away. Daisy stood at the door and watched them disappear, her eyes wet with tears. The old man and Jackie sat in the wagon facing backwards, surrounded by piles of baggage. His father was merrily swigging from a bottle, but Jackie sat hunched up like a pixie. His sad eyes seemed to penetrate Daisy's very soul as he waved farewell.

After they had gone Daisy went indoors. She put her hand into her apron pocket and pulled out the roughly wrapped package. Inside was an exquisite, rare uncut opal. Wrapped around it was a love letter from Jackie.

My dear love,

Be careful. Read this and then burn it when I am gone. Dukey is my pal, yet I know him for a hard man as I have often seen him in action. So dearly did I want to embrace you and kiss you farewell but I could see it would be a hopeless situation. And I did not want to leave you a lot of trouble. I never forgot you but it seems our paths lie in different directions. All I can do is wish you happiness. My mother seems set on a farm outside Sydney but as soon as the old folk are settled I will be back on my way to the bush. Promise me, Daisy, that if you ever are alone, you will get in touch with my family. Then I will come and find you.

You were my first and my last love. No one ever took your place in my heart.

Farewell, my love,

Jackie

'Farewell my love,' Daisy murmured, pressing the letter to her lips. She stoked the kitchen fire and put the letter in it, watching it disappear into the flames.

That night after she had tucked her young sons up in bed, and crept into bed herself, she dreamed very deeply of her childhood in Bethnal Green and the corner shop where her daughter Petal was born.

14

Growing Roots

Her time in Australia had developed Rita Murphy's strong character to the full. Her long, grim life in Sydney had done little to deter her from searching for her long lost husband, who had by now been released from the penal colony and disappeared into the bush-lands. Searching for him had been Rita's reason for leaving England with her young family for this unde-veloped land in the first place, though she had not got very far.

After six years she was still working as the house-keeper in Pearly Ladell's brothel high on the hill overlooking Sydney Harbour. She had been saving diligently from her very first pay. There were now half-a-dozen cocoa tins full of golden sovereigns carefully hidden away in the shack she still rented from Mrs Miller, who was a widow since her husband had died suddenly of a heart attack.

The sawmill was now closed and Rita's sons worked instead in the large lumber camp some way out in the mountain. Her niece, Abbey, had married and gone to live in Melbourne, while Julie, Abbey's sister, who was still very shy and a little simple, took sewing lessons up at the convent. She was similar in temperament to her mother's sweet and simple sister. Poor Jane Kennedy had died in a mental home in Ireland, having given up trying to cope with her hard life.

Rita was concerned about her younger niece. 'Oh, she really does bother me, our Julie,' Rita confided in Mrs Miller. 'She never seems to come out of her shell.'

'She certainly is very pretty,' said Mrs Miller. 'Some day someone will want to marry her. Perhaps that will help her.'

'Well, let's hope so,' replied Rita. 'There are plenty of opportunities out here with this shortage of women but Julie never goes far from home so she does not meet anyone.'

'Oh, give her time,' replied Mrs Miller. 'She's a good girl, and that's everything.'

'When I see what goes on up at Pearly's,' sighed Rita, 'I think I'll never rest until Julie is safely and respectably married.'

Mrs Miller was sitting in her usual spot beside the stove. Age had turned her into a thin little woman with neatly bound silver hair. As she spoke her old fingers were busy crocheting fine lace into beautiful doilies which Rita would sell to the settlers' wives for an extra bit of income.

'Did you hear any more about your registration to buy some land?' asked Mrs Miller. 'I was thinking that I might give up this place and get a little house in town if you go, Rita.'

'So far there's not a dog's chance,' said Rita. 'I've tried chatting up the ould fella down at the office but he says that women cannot buy land in their own right, no matter how much they want to pay for it.'

Rita continued to work for Pearly, putting her earnings in the cocoa tins. Pearly had not changed. She was as loudmouthed as ever and was becoming extremely fat. The ones who had changed were the girls. They were not as obedient as they used to be and were fast becoming very slovenly with the customers who were now of all nationalities flooding into Sydney, all seeking a new life in Australia.

While Rita worked for Pearly, she had always been searching for some trace of her husband and news of Jackie, her son who, it seemed, had been swallowed up in the last big gold rush. At every opportunity, Rita would quizz the men returning from the outback. 'Ever heard of a John Murphy or his son Jackie? John was a convict released on licence ten years ago and my son went to look for him. We have had no news of him in three years.' But no one had a clue of their whereabouts. Rita was getting nowhere.

The barracks commander down in the docks told her that he would keep an ear to the ground, for Rita was a popular woman in those parts and knew how to keep secrets. Then one day in the early afternoon, a highland sergeant rode out to Mrs Miller's with a letter for Mrs Rita Murphy. It had been sent to the barracks with a note asking for it to be forwarded to her.

Rita almost pounced on the sergeant as she jubilantly grabbed the letter. It was from Jackie, who it seemed had forgotten Mrs Miller's address! He wrote that he had found his father and that the two of them were in a place called Calpeady, mining opals and doing very well. He added that there was money in the bank in Sydney for her and he would be keeping in touch.

'Yahoo!' shouted Rita. 'Who says I ain't got a man? In fact, I've got two! I'll have that ould fella over the counter when I get to town in the morning.'

Her youngest son Shaun was home from the lumber camp on leave. He was a sturdy boy with thick black hair. He grinned at the sergeant who was still there. 'Yer want a beer, cobber?' he said.

The Highlander, however, could not take his blue Celtic eyes off Julie who was sitting at the table demurely sewing, her golden locks shining in the light of the flickering oil lamp.

'Howdy, mate,' said Shaun, handing the soldier a jug of beer. 'What's yer name?'

'Jamie,' came the reply.

The tall red-haired soldier was suddenly blushing. Julie moved her lips as if repeating his name, and furtively she glanced up to smile at the young man. As for him, he was truly bewitched by her fair beauty.

The next day when Rita got into town she went straight to the land registration officc with her letter and Jackie's bank draft. 'Now, me ould fella,' she said, 'I want no more sauce from ye because I got two good men behind me and money in the bank. I want no more nonsense about me not buying farm land.'

The clerk was delighted. 'Good,' he said. 'Go down and see the bank and I'll start to pull strings for you, Rita.'

'Well, you are a good respectable citizen,' the bank manager said with a smile after he had examined the account. 'We will be pleased to help.'

'Well, you could say that,' grinned Rita, 'seeing as we have met often enough at Pearly's.' She looked away to let the bank manager feel uncomfortable in peace.

At long last Rita was about to achieve her dream of buying land and running a farm just like that one she had been born on in the old country.

Jamie the Scottish sergeant came visiting regularly on Sundays when Mrs Miller would chaperone Julie. They had tea in the cosy parlour and Jamie then walked with them to church.

Rita was pleased, though apprehensive, and she tried to be philosophical about her youngest niece's new interest. 'It's time our little Julie stepped out into the world,' she said.

The political and moral climate in Sydney was beginning to change. The new Governor, a dour Scot, did not like brothels and announced that he wanted the place cleaned up.

One night some wild Scots played merry hell down at Pearly's so the military police raided her establishment and she was heavily fined. This incident caused Pearly to become quite depressed. Clad in a pink outfit which was all furs and feathers, she looked just like a ruffled hen. 'I don't know why, but it's flaming well coming down in class here. I run a good clean respectable house, and have done for ten years. What have they got to complain about? I'm always bunging them buggers, I am. They've had a bleeding fortune out of me, those policemen have.'

'Well, Pearly,' said Rita, 'maybe it's time to quit. And you know that I will be leaving you as soon as my land deal comes up. Then it's back to the good old earth for me, where I belong.'

'Yer know, I have got a bloody good mind to quit, just as you say,' declared Pearly.

Pearly was as good as her word. About a month later, she hired a carriage and a wagon. With a few bits of her best furniture on board and the rest of her girls, Pearly prepared to set off to the western gold fields. She was very drunk and the long blue feather in her wide bush hat wagged up and down as she yelled drunkenly: 'Come on, gels, thars gold in them thar hills!'

The men from the nearby tavern came out to give them a send-off. The yelling and screaming girls kicked up their legs and cavorted about in the back of the wagon, as the men cheered and waved goodbye and threw money for them to fight and scramble over. Pearly's send-off was an exciting event which Sydney Harbour remembered for a long time to come.

Back home at Mrs Miller's Rita awaited the agreement notice for her farmland. She wrote to Jackie telling him to bring his father home. He had wandered long enough, she told him, and it was time for him to settle down. Besides, she was about to acquire a farm.

It was spring before Rita's dream finally came true. The farm was a tumble-down old dwelling place on a tract of land. It had been pioneered by an old couple who had since died, and was many miles from Sydney.

Rita said goodbye to Mrs Miller, who had decided to sell up and move into town, and with Shaun and young Julie, travelled out to their new home. It was a lovely place. There was a good well full of water, rows of peach trees and a lovely view of the mountains that lay behind them. With her ferocious energy Rita soon settled in. She employed native labour, bought laying hens, a flock of sheep, acquired cows and horses and rode on horseback around this stretch of wild country which she called Inchalee after her old home in Ireland. She felt happier than she had been for years.

Shaun married an Australian girl and set up home nearby, and Abbey often came visiting with the grandchildren. Every evening Rita would stare proudly over to the line of blue hills and the fertile valley which she now owned.

'This is mine,' she would declare. 'No man can take it from me. I am at last a happy woman.'

Jackie wrote to her again but he still did not come home, being happy at the mines in Calpeady. Little Julie seemed to have become withdrawn again. She was missing Sydney and her young lover, the Highland sergeant, Jamie. She had been loath to leave at all and was still pining for her lover. There were so many miles between them, and they kept in touch sending love poems to each other.

'Has he proposed to you yet?' Rita would ask.

Tears would come into Julie's eyes. 'Not yet,' she would reply sadly.

The next summer Rita took a stall in the haymarket just outside the town. Here she sold her farm produce – eggs, butter and cheese – and it was very successful and soon Julie took charge of the stall a few days each week.

'That will stop her moaning,' Rita told Shaun.

Rita herself had a full life. She was still a magnificent looking woman. She walked with a stately grace, and with her white skin and very dark hair, she looked considerably younger than her years. Plenty of men were interested in her but she rejected any advances with her usual straightforwardness. She had no time for such things.

Nowadays she wore breeches and a checked shirt and rode her horse with the haughty air of a queen. She did all her business with the bank manager and rich traders directly, and was becoming known in the district as a shrewd, honest businesswoman. The rough communities were developing into more sophisticated states. Trade councils were being formed and places became less wild as crime and vice were contained by battalions of soldiers who were sent to inhabit the towns. Women were acknowledged a little more and allowed more status, and Rita shone like a star above the other settlers' wives.

And all the while, her son Jackie and his father stayed out at Calpeady digging for opals.

'Oh well, said Rita, turning down another offer of

marriage, 'at least I am not a widow. I've got an old man but God knows when he will come back to me!'

One day as Rita and Julie stood at the stall selling their produce, there was the sound of bagpipes in the distance. The wailing sound came closer and closer as the Southern Highlanders marched into town with their kilts swinging, their pipes before them. And in the middle of the battalion was Sergeant Jamie.

'Well, I'll be blowed!' 'Tis the ould fella himself,' jested Rita. 'Strikes me that wedding bells will be ringing soon.' She squeezed Julie's arm affectionately.

Julie was blushing and looked down at the ground in her shy way. But suddenly the excitement was too much for her. Picking up her skirts, she ran out into the street to run alongside the marching soldiers. And to her aunt's astonishment, Julie even started to call out to her fine man.

It was a good summer that year. Many parties and musical evenings went on in Inchalee, Jamie and Julie were now openly acknowledged as lovers and the sight of Julie in love was wonderful for everyone to see.

Every evening Jamie would slip out of the barracks to see Julie in the market place. She would leave the stall in the care of one of the native boys and then she and Jamie would stand close together in the shade of a gum tree in the centre of the haymarket. With the setting sun shining through the leaves to give a dappled shade, the two of them looked like fairy story lovers. Jamie would be in his full highland dress, his flame-coloured hair glinting in the sun, and Julie would be in a blue cotton dress with a white sun bonnet covering her long golden curls.

On Sundays Jamie came to Inchalee for tea. He was always welcomed by Rita. But one day he and Julie went riding out into the hills and were missing for two days. Rita was worried but she guessed that they were probably safe. To contain her worry she became angry. Then she went down to the barracks to complain that Jamie was not doing the right thing by her niece.

'When they return,' she said to Jamie's commanding officer, 'please God, I want that young man's word that he will marry my niece. This courting has gone on long enough, and no one is doing the dirty on my family.' She raged.

The officer looked at her with a compassionate look in his eyes. He sighed gently. 'Sit down, Rita,' he said. 'I've got something to tell you.'

'I don't know what he is hanging about for,' Rita continued to grumble. 'He's been courting her for three years and it's time he proposed.'

'That will not be possible in his case,' said the officer shaking his head. 'He is already a married man. I am sorry that you were not warned but we pay maintenance to a woman and child in Liverpool whom he married before he came overseas.'

Rita's face blanched. 'Oh, dear God,' she cried. 'It will break her heart, my poor little Julie.'

'He is a good officer,' continued the soldier, 'but now he is absent without leave, and he will be disciplined on his return.' He added, 'I am sorry Rita, but it is not in your hands any more. We will be dealing with the situation.'

'More's the pity,' cried Rita, her Irish temper to the fore. 'He deserves a good horse whipping.'

'I am sorry about your niece but I'm afraid that that is not our affair.'

Rita rode home in a terrible rage and found Julie there looking very tearful.

A rush of love came over Rita as she hugged her niece. 'Oh, my darling, I am so glad you are safe,' she exclaimed.

'We got lost out in the hills,' Julie said quietly.

Rita put an arm around her. 'Jamie can't marry you, darling,' she said. 'He has a wife in England.'

A sob escaped from Julie's throat. 'I know. He told me,' she said. Now she began to weep, the heart-breaking sobs pouring out.

Rita cuddled her saying, 'It's not the end of the world, baby,' she said. 'There are many more fish in the sea.'

Jamie was severely punished. He was tied to a gun wheel and left out in the sun, then given fifty lashes and finally sent to Tasmania. He was never seen or heard of again.

Julie pined for him and refused to go into town anymore. Instead she just sat around at home with heavy eyes and a long face.

'I will look around for a nice farmer husband for you,' said Rita, trying to cheer her up.

'No, thank you,' replied Julie listlessly. 'I would prefer to go and live in the convent.'

'Oh, don't be such a fool!' snapped Rita. 'Women have to be strong out in this rough country. You can't afford to go mooning around and falling in love.'

Julie stared at her aunt with a tragic look in her face but she did not reply.

Not long afterwards Jackie and his father finally returned home to Rita. They had left Calpeady several days before and arrived dirty and unshaven with swag bags on their backs. When they came up the path to the farmhouse, Rita did not recognize them. 'It's a couple of bushwhackers,' she muttered, reaching for her shotgun from the wall.

Gun poised, Rita waited for these strangers to come closer. Suddenly they looked familiar, and her spine twinged as she realized the identity of the older man in spite of his long brown beer-stained beard. 'Oh,' she exclaimed 'My God! Spud Murphy! Is it really yerself? And Jackie!' She embraced Jackie but as she turned to put her arms about her husband, old Spud pushed her off. 'Get some food, woman,' he said gruffly. 'We're tired an' 'ungry.'

For the first time in years, tears pricked Rita's eyes. She sniffed, turned away. 'Well, can't expect much more from a man like that,' she muttered. 'He's been roaming more than ten years now.'

Rita prepared a meal and the men settled in. Old Spud found a spot near the fire where he plonked down his bed roll. He scoffed up the meal Rita had cooked him and every time she began to make conversation, he growled: 'Hould yer whisht, woman!'

Far from being offended, Rita laughed heartily. 'Well, this is really like old times,' she said. 'I'd forgotten what a grouchy old bugger ye were.'

From then on Spud slept on the floor, and went

into town every evening to get drunk and play cards. He took no interest in the farm at all.

This went on for a few weeks until one dark night when coming home drunk, his horse threw him. Spud fractured his collar bone and broke a leg. After that he was propped up in a rocking chair and placed out on the balcony because he could not bear to be shut indoors.

Rita robbed her husband of his opals and put them in the bank while he swilled whiskey from a bottle and sang Irish songs very loudly till late into the night. The quiet native boys looked after him, and the rest of the family ignored him.

Jackie was not delighted by the atmosphere at home and was getting itchy feet. He was eager to move on soon but he wanted to get to know Julie, who intrigued him. Julie was like a little sister to him even though she was actually his cousin. They liked each other and went riding and Jackie tried hard to draw her out of her shell. And his patience paid off. Eventually Julie did open up and tell him of Jamie, her lost lover, and how they had spent two nights out in the hills. But now, she confided in him, she feared she was pregnant.

'Phew!' said Jackie. 'Does Mother know?'

Julie shook her head. 'Not yet, but I think she suspects something. I wanted to go into the convent but now it will not be possible.'

Jackie frowned with concern. 'What will you do, Julie? Is there no one who will marry you to give your child a name?'

She hung her head sadly. 'I never mix with the lads,' she said. 'I could not bear to because I still love Jamie.'

Jackie was touched that Julie dared tell him her secret. Now he told her of his plans. 'I want to get back to the bush,' he said. 'I only came here to bring the old man home. He is getting too old to rough it out there.'

'Is there a woman in your life, Jackie?' Julie asked.

Jackie sighed. 'Well, there was, but she is now married to my friend.' He looked sideways at Julie and an idea suddenly came to his head.

'I'd like to marry Julie before I go back to the bush, Mother,' Jackie said to Rita that afternoon.

A frown appeared on Rita's forehead. 'But son, it is not your responsibility.'

'I want to,' said Jackie. 'I'll protect her from the world and I know you will take care of the child.'

Rita was close to tears. 'Jackie, what did I do to have such a sweet boy as you for a son? I don't deserve you.'

'I'll never marry otherwise, Mother, and all this money I have made must go to someone. Marrying Julie is my wish.'

Rita knew that Jackie had her own streak of stubbornness; once his mind was made up, there was no changing it.

Jackie had also made up his mind to return to the bush. His marriage to Julie would not change that; he had married her out of kindness and a sense of duty. That was as far as his feelings went. So while the neighbours still celebrated downstairs, Jackie gently took off the wreath of flowers and the white veil from

Julie's fair hair, and kissed her on the brow. 'Goodbye, darling girl,' he said. 'I must go.'

Julie wept. 'Stay with me, Jackie,' she sobbed.

Jackie shook his head. 'I won't be far away and Mam will care for you and the baby. Some day I will be back, so take care of yourself.'

Rita came in and swept Julie into her warm arms. 'Now, now, my love,' she whispered. 'There's nothing to cry about.'

Jackie took off his town clothes and put them away in the cupboard. Then he pulled on his old breeches and big bush jacket. Picking up his swag bag, he mounted his horse and rode away into the bush in search of adventure.

The stars shone bright in the dark sky and the cool misty night seemed to close in on him. At last he was free again to ride to unknown territory. He was gripped with wanderlust and felt compelled to ride on and on. As he rode, he thought not of the young bride he had left behind, but of the luscious Daisy, his first and life-long love.

15

Goodbye, Dukey

Far away in Calpeady, Daisy was sitting desolately beside the fire. Next to her, on a low truckle bed, lay Dukey, gasping for breath. Several hours before he had been brought down the mountain with a bullet in his lung. Now he was semi-conscious and fighting for his life. Daisy just could not believe what had happened.

Earlier that evening, Dukey had gone up to the mine for his beloved game of cards but this time there had been trouble. A fight had broken out between some newcomers to the mines and the old timers who had pioneered the territory. Shots were fired and Dukey was hit.

The doctor who removed the bullet could give no guarantee to Daisy that Dukey would live.

Although Daisy nursed Dukey day and night it became obvious that there was no hope. Twenty-four hours later, he died. Her strong man left her and her three sons to fend for themselves in the hot and violent township.

When she went through Dukey's belongings, she found a gold ring with a crest. At first she thought he probably won it gambling, but there were also some documents suggesting that Dukey had inherited some property in England.

'I was astonished,' Daisy said to the lawyer she had hired to sort out her affairs. 'I had an idea that Dukey came from a grand family but I didn't think he had any links with them at all.'

'This letter is rather important,' said the lawyer. 'It seems that your late husband's family have considerable estates in France, Guernsey and London.'

Daisy was looking magnificent in her widow's weeds. The long black veil trailing from a tall black hat revealed glimpses of the shiny roll of chestnut hair beneath. The lines on her tired face had not aged her at all. In fact, Daisy in middle age had matured into a lovely woman. Now she was all alone in this God-forsaken hole but she was sure that she would stay put.

'Go back to Europe and take the boys,' suggested the lawyer. 'Your late husband left no estate here that would be of use to you. All he left is a list of I.O.U.s which you might never be able to pay. It might be wise to sell the shop, pay your passage to England and claim the inheritance, if only for the sake of your sons.'

Daisy stared at him in horror. 'Go back to England? No, I'll never do that. There is nothing left for me there. I am an Aussie now, and I've been out here too long to go back.'

'Well, Madam, it is up to you,' replied the lawyer. 'I will give you time to think about it and then I will contact your solicitors in England. It is of course possible that your passage will be paid, once they have properly established your identity.'

'Oh, stop it,' cried Daisy irritably. 'I can't digest all them bloody big words. I'll have to talk to the boys about it. Meanwhile I have a living to earn and I've no help in that bar, so I'd better get on with it.'

Six months had passed and no decision either way was made by Daisy. 'Perhaps it would be a great trip to go back to England but I am not sure I would stop there,' she would mutter occasionally. 'I like Australia, it's my own home now. Let all those lawyers sweat for a while. I can't see what I have to gain by going back. At least I know how much I can take behind the bar and that it's all mine.'

So Daisy went on living in her merry fashion. She was very attractive and she did not lack admirers. She tried one or two associations with other men but she was not impressed. 'What a bunch of weaklings,' she told a friend. 'If I hitched up with one of them, it would be me carrying them, and that I'll never do, not while I can get by under my own steam.'

Opals had become popular all over the world. Prospectors from all over the place were coming to Calpeady, so the little shanty town expanded constantly, spreading outwards and becoming more prosperous as the years passed. Modern houses were built and new bars started up with dancing girls providing popular entertainment for the lustful miners. Now Daisy's little old wooden bar just out of town was often by-passed by people who preferred to go to other establishments.

The rough old diggers frequented the bar and

Daisy still ruled it with a rod of iron but trade was not so good.

One day, a weary traveller walked in. He put down his swag bag on the floor and came up to the bar. There was a thick growth of whiskers on his chin and his clothes were worn and dusty.

'Hullo, matey,' Daisy greeted him. 'Down on your luck? Here, have a cool beer on the house.' She briskly pulled the pump allowing the beer to froth into the tankard. Two bright blue eyes stared quizzically at her from under that bush of hair. Daisy had opened her mouth but no words came out. The beer began to froth out all over the counter.

The man put out a gentle hand towards her. 'Yes, Daisy, it's me, Jackie. I was sorry to hear about old Dukey,' he said.

Then Daisy found her voice. 'Oh Jackie,' she said with a broad smile. 'It's great to see you.'

'I've just come back from the west coast,' said Jackie. 'I'm sorry, Daisy, if I look rough but I've been travelling a long time.'

'I'll say you look rough!' Tears were running down her face but she looked happy. 'Now, you get yourself under the counter and through into the back room, Jackie Murphy, and I'll see you get cleaned up.'

Jackie took a swig of the beer and then ducked under the counter as Daisy lifted the wooden flap. With a wide grin, he followed her into the living premises. He sat down while she pulled off his sweaty smelling socks.

'Phew! How long have you been wearing these, Jackie?'

Then she yelled for the native girls to get a bath ready. 'I'll shut the bloody bar,' she said. 'It ain't doing so good these days, anyway. I'll be back with you in a minute, Jackie. It's been a long time since we had a chat together.'

When morning dawned and the red sun came up over the mountains, another long hot day had begun in the bush. Daisy lay in her bed with Jackie's black burly head cuddled to her breast. She had been reunited with her long-lost lover. He was nothing like her strong virile Dukey but he was hers, little Irish Jackie who had fathered her first child. All the misery of the past few months seemed washed away and Daisy felt so content.

For his part, Jackie was ecstatic except for one thing: Daisy was free to marry him but he was no longer free to marry her. How cruel fate was! If only he had not been so rash. How he longed to be wedded to this wonderful woman, the mother of his own child, back in England. With happiness always had to come sadness.

During that long hot dry summer in Calpeady, Daisy was happy with Jackie at her side. She was blooming, now involved in a passionate love affair and catching up on all those years of separation. It was almost as if Dukey had never existed.

Daisy still ran the bar with Jackie as her aid. He was a tough little man and a good asset when the drunken miners started a fight. But the bar was still not thriving. The very respectable miners' families who had now migrated in droves to the new town did not approve of Daisy or her shack-like bar and shop. They bought their provisions from the larger company which now owned the mines and transported all the necessary commodities up the river and sold them at lower prices than Daisy could manage.

Calpeady was slowly becoming a civilised community, as the company built cool brick homes deep in the shade of the mountain. And the church-going wives did not care to associate with the likes of Daisy. Many had been shocked by Daisy's decision to ignore the usual one year of mourning. It was considered proper in such circumstances to dress in simple black and wear a heavy widow's cap for all occasions. Daisy, however, wore a white lace collar on her black dress and discarded the quaint cap to display her abundant chestnut hair. With the large gold nuggets swinging in her ears, she laughed and joked with the customers. But propriety could not be thrown aside like this. In protest, the women boycotted Daisy's store and would not allow their men to come in the bar or drink her beer.

'Who cares?' said Daisy defiantly with a shake of her head.

But it was her eldest son Charles who quarrelled with her about her behaviour and hurt her the most. 'Mother,' he said, 'how dare you take another man into our father's bed, and so soon too?'

'Your father was a generous man,' replied Daisy. 'He would not have begrudged me my happiness.'

'Well, you get on with it,' declared Charles, 'but I'll not come home. I'll live on the range.' So saying, he packed his saddle bags and rode away into those misty blue hills.

Daisy wept as she watched him go, her fine son with his saddle bags slung over his horse's back. He left her without even a backward look.

Next it was Frederick's turn to leave. He liked the sound of city life and was very good at cards, like his father. Following his elder brother's example, he soon took off for the bright lights of Sydney.

Daisy was hurt but she did not try to stop him. Next it was the little one, John, who announced that he was leaving. He was studying at the Monastery. 'I want to be a priest, Mother,' he said, 'and it is necessary for me to actually live up there. I hope you do not mind.'

So with big tears trickling down her cheeks, Daisy parted with her youngest son.

Jackie felt sad. 'It's all my fault,' he said. 'Perhaps it is I who should push on, Daisy.'

'No, you won't!' cried Daisy. 'I'll stick it out here. They will come home and next year you and I will get married.'

Jackie's long dark lashes veiled his eyes and he did not reply. How could he tell her that this would not be possible? His act of kindness to Julie was one of gross cruelty to Daisy.

'This year,' wept Daisy. 'I have lost my fine husband and now my three lovely sons. I'll not lose you, Jackie. Oh God! What else can happen to me?'

Jackie cuddled her close. 'Don't cry, darlin', I'll not leave you.'

Daisy held on to him. 'Promise me, Jackie.'

'No, darlin', now that I've found you, nothing will ever part us,' he whispered.

That summer there was a terrible drought. Cattle dropped dead from lack of water on the dry land and huge fires raged through the bushlands.

'Oh, what a God-forsaken country this is,' complained Daisy. 'I feel like packing it all up and going home.'

'Bedad, that's all talk, Daisy,' said Jackie, 'you are the last one to give in.'

Although Daisy had not the slightest intention of following up her threat, fate made its own decision for her when a stranger walked into the bar one day. He was in his mid-twenties and wore a city suit and a top hat. He also had a little tufted beard and steel-rimmed spectacles. He looked like a townie and this raised a lot of curiosity in this outback where everyone knew everyone else.

As Daisy served him his beer, she scrutinized him. 'Stranger to this place, ain't yer?'

The man nodded. 'I've travelled up here from Sydney. But I came from England earlier this year.'

The stranger's speculative gaze bothered her. 'What are yer doing in these parts?' she asked, for she believed in being direct.

'If you are the proprietress of this establishment and you go by the name of Mrs Daisy Dukes, then I have been looking for you,' he said.

'Ger away!' cried Daisy. 'Wot d'yr want me for?'

'I am a lawyer and have been sent over from London to straighten out your husband's affairs.'

'Affairs?' snorted Daisy. She narrowed her eyes suspiciously. 'My husband didn't have time for affairs,' she sniffed. 'He was only forty-five when he went to his grave.'

The man smiled politely. His teeth were uneven. 'His family has the welfare of his sons at heart,' he informed her.

'His family?' snorted Daisy. 'Dukey did not have anything to do with his family.'

'If you will kindly allow me to enter your home so we can talk privately, I should be grateful,' the man said.

'Oh, come inside,' Daisy snorted impatiently, lifting the wooden flap. Then she yelled out of the window in a loud voice: 'Jackie! Come you here and mind the bar.'

She and the lawyer sat at the kitchen table.

'Well, wot's this all abaht?' she asked.

'You may or may not know it but your eldest son is next in line for the title.'

'What bloody title?' asked Daisy irritably. It was hot and she wished that this young man would get to the point.

'Your husband came from an aristocratic family and they have been trying for years to trace him. It was only the registration of his death that put me on his track.'

'Well, then, wot's that make me, a bleedin' duchess?' Daisy's smile was preceded by a rich giggle.

The man looked shocked at this lack of enthusiasm. 'Well, actually, yes,' he said. 'Your late husband's family are the English Beauclairs. In fact, this means that you are the Dowager Duchess of Beauclair. Your eldest son will now be the new Duke.'

Daisy's lively brown eyes surveyed him in amusement. 'You've gotta be joking,' she said quietly.

'No, madam, the Beauclairs are a family of long lineage. They have property in England, Guernsey and France.'

Daisy was staring at him more seriously. 'Guernsey? Dukey used to talk about that. He lived there as a boy.'

'Yes,' said the lawyer patiently. 'There is considerable property and a title descended from the Normans.'

'Oh, dear, I can't believe it,' cried Daisy. 'Jackie!' she yelled, 'shut the bar door and come in here. We got something to tell you. By the way, young man, what is your name?' she asked.

'I am Joseph Feldman,' he replied.

'Yer don't sound like a Londoner to me.'

'I am a naturalized American,' he said. 'And I came to London to study law, hence this assignment.'

'It's funny,' said Daisy, 'but every time I look at you I think I know you but that can't be possible. Wait now and I'll get old Dukey's saddle bags. That's where he kept all his papers. We had a lawyer read them soon after Dukey died and he said something about some property in England. But to tell you the truth, it seemed like such a wild idea that I could not take it very seriously.'

She produced the old saddle bag with Dukey's possessions carefully wrapped up inside.

The young man picked through the contents. 'Well

there is good proof of your marriage and the births of your children. Now, this gold ring carries the Beauclair crest. This is all we need.'

'Well, what happens now?' asked Daisy.

'You, madam, will have to travel back to England with me and your sons. All expenses will be paid but you must establish your identity or the estate will go into Chancery and lie unclaimed.'

'Oh, cor blimey!' said Daisy. 'I can't do that.'

'Well, I will call back tomorrow. In the meantime, you must contact your sons, for it is important that they travel with us.'

'Oh dear, Jackie,' cried Daisy when the solicitor had gone. 'Wot an ow-de-do! I don't think I like all this.'

But Jackie could see the importance of what the young man had said. 'You need not go, Daisy, but you cannot deprive your sons. I'll ride out to the sheep station tomorrow and bring back Charles and collect John. Meanwhile, you must send a message to Sydney to tell Fred to come back.'

'But what about you, Jackie? I can't go without you. Let's get married.' She looked at him expectantly.

Jackie squeezed her hand. 'Daisy, I can never marry you,' he said. 'I have a wife and she is expecting a child.'

Daisy sat down heavily in a chair. 'Well, I'll be blowed! It's just one damned thing after another. Why didn't you tell me?'

Jackie sat down beside her and told her the story of his gentle cousin Julie whose tragic love affair had ended in her pregnancy and her lover being sent away.

He told her how he had married Julie to give her protection and give the child a name. He added that Julie was very delicate and she was best left at home with Mother to look after her.

'Oh, Jackie,' cried Daisy, wiping away her tears. 'Life is very strange, isn't it? You must go home to look after them.'

'No, Daisy,' said Jackie, shaking his head. 'I'll never do that. You are my love and always have been. Julie is my cousin. We respect each other, that's all.'

'Right, then,' declared Daisy. 'You come with me to England or I won't bloody well go.'

'As you wish, darlin',' smiled Jackie, giving her a long kiss.

If the circumstances were not perfect, and Jackie was unhappy about leaving Australia, at least he was at the side of Daisy, the woman he loved. Nothing could take her from him now.

Two months later, Daisy and Jackie walked up the gangway of a big ship which would take at least three months to reach England. Behind them came Daisy's three sons, all dressed in their new clothes. Daisy's store and bar had been sold and the money used to pay their passage and kit everyone out in clothes worthy of people going to claim their inheritance.

From the deck, with the breeze in her face, Daisy looked back over the harbour to the mountain beyond, her heart was heavy and she held back tears as she cried: 'I'll be back. Don't forget me!'

Thus Daisy, now a rich widow, her three fine sons and Jackie, her lover, all sailed away to a new life. What was held in store for them they were unable to imagine.

But unknown to him, Jackie's own life was to be made further complicated by the tragic death of his wife Julie a few days after she had given birth to a son, whom she called Alastair. To nobody's surprise, it was Rita who took on the responsibility of raising the child, just as she had raised poor little Julie.

BOOK TWO

16

Working Girl

Maxi Feldman wiped the sweat from his brow with a big silk handkerchief. He had put on so much weight recently that he could not stand the heat for very long. All that rich food he had eaten while living in Paris put pounds on him! He was now at least eighteen stones and almost as wide as he was high. Relatives remarked that he was now the same shape and size as poor old uncle Harry who popped off very quickly, gasping and wheezing for breath, having become too obese to enjoy the good things he could have bought with the money he had made in his lifetime. Still, old Harry had done well by Maxi. He had left his nephew his big successful East End store and Maxi had made it even more successful.

With a self-satisfied sigh, Maxi patted his large paunch and lit up a cigar. It was very pleasant indeed to be prosperous but he had worked for it, keeping his nose to the grindstone. How different life might have been if he had wed his first love, beautiful chestnut-haired Daisy! But so much water had flowed under the bridge since then, and there had not been one sign of her in fifteen or twenty years. But Maxi often wondered how she fared.

The big gold watch on his fat wrist informed Maxi

that it was time to open the store. Every morning he did a routine inspection of the staff at Feldman's Store. Every morning he walked past those neat young ladies dressed in black dresses with white collars standing to attention and waiting for the boss's approval before the long day's grind. They were not bad-looking, these assistants. Maxi grunted his approval as he eyed them up and down. Yes, he still liked a green leaf, as old Greta used to say. How mad she got when she caught him at it! At times he thought that he should never have married that old hag but at least he had come by her fortune when she died.

Puffing the cigar smoke carelessly into the faces of his working girls, Maxi waddled down the line. At the end of the row he found himself confronted by a pair of intensely bright eyes staring at him from under a smooth white brow. The owner of the eyes was tall and slim with black hair brushed smoothly around her head. There was something curiously familiar about that haughty look coming from the heavily lashed blue eyes. Why, it reminded him of Daisy, though her eyes had been deep brown and her hair bright chestnut. Maxi grunted. He must be in a nostalgic mood this morning.

'Right, start work,' he barked.

As his employees moved swiftly to their respective counters, Maxi asked the supervisor about the owner of the lovely eyes.

'That is Miss Ramsey,' the supervisor told him. 'She is new. She's been taken on in the fashion department on one month's trial.'

'Never mind the Miss,' said Maxi. 'What's her name?'

'It's a strange one, I can tell you,' the supervisor sniffed. 'Petal! Never heard it in my life before!'

'Nice, nice,' muttered Maxi, eyeing Petal's smooth shape as she walked by. 'Where's she from?' he demanded impatiently.

'Oh, she lives around here,' replied the supervisor, 'but she is not the usual type. She's well-spoken so we have put her in the best dress department.'

After that Maxi visited the fashion department every morning to watch Petal bending down gracefully as she placed the garments on the model, and he would stare at her trim ankles under that long black skirt and note the tilt of her head as she moulded the material over the shape of the dummy, her mouth full of pins.

'Yer all right?' he asked one day. 'Do ya like it here?'

'I am perfectly happy, thank you, sir,' Petal replied. She pronounced her words clearly but there was not even a ghost of a smile on her full red lips nor a hint of emotion in those lovely eyes. The only expression in her beautiful face was one of scorn, particularly since the smell of pickled onions emanating from him made her wrinkle her pert little nose.

Although Maxi decided that Petal Ramsey was an ice-cold bitch, he still came to the fashion department every day to scrutinize her.

In the dress department it was often quite quiet. It was here that the fashionable women of the day came to be fitted for the new models, the long flowing gowns in feathers and lace. For this was the age when the newly rich merchants' wives and bankers' daughters were all ready to ape the aristocracy. They came to buy and young Petal was just the young lady to assist them.

Maxi was getting more familiar and often stood very close to her.

'Don't encourage him,' the other girls warned her. 'Maxi's after you, and we all know him for a dirty old man.'

But Petal's lips were hard. 'I can cope with him,' she said confidently.

'Where do you live?' Maxi quizzed her one day.

'Mirander Street, Bethnal Green,' Petal replied coolly.

'I knew a girl once who lived around there, a real beauty she was. Have you got a young man?'

'No,' replied Petal. 'I support my mother who is a widow.'

'Where did you get that posh accent?' Maxi asked. 'They don't talk like that in these parts.'

'I went to a private school for a few years until my father died suddenly.' She did not tell him that her father had committed suicide. 'Then I had to find a job.' She spoke clearly and precisely, her tremendous, deep-blue eyes staring at him unhesitatingly.

'Pity, pity,' remarked Maxi, but he was not particularly interested in the details of Petal's life, only the details of her body.

He continued to visit her every day and Petal blithely held his scrutiny. In fact, when she realised that she had a certain power over him she began to enjoy his attention.

Then one day he whispered in her ear: 'What about a nice posh nosh-up, up West – just you and me, Petal?'

Petal stopped herself from drawing back from his foul breath and just flicked her long black lashes. 'Why not?' she said smoothly.

Maxi could not believe his luck but did not show his surprise. 'Right, then, tomorrow night I'll send a cab for you. You can borrow any clothes from the store you fancy, so tog up well. I'm going to show you off, my young beauty,' he added jubilantly.

As Petal walked along the wet street on her way home that evening her legs ached after the long day. She felt unusually confused. Was it right for her to encourage that lecherous old swine? It was hard to say but what she did know was that she was determined to rise from the gutter. She thought of that cold untidy house in the back street behind Gardener's Corner with its faded wallpaper, the smell of rising damp, and the wet washing permanently strung across the room. And she thought of Harriet who was always grumbling of the cold or complaining of the shortage of money to buy the gin to which she had become addicted.

'I spent good money on your education, I did,' Harriet would whine to Petal. 'I brought you up to be a lady and little thanks I get for it.'

'Oh, be quiet, mother!' Petal would say irritably. 'It's not my fault that Daddy squandered all his money. I am doing my best for you now.'

'I had me own shop,' Harriet muttered pitifully, 'but now there's nothing left.'

Although Petal sometimes wondered why she did not feel any love for her parents, it did not worry her that she cared so little for her mother. She was a hard nut and she had never even felt remorse when her poor father had been found dead soon after he had gone bankrupt, having invested a vast amount of money in a new shop which failed. How she hated this poverty, the squalid street and all the poor ugly people!

Her formative years had been spent at a posh boarding school, paid for by her parents during their richer days, and Petal now found it impossible to feel sympathy for the whining grizzling mess that her mother was becoming. For Harriet had never recovered from her husband's death or the debt collectors who had taken her home. For the self-possessed, respectable Harriet, it had all been too much.

Conditions in the East End during that time were terrible. The rich, the merchants and bankers, spent money ostentatiously everywhere they went, while the poor rotted in tenements. There was no welfare or provisions for the old folk. If someone could not support himself or his family then it was the workhouse for them all. And anyone born into poverty was most likely to stay there while the rest of society ignored them.

It was this gutter of poverty that Petal was determined to rise out of. She had been to school with young ladies who had never had to worry about a thing. When they left school they expected to marry into monied families. Even if Petal had not had to leave this school early when her father died she would still have had to work or starve. There was no one to help her but also no one to stand in the way of her plans. So, her fat old boss fancied her! Well, no one else did, so what did she have to lose?

In this cynical frame of mind, Petal went to the stock room and chose a blue silk dress and a feather to wear in her hair. Then she waited for the cab to take her to meet the boss.

Her actions did not go unnoticed by the rest of the staff. They had seen this sort of thing many times before and with smiles and sniggers they watched Petal go.

On Saturday night Petal sat at a table in the Café Royal, a tip-top West End restaurant. She looked very smug as she faced Maxi across the table. He was smartly dressed in a black evening dress suit and bow tie. His bald head shone and his gold teeth flashed in the light.

Petal was very pleased to be there, amongst the rich middle classes who frequented this restaurant on Saturday nights. And she looked ravishing in the blue silk décolleté dress with a pink feather in her hair to match the quivering pink feather boa draped around her fair shoulders.

Petal daintily consumed her fresh salmon and sipped her champagne as though she had been used to them all her life. The other customers, who were used to Maxi's young ladies, gazed at her with approval.

'You got class, you have,' said Maxi, squinting at her

boozily. 'I knew it as soon as I saw you. Yer not the average, I said to meself.'

Petal made no reply but returned his look with cool appraisal. Inside she felt pleased with herself. She had set the bait and now she had him hooked. It had worked out as planned.

'What abaht a little drink in my flat before I take yer home?' said Maxi as they finished their coffee. An artful expression had crept over his fat face.

This was just what Petal had been waiting for. She lifted her dark lashes and stared steadily at him with a quizzical smile on her lips. 'And what then?' she asked in a husky voice.

'Now, girlie,' laughed Maxi. 'Yer ask no questions yer hear no lies. You know what it's all about.'

Oddly enough, for all her cockiness, Petal did not actually know what it was all about. Her posh school had forbidden all talk of sex and it was drummed into her there that nice ladies waited until they were married to find out about it! Her mother certainly never talked about sex.

She looked now at this fat drunken man and she momentarily felt that she was losing control of the situation. A thrill of terror shot up her spine and made her shiver. But there was no going back now. Arranging her feather boa elegantly around her shoulders she walked like a queen through the restaurant and out to the hansom cab waiting at the door.

Maxi seemed very excited and was breathing heavily like an old horse. He tried to fumble with Petal's neck as they sat side by side but Petal raised her elegant eyebrows indicating that it was not appropriate behaviour.

Once they were inside Maxi's over-furnished flat, Maxi plonked himself down on the *chaise longue* and pulled Petal on top of him. His breath smelled foul and Petal was repelled by his groping. She gave him a great push and he fell heavily to the floor.

'Blast you, bitch!' he shouted. 'What d'ya do that for?'

Petal straightened her dress and stared haughtily down at him. To her amazement, she saw that fat Maxi was as helpless as a beetle on its back.

''Ere, give us an 'and up,' puffed Maxi. 'I can't make it on me own.'

'Well, dear,' she said smoothly with a smile, 'you will have to stay down, won't you.' With that she swept out of the door.

With a pathetic and disbelieving expression on his face, Maxi watched her go. He knew she would not return.

On Monday morning Petal was there at the end of the work line as always, bright, neat and alert. But the boss had sent his regrets; he would not be there that morning. Petal resumed her place in the showroom and got on with her job in her usual efficient manner, having carefully replaced the blue silk dress and its accessories in the stock room.

Her fellow workers looked at her in puzzlement. They longed to know what had happened but they knew better than to ask her about her adventure, for Petal was not the type to gossip.

Maxi stayed out of sight for over a week. Then he arrived one morning looking decidedly seedy. He looked surprised to see Petal standing so proud and erect at the end of the line, and she delivered him such a wide bright smile that again his memory of little Daisy was stirred. This bothered him.

Later that day he came waddling into the showroom. 'Good morning, Miss Petal,' he said.

'Good morning, sir,' she replied breezily. She seemed to emphasize the 'sir', a title she rarely used.

Maxi stood looking uncomfortable, his hands in his trouser pockets. 'I am a clumsy old sod,' he said at last. 'I am very sorry about our last meeting.'

Petal got busy folding a length of bright silk, her slim hips moving rhythmically as she did so. Her hair was shiny and black and rolled into a smooth roll with not a hair out of place. 'Well, I think you are well past it,' she said. 'Only a foolish old man would behave in that way.'

Maxi grinned at her forthright tone. 'Oh well, Petal,' her said. 'You could be right. Now come and have some lunch at Sammy Isaac's. It's nice Kosher food and no strings attached.'

Petal stopped folding the silk and looked squarely at him. 'All right,' she said evenly. 'My lunchtime starts at one o'clock.'

Big slices of smoked salmon with salad, washed down with plenty of wine went down a treat as Petal lunched with her boss in Sammy Isaac's Kosher restaurant. At the counter a huge man was carving off slices of succulent salt beef to be served at tables laid with red-and-white checked cloths to all the business-men talking about deals.

'Look 'ere,' said Maxi, 'let's make this a platonic friendship. It's not my usual style but there's something about you that appeals to me, something different. I know I am well past the sex drive so there's no sense in spoiling a lovely young filly like you.'

Petal's full red lips gave a little twitch of amusement but that was all.

'I got a good idea about you,' continued Maxi, 'and I am seldom wrong when I get a hunch. That's how I make money, whether it's a horse or a woman, I can always see a winner in the making.'

Petal slowly sipped the excellent coffee. She had just demolished a very nice pastry and was feeling pleasantly full. 'Well, what is all this leading to?' she asked.

'Well,' said Maxi with a thoughtful look on his face. 'How would you like to be a mannequin?'

'What is that?' Petal looked surprised but interested.

'That, my love, is a new idea in the rag trade. Beautiful gels are trained to show off the newest models and the rich stupid women buy them like hot cakes. All them scraggy old gels think that if they wear the dresses they will look just like the mannequins.'

'Oh, I see what you mean,' said Petal. 'A model to wear the finished dresses.'

'They calls them mannequins in France,' replied Maxi, 'and they are all the rage out there. Many of the mannequins end up marrying millionaires themselves, and I think that's the right spot for you, my beauty.'

Petal was decidedly interested. 'And who arranges it all?' she asked.

'In your case, I do,' Maxi replied. 'No, you will have to be led by me and me alone.'

Petal narrowed her eyes and looked at him a little suspiciously.

'Nah, nah,' Maxi waved his hand. 'Not that, what I mean is that I'll manage you just like I had a share in a racehorse. I'll get you trained and you will get your cut and I get mine.'

'Sounds complicated,' said Petal. 'What is your first idea?'

'I know a woman calls herself Madame Adelaide. She says she is French but she is a Russian Jew like meself. Well, she's got an agency that trains these girls for the big dress companies. I'll take you over there and introduce you. How about it?'

'Sounds all right to me,' said Petal. Her quick mind was thinking that this could be her chance to get out of the East End gutter.

'We all came from humble beginnings,' Maxi was saying, 'and some of us are very proud of it. Besides, I am sure that you are just the type Madame Adelaide is looking for.' Petal's blue eyes stared very intently at him. For the first time in her acquaintance with him she felt the warmth of friendship in this fat old man. He was not so bad, she thought. Perhaps she should have been kinder to him. 'I am sorry I let you down before,' she said quietly. 'It was not an easy decision to make to come out with you but I am fed up with being poor. I get quite depressed about it sometimes. I long for nice food to eat and good clothes to wear.'

Maxi patted her hand in a paternal manner. 'Quite right too, my dear,' he said, 'and Maxi will see that you get it. Trust me.'

'Well, what is it you want me to do?' Petal asked.

'Right, the first thing you do is hand in your notice, a month ain't it? But don't say nothing about me, just say you got another job.'

'Leave my job?' Petal gasped. 'I can't possibly do that, I have to support my mother.'

'Nah, nah, not to worry,' said Maxi, reassuringly. 'I'll give you all you need. That is, until you start earning for yourself.'

'But how will I do that?' Petal cried in alarm.

'I told yer,' he hollered. 'As a mannequin. Yer just the right kind for it and there is plenty of money to be made at it.'

'If you say so,' she answered dubiously.

'Next week I'll introduce you to Madame Adelaide. She's got a salon in Sloane Square where she trains beautiful gels like you to display all the best designed garments in the country.'

'What do you get out of it?' Petal asked shrewdly.

'Me?' Maxi waved his hands about. 'I told you. I get a good commission on you, dearie, just like a bloody good racehorse. You will make a pile for me and a good living for yourself.'

'Oh well,' sighed Petal. 'What can I lose?' she looked at him sideways. 'But there's to be no funny business.'

Maxi shook his head with an innocent look on his

face. 'Not me, dear, not from me you won't. I like women to be soft and you are as hard as a rock. A real diamond, in fact!'

So Petal left the store in Whitechapel and Maxi took her up to meet Madame Adelaide.

Madame Adelaide was very haughty and wore a black silk dress and a collar laced with pearls which seemed to choke her scrawny neck. She had long earrings, strings of beads and a scarlet lace shawl over her shoulders.

A pair of eye glasses hung on a string and lay balanced on her high bosom. She picked them up and stared through them to examine Petal from head to foot.

Petal felt oddly relaxed. Looking tall and beautiful, she stared coolly back at this woman with her large blue eyes.

'Walk over there,' said Madame, 'and then come back towards me.'

Petal glided across the large room and then turned to come gracefully back towards Madame. She held her head high, and her facial expression was as composed as always.

'Hmmm!' muttered Madame Adelaide, 'very nice.'

'What did I tell you?' cried Maxi exuberantly. 'Ain't she beautiful?'

This tall dark graceful girl had a great inheritance – the queenly grace of Irish Rita and the shapely beauty and supreme courage of her mother, our Cockney Daisy. Yes, those seeds had produced this phenomenon of grace and beauty.

'Well, Maxwell,' said Madame Adelaide in a crisp tone of voice, 'where exactly do you fit in here?'

'Business, purely business,' cried Maxi evasively.

'And who will pay for her training?' demanded Adelaide.

'Me, of course!' cried Maxi. 'I get ten per cent when she starts earning and I'll put plenty of business your way, of course.'

These words seemed to satisfy Adelaide. She turned to Petal. 'Well, my dear, I will train you and find work for you but you must break all home ties and live up here with the rest of my girls. I'll have no irate parents challenging me. It must be a complete break. I will find you an apartment and Maxwell will pay the rent for you. It will be hard work but worth it if you want a good future.'

'Thank you, Madame,' Petal replied, feeling a little dazed by the speed of these decisions. In the cab going home, she recovered her senses and argued with Maxi. 'I cannot leave my mother,' she said. 'She relies on me.'

'We will give your mother an allowance. Don't be a fool,' said Maxi. 'When you are earning good money she will also get the benefit.'

Petal did not need much persuading. 'Oh, I suppose you could be right,' she said. 'I am really fed up with that miserable old house.'

'Nah, nah,' announced Maxi. 'I will give you a small bank balance to start off and we will write a cheque for your Momma once a month. That should suit her and I got a place I don't often use not far from Sloane Square. You can have it but as long as I can come and go freely. I won't bother you.'

Petal looked at him with suspicion. Maxi was very secretive about his own affairs.

Maxi could see her perplexed expression. 'Look, I stay up here gambling some nights,' he said. 'You'll have no need to worry. Just get on the right side of old Adelaide and we are in good business. Like I told yer, it's a coming thing, these mannequins, and I should know. Always has one ear to the ground, has old Maxi,' he cackled, lighting a big cigar in a very self-satisfied manner.

Petal stared coldly at him. For a moment she had an urge to reach out and smack that big podgy face but calmly she said: 'Oh well, you make the final arrangements, then I'll go home and face mother. I am damned well not looking forward to that, I can tell you.'

Harriet snivelled at the news and demanded to know why Petal wanted to leave home. 'I brought you up to be a lady,' she said. 'I went without meself for your benefit and now you're deserting me.'

Petal looked coldly at her mother's shapeless body and her dirty tousled hair. 'You will be better off now,' she said, 'and have plenty of money to spend on gin with that old bag next door.'

'Oh, you wicked girl!' howled Harriet. 'Sometimes I wonder if I ever did know you. You're just like our Daisy, and she went wrong, she did.'

'Who is Daisy?' asked Petal, throwing a few of her belongings into a tatty suitcase.

'My young sister, she was, and too good-looking, just like you. Men was always chasing her.'

'Oh, well, it seems someone caught her if she isn't

here now,' replied Petal with dry humour. 'Anyway, you will get a cheque every month but I will leave you all the money I have got at the moment,' she added a little more kindly, 'so you will not be without.'

Harriet huddled in her chair, her red-veined eyes seeking Petal's. But Petal avoided her glance. Climbing the stairs to bed, she said: 'Well, so long, I might not see you. I am leaving early in the morning.'

Thus Petal began her new life away from the poverty and squalor of her upbringing. Her conscience did prick her about leaving Harriet but not enough to make her change her mind.

'Maxi is right,' she told herself, 'I am a hard cow,' and she settled herself into the comfortable apartment with its big bathroom, two bedrooms and a large sitting room full of red plush overstuffed furniture. It was none too clean but Petal began to wash and polish and generally tidy it up.

Maxi was no trouble at all but he tended to arrive at the flat in the middle of the night when, full of good food and wine, he would just plonk himself on the sofa and not trouble to go to bed. He was often still there in the morning when Petal went to work.

Petal herself worked hard, for Madame Adelaide was very strict about time-keeping. At eight o'clock her girls all met in the office. There were seven of them in all. Some had been actresses and some, like Petal, were simply working class. Only one girl was a real toff from the top shelf, *related to royalty*, another girl informed Petal.

The day would start with an exercise class, marching

hands up, knees bent, in true army style. Then they had a light breakfast of orange juice and a brown roll before having a rest period in which they all lay about on *chaises longues* and chattered until Adelaide arrived at eleven. Then they had a posture class and paraded about with piles of books on their heads. Then they would try on various garments and have lectures in skin care and personal hygiene. Oh, Madame, Adelaide trained her girls very thoroughly indeed!

From the very first day Petal loved it. She enjoyed mixing with this company of young ladies and lapped up all the curious lessons in cosmetics and hairstyles.

Madame Adelaide was very pleased with her progress. 'You learn quickly and very well,' she told her. 'And you have a lovely name which you must keep. I often give my girls a nom-de-plume but you will remain Petal, it has a beautiful sound.'

Petal smiled, pleased with the praise. 'I think I was called Petal because my mother had a sister called Daisy who, incidentally, went wrong,' Petal explained.

Adelaide's lips twitched for a second, then she stared severely at the girls through her spectacles. 'I take good care that none of my girls go wrong,' she warned them.

It seemed no time at all before Petal was out on the floor modelling the latest fashions. Tall, slim and willowy, she walked back and forth in front of London's society women, rich men's wives and mistresses, all out to compete with each other. At every ball, at every social gathering, they had to look their best. They were fed up with black gowns and Victorian bonnets, now fashion was booming and there were many exotic materials, beads, corsages, long trailing skirts, feathered hats and high busts supported by tight corsets. Yes, feminine beauty was becoming glamorous as women began to spend their newly acquired wealth on themselves without any restraint.

Merchant bankers and foreign traders all poured into London's West End and their women rose to each social occasion, dressing themselves up like birds of paradise. The times were very gay. The rich liked to enjoy themselves and there was a little more mixing of the social classes since it was well known that the Prince of Wales was *very fond* of actresses.

The new models found their own position within this high society but they still had to know their place as they were still considered working girls.

17

Victor

Now aged twenty-five, Petal's beauty had increased. She had a remarkable natural look and, thanks to Madame Adelaide, she knew exactly how to dress and behave in this decadent world.

Madame Adelaide was very old-fashioned. She would have no nonsense from her girls. At the slightest breath of scandal, they were out. Her girls were there to amuse and entertain society, not to join it.

Madame's mannequins would travel up and down the country to the big stately homes where they would put on dress parades for the idle rich.

Madame chaperoned her staff very carefully. Petal was still a virgin. She had received many propositions but had been protected by Madame Adelaide's watchful eye. Petal did not mind, for in her eyes these rich men were foolish, overdressed and not to be trusted, though she did wish that she could keep some of the presents given to her by admirers. Madame Adelaide always returned such gifts immediately.

'Don't get involved with them, Petal,' Madame would advise her. 'One day your man will come along. For the time being, remaining unmarried is best if you are going to make a career for yourself.'

Many of Adelaide's girls dropped out, some got into trouble, but the cool, calm Petal never stepped out of line and she steadily built up a reputation in the profession. Maxi was very proud of her. Together they began to make a lot of money. Maxi was still very obese and as self-indulgent as ever but a good relationship had developed between them. Now he often took her on business trips with him to France and frequently gave her advice. 'Use your head,' he would say. 'It pays to be seen in these rich circles.'

Harriet had died the year before when she fell out of bed dead drunk. Petal just took one day off work to sort out the old house and to get rid of the old furniture. The only thing she brought out was a box full of family papers Petal barely glanced at. There were also some old photographs, including one with the name 'Daisy' written on the back. There was a pretty girl of about sixteen staring back at the camera.

Petal stared at it for a few moments and thought how lovely her aunt was. At first she thought she might show it to Maxi but then she decided that he would not be interested.

That autumn, Maxi suggested a trip to France. 'We will get back in time for the high season, so come with me and relax a bit. I've got business in Paris and then I thought I might stay on for a spot of gambling.'

Petal felt eager for another trip and set off with Maxi, complete with fashionable wardrobe, for the sights of Paris. With Maxi she did the town, going to the *Folies Bergères*, Maxim's and the Paris Opéra, where they would rub shoulders with the writers and actors of the time, as well as the dross which frequents those big cities.

At every moment, Petal concentrated on her appearance. She and Maxi had separate hotel rooms but he frequently popped in to her room to find her yet again at the dressing table. 'Wot yer doin', gel?' he would ask teasingly. 'My life, first yer gettin' ready for breakfast, then for lunch and then for dinner. It's wonder you get any time for anything else.'

Theirs was a comfortable association, which they both enjoyed, and to the rest of the world, he was what he really was, her agent and protector. That suited them too.

One night, Maxi had been unlucky at the gambling table and he had not gone home.

Instead, he kept gambling and gambling in the hope that his luck would change.

Back at the hotel, Petal waited for him. She was dressed in a long white-and-blue décolleté dress which she had worn that night for the opera. Now she sat outside on the hotel terrace. She was a little bored and, as she mused, her lovely silk shawl slipped to the floor.

Immediately a distinguished-looking young man stepped forward and picked up the scarf. He replaced it around Petal's bare shoulders. 'Pardon me,' he said.

'Oh, thank you, I was feeling a little chilly,' Petal murmured.

'Allow me to introduce myself,' he said. 'I have seen you often both here and in London. My name is Victor Foster, and I know that you are the lovely Petal, who models fashionable clothes.'

'Well,' said Petal coolly but with interest, 'you have done your homework, I must say.'

'May I join you?' Victor asked politely. 'I am also tired and very bored waiting for my friends to come back from the casino.'

'You do not play?' she asked.

'No, I am afraid not. I cannot afford to gamble,' he said.

Petal stared at this young man who had the courage to admit that he was not affluent.

'I am an actor,' said Victor, 'and that means more rest than work, I'm afraid.'

'Oh, pity,' Petal replied.

'Would you care to join me for a stroll?' he asked.

With a graceful bow of her head, Petal allowed Victor to take her arm and they strolled along the terrace, stopping at the end to look out at the city's bright lights.

'I have wanted to meet you for a long time, Petal,' he said looking closely at her perfect profile as she looked out into the night.

'Indeed, why?' she queried.

Victor's hand on her arm tightened its hold, and Petal felt a tug within her. She did not pull back but allowed her clear blue eyes to stare up at him.

'Oh, God, you are so beautiful,' he murmured.

To her own surprise, Petal felt a blush creep up her neck. She looked bashfully at the ground.

Victor smiled to reveal a line of perfect white teeth under the well-trimmed moustache. He had long dark fashionable side-burns and was sleek and slim in his evening attire. 'I have been touring Italy with some friends,' he said, 'but now I am going back to London. May I call on you there, Petal?'

Petal had no time to answer, for at that moment Maxi came rushing along, having left his casino after a row with the croupier, and arrived back at the hotel. He looked quite hot and bothered as he waddled along, and without a word, Petal drew away from Victor to join her fat friend.

The journey between Paris and London was long and tedious. The trains were always very crowded with people and their luggage and servants. And the boats were even worse. Worst of all was the slowness of it all.

Maxi was a bad traveller. He complained constantly of his upset stomach and barked and belched wind to an embarrassing degree. So Petal stayed well clear of Maxi. While he sat engrossed in an endless card game on the London train, she sat in a first-class compartment for ladies only, and dreamed of the handsome young man she had met on the hotel terrace. She could still feel his soft touch on her arm and see the passion in his eyes when he looked at her. Something stirred inside her: never before had she felt this way. Something about him had affected her in a way no man ever had before. It made her feel good just to think about him.

On their return from Paris, Maxi took himself off to a spa for a health cure. He did this once a year nowadays and had great faith in his annual retreat.

Petal was therefore entirely alone in the flat and quite relieved to be rid of Maxi's large presence for a while. One morning roses arrived at the agency for

Petal. Adelaide immediately returned them to the sender with a severe note attached stating that her ladies were not allowed to receive favours of any description.

'I am surprised at you, Petal,' she said.

Petal sighed. 'I don't know why you should worry,' she said. 'I am already classed as the perfect old maid among our acquaintances.' But inside her heart was singing, for she knew who had sent those roses.

Adelaide smiled. 'The time will come for you,' she said, philosophically.

And Victor did not go away. He was always in the background. Whenever they put on a dress show, Petal could feel his eyes piercing her flesh. Everywhere she went, she was aware of his presence. Then one night as she got into her personal hansom cab, which took her home late at night, Victor slipped in beside her. His tall body was enveloped in a long opera cloak and he wore a tall silk hat.

Petal gave a gasp of fright but Victor put a finger to his lips and ordered the cabbie to drive on.

'Well, you have got a nerve, I must say!' Petal stared severely at him. Victor's eyes held her own. 'I had to see you,' he said. 'And I will go mad if you reject me now.'

Some surge of feeling made Petal speechless and the warmth of Victor's body beside her seemed to make her own burn with excitement. She smiled sweetly. 'All right, you can come in for coffee,' she said, 'but that is all.'

Victor helped make the coffee and they sat together

on the sofa. Petal felt quite warm and began to untie the velvet collar arrangement about her neck. Swiftly Victor's fingers untied the velvet string and even more quickly, his lips brushed her long white neck.

'Now behave!' Petal giggled. But her body wanted to lean towards him.

'Relax, darling. I love you, I want you.' Victor's voice sounded quite urgent.

Petal for the first time in her young life really wanted a man. Now Daisy's blood was hot in her veins.

Victor bent her backwards. As his lips touched her delicately along her neck and his dark moustache tickled her white breast, Petal felt lost.

'Let me stay, darling,' Victor gasped.

As she made no motion to reject him, he got up and carried her to bed. There, in the sweetest state of mind she had ever experienced, Petal surrendered her virginity to this passionate and gentle young man.

And so began Petal's love affair with Victor. She gave him a key to her apartment and informed him of the times when Maxi was away and it was safe for him to come.

Victor seemed besotted. He could not keep his hands off her. 'You are my woman,' he would say. 'I never ever loved anyone before you, Petal. You are my destiny. Let us go away together, my darling girl.'

Woozy with love and feeling so happy, Petal would smile. 'I will think about it but in the meantime let us just be together when we can.'

This love affair was a secret to all who knew Petal. No one could have imagined that the cold calm Petal was capable of feeling with such great emotion. But whenever Maxi was well out of the way, Victor was invariably in bed with Petal.

Petal adored Victor yet there were times when he puzzled her. He told her that he was an actor and although he never seemed to have any regular work, he dressed extremely smartly and spent freely and lavishly. He also had an unusually flippant attitude towards life.

'When do you work?' she asked one day.

Victor laughed. 'My dear, work is the curse of the working classes.'

Petal's clear blue eyes narrowed. 'Well, I am a working girl and if I don't work, I don't eat. I think your attitude is silly.'

Victor's fair skin flushed but he smiled. 'Do not worry your pretty head over me,' he said, 'but in the meantime, my darling, let us love each other while we are still young and you are beautiful.'

Petal had just come in from a late evening engagement and still wore a silk dress with a low neckline and a froth of frills that swept the floor. Victor helped her out of the dress and as his hands smoothed her silky skin, the long slip slid from her shoulders.

'Oh, my darling,' Victor gasped as he knelt before her in homage. As he kissed her full breasts. Petal stroked his curly hair in a whimsical manner. 'Oh my God, how I desire you,' she murmured, 'but where is all this going to end?'

It was the high season and Petal was having to work particularly hard. This and her demanding love affair were beginning to make their mark as Petal lost weight and her beautiful face took on a drawn look.

Adelaide stared at her one day through her eye glasses. 'Petal,' she said, 'what are you up to?'

Petal stared at her coolly. 'Whatever do you mean? I am just working hard. Does that not please you?'

'Your face is wan and you are getting scraggy,' replied Adelaide. 'This is no good. You need good health and a perfect complexion to model these new fashions.'

'I'm getting old, I suppose,' said Petal. 'I have been with you six years now.'

'Perhaps you should take a holiday,' suggested Adelaide. 'Take some time after Christmas when it all becomes a little quieter.'

Petal thought this was a good idea and began to plan an escape to the Scottish Highlands with Victor. It gave her much pleasure to think about it so she was not at all prepared for what Maxi was to spring on her one might.

He blundered in from his gaming club. 'Get up, Petal!' he shouted. 'I got to talk to you.'

Wearily Petal pulled herself out of her bed and put on her Chinese kimono. 'What is it?' she asked rather crossly. She did not like being disturbed so rudely.

Maxi was gesticulating with his hands. 'What is this I been hearing?' he demanded, 'that you got a lover?'

'So?' Petal lifted her chin defiantly. 'What do you expect of me? I am, after all, twenty-five years old and I don't think that I am cut out to be an old maid.'

'Nah! Nah!' yelled Maxi. 'I don't care who you sleep

with, really, but what's this I hear? That fellow is a bloody playboy. I got the news today at the club that you are having an affair with Victor Foster. I just could not believe my ears.'

Petal stared coldly back at him. 'Well, now, you can believe it because it is quite true. We are in love and hope to marry.'

'Marry! My life, he won't marry you! Victor Foster is a playboy and, what's more, he's had more men than women and more of those than I've had hot dinners. My guess is that he's after you for your money and nothing more.'

Petal's face hardened as she looked at Maxi with an uneasy frown. 'I do not care about his past,' she said. 'I am only concerned with the present.' Her words sounded unconvincing even to herself.

Maxi was now wiping his brow and looking very upset. 'Petal, you don't understand. Foster is a bum boy for a rich homosexual. That's how he gets by without working. Do you understand me? Do yer?'

Petal opened her mouth to speak but no words came out. Now she went deathly pale. 'Do not say such things,' she finally said in a quiet voice. 'Victor is very normal and we are very much in love. I do not believe your filthy talk. I don't want to hear it.' She put her hands over her ears.

Maxi had poured himself a brandy and now he sank down in an armchair. 'I'm sorry to be the one to inform you, Petal, but I move around with that set. It's the way I do business. You know that I love you as if you were my own daughter, so I must tell you what I know.'

Petal turned away to hide the tears pouring from her clear blue eyes. 'It is a lie,' she sobbed. But in her heart she knew it was true.

'I beg you to be careful, my dear,' said Maxi. 'It is a vice-ridden society with so many hazards for innocents like you.'

Petal paled as a wave of nausea swept over her. She had seen the fops all hanging around the dress shows, effeminate artists who aped women and had their train of boy lovers.

'Go away,' she said quietly. 'Leave me alone.' She went back into her bedroom and shut the door.

The next day Petal cancelled all her appointments and spent the day sitting on the edge of her bed and thinking about the shocking things Maxi had told her. That night, when Victor walked in through the door, Petal was standing before him, tall and majestic, her eyes red with weeping.

Victor looked a little drunk. He moved lovingly towards her. But Petal held out her arms to push him away. 'It is all over,' she said briskly, trying to swallow the lump in her throat. 'I feel nothing but contempt for you. I have just received an account of your true way of living.'

Victor's face seemed to crumple and he fell on his knees. 'Oh, my darling,' he said. 'Please don't let it spoil our life.'

'How contemptible you are!' she said angrily. 'It seems that I am just a novelty between your other activities. I am told that you are a male whore. You disgust me. I gave my heart and my body to you without question. And you took them and made me believe you loved me.'

Victor got up from the floor. 'That life is all in the past,' he said. 'Since I met you I have changed my life. I was corrupted when a little boy. I never knew true love until I met you.'

'You really expect me to believe that?' Petal cried. 'Well, I don't. Get out of my life and stay out!'

Victor had begun to cry. He hung on to her flowing skirts plaintively. 'Darling, do not reject me,' he begged. 'I love you.'

Petal shook her head. 'I do not believe you,' she said, giving him a push with her dainty foot. 'Now go!' she ordered him. 'Get out, or I will call someone to throw you out!'

Gathering up a little of his pride, Victor backed away. He stared at her for a moment and then turned and walked out.

Petal rushed to the door and bolted it. As she leant against it, she could hear his sobs as he went down the stairs.

Petal went into her bedroom and sat at her dressing table. For several minutes she stared at herself in the mirror. Her face was expressionless. Picking up the silver-backed brush, she smoothed her long hair and began to brush it over and over again. In her reflection, her face was calm but inside, her heart was breaking.

The next day Petal was working hard as though nothing had happened. It was Christmas and she was very much in demand. Work was the only way to blot out the hurt she felt inside. After Christmas Maxi joined Adelaide in urging Petal to have a holiday.

'Come to New York with me, my dear,' he said. 'You will be a sensation out there.'

Petal looked at him mournfully, thinking that he was the only true friend that she had. The world outside had disillusioned her; she felt so cold and empty inside.

Maxi placed a podgy hand on her arm. 'Travel with me to America. I got relations out there. They've done very well, and now they have a number of stores all over New York state. They will welcome you with open arms, Petal, so do come.'

Petal sighed wearily. 'All right,' she said. 'A sea trip might buck me up.'

Maxi's fat face beamed. 'Good,' he said. 'And I know Adelaide will plan a magnificent wardrobe for you to take. You will take New York by storm.'

18

A Yiddish Family

Petal was enjoying the Atlantic crossing to New York. She and Maxi were travelling first class and she loved to show off her expensive wardrobe to the other rich passengers. She enjoyed talking to them and she made a lot of friends and won any number of admirers.

Over the weeks, Maxi told her about his family. 'You will like them all,' he said. 'Sometimes I feel sorry that I stayed in England without them. They have all done very well for themselves. My sister Ruth was married to a millionaire. She is a widow now but since she started out as a factory girl, it's not bad.'

Without being able to put a face to all the people he talked about, Petal was a little bored by Maxi's rambling family history. 'We came across the snow plains from Russia into Germany. My mother had her last child as we fled the pogroms. But the poor little bubba never was very strong, and we dumped her outside a convent in Germany. We had to as they would never have let us through immigration with a sick baby.'

Petal raised her elegant eyebrows. 'You mean your mother left her child behind?' she exclaimed. 'How dreadful.'

Maxi shook his big head. 'Oh, Momma never knew. We kept it from her. My brother Yos had to do the deed. But times were very hard then, you know. You could not imagine how terrible it all was. As I get older and think back on my life I can barely believe that it all happened. But it did and we must not forget it. Jews are a special race and an asset to any country they enter. I am not a good Jew but still am proud to be one.'

'I cannot see the point,' said Petal. 'What is the difference? A Jew is a Jew, what else is there to know?'

'Never mind, dear, I wouldn't expect you to understand but Ruth, my sister, is very strict and I have to mind my p's and q's when I stay with her. She has got a big mansion at the top of Fifth Avenue where she entertains all the top folk, does our Ruth,' he added proudly.

'I had better stay in a hotel, then,' said Petal looking bored.

'It might be for just a week until I get you established,' said Maxi. 'I got another sister called Rosa. She is a bloody blue stocking and bores the pants off me, she does. She works for some society but for years working down in the Indian reservation trying to get education to those natives. We never knows what Rosa will be doing next.'

'She sounds very interesting,' remarked Petal.

'Don't know about that but she's got a lot of jaw. Last time we met she was on about the emancipation of women and their right to vote.'

'What's wrong with that?' asked Petal innocently. 'I've always thought myself equal to a man.'

'Nah! Nah!' yelled Maxi. 'Now don't you start! Women will always be the weaker sex. They lose their charm if they start acting like men.'

'Well, I do believe it was Eve who was brave enough to take the first bite of the apple,' grinned Petal.

Maxi sniffed. 'Oh, forget it,' he said. 'While there are beautiful women like you in the world it will still go round for me. Anyway, let's go for a stroll on deck. The weather's good and the captain says we should spot Newfoundland tomorrow. That will be the first glimpse of land since we left home.'

Petal took Maxi's fat arm and together they strolled around the deck happy in their harmonious relationship that had stood them through the years.

A few days later their ship sailed down the Hudson River. Bubbling with excitement, Maxi pointed out the landmarks of the promised city, as the Jews had seen New York. 'That's Ellis Island over there,' said Maxi, pointing to a desolate looking island with gloomy government buildings on it. 'So many poor devils have perished out there,' he said. 'It gives me the jitters just to look at it.'

Petal screwed up her lovely eyes to stare across the wide flowing river, at the lines of low buildings. 'Yes,' she said, 'it does look creepy.'

Maxi pointed in the other direction to the great Statue of Liberty rising majestically out of the water, her torch held up high. 'That, my dear,' he informed Petal, 'symbolizes the freedom sought by all the refugees and immigrants.'

Petal stared at the massive statue in awe. 'How romantic,' she murmured, genuinely impressed.

No sooner were the two of them ashore than they were hit by an enthusiastic welcome for Maxi from his relatives. Petal was even pushed and jostled as they swarmed around him – large, well-dressed women, small children and bearded men with little flat caps all smacking Maxi on the back and kissing him on both cheeks. They all shouted and talked at once.

Petal stood at the side feeling a little bewildered until the ever-vigilant Maxi introduced her to everyone and put an avuncular arm around her. 'Manny,' he said to a bright-looking youth, 'you take Petal to Sam's hotel and get her settled.'

Manny grinned in welcome showing a mouthful of teeth.

'This is my brother's son,' explained Maxi. 'He will book you in to a good hotel in the town. I know it's good because it belongs to my nephew. I'll come along later and get you for dinner,' said Maxi as the relations whisked him away.

Manny got them a cab. Petal found that he was a shy boy but most attentive. 'I'll take you to Le Royale,' he explained. 'It belongs to Sam. He will be home soon, he has been travelling in Europe himself.'

Petal was soon installed in one of the best suites at Le Royale Hotel. It was a beautiful room with pretty furniture. There was Nottingham lace, velvet drapes and aspidistras, gilt fittings and red carpets. Everywhere, bunches of flowers sat in precious-looking vases. It was indeed a posh hotel. The biggest bouquet of all had a gold-edged card leaning against it. Petal was touched when she read the words: 'With the

compliments of Sam Feldman's family.' It gave her a
warm feeling. But really she should not have been
surprised to find Maxi's family as warm as Maxi
himself. She began to relax. She took a bath and then
looked out of the window of the tall hotel. Down below
in the street hundreds of people were milling about
and the noise of the traffic was more than anything she
was used to in London. There was a thrill in the air
that caught her imagination. What an exciting place.
Petal was sure she would like it here.

A few hours later, Petal had fixed her hair and was
all dressed for dinner when Maxi arrived to collect
her. He was looking very red-faced and in a happy
mood. 'Yer like Sam's hotel?' he asked. 'Bright boy, our
Sam, he plans to buy them up all over the place.'

'Yes, it is very nice,' Petal said. 'How old is Sam?'

'Now, let me think,' said Maxi, scratching his bald-
ing pate. 'He's about twenty-five, I think. He's Ruth's
only son. She thinks the sun shines out of his backside,
but between you and me, he's a bit of a rake. But I have
to admit that he's a real businessman, like his father
was. Now, I'm gonna take you to dinner at Ruth's
house. She's already given me a ticking off for not
bringing you straight off the boat. I expect she will ask
you to stay with her.'

Petal raised her eyebrows. 'I am not sure that I
would want that,' she said. 'I would like to be free to
explore this exciting place.'

'Well, we will see,' replied Maxi.

Petal placed her pretty fur stole around her shoulders. She was dressed in a striking silver-grey dress

which had a froth of white lace dropping from the knees to the hemline. The skirt clung snugly around her slim figure and swung pleasingly as she walked. Her hair was put up on her head in black shiny curls and her long swan-like neck was wreathed in pearls – not real ones but the paste ones that were so fashionable at that time.

Maxi nodded at her approvingly. 'I must say, you look like a princess,' he said. 'So make your entrance, ducky, that will knock some of those frowsy old dames stone cold,' he cackled as he escorted her into a cab.

Ruth's house was very smart. Petal was impressed as their cab pulled up outside. All the windows were lighted up and a big balcony ran across the front, groaning with an abundance of plants and flowers.

They were shown into the house by a butler and Maxi's sister Ruth came to greet them in the long cluttered drawing room.

Petal had been expecting to see someone who resembled Maxi. But far from being big and fat, Ruth was extremely beautiful. She was tall and well-built but slim and she held herself very upright. Petal guessed that she was about forty-five. She had lovely white arms and a big bosom. Her smooth, white face was topped by a tremendous hair-do of white gold curls above a pair of deep-set, icy-blue eyes.

'Ah, Petal, my dear,' Ruth had a slightly guttural accent but she sounded warm and friendly. 'I haff waited so long to meet you. Welcome to my home.' She kissed Petal warmly on both cheeks. 'Come, I will introduce you to my friends before we go to dinner.'

Petal now noticed that the room was full of large ladies in heavily beaded gowns. They all seemed to have fat bottoms, wide hips, too much make-up and loud, vibrant voices. They were all very friendly.

So this was Petal's first impression of the Jewish community of New York. They were a happy, extrovert crowd and a refreshing change to the young Petal after the stiff English society who always made her feel that she was still only a working girl.

In the dining room, the long mahogany table was laid out with fussy, old-fashioned silver and outrageous decorations. Over the delicious food, Ruth's guests all talked rapidly of the theatre, of London and the Royal family. They were very interested in Petal and her work, which surprised and pleased her. They all seemed so free and easy with no thoughts of class distinctions whatever, and Ruth was the magnificent hostess. Petal felt much admiration for her.

To Petal it was one of the nicest evenings she had ever spent, and she told Maxi this as he escorted her back to the hotel in one of Ruth's carriages.

'Ruth told me that she wants you to go and stay with her,' Maxi said. 'So if you want, I'll check you out tomorrow and take you up there. You will meet most of New York at Ruth's parties.'

Petal nodded. 'I should like that very much. I do like your sister. What happened to her husband?'

'Old Barney was a war profiteer,' said Maxi. 'He went down South snatching up property after the civil war, and that's how he made his fortune. He died a few years ago and Ruth's not silly enough to get pulled in by some guy for her money now. She lives only for her son Sam.'

So, with her big trunks containing her wardrobe, Petal moved up to Ruth's house the next morning. They drank sweet coffee and liqueurs out on the balcony and Ruth told Petal her plans with enthusiasm. 'Oh, it will be such fun,' she cried effusively. 'We will put on a dress show. Many of my friends are so old-fashioned out here and afraid to spend their money. One ball gown has to do for several seasons. It will be so exciting to try and change all that, and good for business,' she added. 'Our brother Yossel has a big store and he will probably like you to put on a show there.' Ruth waved her hands about as Maxi did but with more graceful gestures. Petal watched her and thought that but for her slightly shapeless nose, Ruth would be a perfect beauty.

That afternoon they had to take tea with Momma, who lived in a remote part of the house in pleasant rooms which led out to the lovely gardens.

'Momma is nearly eighty now,' Ruth explained to Petal. 'She was one of the very early immigrants. Her eyesight is fading now but her memory is still excellent.'

Petal shivered a little at the sight of this tiny white-haired old lady in a chair beside a great big bed. Soft-footed nurses glided around as Momma put out a small wrinkled hand to Petal, who held it gently.

Her eyesight was clearly going because when she squinted at Petal, she said: 'Tell me, dear, are you as beautiful as they say you are?'

Her voice was thin and cracked and had a thick foreign accent.

'Well, I am passable,' laughed Petal.

'I haff a goot familee,' said Momma. 'They take goot care of me. But soon I go to my Maker.'

'Hush, Momma,' said Ruth. 'You know we don't like you to say that.'

'I haff known hard times and great poverty,' said Momma, ignoring Ruth. 'My husband was a great man, a butcher, and we came here on a big sailing ship from Germany.'

As Petal gently squeezed her hand, she suddenly found herself thinking of her own mother, who had died a squalid death by falling out of bed, full of gin. Here, on the other side of the world, was this mother, being cared for lovingly by her family and in the utmost luxury.

'Maxwell is my eldest son,' Momma was saying. 'He remained in England, so we did not see much of Maxwell. I had a lovely baby once, too, who died in Germany . . .'

On and on the old lady rambled until Ruth signalled to Petal that it was time to leave. 'Momma likes to talk about old times,' sighed Ruth.

'She is a sweet old lady,' said Petal. 'And what is left for her if not her memories? But thank you for letting me meet her.'

Ruth was very fond of classical music and was a devoted patron of the arts. After dinner every evening there was always someone to play the piano or sing. But outside Ruth's sophisticated household, Petal was discovering that New York was a busy exciting city and she really loved it. She loved the theatre, the restaurants and the clubs. But best of all, she loved being included in Ruth's family's social gatherings, weddings, engagements and barmitzvahs.

To someone who had never experienced much of a family life, the warmth of this society was marvellous. 'Is all New York life just for the Jews?' she asked Maxi one day.

'Nah, nah, my dear,' he replied. We only have our own community life. It is pretty much cut off from the rest of New York society, where Jews are not so welcome.'

Petal was intrigued by all the unspoken rules of New York society, it was similar to the rigid class differences at home, after all, but also very different.

'Anyway,' said Maxi, 'we shall be having a huge family gathering next week when Rosa and Sam arrive. After that, you and I will head off for a little travelling so that you see more of America than just New York.'

This big family gathering was a banquet held in Sam's hotel. It was a glittering affair with a delicious dinner followed by a grand ball that went on long into the morning.

Petal was introduced to famous musicians, and opera and ballet stars. She was impressed by it all but her interest was chiefly centred on Rosa, the sister she had not met.

Rosa's hair was iron grey and fixed in a roll around her head. Her features were uneven and she had penetrating eyes, but she had a sweet and attractive smile.

In comparison with the other guests, she was dressed very simply in a white blouse and a navy skirt. She was also accompanied by a lovely young girl with red-gold hair and the most beautiful complexion Petal had ever seen. She was very slim and also plainly dressed.

'Come, Petal,' said Maxi. 'Meet my sister Rosa and this is her niece Zvia.'

Petal smiled as her eyes met Rosa's hard stare, and she felt an odd sensation in her body.

Rosa smiled back. 'Ah!' she said, 'I am so pleased to meet a real working woman among this bunch of parasites.' Petal could not tell from her tone whether Rosa was being serious or not.

Zvia gave a gentle smile and put her soft hand on Petal's. 'Welcome to New York,' she said quietly. Petal noticed that her eyes were a lovely shade of blue.

'We are staying at this hotel, courtesy of my nephew,' said Rosa. 'Come and have tea with us tomorrow, Petal, and in the meantime, don't let this lot spoil you.'

Maxi laughed. 'You're just the same old Rosa. What are you now, then, a bloody socialist?'

'You mind your own business, Maxi!' retorted Rosa. 'You just stick to your money-making.'

This exchange was quite genial, which pleased Petal; she had rather taken to Rosa.

The rest of the evening was quite hectic. All the young guests danced and Petal had so many partners that she was getting tired. Just as she hoped to have a little rest, a sleek young man approached her. 'Is there a dance left for me?' he asked.

'I do believe it's the last, and that it's a waltz.'

Petal hesitated for the waltz was still a shocking dance to do with a stranger. But no one seemed shocked as this young man placed his arms around her and began to circle the smooth floor to the tune struck by the orchestra. Other dancing young couples were also joining in while the older guests watched from the sidelines. Gliding like silk, Petal's dark young man waltzed her round and around until she felt quite giddy.

At the end of the dance, there was loud applause from all sides as the music ended and the young man bowed. The young man smiled as he led Petal back to the seats. 'I knew you would be able to dance the waltz so well, since it is all the rage in Europe.' He had even white teeth and deep blue eyes under dark lashes. 'I am the elusive Sam Cohen,' he said, with another bow. 'I am happy to meet you, Petal,' his hand still held hers.

Of course! Petal saw the resemblance immediately. 'Oh, you are Ruth's son,' she said. 'I have heard all about you.'

'Good things, I hope,' he laughed. As Petal settled into her seat, Sam bowed graciously to his mother and aunt then disappeared again. Petal did not see him again that evening.

'My goodness,' cried Ruth, waving a feather fan, 'how you can find the energy to do that dreaful dance, Petal, I do not know. It is very unbecoming to dance so close. I'm not sure that I really approve of it.'

'Bosh and twaddle!' shouted Rosa. 'You are just too old-fashioned for your own good, Ruth.'

It seemed that Zvia's role was to keep the peace between the sisters. At this moment, she got up. 'I will get some ice cream. Would you like to come with me, Aunt Rosa?'

Petal felt the atmosphere of a family squabble brewing and decided that it was time for her to leave. 'I am tired,' she said to Maxi when he came by. 'Shall we go home?'

Maxi dropped Petal off at Ruth's house and prepared to go on to his gambling haunts. But he guffawed with laughter when Petal mentioned the tension between Rosa and Ruth. 'You ain't seen nothing yet,' he said. 'Just you wait, they can really go to town when they start. It all began years ago when Barney Cohen became a carpet-bagger. Rosa did not approve.'

Petal yawned wearily. She was feeling too tired to hear any more about Maxi's family for the time being. She said goodbye to Maxi and then settled down in Ruth's drawing room for a while.

Just as she had slipped off her shoes, Sam came in, much to her embarrassment.

'Hello, Petal,' he said. 'Let me order you a cool drink.'

They drank champagne, and although Petal felt that she should not be sitting there with him without a chaperone, she was too tired and tipsy to care. He was obviously attracted to her and was not afraid to let her know it. His hair smelled of expensive perfume, as Petal allowed him to take her hand and tell her how lovely she was. There was something very warm and affectionate about this young man. Although they were similar in age, she felt years older than he, because his youthful manner made her want to pet and fuss him.

The sound of carriages rattling down the drive, and doors opening, signalled the return of the rest of the family.

'Oh, here they come,' said Sam. To Petal's astonishment, he put her hand to his lips. 'We will meet again soon, Petal. This lot are too much for me,' he added, moving quickly to the French windows through which he disappeared.

The next day when he and Petal met for a stroll together, Maxi said: 'Well, my family really love you, Petal. I've never known them to get so fond of a Gentile before.'

'They're very close, your family,' remarked Petal.

Maxi laughed. 'I'll say! In my view, they're a little too close, and young Sam feels that way, too. That's why he stays away. He's like me, in fact, and likes to live his own life.'

'Tell me about Zvia,' Petal said a little later. 'If she's Rosa's niece, is she yours too?'

Maxi shook his head. 'She's not even related to Rosa,' he said. 'Why, she's half Indian.'

Petal stared at him with astonishment. 'Really? But how?'

'Rosa has been doing good works with the Indians and came across this red-headed girl in an Indian camp. Apparently it was quite common for white women to be kidnapped and kept as squaws. Then, because Rosa was not married, she was not allowed to adopt Zvia, so Ruth brought her up as a good Jewish girl. We all used to think that Sam was sweet on her but that seems to have cooled off now. I think Ruth stepped in and stopped it going too far. She would, she's like that.'

'That sounds like an extraordinary story,' said Petal. 'But Zvia lives with Rosa now, doesn't she?'

'Yes, she is a sort of companion or secretary. She and Rosa buzz around poking their noses into every bloody social problem they can find, from rights for women to education for the Red Indians. She is pretty smart, is Rosa, and self-educated. She earned her way through university as her old folk could not afford it.'

Petal looked dreamily at the leaves of the trees. 'I am so impressed by the warmth of your family. They all look after each other in a way which I have never known. I always felt guilty that I could never find enough love in my heart for my own parents.'

'Yer could 'ave been a love child,' remarked Maxi. 'Yer can never really tell.' He sighed. 'Well, that's one thing I know, that I never left no bastard behind me. After all the women I have had, no one could swing that one on me.'

Petal looked sideways at him. 'How are you so sure?'

'Because the Prussian guards kicked hell out of me when I was just a boy. The doctor told me afterwards that I'd never reproduce.'

'But did you ever fall in love, Maxi? Is there not someone you can never forget?'

He sighed again, somewhat wistfully. 'Ah, yes, there was a little street angel once. She was lovely and I often wonder what happened to her.'

'Why did you not marry her?'

'Dearie, I am Jewish, so I married some old hag of the same faith for her money and regretted it to this day. And that is the way of the world.'

'Yes,' sighed Petal. 'I suppose none of us gets what we really want.'

Later that afternoon, Petal was relaxing in the drawing room alone when Sam appeared. Her heart jumped as she saw him and she could feel it beating much faster.

'Hello,' she said, surprised by how shy she felt.

Sam came over to her immediately, his beautiful youthful face looking down at her. Without a word, he sat down beside her and kissed her hand gently.

Petal could hardly believe that her movements were beyond her control. She felt herself leaning towards him. Sam's arms folded around her slim body in a warm and yet passionate embrace. Petal had a strange feeling that this was all meant to happen.

So under Ruth's very roof, Petal's love affair began with Sam Cohen. When they were with the rest of his family, they hardly spoke to each other, but they took every other opportunity to steal a kiss or hold hands. And then, late at night, when the whole house was asleep, Sam would slip into Petal's room where she lay waiting for him perfumed and powdered in her bed.

Petal blossomed. The bloom on her cheeks was evident to everyone else, who commented on how well she looked. A gleam of pleasure would flash in Petal's blue eyes as she thought of the reason why, her secret, of Sam's arms around her naked body, his lithe body on hers. Yes, she was a fallen woman now, but how wonderful it felt to be so!

19

The Chestnuts

Ruth regularly paraded Petal around the big dress houses getting her to choose the latest styles for the coming season. She was eager for Petal and Maxi to prolong their stay as much as possible. 'Oh, there is going to be an exciting new opera company here in the coming season. It's making its first trip to New York from Germany and there are so many German immigrants here now that it's going to be very popular. My dear, I am so busy with it all,' she added in a mock-flustered manner.

Petal showed only polite interest. She knew very little about the art of the opera but she did think it a good idea to stay longer in New York.

She had put off thinking about her departure because the very idea was too depressing. But now Sam had gone off on a business trip and she did not know when he would return, while poor Maxi had suddenly developed bronchitis and was laid up in bed. His coughing and spluttering was repulsive to Petal, but he had been a good friend to her so she did her best for him. The house without Sam seemed dreary and rather like a sick house what with Maxi and then old Momma in her room muttering on about her old home in Russia and about the baby she had lost so many years before. The monotony of it all was beginning to get on Petal's nerves, this big house which ran so smoothly, with meals on time, big gatherings every evening, musical afternoons and Ruth the queen of all she surveyed. A bitter little streak inside Petal suddenly resented the easiness of this life. It could never be hers, she knew that. She would not be sorry to go home.

But Maxi was still feeling very ill and was not up to the voyage home as yet. So Petal had no choice but she wished Sam would return.

Her wish was granted a few nights later as she lay in bed dreaming. Suddenly she felt her toes being tweaked. She sat up with a start. It was, of course, Sam, looking suntanned and healthy. With a wide grin, he placed his finger to his lips for her to be quiet. The next moment he was in bed with his amorous arms holding her close.

'Oh Sam, you are a naughty boy,' she whispered.

'I know,' smiled Sam, nuzzling her neck. 'But that's what you like, isn't it!'

After making love, they talked. Sam told her that he had a new boat moored off Long Island Sound. 'We can sneak away there,' he said. 'I will send a carriage for you every afternoon.'

Petal shook her head. 'Oh no, it will be too dangerous, Sam. In fact, I can't let this affair go on any longer. Suppose your mother found out. What would she think?'

Sam laughed. 'I am a big boy now and she is too busy to worry over me.'

Petal frowned at his selfishness. 'Have you given thought for me, Sam? I would be ruined if word of our affair got out.'

The thought had obviously never occurred to him. Now he did look concerned. 'I will stick by you, darling, if that happened. You know how much I love you.'

'But you won't marry me, will you, Sam?' she asked slowly.

Sam looked away. 'No, Petal,' he said quietly, 'but I will always take care of you. You see, it is different for us. My wife was chosen for me when I was sixteen, and I am due to marry her next year when she comes of age. She is an heiress.'

Petal looked annoyed at this news. 'Well, I think you have some cheek. I resent being treated like a cheap whore.'

Sam pulled her to him and stroked her soft cheek. It pained him to see Petal's lips trembling. Her pride had been hurt and she was close to tears.

'Darling, do not weep,' he said. 'I cannot bear to see a woman cry. Come out to the boat and we will love each other. At least we will always have our memories.'

Petal felt a tight knot inside her. 'No, Sam,' she said. 'If you must sow your wild oats, it will not be with me.'

Sam held her closer. 'I have something for you,' he said. 'I bought it from Canada. Come tomorrow, please Petal. Come and see my new boat.'

She wavered and gave in. 'All right, but that will be the last time, Sam. As soon as Maxi is fit enough, we are going home.'

In spite of her resolution, Petal spent a great deal of time with Sam during those last weeks. They sailed in the boat and strolled in the park and walked up Fifth Avenue together. And at every opportunity, they made love, passionate love that Petal could never have imagined to be so wonderful. She felt so happy with Sam and not just because he loaded her with gold jewellery, diamond rings, furs and orchids. Deep in her heart she suspected that she was enjoying herself so much precisely because it did all have to end.

Ruth had begun to look very suspiciously at Petal and her attitude towards her changed. Perhaps it was because Petal chose not to accompany her any more, preferring to be with Sam, but basically she knew Ruth had guessed, that she knew the truth.

Ruth no longer urged her to stay. In fact, the opposite was true. 'I will have a house full of guests come September,' she said. 'I might need the spare rooms. And I need to know as soon as possible if you and Maxi will be returning to England before then or not.'

Petal did not meet Ruth's cold gaze. She felt deeply guilty, for she had not behaved well towards Ruth. Ruth had been so generous and Petal had taken her son. But nothing was said. Manners ensured that no scenes were made and there was just polite conversation until the day they left.

London was looking particularly dismal months later on the day their train pulled in at the station. Petal was also feeling dismal. She had been continuously seasick on that slow voyage home and still felt very queasy.

This was not like her. She also looked very pale with dark rings under her eyes.

In contrast Maxi had perked up as soon as they arrived in Liverpool. 'Ah, there's no place like home,' he said. 'I don't think I'll make that trip again. I'm beginning to feel my age.'

'Well,' snapped Petal. 'You just eat and drink too much and stay out all night gambling. What do you expect?'

'Oh my, you got out of bed the wrong side this morning,' said Maxi, shaking his head. 'You had better get back to work.'

'That is my intention,' retorted Petal. 'And I have also decided to look for my own apartment. Everyone seems to think I am your mistress, what with us living in the same place.'

'Well, that's far from the truth,' grinned Maxi, 'but please yourself, you are your own boss.'

But Petal said no more. She just wanted to get home as quickly as possible; she felt she was going to be sick at any moment.

A week later Petal was slouched in a chair feeling sorry for herself. A visit to the doctor, under the name of Mrs Ramsey, had confirmed her fears. She was indeed in early pregnancy. Petal was devastated. What a fool she was! Each time she had let men use her and she always lost out. Now her career was finished. The disgrace would be terrible. What was she going to do? Whom could she turn to? Would Sam come over and marry her? She knew that the answer to that would be no. It could only be a dream. The thought of her return to the gutter appalled and depressed her, and she could neither eat nor sleep.

When Maxi came to see her, having made himself scarce for a few days, Petal was only a shadow of herself. 'What the bloody hell have you been up to?' he yelled. 'Yer look like a walking death.'

Petal's nerves were shattered, and she broke down in floods of tears.

Maxi was very taken aback. His cool calm Petal in tears? He just could not believe it.

'I'm sorry, dearie,' he said gently. 'What's upset you? Aren't you well?' he cried.

'Oh, Maxi!' Petal sank further down in the chair and put her hands over her face. 'I have made a complete fool of myself.'

'Come, so that's it? With Sam, you mean?' he muttered.

Petal looked up at him in astonishment. 'How did you know?' she demanded.

'Well, it was pretty obvious with you two. Certainly Ruth guessed and was anxious to get rid of you before there was trouble. Betrothed to a million dollars, is Sam. She didn't want to risk losing that.'

'Oh,' wailed Petal, 'don't rub it in, Maxi. Now I am pregnant and what am I going to do?'

Maxi's face scrunched up in a smile. 'Well, do what they all do, get married. You need to find a father. A few well-placed quid should do the trick and then it gets brought up respectable.'

Petal shook her head. 'Oh, Maxi, do not be so crude and horrible. Think what I will have to go through . . .

I'll lose my figure and I might never get my shape back. Then I will never find another job.'

Maxi shrugged. 'Well, it's been done before and women do get their figures back into shape,' he replied. 'Though I've always thought that all them mannequins were too skinny anyway.'

'Oh, please do not change the subject,' Petal wailed. 'You are the only true friend I have got to advise me.'

Maxi walked about the room and then fixed himself a drink. Taking a deep breath, he said: 'There is one solution. You can marry me.'

Petal stared at him open-mouthed.

'I know I am no oil painting,' continued Maxi, 'but I am not without the wherewithal to support you and I am very fond of you, Petal, you know that.'

Two big tears like crystals coursed down Petal's cheeks. 'Oh, Maxi,' she cried, 'I am grateful but I could not do it to you. You like to be a free man, to come and go as the will takes you. No, I will not burden you with my problems.'

Maxi placed a fat arm about her. 'Now, cheer up,' he said. 'No one will be in the least surprised about us. Though how I managed to knock out a nipper is going to make them laugh. But let's get on with it, Petal.' He paused and added: 'It's for the best anyway. You know that. Sam's a bloody playboy and would never have been good to you.'

'Yes, I know,' said Petal sadly, 'he did not really love me, but I easily fell for him. I must be a complete fool as far as men are concerned. But anyway, Maxi, if we marry, I promise on my honour I will stay near you and look after you as long as you want me to.'

'Nah! Nah!' yelled Maxi. 'I don't need no bleedin' rash promises. Let's just get it all organized. Boy, this is going to amaze sister Ruth!' he cackled.

It was a civil ceremony and a secret wedding, with just two old friends of Maxi's as witnesses, an old couple he had known all his life. They kissed the bride and wished her luck. As they did so Petal nearly cried. She felt all alone in the world.

She was quite relieved when it was all over and they could go home. Now she focused on the little baby inside her. This unwanted life did little to make her happy.

Later that evening Maxi said: 'I'll clear out of the flat, Petal, if you want me to. You might like a bit of privacy.'

'No,' she said. 'Do not go away. Let us face our lives and the hash I have made of them.'

'Well, it can't be so bad having a child,' Maxi said cheerfully. 'As a matter of fact, I've always regretted not having a son and heir, particularly since I've been thinking that I might sell the store and settle down to retirement. I've still got a few investments which will keep us going.'

'I have my own money,' Petal said. 'And the jewellery Sam bought me must be worth something.'

'We could buy a nice house somewhere,' Maxi enthused. 'I like Stamford Hill. It's got a good Jewish community up there,' he said. 'After all, this baby is my own blood,' he added.

Petal smiled. 'Maxi,' she said, 'you do as you wish. I hope for your sake that the baby is a boy. I am not the motherly kind, so he will need you. When this is over I intend to make a career for myself, come what may.'

Maxi suddenly got very busy. He sold his East End store to a big combine, a new co-operative which specialized in drapery.

They argued a little about where to buy a house.

'Let's go and live in Chelsea,' suggested Petal.

'Nah, nah,' yelled Maxi, 'there are too many ponces and nancy boys around there. We want a good solid background for our nipper.'

Petal smiled as she sat polishing her nails in a graceful manner. She was touched by Maxi's enthusiasm for this child for which she had not the slightest feeling.

Maxi got his way and chose Stamford Hill. This was an area just on the rise as one went out of London towards Essex. It had recently become popular with the Jews as they made a better life for themselves. They left the East End and moved up onto this big open land near to the river Lee, building big comfortable houses and a synagogue, and soon it had become a thriving Jewish community.

In those Victorian days that area was very rural with great sycamore trees and small green squares where the elderly gathered to discuss their own affairs. The butchers were Kosher and Orthodox Jews dressed in their black hats and robes were a common sight in the High Road. It was a peaceful and prosperous place and it was here that Maxi chose to retire.

The house they bought was called The Chestnuts. It was relatively new but it had a strangely old-fashioned garden with peculiar stone figures and terracotta pots with large ferns.

Petal did not like the garden. 'These statues and pots look creepy,' she said. 'I'd rather have a nice green lawn.'

'Nah, nah' said Maxi, shaking his head. 'I like it, it gives it a posh look and a nice bit of privacy.'

The house was double-fronted with bay windows and a wide central hall with rooms leading off on each side.

'Well,' said Maxi, 'let's say that's your side and this is mine. You can do what you like in your part and I do what I like in mine.'

Petal giggled. 'That is very generous of you, Maxi.' She stared about the big empty rooms. 'It will need a lot to keep it clean. How much help am I going to get?'

'I got all that laid on,' said Maxi. 'We have come to Annie. She was my friend's gel for years but they are now going to New York to live with their son. So Annie will be out of a job. You will like her. She's the nearest thing to an Irish Jew I've ever known.'

The West End flat was let and Mr and Mrs Feldman moved into The Chestnuts. Petal was feeling rather low for her pregnancy was now in its seventh month and the big lump of a stomach depressed her. She did not feel like doing anything except lazing about.

Maxi, however, had taken on a new lease of life. He laughed and joked constantly as he moved all sorts of junk into his part of the house. They had divided up the house so that they each had their own bedroom and sitting-room but they shared the dining room.

When they arrived at the house Annie had been waiting to greet them. She was the maid of all work, six feet in height, big and brawny, and she wore a bright pink cotton dress with the sleeves rolled up to the elbows displaying her muscular freckled arms. Her big moon face was wreathed in smiles under a lopsided maid's cap.

'Ow,' she said in a broad Cockney accent. 'Yer got 'ere, then.' Taking Petal's case, she said: 'Now orf yer go and 'ave a nice quiet lay dahn on the sofa. I'll make yer a strong cuppa, there's a good gel.'

Not having expected such familiarity, Petal stared at Annie a little haughtily but she allowed herself to be pushed and prodded into the sitting-room where she was made to lie down on the sofa.

Maxi roared with laughter. 'Nah, nah,' he cried. 'See what I mean? You'll be in good hands with Annie around.'

''Op it, you fat old sod,' said Annie, 'and let that gel 'ave a bit o' rest.'

Maxi roared with laughter. 'I'm going, Annie, I'm going,' he said and went on his way.

Petal closed her eyes and relaxed while Annie brought tea on a tray with little sweet biscuits. These she served silently and expertly and then she pulled back the drapes so that Petal could see the huge chest-nut tree in the front garden.

'It's nice and peaceful 'ere,' said Annie.

Petal smiled and nodded. Something about Annie had got through to her. She liked what she saw.

As their association continued, Petal got very fond of Annie and relied very much on her. She was quick, clean and thorough in all she did, and she showed little respect for authority of any sort. Annie assumed a very motherly attitude towards Petal from the beginning but Maxi she bossed around shamelessly. She nagged him without hesitation and was always ready to start on a slanging match with him in Cockney and Yiddish.

Maxi loved it all. 'Oh, she is a great character, is Annie. I've known her twenty years, ever since she came to the Goodmans from an orphans' home. And don't you worry about her arguing with me. She's always done it. She don't seem to like men for some reason.'

Another woman came daily to help Annie clean and the house was soon sparkling and well kept. Annie was also the cook. Food was cooked to perfection and served just as Petal and Maxi liked it.

'If yer want Kosher, that's all right with me,' said Annie. 'I've been with Jews all me life so I knows their ways.'

'I really don't mind,' said Petal, 'as long as it is eatable.'

Lazily Petal awaited her baby's birth while Maxi went his own way, enjoying himself. He came and went and sometimes brought in friends for a game of cards. But he also began to observe the Sabbath, for he had suddenly decided to be a good Jew. He went to the synagogue and joined the various groups of Jewish businessmen in the district. He also kept busy buying and bringing home huge pieces of furniture which he placed in his own sitting-room until it was practically overflowing. There were knick-knacks everywhere on the three heavy mahogany sideboards. 'There's money in them, dearie,' Maxi told Petal. 'Won't lose their value, they won't.'

Petal kept her own part of the house fairly clear. She read books and did her sewing while Annie relayed all the gossip of the day, brought in by the tradesmen. Ever busy with a big yellow duster always in her hand, Annie would stride around the room swooping on each speck of dust with ferocious intensity.

Lying on the sofa during these last weeks Petal felt a little forlorn. She found Annie's chatter very amusing, and loved to hear about her latest battles with the tradesmen. Annie had enormous respect for the queen and was very concerned with the welfare of the royal family. That morning it seemed she had had a bitter argument with the milkman. 'He said that it was time "that old lady let go". "Wot?" I says. "She's bin a great queen to us and that son of 'ers ain't no good. 'E does nothin' but fancy women and 'orses."

'"Wot's it to you?" he says. "You're only a bloody skivvy!" Oh, was I mad! I give 'im a good thump I did. "Push orf," I says, "I don't want none of that disrespectful talk around 'ere." '

So it went on. Every day Annie had a fresh row with somebody and hearing about it helped Petal to while those last long days away.

'I'll look after you when it's time,' Annie assured. But Maxi was having none of it. He insisted on a local nursing home. 'The family would never get over it if I allowed you to have the baby at home,' he said. 'No, you go to the Jewish Mother's Home, because we help to support it.'

Petal gave in and on a very hot summer's day when a haze rose over the whole of London, Petal gave birth to a bonny bouncing boy. Maxi, the proud father, went wild with delight and was celebrating from Stamford Hill to the East End for a whole week.

When Maxi came to visit Petal, loaded with flowers and fruit, he asked her why she was not smiling.

'This is the happiest time of my life,' he said. 'It must be yours too.'

'But why is he so fair?' Petal asked. 'Both Sam and I are dark.'

'Nah, nah, nothing to be bothered about,' cried Maxi. 'You ain't forgot, have you? He's a Feldman. Why, Ruth is very fair and my younger sister had red hair. Not all Jews are dark, yer know. Oh, he's a bonny boy.' Maxi could barely contain his excitement. 'He's perfect. Now what are we going to call him?'

'Me?' said Petal. 'I call him Buster,' she said, picking up the baby. 'Well, Buster, you are the first and the last, so make the most of it.' The baby cooed as it nuzzled her breast.

'He's got to have a good Yiddish name, you know that, Petal,' insisted Maxi.

Petal was quite unconcerned. 'Please youself,' she said. You choose. Call him Maxwell, if you like.'

'Nah, nah,' shouted Maxi, his voice ringing around the room. 'No thanks, we've got to have a nice modern name, and not Sam. So what about Morris? Now that's nice, very posh and it's not old-fashioned.'

Petal smiled at Maxi's excitement.

Morris was four days old when Maxi came to visit and had a sheepish expression on his face. 'Petal, today my son is to be circumcised. According to the faith, it should be done before he is eight days old.'

'What?' Petal cried, holding the baby protectively to her breast. 'You can't hurt him, I will not have that!'

'But you promised to let me bring the boy up as a Jew, so it must be done. The mohel is a man who does it and he will be able to do it today.'

The debate went on all day. 'I know I promised,' said Petal, 'and I did because I have got no interest in religion myself. But no one is going to cut my baby about.'

It was Annie who finally persuaded her when she came to visit. 'Petal,' she said, 'get it over with. If I know them, they will persist, and the older the baby gets the more it will hurt him. Now, I'll go with Maxi when he takes Morris down. I've stood by all the Goodman babies, so I can take care of yours.'

So Petal let Maxi take the baby off to be initiated into the Jewish faith. All these ceremonies seemed so strange to her.

Ten days later, Petal was back from the nursing home and had settled down at The Chestnuts with her baby Buster. Annie clearly loved infants and the two women were very content to sit out in the garden with the baby in his crib in the shade. Petal felt oddly pleased and was surprised to find that she really rather liked the baby, though she was very contented to let Annie do all the work of looking after him.

Maxi was a happy man and not a lot of bother. He came and went in the usual manner and seemed to be doing a lot of secret business concerning the Market Traders' Society. He and Petal often had breakfast together in the dining room where he always read out any letters that came from the family. One day there was a very angry one from his sister Ruth, who wrote that she was disgusted that Maxi had married out of the faith and that he should insist that Petal converted. That, she thought, was the only way this dreadful situation could be saved.

'Tell her to mind her own business,' declared Petal. 'I have no intention of converting to any religion. I don't believe in my own religion, let alone a foreign one, and I'm no hypocrite.'

Maxi smiled sympathetically. 'All right,' he said, 'it's agreed.'

One morning a long letter arrived from Rosa enclosing a newspaper cutting of Sam's wedding. It had obviously been a tip-top affair. Petal stared disdainfully at his bright-eyed bride and hardened her heart as she looked at Sam at her side.

'Well, let's hope he got what he was looking for,' Petal said bitterly.

'Nah, nah,' said Maxi, 'it won't last. It's all the money she inherits that he's after. Sam's done for most of old Barney's money with his lecherous ways, but he's a good businessman and still owns his hotel. Her money will be made good use of.'

'It all sounds a little disgusting to me,' said Petal. 'I wonder what she would say if she knew he had a son.'

'Nah, nah, Petal,' said Maxi, looking sideways to see if Annie was within earshot. 'Yer won't break your promise to me, will you?'

'Sorry, Maxi,' Petal replied, very contrite.

'Rosa is thinking of coming over to visit,' said Maxi perusing the letter. That will be a change. There's usually a lot going on wherever Rosa is.'

The Chestnuts household settled down that winter. Petal took up sketching various styles of dresses and began to make a few samples to show around. She was good at it and some of her styles were taken on by dressmakers. Slowly her reputation grew.

One day Petal said: 'I'd like to take up some career, Maxi. Now that Buster is thriving and very happy with Annie, I need something to keep me busy.'

Maxi nodded thoughtfully. 'Well,' he said after some time, old Adelaide is thinking of retiring. She's worked up a good business there, and her girls are famous all over the world.'

Petal momentarily looked sad as she remembered herself as tall, slim and very beautiful. She had filled out a little since Buster's birth and tended to take less care of herself. 'All that's over for me,' she said. 'I'm getting too old to be a mannequin.'

'Yes,' replied Maxi. 'But you know the business. Why not try to buy out old Adelaide? We should have enough between us,' suggested Maxi.

'It might work,' she said. 'I have still a little money and plenty of jewellery. Yes, why not? Are you willing to trust me?'

'Haven't I always trusted you?' he asked with a rare note of affection in his voice. 'I'll go see Adelaide tonight and see if I can make a deal with her.'

As with all Maxi's business deals, he quickly pulled it off. Within a few days, Maxi and Petal had bought the business and the premises in the West End and set up as partners.

Petal sailed out into the world once more full of brilliant ideas. Soon she was completely taken up with running her grand emporium, which was becoming very famous. Her artistic designs had taken off. The furbelows and grand ensembles favoured by the new society were often designed and completed by Petal, and modelled by her young mannequins. Petal soon became very skilled at pleasing wealthy women.

A famous actress was one of Petal's best customers, and since it had become known that this actress was mistress to the Prince of Wales, other women, of course, copied her styles, and so Petal's clothes became all the more popular. Within a few years, her business was making a considerable amount of money and Petal was the independent woman she had always wanted to be.

The Chestnuts was a haven for her with such a busy life and she still got on very well with Maxi. Maxi was now fully retired and had devoted his life to young Morris, and giving him a good Jewish education.

Morris was a bright and intelligent child and could

converse in Yiddish from the age of three. He was a nice-looking boy with reddish hair and dreamy brown eyes. He was often to be seen holding his Poppa's hand as Maxi, moving rather slower these days as his weight had increased, proudly presented Morris to his old friends as they went back and forth to the synagogue.

Back at home, because Petal was seldom there, the Jewish atmosphere of the house had increased. On Friday nights, the little celebrations were held when the poorer Jews popped in for a glass of wine and a sing song. Maxi was very proud and pleased to welcome them.

'Oh, don't bother me about it, Annie,' pleaded Petal, whenever Annie tried to ask some detail about such evenings. 'I am not interested in religion. You just get on with it.'

'Well, you should be interested,' grumbled Annie, 'for the sake of your lovely son.'

'It's too much bother,' sighed Petal. The whole business of religion really bored her and she generally tried to stay at work on Friday evenings for she knew that the house would be full of people all trying to talk at once, eating and drinking their heads off.

Family news still came back and forth across the Atlantic but nowadays no one even mentioned Petal. They did all send their love to young Morris and often wonderful presents would arrive.

Rosa's letters were the most informative. A little while after Maxi had heard the news of his mother's death, Rosa wrote a letter to tell him about some of the details. 'Momma died soon after a peculiar incident at

Ruth's house. The famous German opera singer, Ursula Joseph, came to dinner and met Momma there. Momma went all funny and gabbled away in half Yiddish and seemed to suggest that the singer came from the same German town where her baby had been buried. We all felt a little uncomfortable and it was very embarrassing. Anyway, I like Ursula and we have become good friends in spite of the incident and in spite of the fact that she is a devout Catholic. We get on so well that sometimes I fantasize that she is our poor little sister we abandoned.'

Maxi would read some of these letters out to Petal over breakfast. 'That's typical of Rosa to believe that a complete stranger is a relative. She is such a dreamer! Rosa says that she might come over next year now,' he added, folding up the letter and laying it beside his plate.

Petal sniffed. 'Oh, she's always saying that and she never does. I'm not going to change any of my plans just in case she comes. In fact, I might go to Paris next year. One of the big designers out there has invited me.'

Maxi sighed. 'Please yourself, dearie, we will carry on just the same, Morry, Annie and I.'

Petal, slightly guilty, snapped defensively, 'Is that not what you wanted?'

And Maxi's silence gave her the answer.

20

Rosa

Rosa sat in her high studio flat in Greenwich Village, staring down at the people bustling about in the street below. Her hair was now very grey and her body wide and shapeless. But there was a hint of her early beauty about her as the strength of her character shone through. She was in a rather quiet, nostalgic mood as she thought about her life in America since her family had arrived on those shores.

Zvia was sitting on the sofa looking very pretty with her red-gold hair bound up in a chignon. Rosa turned to look at her, her eyes misty with memories. 'I remember the day when I stood down at the Battery waiting for the other immigrants to land. Most were in a much worse state than my own family had been. Most of them were lost souls, and could not speak the language. And they had only the clothes they stood up in. They were all absolutely worn out with their long voyage across the Atlantic.'

Zvia smiled. 'Well, you have got it all written down, so it will not be forgotten.'

But Rosa looked troubled. Gazing back through the window, she said: 'I do think that it is time to leave New York. I am no longer happy here and I yearn for Europe in some strange way.'

'Aunt Rosa,' said Zvia, 'you have helped many people over the years and now it is time to think of yourself.'

Her voice was calm, cool and sweet and revealed a genuine affection for her Aunt Rosa. For more than fifteen years she had devoted her life to Rosa as companion and niece and there was a strong bond between them.

They had spent several months finishing a book about early America which Rosa had written.

'Yes,' said Rosa. 'We should leave for Europe as soon as we can. I have to do this for two reasons. One is to meet the Irish women who have formed an organisation to fight the English landlords and defy the evictions. And they must do it,' she added. 'Women do not give up as easily as men.'

'And the second reason?' asked Zvia.

'I want to try and find somebody I used to know,' continued Rosa. 'A very dear friend who came over on the same boat. Then she worked with Ruth and me in the old sweatshops where we sat sewing uniforms for soldiers during the war between the states.'

Zvia nodded with interest.

'Her name was Eli Lehane and she married a David Kennedy. I just wonder what happened to them,' mused Rosa. 'You see I heard that they returned to Ireland, so I will have a good try at finding them. Eli was such a sweet little girl and so very religious, a Roman Catholic.' She paused and regarded Zvia thoughtfully. 'Have you still got those ivory beads and the tiny baby's shirt I gave you when you were young?'

Zvia frowned now. 'Yes, but please don't drag all that up again,' she begged. 'I have tried desperately to forget my past. It is not everyone who is a Red Indian Jew, you know . . .'

But Rosa could not be stopped. 'When I found you out in that Indian mission, I knew instantly that you were at least part white. You had the rosary beads around your neck. They were familiar to me because they were like the ones that Eli had used to pray with. Oh, she was so devout, I can see her sincere little face before me now. Bring the box here, will you? I am in the mood to look back down the road.'

Zvia's slim shape left the room and she returned clutching an old wooden box which contained all her treasures. Opening it up she removed a package of soft paper inside which were some ivory rosary beads.

Rosa held them up affectionately and looked again at the name scratched on the little medallion, the name: Foley.

Then she unwrapped another little parcel Zvia handed her. Inside was a very old and slightly discoloured baby's vest. It was made of flannel with a bunch of violets neatly embroidered at the neck. It smelled strongly of spices and Zvia wrinkled her nose.

'That is what you were still wearing when I found you,' Rosa told her. 'The Indian tribe had been wandering for days before they got to the mission. They were just old folk, women and children, because all the war braves had been killed. They were a terrible sight, so hungry and weary. I will never forget it.'

Zvia wrapped up the little garment again. 'I don't

know why I even keep these things,' she said. 'They always upset me. Look, Aunt Rosa, you have this. I don't want to see it ever again.'

Rosa wrapped the vest up gently. 'I will take it to Ireland with me,' she said.

'What good will that do?' snapped Zvia. 'I do not want to know where I came from. I belong here amid the New York Jews. What do I care about some other strange religion?'

'Well,' said Rosa, 'religion is not all of it. There are many other paths to tread in life, Zvia.' Rosa got up from her desk. 'I don't know about you, but I feel like having a stroll. We should enjoy New York if we are to leave it soon.'

In the spring of 1895 Rosa and her companion Zvia set sail from New York harbour with a great send-off from the ever-increasing Feldman family. Yos was there with his wife, children and grandchildren, as was Ruth, moving slowly now that she had grown so fat.

Only Sam was missing. His new actress wife kept him moving and spending time away from his family. So far he had not produced any children. His first marriage to Sadie Shuster had ended in a much publicized divorce which made Ruth very ashamed. Now there was the Austrian-born Gabrielle who had no intention of having any children. Ruth pined to be a grandmother and was most envious of her sister-in-law with her big brood.

The ship Rosa and Zvia were travelling on was one of those new huge transatlantic steamships and called the *Kaiser Wilhelm*. The Feldman family all threw streamers and uttered wild cries as the great ship left the dock, heading back to the lands where they all had their roots.

Rosa stared over the rail at her relatives with their furs and diamonds and the exuberant farewells, 'Anyone would think I was never coming back,' she grinned.

Zvia shivered. 'Oh, Aunt Rosa, don't say such things!'

Rosa gave a hearty laugh. 'Oh, my timid little Zvia. There is nothing to worry about. I came over on an old tub that only just made it and travelled steerage. Today we are first-class passengers and this is a great new modern ship. Don't worry. I could do this crossing standing on my head.'

'Well,' said Zvia a little sarcastically, 'that should amuse the other passengers.'

Rosa's hearty laugh rang out over the water. 'Well, with my big bottom, it should!' she replied.

Zvia hugged her. 'Oh, what would I do without you?' she asked gently.

The voyage was long and uneventful, but Rosa managed to liven things up by having arguments in a loud persistent voice with the sedate upper-class ladies on the upper deck. The women were upset and the men bored to tears, but that was Aunt Rosa, and nothing would change her.

Every night Rosa sat down to work on the speech she intended to make to the Ladies' Land League once they reached Erin's poor distressed Isle. She was in a reflective mood that last night before they arrived at Cork harbour.

'It is strange,' she said to Zvia, 'no matter who you meet at home, if they are Irish they still remain so. They are always talking and dreaming of the "ould countree", so I can't wait to find out about it. At times America seems to be snowed under with immigrants and yet still they come.'

'Well, it is a big underdeveloped country,' said Zvia, 'and they hope to find room for them somewhere.'

'Who knows,' replied Rosa, 'but it seems that the Irish have quite a lot in common with us Jews.'

The next morning, the big liner sailed slowly in to Cork harbour. As their luggage was being sorted out, Rosa and Zvia stood up on deck looking out at the green and misty island and watching the second- and third-class passengers pour out of the lower decks to be greeted with great warmth by their friends and families on the shore.

'It is interesting to see how many do return to their homeland,' remarked Rosa. 'You would think that having made it to America, they would stay there.'

'I suppose everyone is drawn back to the place they came from,' Zvia said wistfully. How she would have liked to have had a permanent home instead of roaming America with Rosa. Now it was to be Europe, where would it end?

The hilly streets of Cork were crowded with poverty-stricken people – women in ragged plaid shawls, men in stove-pipe hats and creases to their pants, and grubby little urchins running hither and thither offering to carry luggage or trying to scrounge a penny. On their way to the Hotel Cork, Rosa stared from the window of the hansom cab. She could not believe her eyes when she saw the soldiers in red coats standing guard with fixed bayonets and the crowd of weeping women outside the prison gates reading the notices of those due to be hanged the next day. Their only crime, it seemed, was defending their home from eviction by the English landlords.

In a rage, Rosa read all the newspapers that night and then wrote an inflammatory letter to the *Cork Examiner* to let the powers that be know she had arrived in town.

The pleasant hotel and the smooth flowing river mellowed Zvia as she sat at the window reading Jane Austen which she had found in a bookshop nearby. The damp cold mist that crept up over the hills made her feel good, as though mystery and romance were in the air.

All that Rosa could find was trouble. She had visited the barracks and had an argument with the captain in command. Then she wandered down dangerous-looking alleys and handed out coins to the ragged kids who followed her about in droves talking in a quick gabble which no one could understand. It was all very wearing for Zvia who felt that perhaps she would not be sorry when they sailed away once more.

One morning Rosa looked jubilant: 'They are out in the country, in a place called Bannateer.'

'How do you know?'

'I learned it at the League,' she replied. 'The Ladies Land League have very secret meetings because they are strictly illegal. They meet in each other's houses. I was asked to a meeting last night down by the coal quay and there I met two very lively young women. One was a hospital nurse and the other one was her cousin, a farmer's wife called Sheila Kennedy. She informed me that there is a big family of Kennedys and they are all very close to each other, and all working for the cause. Now, she told me that her father-in-law, David Kennedy, works for the railway and is married to Eli Lehane, my friend. Is that a coincidence or not?' cried Rosa jubilantly. 'Tomorrow morning we are off to see them. I've made all the arrangements. We travel by train to Shasla Farm and proceed from there.'

'Oh dear, must we?' protested Zvia who felt nicely settled.

'We must, dear,' said Rosa firmly. 'I cannot afford to let this opportunity pass. Anyway, it will be a good chance to talk to the women in the countryside. They are doing great work. It seems to me from what I have heard that these damned English oppressors are even worse than the Prussians. It's time someone stood up to them.'

Zvia looked sad. It had been so peaceful here in Cork and now they were heading off again for unknown territory. How she longed to stop in one place and put down roots.

As they left the hotel, little ragged urchins ran forward to carry the luggage but the hotel porter drove them away. Ignoring him, Rosa tossed them a coin.

'Begorra!' said the hotel porter. ''Tis the eyes out of your 'ead they will have, proper wee rogues.'

'It is poverty that has caused it,' announced Rosa in a powerful voice. Then she was quiet as her attention focussed on a little lad with bare feet and an untidy shock of red hair. A ragged brown cap lay at his bare feet and his small head was lifted high as he sang in a sweet voice:

> If they ask you what your name is,
> Tell them it's Murphy,
> For where's the shame,
> There is no blame,
> In an Irish name, me boy.

Rosa stood rooted to the spot, impressed by the defiance in the boy's tone and his proud partisan manner. Throwing a half sovereign into his hat, she gave him a wide smile indicating to him to continue. As the porter placed their luggage in the cab, the boy went on:

> If they ask you where you came from,
> Tell them friends or foes,
> Twas Killarney's lakes and dells,
> That land where the shamrock grows.

The end was spoiled by the sound of clattering feet as the soldier at the corner, having come out of his doze, came running headlong at the small lad roaring out in a loud Cockney voice: 'Sod orf! I told yer not to 'ang abaht 'ere!'

Swiftly the boy picked up the coin and plonked his cap on his head before charging off down the street on his thin legs.

Rosa gave the soldier an icy stare as she picked up her long skirt and flounced into the cab speechless with anger.

'The Philistines are still around,' Rosa muttered to Zvia when she had calmed down. 'They knock down and destroy what they can. Will it never end?'

'God save Ireland, the heroes said,' whistled the cabbie with a grin on his face.

'Oh dear, Aunt Rosa,' sighed Zvia. 'We have certainly arrived in the right place. Perhaps it will be more peaceful in the country.'

'I doubt it,' cried Rosa. 'Not while the bloody English occupy this lovely Ireland. Its beauty will lie dormant until it is free.'

Zvia smiled. 'You sound like an Irishwoman now,' she remarked.

As the cab left Cork's winding streets the emerald green of the countryside gradually came into view. They crossed a rickety bridge over a wide, swift-flowing river. Everywhere there were signs of the English occupation – at a castle with an armed guard, soldiers patrolling the bridge held them up for their papers.

Rosa was disgusted and became very hostile to the soldiers. But the old cabbie took it surprisingly calmly. His brogue, however, became unintelligible at times, when he wanted to hide an insult.

'Speak English, man!' ordered the sergeant. 'You know that Irish is forbidden.'

'Oh, 'tis English oi spake, every blamed word,' protested the cabbie.

'Why isn't he allowed to speak his own language?' demanded Rosa in loud tones. 'We are American citizens and you have no right to interfere with our journey.'

'Sorry, ma'am,' replied the soldier, 'but there has been trouble here. A prisoner has escaped from the castle, so we have to do this. Where are you bound for?'

'To Bannateer, out in the country,' Rosa replied. 'Now, man, let us go on, and don't waste our time.'

The soldier waved the old cabbie on.

'How many miles is it from here?' asked Rosa of the cabbie.

'Well, ma'am, I can't go all the way because the old nag can't do thirty miles in one day. But I am goin' to set you down in Blarney and D.D. will be there to collect you.

'Who the devil is D.D.?' Rosa cried.

'Oh, Dan Kennedy, so he is,' replied the cabbie. 'He is the brother and he lives in Blarney.'

'How did you know that I was going to see the Kennedys?' demanded Rosa.

'Well, ma'am, 'tis a very dangerous country, so 'tis. We know each other's business. We Irish folk hang together, like. Sure I know the Kennedy family very well, as well as their cousins in Cork, the Woods.'

Rosa was a little amazed 'Well, now, that is very nice,' she said with a smile.

'Ah, mebbe,' said the old cabbie, 'but I tell ye it can be very nasty too.'

All this time Zvia sat silently watching the huge haunches of the old nag as it ambled along through the long shady lanes which were so moist underfoot, and gazing up at the undulating hills rising up from the surrounding mists. She suddenly had an odd little feeling as though she had been there before. It frightened her a little and she shuddered. It felt ghostly and creepy.

The farm labourers were going home across the wet fields, walking wearily as they carried their farm implements on their shoulders. The evening air was cool and neither Rosa nor Zvia was sorry when they pulled up at a coaching inn in the small town of Blarney. It seemed a relatively prosperous place. There were some smart carriages outside the inn, and dotted about there were some well-built houses. Looking down over the town was a tall castle.

'Well, ma'am, here y'are,' said the cabbie. 'You will be staying here till D.D. collects you tomorrow. They said that's what to tell you.'

'How much do we owe you?' Rosa asked as he carried their bags into the inn.

The cabbie waved the money away. 'No, ma'am,' he said. ''Tis all been paid for.'

'Well, for God's sake, man, take something for your own trouble,' Rosa ordered.

The cabbie looked at her in astonishment and his old face crinkled into a smile under his bushy moustache and a big horny hand came out to clutch the sovereign. 'Well, well,' he said. 'I'll not mind taking a drink of ye,' he grinned. 'Then I'll rest me old nag and get back home afore it be dark for me, fare thee well, ma'am.'

'Goodbye,' replied Rosa, 'and thank you for everything.'

Zvia was feeling very cold and travel weary. She was never happy about Rosa's familiarity with strangers, it always made her nervous.

The next morning, soon after Rosa and Zvia had eaten their breakfast, a tall, fresh-faced youth arrived and announced that he was David Daniel Kennedy come to collect them.

Rosa was astonished when she saw him. 'Why,' she exclaimed, you are the image of your Pa. I knew him when he was your age and a tall string of a youth he was just coming into America.'

D.D. told them he was Eli's second son and a twin. His elder brother, Con, had gone to England, while his twin, Hesty, had married young and now had a small farm. His wife was Sheila O'Shea who was a descendant of the cousin O'Shea who went with his father and mother out west in America. Sheila was the one Rosa had met already. 'You see,' he smiled quietly, 'I know the whole story. Why, the folk have never stopped telling it since I was knee high!'

Rosa laughed heartily and kissed him. 'To think little Eli should have such fine sons.'

'There are two more boys, younger than I, and a sister,' D.D. added.

'Oh, I can't wait to meet her again,' cried Rosa. 'When do we leave?'

'Any time you are ready,' replied D.D. 'I have hired

a carriage to take us home. This is my day off. Unfortunately, I work for the English up at the castle. I'm a groom there.'

'Why unfortunately?' quizzed Rosa.

D.D. gave her a strange look and shrugged. 'Oh, it's the times, I suppose,' he said.

Rosa was still a little puzzled but she asked no more questions. D.D. pointed out the big castle to her and Zvia.

'That is one of our famous landmarks,' he said. 'Up there in the battlements is the Blarney stone. If you kiss that you will get the gift from the ancient gods, or so they say.'

'I have heard of it from the people I travelled over to America with,' Rosa informed him.

'The English closed it down to the Irish peasants so it's only for the nobility now,' he said sadly. 'All our good men are in exile.'

They all sat close together in the cramped seat of D.D.'s carriage. The red-faced driver never said a word to them but he wheezed a lot and had a deep rumbling cough.

'As we left Cork,' Rosa said to D.D., 'I heard a boy singing outside our hotel. I can't remember the words but the tune was quite haunting. In fact I felt that I might have heard it before.'

'That must be Billy O'Reilly singing "The Son of the Exile",' D.D. laughed.

'You know the boy?' Rosa was surprised.

'Yes, indeed I do. Billy does good work for us.'

'I would love to know all the words,' said Rosa. 'Will you teach it to me?'

'Why not? You probably hear it sung in America. So many of our compatriots are out there at the moment. One day I'll get out but at the moment I don't like to leave my parents.'

'Get out your notebook, Zvia,' said Rosa, 'and write down the words so that we don't forget.'

''Tis a prohibited song,' D.D. explained. 'To be sung when there are only friends around. What say you, Paddy?' he called to the old driver.

Paddy grunted and waved his whip in assent.

Then in his sweet Irish voice, D.D. sang the song and Zvia took down the words of the exile: 'I am thinking of the many who left old Erin Isle, My father and mother stood in the cabin door . . . And many years I've wandered in this land so lonely and cold.'

As the pathetic words rolled off D.D.'s tongue, Rosa's tears ran down her cheeks. Zvia looked at her in surprise for Rosa seldom cried.

'I remember now,' Rosa said in a choked voice. 'I remember where I heard it. It was Eli's grandfather singing it below decks in that horrible old ship we went over to America in.'

'Why, Grandpa Foley was my old grandfather,' said D.D. 'So you did know him well. Mother is going to be so thrilled to see you again!'

Two hours later the carriage drove into a straggly little village of several cottages which wound up the hill to a high mountain. Noisy ragged children played in the streets but otherwise there was an air of peaceful tranquillity.

They drove halfway up the street and stopped at a

small red-brick cottage by a stream. Standing in the porch waiting for them was none other than Eli Lehane.

Rosa would have recognized her anywhere. Her face was still good-looking and, in spite of her child-bearing, her trim little figure was the same as it was twenty years before.

Rosa clasped Eli affectionately in her arms, just as she had done in the Eastside tenement. After the tears and greetings, the party went inside the cottage for tea.

A table was set with a beautiful lace cloth under plates of bread and butter, and potatoes. A huge side of home-cooked ham sat in the middle. The knives and forks were all set out neatly and daintily as had always been Eli's way.

'I'll go down for a beer and tell Pa that we're here,' said D.D. He withdrew to leave the women to talk about old times and settle down.

21

A Mountainside Cottage

The evening was drawing in. The birds twittered in the eaves and a vast red sun hung over the mountaintop. Eli and Rosa sat hand in hand outside the cottage on a rustic seat. Roses and honeysuckle climbed up the walls of the house, their fragrance intermingling with that of the sweet peas. It was an idyllic place – so quiet and peaceful. One could hardly imagine the terrible events going on elsewhere in the county from this spot. Eli explained that her many children were staying at Hesty and Sheila's farm to make room for the American guests in the one spare bedroom. But Rosa and Zvia would meet them soon, she hoped. Eli apologised for the tiny size of the cottage.

'Oh, it is so pretty,' cried Rosa. 'Eli, I am so pleased for you.'

Eli smiled her sweet smile. 'I have my David and the family and this nice cottage. The railway company built this house for David when he worked on the Irish railroads. He is a foreman now working on the Cork-to-Dublin line. He works very hard and does not get home until late, but then we are fortunate that he has a regular job. There is terrible poverty all around here and folks are still leaving for America. America is all they talk about. But you know, I have never been sorry that I came back. Once I had lost my baby there, I hated the place. I was never in such good health until I returned: you will see what a fine family I have reared. My baby will never be replaced but thank God I have such a fine brood now.'

'I agree, Eli,' said Rosa. 'I remember that you lost a baby there, and that's sad, but I still think you would have got on well in my country if you had stayed. I know that David would have succeeded at anything.'

Eli smiled proudly. 'Oh, yes, my David is a fine man and I am very proud of him. But I never want us to go out into that world again. I am quite content here. I know we live under the English yoke but I want so much to live in peace. I cannot bear all the troubles that are still going on.'

Rosa smiled. 'Still the same timid little Eli,' she said teasingly.

Eli raised her chin. 'Oh, no, not timid,' she replied, with a little defiance. 'I will fight if need be but only for my own family. I am not like you, Rosa. I cannot get involved in everyone else's battles.'

Zvia was strolling around the garden when she heard Eli standing up to Rosa. She turned to look at her, admiration in her eyes.

Eli smiled at her. Her hazel eyes were still so bright, and she had lovely rosy cheeks and her trim figure. It seemed that Eli was everything Rosa had expected. For some unexplained reason, looking back at Eli and seeing Rosa so happy and content made Zvia feel more lonely than she had ever felt before.

'She is a handsome young woman, your nice, Rosa,' said Eli. 'She has such lovely colouring, just like the Kennedys.' She cried out suddenly and rose from her chair. 'Talk of the devil! Here's my David.'

As Eli ran to greet him, David picked her up in his arms, just as he used to do out there on the Eastside of New York. He was still a huge man, with still not a trace of fat on him even at middle age. He was six feet two and all muscle. His red hair glowed in the setting sun, and his ginger beard and moustache framed that cheery face. He had just one blemish, a deep scar over his eye that Rosa had not seen before.

Eli fussed and giggled like a young girl. 'Put me down, David, we have guests!' she cried.

Smiling broadly, David shook Rosa's hand. His was a grip of iron. 'Well, I'll be blowed!' he said, ''tis a fine women ye are now. And who is this pretty gal with you?'

Zvia came forward shyly and blushed as David cast an admiring glance at her. 'So this is the little lady from America,' David said, holding her hand rather gently.

Zvia felt very strange and a peculiar wave of emotion went through her. She suddenly wanted to throw herself into those big strong arms. It was an outrageous thought and she felt embarrassed as she stood shyly looking at him.

That night there was a merry supper. D.D. came up from the pub a little tiddly. Hesty and Sheila came over having settled Eli's smaller children with their own child.

The men drank poteen and got very merry. The women drank wine. They all sang songs and danced a jig or two, and even shy Zvia joined in. Several neighbours popped in to meet the Americans and tales were told of the folk they knew and family stories of wakes and weddings. Even the old priest dropped by and slyly partook of the strong poteen. Everyone was in good spirits. No one was down at heart, and no one mentioned the troubles or evictions that were taking place. It was just a happy evening to be remembered.

Everyone fussed Zvia and some young lads were quite attentive to her. Zvia smiled more that evening than Rosa had ever seen her do.

The party quietened down, Sheila returned to the farm and Hesty had decided to stay at her parents. The remaining crowd sat around the big fireplace. A huge block of peat sent out a tremendous heat and the black iron kettle hung on a hook over the blaze.

As the Kennedys talked, Rosa was pleased to realize that she was beginning to understand the quick gabble and the thick Irish brogue. How she laughed! And how well they told stories. Everyone had some tale to tell, often a little sad, particularly when they spoke of loved ones in exile. 'I have another son,' Eli told Rosa. 'He is in exile in England. I worry about him because I do not hear from him very often. He is the son who was born when we were coming home. His name is Cornelius Erin after the ship and its captain, a Dutchman.'

'You must miss him,' said Rosa gently.

Eli nodded and she bit her lip as tears welled up in

her fine eyes. 'Now, Eli,' said David. 'No tears tonight. Give us a song D.D.'

'Oh, David, sing that lovely song, the one your Grandpa used to sing,' said Rosa. 'I really must learn all the words by heart.'

So in a full but drunken voice, D.D. sang the 'Ballad of the Exile'. By the time he had finished tears were pouring down his face.

Rosa was impressed. 'How strong are one's roots,' she said. 'Once Irish, always Irish it seems, no matter where you be.'

'That is so,' David nodded.

'Me, I am a wandering Jew,' said Rosa. 'I was born in Russia, grew up in America and I am still travelling.'

The conversation turned to the little boy Rosa had heard singing the song.

'You tell them Billy's story, D.D.,' said Eli. 'They will be very interested, I think.'

'Billy is from this place,' said D.D. 'His father was our minstrel boy when his uncle was on the run hiding in the mountain. You see, 'tis the singing that tells the word.'

''Tis a warning sound,' broke in David. 'And they sing in Irish to tell us the latest happening. 'Tis been like that since time untold.'

'Well, Billy O'Shea's father was killed in that last bit of trouble during father's time and his wife and two children were hounded out of the village and ended up in a work house in Cork. The woman died in there and Billy and his sister were left orphans.'

'The girl is called Minnow,' broke in Eli. 'Isn't that a pretty name?'

'O'Reilly loved the river,' continued D.D. 'He was always fishing, so maybe that was why. Well, Minnow is eighteen now and working with me at the castle.'

Hesty, a big burly man with bright red hair, gave a big roar of a laugh. 'And don't he wish he were a big king salmon, so she will fancy him!'

'Well now, Hesty, behave yourself,' said David sharply as D.D.'s face reddened in a blush. 'The story goes,' he said, 'that the English sent little Billy off to an orphanage in England – you know how it is with these do-gooders. But Billy escaped and stowed away on a coal ship and came back to Cork. He's been running the streets of the city ever since.'

'He was so black from sleeping in the coal quay,' added Hesty, 'that no one recognized him when he returned.'

'Will they hurt him if they catch him?' asked Rosa.

'No, he is accepted as he is now. He has his father's musical gift which he uses, and he scrounges round the barracks and the church when he can.'

'Billy's an astute little devil, he'll get by,' said Hesty.

'And he is very useful to us,' said D.D.

Rosa was interested to notice warning glances were passed around the room as though too much had been divulged. Quickly she changed the subject. 'So what about Billy's pretty sister?' she asked. 'D.D., are you sweet on her?'

D.D. glanced at his feet sadly. 'Oh, Minnow will not look at me,' he said. 'I am only a groom, and she has eyes for the gentry.'

'I have heard that she has strange powers,' said Eli. 'And I believe it, for she is a direct descendant on her mother's side of our great Aunt Mair Owan.'

There was a soft groan from the men.

'Oh, Mother!' Hesty said, 'don't start on about Mair Owan.'

'Well now,' said Eli, ignoring them. She was thoroughly enjoying herself. 'Mair Owan was a very small wee woman and lived up in the mountain in a kind of cave, so she did. All the village folk would go to her for advice. If they were ill she would mix up all kinds of herbs to make medicine and to have their fortunes told as well.'

'Well now, she must have been some kind of a witch,' said David. 'And every time you tell the story, Eli, Mair Owan gets smaller, so she was also some kind of dwarf.'

'What do you mean by power?' asked Rosa.

'Fey, my dear,' whispered Eli in Rosa's ear.

'Oh, you mean black magic,' exclaimed Rosa. She was embarrassed to see that everyone looked very shocked.

'No, darlin',' said Eli. ''Tis the fairies. Have you never heard of them?'

Rosa shook her head in amazement and there began a long digression about leprechauns, the little people. Then more amusing stories were told by the family until it had become very late. The women went off to bed and the men put more sods of peat on the fire and lay down on rugs in front of it to sleep until the morning.

As she climbed the ladder stairs up to bed, Rosa asked sleepily: 'What did happen to Mair Owan?'

''Tis the bloody English what kill't her,' growled David. 'Took her forcibly down the mountain, they did, and put her in gaol. Kill't her, it did.'

'Oh Pa,' said Hesty, 'she was ninety years old and I did hear she gave her medicine to the English soldier and kill't him.'

'It's not true, 'tis only hearsay,' replied David as he lay with his big head down on the sheepskin.

Rosa and Zvia settled down for the night in Eli's guest room, which had been specially prepared for the American guests. It was scrupulously clean with low beams overhead and white-washed walls. The bed linen was spotless and was covered with a beautiful lace bedspread. On the walls were religious pictures, and at one end there was a tiny window which looked out on to the big shadowy mountain lighted by a silvery moon.

'It's heavenly,' whispered Zvia as she undressed for bed. Her speech was a little slurred from the wine she had been drinking and she felt the strong masculine presence of the three Kennedy men.

As Zvia slipped into her side of the double bed in the room Rosa was already half asleep. But she murmured. 'Yes, I suppose so, but it's not. They have had a lot of unhappiness and a real undercurrent of sorrow is there all the time.'

Zvia frowned petulantly. She did not want Rosa to spoil her vision of the Kennedy house. 'Well, I love it,' she said, 'and tomorrow I must get up early. I am going up that mountain with D.D. and Hesty.'

The sky was still pink with the dawn when D.D. and Hesty, who were out in the yard washing their faces under the pump water, whistled to Zvia to rise and join them.

Rosa was still snoring as Zvia put on an old skirt and jumper and some strong boots. She crept out of the room and downstairs to meet them.

Hesty was carrying a gun. David, who had also risen and was getting ready to go off to work, called to him quietly: 'Do you have to take that gun?'

'It's all right,' replied Hesty. 'I'll bag some game for dinner tonight.'

'Well, be careful, lad,' warned David. The use of firearms by the Irish was illegal, although farmers kept a gun. Poaching for game or fishing for salmon was common; no English landlord was going to stop them.

Zvia was feeling very excited as she climbed the steep slope with these two strong lads. The sun came up over the mountaintop and, looking back, the village looked like toyland with its tiny houses dotted about. When they reached the top, they rested and ate sandwiches, drinking fresh water from the stream.

Hesty disappeared for a while and there was a marvellous silence all round. Suddenly, there was the sharp crack of a gun, and again.

Minutes lates, Hesty crawled back through the bushes carrying two freshly killed partridges. He stuffed each one down his trouser legs to hide them from the prying eyes of any gamekeeper.

Zvia was amazed. She felt sorry for the birds and said so. But Hesty was blunt, 'It's the way we live out here. It's just a matter of survival. See that stream? That is the beginning of the big river, Black Water, which flows through Cork.'

'Come, we'll show you the pools where the salmon spawn. We catch them at night to avoid the gamekeepers.'

Zvia gazed into the deep silver pools and saw the big salmon lying lazily at the bottom. Occasionally one took a big leap out of the water, at which she clapped her hands with glee.

'They are like travellers,' Hesty told her. 'They've come all the way over the Atlantic back to their place of birth just like you.'

Zvia was puzzled. 'But I was not born here,' she said quietly.

'No, I'm sorry,' said Hesty quickly. 'I just keep thinking that you are one of our cousins. I don't know why. It's the colouring, I suppose. My little girl Maggie has the same red-gold hair and so has Pa. In fact, most of the Kennedys have.'

Zvia snuggled close to him. 'Oh, how I wish I was your cousin,' she said longingly.

Hesty grinned and put his arms around her.

'Now, brother,' said D.D., 'you are a married man, so watch it.'

'You are just jealous,' said Hesty. 'Come, Zvia, we will go down now. It's time for me to milk the cows. I'll see you again before you go home.'

Zvia stood on tiptoe to kiss these tall men. 'Thank you for a lovely time,' she said. 'I'll never forget this place.'

Rosa was sitting out in the garden drinking tea with Eli when they returned. 'I left your breakfast all ready for you,' Eli told Zvia. 'There are some nice new laid eggs and grilled ham in the oven. Maggie has come up from Sheila's. She will look after you.'

Maggie was Eli's only girl. She was about seven years old and very adult in her ways. She had long dark hair and the same colour eyes as Eli. She buttered the bread and took the plate of food from the warm oven. Then she sat down and watched Zvia eat it.

'I've had mine,' she said. 'We have oats most days but seeing as we got visitors, today we have eggs and bacon.'

After breakfast Rosa and Eli gossiped away about the old days, while Maggie took Zvia to feed the ducks and hens and then the old sow in a sty at the end of the garden.

'She's in litter, you know,' said Maggie, dumping the bucket of swill on the ground. 'It's the second lot this year.' She paused and looked thoughtful. Then she said, 'Why do pigs have so many babies?'

'I am not sure I know,' said Zvia with a smile.

Maggie was a sweet sort of child with a quaint, adult manner.

Later that morning, they all began to shell peas for lunch. This business of working went on all the time, and it was interesting to Zvia who had lived in hotels and big houses with servants all her life. The mysteries of household tasks were unknown to her.

Maggie busily explained how to split the shells and get out the peas. 'If there is a maggot, you just take the bad one out,' she said. 'You mustn't throw all the peas away because of one little maggot.'

'She is a right one,' mused Rosa. Rosa was not fond of young children, especially precocious ones.

'If you like, you can stay here and be my sister,' Maggie said to Zvia. 'I haven't got a sister.'

'Now, Maggie,' Eli reprimanded her gently. But she was clearly proud of her Maggie. 'Wasn't I lucky to have another little girl?' she said. 'Four boys I had first, and then Maggie. But I shall never forget my lovely little Violet who died in America.'

'What baby? Who died in America?' quizzed Maggie.

'Now, Maggie, go and get ready for school,' said Eli. Perhaps she should not have mentioned it. But Maggie was old enough to be told all the facts soon.

Maggie kissed Zvia on the cheek and went obediently.

'I am so happy to have found you, Eli,' said Rosa, 'but there is another reason for my search for you. I lost touch with you when you went out west, but I did hear about your tragedy. Now I have got something to show you.' She opened her big handbag at her side and rummaged around in it.

Zvia's face went rather pale. 'Do you have to, Aunt Rosa?' she protested.

'Now, Zvia, I'll get to the bottom of this,' Rosa said as she unwrapped the crumpled paper. Before Eli's astonished gaze, she held up the rosary. 'Have you seen that before?' she asked.

But Eli's eyes were fixed not at the rosary but on

the little flannel shirt embroidered with violets around the neck. 'Dear God,' she whispered. 'Where did you get it? That was my baby's vest. I made it so many years ago.' Her hands trembled as she reached out to touch it.

Rosa waved the rosary beads with the scratched name. 'If I remember correctly, wasn't your Grandpa's name Foley?' she asked.

Eli's face was white as she took hold of the beads. 'Where did you get it?' A muffled sob escaped from her throat. Zvia got up and went over to Eli to place her arms around her.

'Why,' exclaimed Rosa. 'I knew it was right! She sounded trumphant.

'Why don't you be quiet?' hissed Zvia. 'Can't you see you are upsetting her?'

Eli's head rested on Zvia's shoulder. 'Come, let's go inside,' Zvia said.

Eli clutched the little vest to her heart and held tightly on to the rosary beads. She was guided in to the house and sat in the armchair by the fire. Zvia knelt down beside her. 'There is more to come. Now, don't be upset. If you don't want to hear it I'll stop Aunt Rosa.'

'Please tell me where you got them,' said Eli. 'These things were buried with my baby in that terrible place out west.'

By now, even Rosa was tearful. 'I am sorry I sprung this on you. I should have waited until David was here, but now, darling, listen to the story. I think it will make you very happy.'

Zvia sat on the floor beside Eli and held her hand.

'You remember,' said Rosa, 'that I worked for the immigration society down in the Battery? Well, after I got my college degree, I went to the south-west to work with the Indian refugees. They were putting the tribes into reservations. The men were mostly all dead and conditions were terrible for the rest of them – old folk and women and young children. One day in Arizona I was working at the mission looking after a group of these lost children. Some were white, having been captured by the Indians, and some were half white. We welcomed them and fed them and tried to find their kin folk. But one little girl was wearing this vest and nothing else and around her neck were these rosary beads. She looked like an Indian child and she did not speak any English. She was very thin and undernourished. She had worn that little vest for ages. It was absolutely filthy and the front was cut to make it fit her. That's Indian stitching around the edge.' She pointed out to Eli the stitching done Indian fashion. 'Well, I washed the filth from her hair and it was a golden blond. Her skin was so lovely and fair I could not believe it. No one claimed her, so I took her under my wing. Then, when I left for New York, she came with me. My sister adopted her and brought her up, and we called her Zvia.'

Zvia's hands were over her face hiding the tears that trickled down her cheeks.

Eli was as pale as death but she took Zvia's hands gently from her face. 'Dear God,' she cried. 'I have always believed that you were murdered by the Indians.

I have believed that ever since. But when I see the little vest and the rosary and then I look at your violet eyes and the colour of your hair, I know that years ago I wasn't told the truth about your fate. I do now believe it. You are my own lovely daughter.'

Zvia put her head in Eli's lap and sobbed broken-heartedly.

Rosa sat bolt upright in her chair looking both tense and forlorn.

'Why is everybody crying?' said Maggie, who had now got dressed for school.

'We are crying because we are happy,' said Eli. 'Come and meet your real sister.'

Maggie squealed with delight. She took it all in her stride. 'Oh, I told you I wanted one,' she said, flinging her arms around Zvia. 'I shall see you after school. But I am not sure I like your name. I might have to call you something else.'

Rosa laughed and even Zvia released a smile as Maggie stomped away in her boots, on her way to school in the village.

For most of the morning they sat talking of this extraordinary coincidence, and of Zvia's reluctance to tell anyone that she was born a real Indian. 'Well, and after all that, it turns out that I am Irish. It's certainly confusing.'

The old priest was sent for. He was to be the first to know the news of Eli's long-lost child. He said a prayer over them and blessed Zvia.

'Don't waste your time,' muttered Rosa. 'Zvia was brought up a strict Jewess.'

The old priest looked rather shocked. 'I know little about your religion,' he told her, 'but I will instruct her now in her true faith.'

'Well, that will be up to her,' said Rosa in a hard voice. 'I will be going in the morning.'

When David came home that night expecting to find the usual happy home, he found a tearful Eli, Zvia quite silent and a very aggressive Rosa.

Once he had discovered why, he filled in the gap in the story. He explained to Eli how the child she had been told was dead could be before her now. 'Eli, darlin', I never told you the truth that she had been kidnapped because I loved you and it would have only been harder for you to bear.'

'I know, darlin',' said Eli, sliding into his arms.

David looked shyly at Zvia and said: 'Well now, it seems we have another fine daughter.'

But Zvia and Rosa could tell that he was not very happy that his secret had been unearthed and that he was worried about it. He was a man who lived for his happy home and never ever wallowed in the past. 'Now, let's have supper, shall we? And off to bed with you, Maggie.'

Maggie had not left Zvia's side all evening, plying her with questions all about America. 'Will you stay here with us or shall I come back to America with you? I would like that. I have heard about Buffalo Bill. I would like to see him.'

Maggie was hustled off to bed and Zvia sat very quietly in the chair. Her thoughts were miles away. Did she want to stay here? They were a warm and devoted family but what would Rosa do without her? And this Catholic religion they all believed in, was it right? She was a good Jewish girl and even though Rosa was slack about keeping up with her own religion, it had always been her way of life. Inside her chest, Zvia's heart beat with a sudden fear like a trapped bird.

'I must leave tomorrow,' said Rosa. 'I have a date in England with some of the suffragettes.' She smiled at David. 'And I have also promised Eli that I would look up your son Con while I was there.'

David smiled. 'Still the rebel, Rosa,' he said, not unkindly. 'And I'm grateful to you for looking up Con. It will mean a lot to Eli.

'Zvia will stay with us and be very welcome,' he continued. 'The boys will be happy. I know that she made a real impression on them.'

'I hope you will find happiness here, Zvia,' said Rosa. 'I will miss you, darling, but I must push on. There is plenty of work for women to do out in the world, even here. If only they were a little more appreciated. For this is a man's country and very much under the British yoke. I shan't be sorry to go.' Having said her piece, Rosa went heavily off to bed, leaving Zvia with her new family.

That evening Hesty and Sheila came over to hear the news. They were thrilled, as was D.D., who came in later. But they were all sad to learn that Zvia had decided not to stay with them after all. 'I will go with Rosa tomorrow,' she said. 'I hope you don't mind. I will love you all and not forget you but my life is with Rosa, as it always has been.'

Quietly they understood and did not try to change her mind. Eli got up and wrapped the rosary beads with the little vest and offered them back to her.

Zvia shook her head. 'You keep them, mother,' she said with a warm smile.

'Oh, thank you darlin',' cried Eli. 'I don't want you to leave me but I do understand.'

'Pour out a drink, Hesty,' said David in a choked voice. 'We will give Zvia a send-off and may she come back soon. This is her home whenever she wants it.'

Rosa and Zvia rose early and while the cabbie was at the door, Hesty piled in the luggage. Rosa sat in the cab staring moodily in front of her as Eli waved goodbye. Then Hesty helped Zvia up and gave her a quick kiss. 'Come back again soon,' he said, and the old cabbie whipped up his horse to take them to the railway station. From there they would take a train to Dublin and then they would board a ship for England.

Zvia glanced sideways at Rosa and then reached forward and clasped her hand.

'This is not entirely for my sake, is it?' said Rosa in a choked voice.

'No,' said Zvia with a gentle smile. 'I would never have got used to their odd religion.'

Rosa started to laugh loudly. 'I might have known,' she said.

Zvia hugged her quickly. 'But thank you for finding me my place in the world.'

Travelling from Cork to Dublin on the new railway line took a long time. The carriages only had hard wooden seats and most far-sighted passengers had brought bundles of cushions and rugs with which to make themselves comfortable before nodding off to sleep.

As the train rattled along, Rosa and Zvia gazed forlornly out of the window at the green boglands and the humps that rose up out of the misty glen. At one point the train had to stop because of a cow on the line and it waited for two hours until an official finally arrived to shift the animal so that the train could continue its journey. Staring out at the rich green hills and the long stretch of sand at Dungarven, Rosa shook her head sadly. 'I wish to God I understood what all the trouble is about in this God-forsaken land,' she said. 'It seems to me that there is plenty of room for everyone.'

Zvia shrugged. 'But there is no work and nothing grows because the farmers are too poor to cultivate the land and the English landlords continue to evict them.'

'Poor Ireland,' murmured Rosa rather dramatically.

It was a long journey that ended late at night at Dublin's Hotel Imperial. It was warm, cosy and welcoming. There was a bright smiling colleen on hand to wait on them, supplying them with hot baths and a good supper. Outside the streets of Dublin were very noisy and Rosa frowned irritably at the sound of horses' hoofs and carriages rattling by. There were gentlemen in evening dress going out on the town shouting at the beggars and prowlers who had no beds. A squad of soldiers marched through the street.

'Doesn't anyone ever go to bed here?' cried Rosa crossly.

'It is a capital city,' explained Zvia. 'I advise you to go to your bed, Aunt Rosa, and to leave the adventure plans until the morning.'

But the morning brought more noise and chaos, with a demonstration going on out in the street in support of Home Rule for Ireland. There were scuffles as the military broke it up, and shots were fired. The demonstrators were dispersed but they continued to wave their home-made banners with 'Home rule for Ireland' and 'God bless Parnell' printed on them.

'Now, who is Parnell?' asked Rosa. While she was very knowledgeable about anything to do with women and the vote, she was not very well informed about Irish matters.

'Parnell is the Member of Parliament for Ireland,' replied the well-versed Zvia, 'and he's doing a lot of good work for home rule in Ireland.'

Later that day they met a reporter who was staying in the hotel. They fell into conversation and they were delighted to take up his offer of a guided tour around the city of Dublin. At Rosa's request he took them through the poorer part of the city, through tiny alleys and courtways to see the poor dwellings which housed families with so many, many children and all poorly clothed and underfed.

'Why do they have so many children if they can't afford them?' Zvia asked.

''Tis for the faith,' said the young man, whose name was Francis. 'They think that God will find a way to protect his own children.'

'Well, I am sorry,' said Zvia. 'Surely someone will find a way to control this over-population and poverty.'

The young man shrugged. 'Education has enlightened a few but there are some who will never get that chance. Humanity will always be what it is, there is only the choice of good or evil.'

'Sorry,' said Rosa, 'but I don't agree. But then I am an Agnostic. I don't believe my own religion any more.'

Francis put a friendly hand on her arm, 'Well, dear lady, I will pray for you, then. You have told me of the good work you have done in America for the immigrant Jews and Red Indians. When you return to your homeland, I hope you will help us poor oppressed Irish.'

As he spoke, a squad of soldiers marched by, in front of a cart in which huddled six handcuffed young men. 'There you see the problem,' Francis said quietly. 'Our land bleeds its life's blood away. All our young men are shut up in prison or have been sent into exile. One wonders where it will end.'

22

Diamond Jubilee

Maxi had slowed down considerably and was no longer a man about the town. His young son, Morris, a very old-fashioned little boy, spent most of his time with adults and religious Jewish folk who instilled in him the ways and traditions of Orthodox Jews. As he grew older, he became increasingly involved in his religion and very concerned for the welfare of his people.

Maxi was very proud of him and every day he would waddle back and forth to the synagogue to help him take his Hebrew instruction. Puffing heavily, as he was apt to do these days, Maxi would then climb back up Stamford Hill to the safety of the Chestnuts and the warm and comfortable house their housekeeper Annie still cared for.

Petal was rarely at home these days since she was very busy with her business assignments in Paris. Occasionally Morris would receive a big parcel of treats from France and Maxi a sketchy sort of letter, but basically Mama was not often around any more. This did not disturb Morris, for his Papa and dear old Annie were his chief companions and he loved them very much. His Mama had become a pale shadow somewhere out there in the world beyond Stamford

Hill. In fact, he had seldom asked about her since he turned seven.

He was a studious little boy and loved to read. 'Take yer nose outta them books,' Annie would rag him. 'Go play with the other kids in the park.'

'No, Annie,' Morris would reply precisely. 'I have got a lot of learning to catch up on.'

'Tut, tut,' said Annie, shaking her head disapprovingly. Picking up her feather duster she would dust until the furniture shone like glass.

Maxi would have his friends in for cake and wine on the Sabbath, and sometimes for a sedate game of bridge but otherwise the big house was silent. Not even music broke up its peaceful atmosphere.

Petal found the place unbearable. 'Just like a bloody morgue,' she had exclaimed on her last brief visit home.

''Tis the boy that worries me,' Annie had told her. 'Stuffing himself full of all that religion. It ain't natural at his age,' she warned.

Petal was sitting in the chair in her bedroom. She wore a pretty flowered housecoat and smoked a cigarette in a long holder. 'That's how the Jews are, Annie, so it's no good for us to interfere with him now.'

Maxi still received long letters from America, from Rosa who relayed all the family news, while Ruth tended to send polite greetings cards on special occasions. Rosa's letters, however, were always very long and very interesting.

Maxi's obesity had brought with it a form of diabetes that had recently affected his eyes. This meant that

Annie nowadays read the letters from America for him. Peering through a magnifying glass and roaring out the words in her big strong voice, Annie made plenty of mistakes. Her own education at the orphanage had been scant. Morris, sitting a the breakfast table, would burst into hysterical giggles when Annie got stuck on a word and supplemented it with a good bit of Cockney slang.

Rosa's latest letter was being translated by Annie one evening. Maxi settled into his favourite chair while Morris was sitting over his homework.

'Dear Maxwell,' Rosa wrote. 'I hope you are feeling better. You eat and drink too much, and don't say I didn't warn you that it would affect your liver.'

Annie stopped reading and muttered: 'It's not your liver, it's your pangro.'

Morris looked up with a grin. 'Pancreas, Annie,' he said. 'Not pangro.'

Maxi gave a fat chuckle at his son's confidence and cheek.

'Oh, who cares?' sniffed Annie. 'What's it to do wiff yer sister, anyway?'

'Nah, nah,' muttered Maxi with a bit of his old spirit. 'Get on with it, Annie.'

So Annie continued, snorting and sniffing like some old war horse with the heavy magnifying glass close to her eye. 'Zvia and I are coming to Europe next spring.' Rosa had written. 'We are going to Ireland first but then plan to come on to London. I understand that the Royal Jubilee will be taking place around that time. I'm not a fan of royalty, being a republican myself, but you have to admire the old queen for making it this far.'

'Well, of all the bloody cheek!' shouted Annie, throwing down the letter in a rage. 'Who does she fink she is? That's disrespectful, that's wot that is.'

Maxi's huge tummy wobbled up and down as he laughed. 'Well, Rosa is one of those Socialists. She's all for the rights of women and always on the other side, is Rosa.'

'Well, she can keep 'er hopiniuns to 'erself,' sniffed Annie, 'if she comes 'ere.'

'Get on with it, Annie,' pleaded Maxi.

Morris looked up. 'I have to say that I rather agree with Socialist sentiments myself,' he said primly.

Annie spun around with a big scowl on her face. 'Why, you big-headed little sprout!' she cried. 'Now you read the letter, then. I won't finish it.'

So, in his precise little voice, Morris finished reading Rosa's letter. 'We would like to stay with you, Maxi, if we may. I understand that London hotels are very expensive. Sam has been divorced and has married an actress who is squandering every dollar he ever made. It serves him right. She is very fat, like you, Maxi, because of the decadent way she has lived. I wish you well. See you next month, Rosa. P.S. Joe Feldman, our Yos's son, is in London studying law. I told him to look you up.'

By the time Morris had finished reading, Maxi had tears coursing down his cheeks. Annie got up and re-tied her apron strings. 'There y'are,' she said. 'I knew it would depress 'im I'll go and get the supper on.'

Morris went over to his father and put his arm

around Maxi's broad shoulders. He looked lovingly at him with those innocent brown eyes that were so like Petal's in shape.

Maxi put out his hand and rumpled the boy's dark curls with great affection.

'Why does Aunt Rosa not like us?' Morris asked quietly.

'Oh,' said Maxi, 'she loves us, but that's her way. She's always brusque. In fact, you will like Aunt Rosa because she as intellectual like you.'

'And who is Zvia?' asked Morris, who liked to know all the answers.

In a hoarse tired old voice, Maxi recounted to Morris the story of Zvia, the little girl whom Rosa had rescued from the Red Indians and whom Ruth had brought up. 'Rosa took a fancy to this little girl and when she first bathed her, she found that the redskins had covered up her hair with dye and fat. Rosa could hardly believe it when all this red-gold hair appeared.'

'So do you think Zvia is not entirely Indian?' asked Morris.

'No, decidedly not. They used to capture the little ones from the wagon trains and did not often kill them.'

'So the Indians were not so bad, were they?' said Morris.

'They were vicious, all right,' said Maxi. 'They would take off your scalp.'

'But it was their country, wasn't it?' asserted Morris.

Maxi smiled and patted his head. 'You have a streak

of your Aunt Rosa in you,' he said. 'Sometimes I worry about you. You are too brainy.'

In early spring, Morris left the junior school and went down to Mile End every day on the bus to attend the more advanced Jewish college. He was now eleven years old. Watching him set off every morning with his little round cap on his curls and heavy school satchel on his shoulders, Annie was like a proud mother. It was she who waved to him as he boarded the open-deck bus drawn by a team of horses.

After the omnibus had gone off down the hill into the city Annie would then turn her attentions to taking care of Maxi who, though happy and cheerful, was completely housebound.

Then came a terrible day when Morris was attacked by a gang of hoodlums down in a rough area called the East End. They stole his satchel and his little cap, they pelted him with rotten oranges and jeered at him. Morris, who had always received so much love and attention, was completely non-plussed and very upset.

When he got back home, Annie wiped away his tears and scrubbed away the filth the boys had pelted at him. Morris's body was shaking with sobs and he wept copiously. 'Those bleeding Cockneys,' he cursed uncharacteristically.

'Morris,' said Annie, 'don't swear now, and why do you call them Cockneys?'

'They were boys from the market,' said Morris. 'They do it to all the boys if they catch them alone. They call us "long-nosed" and "yidder boys," and I don't even know why.'

'Well, I wish I did,' said Annie, 'but you know fights have been going on a long time. I think you will just have to learn to live with it and then fight back one day.'

'I don't think so,' said Morris weakly. 'I will just try to avoid them in future.'

'Oh, if you weren't born a little angel!' cried Annie, rubbing his black curls affectionately, 'I'll eat my bleedin' 'at.'

'Oiy yoy!' said Morris. 'Now you're swearing!'

The following spring the peace of the Chestnuts was much disturbed by the arrival of Aunt Rosa and cousin Zvia. They arrived in a hansom cab loaded up with trunks and boxes. Rosa was a striking-looking woman in her early fifties with iron grey hair. She wore a dark grey suit of a long skirt and jacket and a strange three-cornered hat like an admiral's. She wore no jewellery but she had a lovely wide smile and merry eyes.

A tall slim beauty in her twenties accompanied her. Zvia was dressed in blue and grey with a froth of lace jabot at her swan's neck. Long drops of tiny pearls hung from her ears under a large brimmed straw hat, and red-gold waves of hair peeped out from under the wide brim. Her wide blue eyes stared out into the world with a very serious expression in them.

Young Morris was very impressed with Zvia. In his imagination she was some mysterious Red Indian princess, for he had recently read the poem about Hiawatha.

Seeing her brother, Rosa let out a loud cry and

flung herself at him. Arms locked in an embrace, Rosa and Maxi wept like rain.

'Oh, oh, poor old Maxi. I can't believe it's you,' Rosa cried.

'Nah, nah,' yelled Maxi. 'Don't rub it in. I know I am an old crock but I ain't dead yet.'

Over dinner, which was served by a new maid whom Annie had hired specially for the occasion, Rosa pontificated about the state of the world and the conflict between rich and poor, capitalist and worker.

Maxi loved every minute. He thoroughly enjoyed himself, and launched into long arguments with Rosa about politics.

Throughout the meal, Zvia sat quietly opposite Morris. Her blue eyes occasionally glinted in amusement but she rarely said anything. Morris was astonished by the animated discussion going on at the table. 'Does the capitalist really gobble up money like Aunt Rosa says?' he asked keenly.

Zvia giggled. 'Not literally,' she said.

'Who are capitalists anyway?' demanded Morris.

'Not your friends. They're your real damned enemies,' cried Rosa, who had drunk a little too much wine.

Morris stared seriously back at her. 'Are you a Jewess?' he asked.

'Of course I am. I'm Maxi's sister, aren't I?' replied Rosa, rather taken aback.

'Well, that does not make you a good Jew,' said Morris, 'because you do not sound like one to me.'

'You've got a real rabbi growing up there, Maxi,' cried Rosa.

Rosa's arrival at the Chestnuts certainly livened up that quiet old house. Annie seemed to be in constant battle with Rosa over the way Morris could or should be treated. The first big battle took place when Rosa took her nephew to visit Madame Tussaud's wax museum where he saw the Chamber of Horrors and the wax effigies of all the most famous murderers.

Annie did not approve. 'He will 'ave bloody nightmares,' she insisted. 'He is a very highly strung boy.'

'Well, who cares if you approve or not?' cried Rosa crossly. 'And don't you swear at me, because if I have to, I can swear as well as you.'

'Ah!' said Annie, 'that's precisely wot I means. You Americans is coarse and common, all of yer, and that boy's bin brought up religious. He don't like to know abaht murders and folks bein' 'ung.'

Rosa sniffed. 'Well, it's time he did. If he is a Jew he will have known plenty of tragedy before he dies,' she said firmly.

'Oh, shut yer face. You ain't natural! You ain't married, and got no chick nor child,' cried Annie, very outraged.

'That's the pot calling the kettle black,' mused Rosa with a sarcastic smile.

'Oh, I knows it ain't,' said Annie. 'I've brung up a lot o' children, I have. And Morris is my boy. Don't you come 'ere interfering with 'is upbringing or I'll walk outta this bloody 'ouse, I will.'

'We could soon replace you,' said Rosa, forgetting her socialist feelings. 'There's plenty who would like such a good home.'

'Ow!' yelled Annie. She burst into tears and rushed out of the room, with young Morris following her. In the kitchen Morris comforted Annie and wiped away her tears. 'Now, Annie, don't lose your temper,' he said. 'Aunt Rosa is an embittered woman. She is an agnostic who does not believe in the words of God.'

'Oh, poor motherless little one,' she cried hugging him to her. 'What would you do without me?'

'Now,' said Morris with great dignity. 'Make yourself a cup of tea, Annie, and I will deal with Aunt Rosa before she starts to upset Father.' Drawing himself up to his full five feet, Morris replaced his little cap on his head and went off to tackle Aunt Rosa.

Rosa had already forgotten about the argument and was reclining on the couch reading a copy of *Forward*, the American Socialist magazine.

With his little hands behind his back and feet apart, Morris stood in front of her. 'I wish to speak to you, Aunt Rosa,' he announced.

'Yes, Morris, I'm listening,' replied Rosa, putting down her paper.

'I would like to let you know that I do not approve of your continually upsetting Annie. She has run this home and taken care of Father and me all our lives.'

'Wal! Wal!' said Rosa squinting at him. 'That's a fine long speech for a little boy.'

Morris scowled. 'That is not amusing.' he declared. 'We are a God-fearing family and Father does not like dissent in the home. It is not good.'

Rosa surveyed him with an amused expression on

her face. She was also impressed. Morris had spirit. 'Do you want us to leave?' she asked.

'No, no, that will not be necessary,' replied Morris. 'I just want you to behave yourself, that is all.' With that he walked stiffly out of the room.

'Did you hear that?' cried Rosa, laughing heartily to Zvia who had just come downstairs. 'Now, there's a man after my own heart.'

After that, the inhabitants of the Chestnuts and their guests managed to live more harmoniously together. Morris went back to school and Rosa went up to London to meet the suffragettes. In no time at all she had got herself arrested at a public meeting and Maxi had to bail her out.

Rosa returned home looking very dishevelled. The brim of her straw hat was hanging around her neck while the crown was still on top of her head. The buttons had all been pulled off her suit and her face and hands were very dirty.

'Oh, my good life,' declared young Morris when he saw her, waving his hands dramatically. 'It is time you returned into the house of God, Aunt Rosa. Women suffragettes? Tut, tut, I never heard of such a thing.'

Rosa was not in the mood for bantering. With a disgruntled expression on her face, she stamped upstairs. 'Aw, nuts!' was her only comment.

While Rosa was living in her London home, Petal was enjoying the attentions of a new lover in Paris. He was an artist who was just beginning to make a name for himself. Petal shared an apartment with Pierre. He was a vain little man but Petal's shrewd business sense very much appealed to him, as did the fact that she knew so many people in the rag trade. She was a useful contact and he specialized in painting lovely women's portraits. Nowadays they were usually painted wearing one of Petal's creations.

Thus together they had moved to the top of society and were welcome guests at all the big salons in Paris and London's drawing-rooms.

This high life suited Petal. She was getting on well and loved her busy social life. She was now past thirty-five but her figure was still good and her appetite for sex just as strong. Icy cool she was with a rumbling volcano inside.

Her association with Maxi had thoroughly weakened over the years. He was now old and obese and Petal, who had never had strong maternal feelings anyway, could not bear her own son priggishly condemning her own business. Sometimes she thought of Sam but she was not one to live in the past and she did not dwell on such thoughts for long, though she did often wonder what he was up to after all these years.

That year in Paris the society talk was all about the Queen's Jubilee in London. It was clearly going to be quite a glittering affair. Almost overnight, dark clothes had become unfashionable and frills, feathers, furs and lace were all the rage. Many Americans had been attracted to Europe for the event, while the English aristocrats were popping back and forth to Paris to buy their dresses and hats.

Going by the unlikely name of Madame de Petaal, Petal had recently opened a new establishment in Paris where she employed several young seamstresses and made the final decision to break with England altogether and stay in France. Pierre was delighted. He was generally a kind, warm and generous man but he did keep Petal's nose to the grindstone in order to make as much money as possible. Petal had begun to feel rather lonely of late. Her cold exterior had always denied her close friendships with other women and she had no friends. But now she often found herself longing to have a woman friend to chat to and confide in.

When a dark-eyed girl called Coco turned up to ask for a position in her salon, Petal was instantly impressed by her vivacious manner. She had a good command of English and an admirable ability to draw. Coco had just left the art academy and, at eighteen years old, was bright and alert and ambitious.

For a while Petal thought she had found the friend she needed. She confided in her and took her out on the town. She invited Coco to supper at the apartment and was pleased that Pierre liked her so much.

At the salon, Petal taught her protégée the trade and allowed her many privileges. She also allowed Coco to run up bills at Petal's expense, which the girl did willingly. But for once in her life Petal felt pleased to have a friend and confidante.

But her new friend was to betray her. Petal failed to notice the growing relationship between Coco and Pierre and she was devastated and shocked when they suddenly announced that they were going to live together and set up their own salon. How could they? Her own lover? Her own best friend? But they had not time for her, they had eyes only for each other.

It was a very disillusioned Petal who closed up her Paris salon and returned to London swearing that she was finished with men forever. Enlarging her London salon, she threw herself into her work and appeared as cool, clever and self-possessed as ever, if a little sad.

A few weeks before the jubilee, a grand dress parade was held at Madame de Petaal's salon in Regent Street. Anyone who was anyone was there. To model her dresses, Petal had a team of very slim young mannequins to delight the society women of London.

During the parade a large, florid woman had been inclined to be rather noisy, making loud comments and guffawing loudly. She looked rather odd, too, with a big pile of red hair pushed up untidily under a floppy and not very stylish hat. An acquaintance whispered that this woman was Australian but was the mother of Lord Beauclair, who had recently married into the Courtenay family.

So, in spite of her irritation at the woman's behaviour, the social connections told Petal that she should not ignore her. At the cocktail party after the parade, introductions were made.

'This is Daisy, Dowager Duchess of Beauclair,' said a crisp English voice.

Petal offered a limp hand which was grasped firmly and pumped up and down.

'Wal, I am sure-glad to meet you,' said the loud

grating voice with a wide smile and flash of good teeth. Two bright blue eyes scrutinized her. 'Yer mean to say that you designed all them marvellous gowns?' declared Daisy.

Petal nodded and smiled. She rather liked this woman after all that. 'And where did you get a name like Petal,' Daisy was asking her with considerable interest.

Petal was a little taken aback by the personal question. She coolly offered Daisy a sherry from a passing tray, and then she sat down beside her to rest her aching legs. 'It is my real name,' she informed Daisy. 'It is not a non-de-plume.'

'You mean to say that is what you were christened?' declared Daisy. She seemed to be quite excited to hear this.

'Yes,' said Petal coolly. 'Now did the grey-green gown interest you? It would do such a lot for your lovely colouring.'

'Never mind,' said Daisy, waving her hands. 'I still want to know about that name and how old you are?'

Petal stared at her aghast. Of all the damned insulting women! Should she snub her? But there was something in the warm grip on her arm and those deep sincere eyes looking at her that made her hesitate. 'All I know is that I was named after my mother's sister who was called Daisy. She seemed to think it appropriate to call me Petal.'

Daisy smacked her lips together in an astonishingly uncouth manner. 'Right, that's it,' declared Daisy. 'And you were born in a little street in Bethnal Green and your mum was called Harriet,' she said in a loud excited voice.

The other guests standing about the room glanced at Petal, concerned as she went a little pale and got to her feet. 'Well, you are a very knowledgeable woman,' Petal said, 'and I am not sure if I can follow what you are saying.' With a cool lifting of her chin, she floated away across the room.

That night, Daisy cried her eyes out on Jackie's shoulder. 'Oh, I know I am right,' she wailed. 'I have scoured London for her and now that I have found her she denies me.'

'Hush, me darlin', don't cry,' Jackie said, hugging her tight. 'You can't be sure that it's her. And if it is, it must have been a bit of a surprise to spring on her like that.'

Daisy blew her nose loudly. 'I know that it was her. I'm sure. Tomorrow you come with me, Jackie,' she said. 'I've got to talk to her. Last time I was out there looking for her, she worked in an East End store, but the place had closed so I drew a blank. But now I know I've found her. She is very refined but she has the right colouring and is the right age.'

'Hush, hush, go to sleep now,' said Jackie gently. 'But has it occurred to you that she might not want to know the truth.'

But Daisy was already asleep.

The next afternoon Lady Beauclair sat in her drawing room having tea and wondering what gossipy old harridan would be calling that afternoon. When the butler handed Daisy a card on a silver salver, Daisy felt almost too depressed to look at it and felt inclined to say that she was not at home. But as she glanced at the card, she realized that Petal had called.

'Oh!' cried Daisy, leaping up to greet her in the hall. 'I had so hoped that you would come.'

'Well, I came,' said Petal a trifle cool, 'because I realized that you could be my Aunt Daisy who went to Australia.'

Daisy swung her arms out. 'Aunt Daisy be blowed!' she cried. 'Why, I am your real mama and my Jackie is your real father. I'm sorry to spring it on you, darling, but I've been looking for you for years, ever since I came back over.'

Petal was reeling with shock. She sat down on a little gilt chair. 'I have always known that there was some mystery about my birth. Although Harriet brought me up and I was told that she was my mother, I never felt towards her what I thought I should have done.'

'Harriet was my sister,' said Daisy quietly.

The maid arrived with tea on a tray.

'Now, darling, we will have tea and I'll tell you a story. Oh, my, what a story it is too!'

As they drank tea and ate sweet cakes, Daisy told Petal about her adventures out in Australia. It was a long and varied story. Both the women shed real tears.

'I have papers and photographs that belonged to Harriet at home. Will you have tea with me tomorrow and bring your husband?' Petal asked politely.

'He ain't my husband,' said Daisy in her forthright

way. 'We haven't managed to make it legal yet,' she cried.

'Oh!' said Petal, a little crestfallen. Then she looked up with a wry smile. 'That makes me a bastard,' she said, with some delight.

The relationship between Petal and her mother strengthened the next day as they sorted out the family letters. Amongst them they came across a picture of Daisy when she was just sixteen.

'Oh, you were really lovely,' sighed Petal.

'Oh well, lovely is as lovely does,' said Daisy. 'Shortly after that photograph was taken I'd got myself in the family way and Jackie was sailing to Aussie land. I was in a right pickle, I can tell you,' she continued in her forthright way.

'Our mother was very strict. She was a small shop-keeper and so terrified of gossip that I was persuaded to pretend that you was Harriet's baby. I ran off when you was a few months old, I just couldn't take it.'

'Oh, how sad,' said Petal.

'Oh, well, I asked for trouble. I could not keep me legs crossed,' said Daisy in her earthy manner.

Petal's cool calm face lit up in a bright smile. 'Neither can I!' she said.

They both began to laugh heartily as a strong bond of affection was formed between them.

'Tell me, am I a grandmother?' demanded Daisy suddenly.

'Yes,' said Petal. 'I have a boy and his name is Morris. I am married to a Jew, you know.'

'Well, I'll be blowed,' returned Daisy. 'I once had a

nice guy who was a Jew,' she said. 'I should have married him but then he did not want to marry me.'

So began a round of visits to the races and grand parties about town. News had soon got in the newspaper that the society Duchess had found her long lost daughter, now a famous dress designer. They were invited to everything and in June they attended Queen Victoria's Diamond Jubilee.

A large balcony in Regent Street above Petal's dress salon was booked by the family for that special occasion, when they would watch the frail old Queen ride in an open carriage to the service at St Paul's Cathedral.

There was Petal and Jackie, and Petal's son Morris; Daisy with two of her sons beside her – the third was in the Queen's Guards riding past in the grand dress uniform of his regiment. Next to Daisy's boys stood Rosa and Zvia, and then even old Annie was there, dressed in a dark service dress with a feather in her best hat. Tears poured down Annie's cheeks when she saw the frail little body of the Queen of England, the woman Annie had cherished all her life.

Everyone was there except Maxi, who was house-bound and being looked after at home by a specially hired nurse while Annie came up to town.

All of London was in a very festive mood. Flags festooned the street. Chinese lanterns hung between the lamp posts; the crowd roared as London cheered Her Majesty the Queen for her reign of sixty years.

Morris and Daisy's youngest son John got on rather well. 'I am going to be a rabbi,' Morris told John.

John looked interested. 'How strange,' he said. 'It has always been my ambition to be a priest. We will end up on different sides.'

'I don't see it like that,' said Morris. 'Surely it is true that there is only one God.'

'That's what they say,' replied John, delighted to have found someone as serious as he in the family.

That evening a grand dinner was held at the Ritz. In her usual flamboyant way, Daisy had invited many guests to dine with her before enjoying the fireworks exploding in the massive bonfire burning in the park. This night was indeed a night to remember.

Daisy's newly united family continued its celebrations for several more days. The day after the jubilee procession, they all met up at Daisy's big house in Onslow Square. This was the town house of the Beauclairs and had been a hundred years earlier.

'It is an old draughty place,' Daisy would declare to her visitors. 'Why, my old shack in Calpeady was warmer than this,' she added with a laugh.

Daisy complained a lot about England. She told Petal that she felt like a square peg in a round hole. 'This house is very uncomfortable,' she said, 'and if it wasn't for the little old nags out in the mews so Jackie and I can ride down Rotten Row, I'd pack up and go back to Aussie land tomorrow.'

In spite of all her moaning, Daisy still stuck it out. But it was sad for Jackie who sat around quietly and uncomplaining, longing for the open bush lands and blue mountains of Australia. He was very excited to meet Petal, his only child, but he was saddened by the coldness of her manner. She did not seem very interested in him.

That particular night a big party was held at Onslow Square. Daisy had employed a well-known chef and extra catering staff for the occasion.

Daisy looked magnificent in a wide flowing gown and a magnificent head-dress which Petal had made and placed on her head with her slim artistic hands.

Daisy roared with delight at the sight of herself. 'What a wonderful hat! Oh, I must wear it! I look just like old Pearly Ladell.' She chuckled.

'Oh, Mother, sit still,' said Petal impatiently. 'And who the devil is Pearly Ladell?'

'Ah, that's another long story,' said Daisy, 'I'll tell you one day. But come on, love, let's go to the ball!'

In the wide rooms the guests had assembled. They were a noisy crowd, made up of some of Daisy's racing friends mingled with the family. Daisy's eldest son, Charles, was there too, with his new wife Vanessa Courtenay. Charles was a fine boy, taller than his Father had been and just as handsome, attired in his red dress uniform. Vanessa looked stony-faced, for she could not tolerate her mother-in-law – and the feeling was quite mutual.

Daisy muttered to Petal. Then, 'She ain't taken long to get herself pregnant.' Like a ship in full sail, Daisy launched herself into the drawing room. She always looked happiest with all her family around her.

Among the young bucks was young Fred, Daisy's second son. He had adopted a confident swagger and was always dressed in the nattiest way.

By his side was a young man dressed in a flamboy-ant embroidered waistcoat, and a gold pince-nez on the end of his nose. It was Joe Feldman, over from New York for the Jubilee, and he was Fred's constant companion, as both were very interested in gambling.

Then there was tall Alastair, Jackie's legal if not natural son, over from Australia, his gold hair and fair skin contrasting with his dark uniform of the Queensland Rifles. While in the far corner young Morris and his cousin John sat close talking to each other about fine ideas.

In another corner sat Rosa, dressed in a heavy serge skirt and white lace blouse. She looked hot and flushed as she argued with everyone about the Boers.

It was Zvia, cool and sweet and dressed in exotic peacock blue silk, who was the centre of attention and attracted all the young men. She looked so appealing and chic that even Petal felt a little jealous of her.

As the band played and the guests laughed and danced with gay abandon, Daisy looked proudly about her. This was her family; the seeds she had sown in two countries had now spread across the world. How extraordinary it was that Petal had married old Maxi Feldman! After all, he might have ended up being her real father. Yes, Daisy thought, it was indeed a small world. And how odd that instead of having a child with Maxi, she had ended up having a grandchild with him – young Morris, her grandson.

Sadly, Maxi had been too ill to come to the party. Daisy resolved to visit him the next day.

At that moment a strange drama was being acted

out at Maxi's home at The Chestnuts. Annie answered the front door to a very smart young man. He was very dark and rather handsome. 'I would like to see Mr Feldman,' he said. 'Please tell him it is his nephew Sam from America.'

Annie squinted at the visitor suspiciously. 'It's not convenient now,' she told him. 'Mr Feldman is very poorly. I've just sent for the doctor.'

As she spoke, a pony and trap rattled up the drive and the bearded old doctor got out.

'Let me come in, please, I might be of some help,' pleaded Sam. 'My uncle has not seen me for years and I came a long way to find him.'

'All right,' said Annie rather rudely. 'Wait out here until the doctor is gone.'

Sam sat on a bench in the hall and waited patiently for the doctor to leave.

The doctor did not stay long but when Annie let him out, she had tears streaming down her face.

'Can I do anything to help?' Sam asked, rising to his feet. 'Oh, stay with him,' cried Annie. 'I've got to get the rabbi. The doctor said Mr Feldman may not last the night. Oh dear, everyone's gone to the party. What can I do?' Sobbing loudly, she pushed her arms into a shabby old black cardigan and trotted out of the door.

Sam walked quietly into Maxi's bedroom. It was in semi-darkness and the smell of disinfectant and death assailed his nostrils. Maxi was lying on his bed, his body swollen to a tremendous size. His lips were blue and he gasped loudly for breath.

Sam went over to the bed and took Maxi's limp

hand. 'It is Sam, Uncle Maxi,' he whispered. 'Ruth's son, Sam.'

Maxi's eyes flickered open and the fingers tightened in Sam's grasp as he showed signs of recognition. 'Hello, boy,' he gasped. He went quiet for a moment and then his eyes glanced towards the door. His grasp tightened more and the dry old lips moved slowly. 'Come closer, boy,' he said. 'I'll tell you something,' His voice cracked and hoarse. 'You must know that Morris is your son.'

Sam look puzzled. Was the man deranged? What was he talking about?

Maxi continued. 'Nah, nah,' Maxi found his voice again. 'I married her, I married Petal. You got her pregnant. You bastard.' His voice was halting and weak. But his words were clear.

Sam drew away, dumbfounded and a little afraid of this swollen mass and the accusations that were coming from it.

Maxi pointed to the bedside table. 'Look, in a drawer. There's a letter for you. I wrote it. No time to send it.' Maxi tried to push himself up but fell back on the pillows in a fit of coughing. He gasped loudly as he fought for his breath.

Still feeling puzzled, Sam opened the drawer and found a sealed envelope addressed to himself. As he pulled it out, Annie and the rabbi arrived. Sam slipped the letter into his pocket and left the bedside to the rabbi.

'Will you fetch young Morris, please,' Annie said to Sam. 'He will want to be by his father's side now, I think. And the rest of the family should know.'

With his eyes full of tears Sam agreed to go and fetch Morris and tell the rest of the family. Travelling in the hansom cab up West, Sam opened the letter he had taken from the drawer and began to read Uncle Maxi's large uneducated scrawl.

> *Dear Sam,*
> *I am about to take off. I don't mind, cos I've suffered too long already. But this you must know. The boy Morris is your son. I married Petal because you let her down. I love that boy. He has been my whole life. Now do your duty by the family and look after him. See that he is brought up a good Jew as I have always taught him to be. Goodbye and don't forget that you owe it to the family.*
> *Uncle Maxi*

Sam's face paled and his hands trembled as he dropped the letter to his lap. So that was how old Maxi at middle age had married the lovely Petal and got a son. 'Oh my God!' he murmured, placing his hands over his eyes.

Petal was the one he should have married! Instead he had ended up with Sadie Shuster who hated him and never bore him a child and the sexless Gabby who cared only for the things money could buy her.

Sam took off his spectacles and wiped the tears from the lenses. Now indeed was the time to stand up and take young Morris into his care.

At Onslow Square, the party was in full swing. When the forlorn-looking Sam walked in, Rosa spotted him immediately. As she came to greet him, he whispered in her ear the news of Maxi's expected demise. Rosa quickly found Petal and soon all the Feldmans were travelling back to The Chestnuts in two carriages. Morris and Petal, Rosa and Zvia, Joe and Sam. Then the family sat through a long night's vigil as old Maxi, that well-loved and fine character, passed into the next world.

Petal's face was paler than death itself; it was the first time she had seen Sam since she left New York so many years before.

The period of mourning was over and Maxi had been laid to rest when Sam arrived one morning at The Chestnuts. He had a very determined expression on his face. 'I want to talk with you privately, Petal,' he said.

Petal looked pale and weary after the long days of weeping. She was dressed in a plain black dress and wore no make-up. 'I am tired,' she said. 'Say what you have to say, Sam, and then leave me in peace,' she added rather irritably.

'No, I insist we talk now. Let's go into the sitting room,' Sam told her. Reluctantly, Petal agreed.

'Sit down,' Sam said, pointing to a chair. 'I am about to deliver you quite a shock.'

Petal looked up warily.

'I have a letter here, Petal,' said Sam, 'addressed to me. It is from Uncle Maxwell.'

Petal's lid flickered but her lips did not move.

Sam's voice rose with emotion. 'Do you want me to

read it out?' he demanded. 'Or shall I just ask you what I want to ask? Why did you not tell me that Morris was my son?'

Petal leaped to her feet. 'Nonsense! That's a lot of old nonsense,' she cried, trying to snatch the letter from him.

Sam drew away, placing the letter behind his back and out of her reach. 'This was signed and witnessed several months ago. Witnessed by Annie and the local rabbi. Maxi tells me in this letter that he married you to give Morris the name of Feldman, to keep him in the family, so to speak.'

'That's not true!' cried Petal, spitting out the words.

'For God's sake, don't keep lying,' said Sam. 'I know it is true and Maxi has given me custody of Morris.'

'I will never allow it,' cried Petal.

'I will go to the law if you don't agree,' Sam replied firmly.

The pair stood facing each other defiantly and then a world of tears washed over them both. Sam moved slowly towards her. 'Oh Petal,' he said gently, 'how I loved you! Why did you do it to me?'

Petal made an effort to pull herself together. 'Oh, don't be a fool, Sam, you know you did not want to marry me.' There was a pathetic edge to her voice.

Sam looked forlorn. She had spoken the truth. 'That may have been so, but how I would have loved our son, Petal. What use is all the money I have made if I have no one to leave it to? Come, let Morris decide. Find him and tell him the truth and I will take him home to America to finish his education.'

'No, you will not!' Petal declared. 'And I will not let him decide. Morris was devoted to Maxi who was mother and father to him. I know that I have not been a good mother but I can assure you that it would break his heart to be taken from me and those who love him. He doesn't even know you.'

Sam reached out to her but Petal pulled away.

'I will divorce Gabby,' Sam said, 'and marry you. I will do anything you want, but let me have my son,' he pleaded.

A protective iciness seemed to envelop Petal at this suggestion. She drew herself up and said firmly: 'I have no wish to remarry,' she said. 'My husband is not long dead, and, besides, I am not a Jew. I know how fussy you Feldmans are about such things.'

Sam looked sadly back at her. He sighed. 'All right, Petal,' he said. 'I will wait a while. I will call before I go back to New York, but if you have not made a decision by then, I have to warn you that I will fight you in the law courts even if it takes every penny I possess.'

With this threat, Sam left the room, banging the door shut angrily as he went.

23

Dark Days

Soon after the Diamond Jubilee, it became obvious to everyone that Queen Victoria, the great ruler, had begun to fade fast. The topic of conversation everywhere was the new regime. At nearly sixty, was not Edward a little too old to take the royal reins which had been withheld from him for so long? How could he cope with being king after so many years as a playboy? And what would it be like having a king on the throne after all these years? Would he be serious enough to take on the great responsibilities of the monarchy? Although he was very charming, Edward read very little, cared nothing for routine, and gathered information from personal contacts. None of this suggested that he would make a good king. On the other hand, he was a great supporter of philanthropic causes and widely popular with all classes.

Whatever the case, Edwardian society was flourishing. The Queen's sombre shades were being pushed aside in favour of the new fashionable colours of purple and scarlet. Everything was flamboyant, including ladies' hats decorated with feathers and gaudy flowers. Skirts had become skimpy and dresses elaborately trimmed, and there seemed to be new styles every year as high society squandered those newly made fortunes drawn in from the big industries. The gap between rich and poor had never been so apparent as it was now. The rich spent the fortunes ostentatiously without a thought for the poor living in squalor all around them.

Petal benefited from society's lavish spending and made a lot of money with her own designs for dresses to be worn in the social whirl. Her mother rarely spoke nowadays about going back to Australia: she seemed to enjoy England too much and she loved hob-nobbing with the lords and ladies at the races where she spent most of her time. She loved to gamble and seemed to be gambling away much of her allowance from the Beauclair estate. This was Daisy Dukes, our bright butterfly, who was determined not to let herself grow old and unsightly, and she wore the latest clothes, her daughter's designs, and was known as a colourful character in the circles she moved.

Sam did not carry out his threat to fight Petal over the custody of his son Morris. Instead, he returned to New York and then turned up in London again with his entire household, wife and all.

'I have come to live in England for a while,' he told Petal on his reappearance. 'It is such a civilized place and I should like to enjoy it.' He hesitated and then added with a sly smile: 'I should like to be near my son, and you, Petal, my darling.'

Petal turned her face away coyly. Could it be that her love for him would be rekindled and be allowed to flare up again? She had had many affairs in her life but no man had ever made her feel so alive as Sam had done.

'I'm pleased, Sam,' she said gently. 'I shall enjoy having you near.'

Sam skipped towards her and took her slim hand. 'I have always loved you, Petal,' he whispered, rubbing her hand against his cheek. 'Let us enjoy each other again as we once did.'

Petal's heart was singing. As she turned towards him, her eyes were wet with tears and her cheeks were uncommonly flushed. 'Oh, yes,' she whispered back, 'Oh yes.'

Meanwhile, Daisy's eldest son Charles and his wife had recently had their first baby. His young wife Vanessa had given birth to a girl. There had been great hopes that it would be a boy to carry on the line of the Beauclairs but it was a lovely girl with her Grandma Daisy's colouring and a long string of names. The principal name was Fleur, which pleased Daisy very much.

'It really takes me back,' Daisy said to Petal, 'to that crummy little room over the shop in Bethnal Green, when I gave birth to you. My mother and sister tried to stifle my cries so as to keep the news of my bad deed from the neighbours.'

Petal was tired of hearing her mother's stories and replied rather curtly: 'Oh, do we have to hear all that again, Mother?'

Daisy puffed out her bosom like a ruffled pigeon and her face became red and angry. 'Look 'ere, my gel,' she shouted indignantly, 'don't you get toffee-nosed with me. I ruined my life having you. But when you came I wanted you to be part of me and my life. I was Daisy and you were my Petal. It was just sad that we had to be parted,' she added.

A forgiving smile spread over her daughter's face. 'All right, Mother,' she said. 'Let's let bygones be bygones. Well, Fleur is a pretty name but the family are all seething. They all wanted a boy.'

'Wal,' declared Daisy, 'frankly they was unlucky. Fleur is a lovely baby and she's got my colouring. They got plenty of time to have an army of boys in their young lives.'

Yet the Gods have decided otherwise. There was not plenty of time at all, for a real war had flared up in South Africa. Most folk knew little about it, and many were not interested. After all, those damned Boers were always causing trouble. 'Our troops will soon put them in their place,' was the arrogant attitude of those in power and the tip-top regiments were sent out to South Africa to sort it out. The war continued to escalate at an alarming rate.

Charles was one of the first to be sent out with his Guards Regiment. The day he sailed away, the whole family gathered down at Tilbury to give him a real send-off. They waved their Union Jacks and sang 'Soldiers of the Queen' as they watched him sail away. With tears in her eyes Daisy waved a last goodbye to her tall dark son, who looked so smart in his scarlet uniform, and so much like Dukey, her late husband.

Queen Victoria died in January 1901 in her

favourite house of Osborne on the Isle of Wight, with her huge family around her bedside.

After one of the longest reigns in European history, the Queen was widely mourned. Under her rule, the country had witnessed a period of incredible expansion and increasing material prosperity. Once more Daisy's family gathered in Petal's West End salon to watch the cavalcade of the Queen's funeral procession draw through the streets. Rosa surveyed the scene seriously, narrowing her eyes at the new King Edward and his young nephew, the Kaiser, as they walked side by side. There they go,' she muttered, 'instigators of the next war. The Queen married her children into every possible royal family.'

'Oh, don't be so cynical, Rosa,' said Sam, who was often with Petal these days. 'Surely it will make royalty a good deal stronger.'

'No,' declared Rosa emphatically. 'It will be the death of all of them.'

Sam gave a good-tempered smile. 'Oh Rosa, you have become a real anarchist. Surely this will always be the greatest country in all the world while there is a royal family.'

'What's that to you, Sam?' sneered Rosa. 'You are an American.'

'Yes,' returned Sam, 'but I feel part of English society. I have a lot to hold me here,' he added enigmatically.

Rosa was about to continue the argument when Petal floated by. She was dressed in a flowing black dress which enhanced her white skin, and she also wore a black-and-white imitation bird on her thick well-groomed hair.

Sam's gaze went straight to Petal in mute admiration. Zvia, who was standing beside Sam, smiled gently and moved over to make a space for Petal next to Sam.

Rosa noticed this and said rather loudly: 'That woman has hooked Sam again. God only knows what will come of that affair. They both seem to have forgotten that he still has a wife and a very vindictive one, too.'

Rosa soon decided that she had had enough of England and that she wanted to travel on with Zvia to Germany, to the big Socialist conference to be held in Frankfurt that year.

'While I'm there, I'll visit my old friend the singer Ursula Joseph,' she said. 'I understand that she has a child now, a girl called Charlotte. I would have thought that her husband was past it, but that's their business,' Rosa gossiped to Zvia. 'It seems that Ursula has given up the professional stage and just works now for charities, while her husband is writing a new opera. She has also converted to Judaism, which amazes me. But, she added, 'I sometimes wonder about her . . .'

'Well, it will be a change of scene,' remarked Zvia with a sigh. 'They tell me that Bernard Shaw is attending the conference as well as other prominent writers form the Fabian Society. It should be very interesting to see what hornets' nest we will find.'

Yes, the gossip published in the society scandal columns about the rich American and the beautiful dress designer was true. Samuel Feldman, they informed their readers, had a worldwide chain of hotels and more money than he knew what to do with. That year Sam had sent his wife Gabby to visit her parents in Austria and had dropped off in Paris to visit Petal. Again he begged her to let him adopt Morris and make him his heir.

'I will definitely divorce Gabby,' Sam told Petal. 'She won't care so long as she gets a good settlement,' he said. 'I am so rarely at home.'

Petal did not believe this and was still adamant about the situation. 'I will not disillusion Morris, Sam,' she said. 'Maxi wanted it this way. Let him finish his training first. He seems so happy.'

But she was happy to see Sam, too. He stayed with her in her Paris apartment, and together they hit the nightspots and the gambling salons. Petal purred like a well-fed cat and revelled in Sam's love-making. He was her man, the only one to have penetrated her icy exterior to her very core. Together they cruised the Mediterranean on a luxury yacht, while society made bets as to when this affair would end.

'I want to keep my freedom,' Petal would declare. 'I love you, Sam, no one else ever touched my life as you have done but I will not interfere with Morris's education. He is doing well at Oxford. It would be unfair of me to spoil things for him. He was never part of my life, after all. He belonged entirely to Maxi and Annie at The Chestnuts.'

'It's a lot of bloody nonsense!' cried Sam. 'What does he want religion for when he can inherit a chain of hotels?' Sam himself no longer observed Jewish customs.

'He would probably give them all away to charity,' Petal replied tartly. 'I should spend all your money, if I were you, Sam.'

'But Petal, I want you too. I love you and need you,' cried Sam.

Petal stared at him somewhat coldly. 'Sam,' she said, 'you have as much of me as you need. You need my body, that is all. I will never forget that you left me to my fate to have Morris all alone. No, I will not let Maxi down, not even from the grave.'

'But Petal, trust me, I have the evidence that Maxi gave me telling me that Morris was mine. I can still take the papers to the New York courts and fight you if need be. But it would be a terrible scandal, and you won't like that.'

'It will be just as much of a scandal with your wife, if she finds out about me,' said Petal coolly. 'No, I am willing to be your mistress but not your wife. I am leaving Paris soon. My mother needs me. She has recently lost two sons – Charles in the war in South Africa and also silly Fred, who disappeared overnight.'

It seemed that the errant Fred had gone to the East End gambling. There was no trace of him but the police did not connect his disappearance with the stabbing of a Peeler down in the Highway near Wapping. Whatever the truth of the matter, it was all very upsetting for Daisy.

The couple returned to London and Sam implemented plans to build another big hotel outside the city. He also bought Gabby a new house near Hampstead Heath.

Sam visited Morris at Oxford and escorted Petal around the town and she was openly acknowledged as his mistress. Petal could take it all well but the terrible threats and cries of jealousy from Gabby's house echoed all over the town. It was all rather unsuitable behaviour but Petal enjoyed the wickedness of it all the more.

The king was now on the throne and in 1906 the Liberals won an overwhelming victory in the elections. There followed a series of reforms aimed at social amelioration, including the famous People's Budget in 1909 brought in by David Lloyd George, the Chancellor of the Exchequer. In 1911, the National Insurance Bill was passed.

Christmas 1911 brought a suicide attempt by Sam's wife Gabby. Sam went to her house in Hampstead to find Gabby beside her bed. Poor pathetic Gabrielle, who had once been slim and beautiful with golden curls falling down her back, now lay like a fat lump in a soiled house gown, her hair thin and grey, spread over the floor with her tear-stained face turned up to the ceiling and in her podgy hands she clutched a photograph of her wedding to Sam taken twelve years earlier.

Sam was appalled and his conscience severely battered. He quickly sent for the doctor who manager to revive Gabby but from that day on the poor woman was a nervous blubbering wreck. Soft-hearted Sam felt that he had to stay with her and she clung to him like a child until he was at his wits' end.

Petal was scornful when she learned of Gabby's

condition. 'I see, so I can only expect you now when you want sex. You don't care about *me*.'

'Don't be sarcastic, Petal,' said Sam wearily. 'I brought on Gabby's breakdown by treating her badly. I am guilty.'

'Nonsense!' snapped Petal. 'She has always been a lush, look at the gin she has consumed and all the pills and potions, and things. She has brought it on herself. I have no patience with such women. And look how obese she has allowed herself to get!'

Sam stared at her in a strange way. 'You are a hard woman, Petal, but one must give way to weakness sometimes.'

'Well, life has made me hard,' said Petal. 'I am not like you, Sam, born with a silver spoon in your mouth.'

Sam came over and put his arm around her. 'Don't quarrel with me, darling, because it is only you that I love, and our son. If you agree to marry me I will take Gabby home and settle her in Los Angeles with her sister. She will like that.'

To Sam's astonishment, Petal nodded. 'Oh, Sam,' she said, 'it has to end. I am also a little tired of this hectic life. It would be nice to roam around the world, just you and I with no commitments. Morris can do what he wants. He is still serious about becoming a rabbi.'

'Do I hear you right, Petal?' Sam's eyes had lit up, and he held her close.

'Yes, you do, Sam, there has never been any man who meant a jot to me but you. So why live in misery?'

'You're right!' cried Sam. 'Tomorrow I will book

our passage on a ship and persuade Gabby to go with me. I will put my affairs in order out in New York and then I shall get a divorce and make Morris my heir. And then you and I, my darling, will sail away to happiness.'

Petal smiled and leaned her head on his shoulder. She suddenly felt overwhelmed with such happiness, unlike any other emotion she had ever experienced. She had given herself to her man and it was good.

They were very close that night, a cold misty December when the streets of London were wet and miserable, when the homeless huddled in doorways with no future in sight. Sam and Petal snuggled down in their comfortable bed with great plans for a life together.

The next day Sam went to Hampstead where Gabby, in a pink robe, sat scoffing chocolates, her hair frizzed up and her cheeks rouged, putting on an act to hold her man. 'Oh Sammy,' she pouted. 'Where have you been? You never went to her, did you? You promised me it was all over.' Tears poured down her chubby cheeks.

Sam knelt beside her and wiped the tears away with his handkerchief. 'No,' he said. 'I will tell you where I have been, to the shipping office to book our passage back home, early in the spring.'

'Oh, Sammy,' Gabby cried, trying to throw her fat arms around his neck. Sam got up, deftly avoiding the embrace.

'We are going on a brand new liner that they claim is unsinkable. It is fitted with every possible comfort on board and is reputed to be very fast indeed.'

'Oh!' Gabby's pale blue eyes widened. 'Will it really be safe?' she asked.

'Of course it will,' said Sam irritably. 'A lot of the best possible people are booking tickets for her maiden voyage and I got in there early.'

'Oh, Sammy,' crooned Gabby. 'You are so clever. When do we sail?'

'In April,' he said. 'We sail on the *Titanic* from Southampton.'

Gabby went back to her chocolates, smiling content-edly to herself. The suicide attempt had worked. At last she was taking her husband away from that slut; she had got him to herself.

Sam and Gabrielle were saying their goodbyes to London. Gabrielle was all dressed up in stunning mink coat and a fabulous hat all spiked with feathers. She posed for newspaper pictures smiling brightly and fingering the fabulous pearl necklace which Sam had bought her. It was rumoured that the pearls were insured for ten thousand dollars. Sam, it seemed, had bought her these pearls as a going-home present and to salve his conscience.

Slim and dark, Sam stood sadly at Gabrielle's side when they boarded the train for Southampton. The night before he had said goodbye to Petal and she was still uppermost in his thoughts. But next to him now Gabrielle beamed, giggled and simpered and held tightly on to his arm. His heart was heavy as they travelled to Southampton to board the splendid new ship, *Titanic*. It would have been even heavier had he known the terrible fate that he and his fellow passengers were to meet a few days later.

When the news reached England, the morning newspapers printed the fact that the *Titanic* had hit an iceberg, along with plenty of false rumours.

Poor Petal did not know what to believe. At first they were reassured that everyone was safe, then the news came that most of the passengers had died in the freezing waters of the Atlantic. She fled round to her mother's house in a terrible state. Daisy tried to comfort her. 'Sam's all right, I'm sure he is,' she said. 'He was a first-class passenger. Why, they gets off first, they do, they don't let the millionaires drown!'

But seven millionaires went down on the *Titanic*, and Sam was one of them. The world was aghast and inquiries into the disaster went on for years.

Petal was devastated. She lost weight and became very pale. Her hair turned grey and she retired from many of her activities. She had truly loved Sam and now he had been taken from her.

The disaster of the *Titanic* seemed to change the lives of many. Joe Feldman had nearly sailed with his uncle but had decided not to at the last minute. He could not help feeling guilty about what had happened. He felt that he should have died instead of Sam. On his return to New York, his doctor sent him to a sanatorium where he got a litle better but for the rest of his life he suffered badly from depression and bad nerves which haunted him.

Sam's mother Ruth died soon afterwards, in

mourning for her beloved son and her many friends who had gone down with the ill-fated ship. Her vast fortune went to her various nephews and nieces – as did Sam's. Legally he did not have a son to inherit the huge estate that he had worked hard for all his life. Papers did exist to prove his paternity of Morris, but all those records had been in his briefcase which now lay at the bottom of the Atlantic along with Gabrielle's famous pearls.

Sam's son and heir was not bothered; Morris was not aware of the fact that Sam was his true father. Still in Germany completing his holy education, he was sad to hear about Uncle Sam, whom he knew as his mother's lover, but his feelings were not strong.

Petal gave up her Regent Street salon and just lived quietly in the apartment over the shop. She still dressed beautifully, always in black, and wore lots of dazzling jewellery. Her greying black hair would be wound about her head and the expression on her white face was tragic.

'Pull yourself together, gel,' declared Daisy. 'One can't live with the dead.'

But Petal would smile her wan smile and say: 'I am all right, Mother, just let me be.'

Daisy's family was battered but still surviving during these years before the Great War. The clouds were gathering and while Daisy ignored as much political talk as she could, it was impossible not to be affected in one way or another. On the whole, though, she entertained herself looking after her little red-headed granddaughter, Fleur, whose mother Vanessa had remarried and, by mutual agreement, had handed over to Daisy the responsibility of the child's upbringing.

In addition to this, Daisy had recently received a letter from Rosa, who was still in Germany. It seemed that in her inimitable way, Rosa had discovered her long lost sister, the famous German opera singer. Rosa asked if Daisy could possibly look after Ursula's young daughter Charlotte as life in Germany did not look very safe at that moment.

'Well, I'll be buggered!' declared the forthright Daisy. 'Ain't I got enough to take care of? What do I want a bloody German girl for?'

Daisy hated writing letters, so it was Jackie who did it for her. 'I'll answer the letter for you, Daisy. I'll tell Rosa that Charlotte can come. We must always look after family, however distant they are.'

Daisy agreed. Of course she would take in Rosa's niece, and she would hope that friends would take in her own family members in the same way.

A few months after Jackie had met the pretty, shy German girl at Victoria Station, a duke was assassinated and the whole world was swept into war.

BOOK THREE

24

Sarnia

Guernsey was indeed an island of strange wild beauty, just as Fred's father had once described it. Charles Dukes, his adored father, had taught Fred to swim, ride and shoot out there in the bush amid the high-ridged mountains of Eastern Australia and given him a strong pride in his own grass roots. Yet Charles Dukes' own roots had been deep in this rocky island, known to the locals as Sarnia. 'Well, boys, I am a Guernsey man and they don't come better,' was all he would say. But he did once sit down with Fred and describe the place where he had grown up. The picture he drew of the place had stuck in young Fred's mind.

When Fred's gambling habits, inherited from his father no doubt, led him into more trouble than he could handle, he hopped aboard an Italian tramp steamer which eventually put him down in Guernsey, a mild and sunny island, with fertile soil and the famous Guernsey cattle, kept pure by local laws.

Fred swung his bag over his shoulder and went ashore into the town, the only town, of St Peter Port. It had a newly built harbour, full of tall ships and small boats. A fishing fleet lay at anchor there, while a small group of fishermen sat playing cards by the harbour wall and others concentrated on repairing nets. They all had long beards, some grizzled and grey from life on the salty sea. Their skin was brown and weatherbeaten, and they spoke a local patois which sounded very odd to Fred as he swaggered past.

The fishermen stared at this newcomer with some suspicion. Although he was dressed in a fine suit and elaborate waistcoat, they were stained and crumpled by travel. He was a handsome young man but his dark hair was long and untidy. He certainly looked unkempt but being Dukey's son, Fred was very proud and his carriage was a trifle arrogant.

'English,' growled a fisherman as he swaggered by. His companions nodded in agreement.

The confidence in Fred's step was inherited, for he was the son of Charlie Dukes of whom no man was a master, and his mother was the strong resilient Daisy who had become one of London's famous socialities. All that high life in London had been the downfall of young Fred. He had found it so easy to fall into bad habits in that fast Edwardian era of vice and gambling. Slow horses and fast women had taken their toll on poor Fred and, at twenty-four years old, he was now on the run from the English law. He had not even had time to say goodbye to his family.

As he reflected on the circumstances that had forced him to flee, he recalled the battered face of the Peeler he had fought with outside the East End gambling house and also the vicious face of the Italian sailor, who had come to his aid by plunging a knife into the

Peeler's back. Fred's last vivid memory of that night was of the policeman, the arm of the law, lying slumped in the gutter, blood oozing from his wound and down into the drain.

The sight had shocked the usually law-abiding Fred and he knew it was time to go. He accepted a lift from the Italian sailor, who stowed him away on the tramp steamer and eventually dropped him off quietly at St Peter Port on the island of Guernsey.

Now here he was on this strange island with very little money in his pocket and not knowing a soul. He walked dismally along the harbour road. The heavy seas were washing over the great harbour wall and a strong wind blew hard about his ears. Ahead of him stood a grim-looking castle built of yellow rock. It had a round tower just like a sandcastle that a child might build on the beach. But the walls looked thick and very solid, and had withstood the passage of time and the winter gales for many years. Armed soldiers walked the ramparts and some were guarding the bridge which connected it to the mainland. One of these soldiers came towards Fred, but Fred strolled nonchalantly by. His heart was beating, though, for he was very wary of authority. Taking a detour, he crossed the main street and went up a flight of steps to a hilly lane where tall stone houses stood huddled together like old people. Around a long market street there were many kinds of stalls and shops. Even though it was mid-winter, there were flowers. Women sat with their baskets of wares, and laughed and gossiped amongst themselves. The cobbled streets were hard on Fred's feet for he wore lightweight boots. He stood outside a bakery staring hungrily at the mouth-watering array of freshly baked loaves and cream pastries. They would go down a treat. He walked in and ordered a coffee and a roll.

'*Non, non,*' said the lovely dark-haired assistant, shaking her head. 'Bread or cake, *non* café.'

Fred gazed at her suntanned face and its halo of lovely dark hair. She did not seem very friendly.

'*Pas de café,*' she shouted. 'Monsieur can 'ave bread.'

'I'll take one of those,' said Fred, pointing to a long stick of bread.

With her long white fingers, the young woman deftly wrapped paper around the bread and thrust it at him. 'Twenty cents, *Monsieur, s'il vous plaît*', she said in a pert French tone.

Fred put the baguette under his arm and fished in his pocket for his last sovereign. He handed it to her.

The assistant looked at the gold coin with suspicion. 'I go to get change.'

As she walked away, Fred watched her swinging hips and the contours of her smooth shape under the snow-white apron with appreciation. There had been many women in young Fred's life but he always had time to admire a beauty like this one with her long graceful neck and thick shiny black hair twisted neatly around her head.

On the girl's return she haughtily offered him the change. Fred took the money and then swiftly raised her outstretched hand to his lips.

The girl pulled her hand away quickly, her dark

eyes flashing. 'Eenglish peeg!' she cried angrily as Fred swaggered out of the shop.

Fred went back to the harbour wall and sat down in its shelter. He consumed his bread and then got up and crossed the road to the bar where he spent the rest of his money on ale.

At eventide as the huge red sun set over the sea, a chill wind blew over the harbour. Fred wandered along watching the sun dip into the sea to line the sky with many colours, and he watched the fishing fleet sail out of the harbour, red sails billowing in the wind. Well, so far so good, but now he had to find a place to sleep, he thought. Then somehow he had to get off this unfriendly island and make his way back to Australia. But how? Meanwhile he had to find a place to sleep. He wandered along beside the sea along the causeway. Finding a huge coil of ship's ropes, he dropped down into it and curled up out of the wind. Within minutes, he had fallen into a sound sleep.

As the dawn light crossed the sea, Fred awoke feeling very stiff and sore to find a big jovial fellow gazing down at him.

'You all right there, matey?' the man asked.

'Oh, I am fine,' replied Fred, climbing out of his nest.

'Missed your ship, eh matey?' the man asked.

'Well, sort of,' replied Fred, well pleased that he had at last met someone who would hold a conversation in English with him.

'Blokes get into the taverns and then lose track of time,' the man continued. 'And the ships don't miss the tide, not in this bay, they don't. It's too dodgy with all them rocks, you know.'

He put out a big firm hand. 'I'm Charlie Duquin, the landlord of that inn over there. You would be very welcome to join me in a nice hot toddy. It's darned cold this morning.'

Fred grasped the man's hand, the first friendly hand for many days, and crossed the road to the Forester's Inn with the landlord. His mind was still a trifle blurred. Had this fellow said his name was Charlie Dukes? No, he must be dreaming.

They entered a warm cosy kitchen where, beside a big brick oven, a buxom woman with wavy blond hair was cooking.

'This is Sally, my wife,' said Charlie. 'Sit down there, my lad, and dry out. Sally will get you some breakfast.'

Fred sat beside the big roaring fire and warmed his wet feet. A big mug of steaming hot coffee was thrust into his hand. 'I'll not have anything to eat,' he said, 'because I cannot pay for it.'

Sally broke into hearty laughter and then in her swift patois said something to Charlie. Charlie smiled. 'You eat breakfast, boy,' he said to Fred, 'and you are welcome.'

Sally handed Fred a huge bacon sandwich, and stood smiling at him with her white teeth flashing. Fred thought there was something familiar about her but he could not identify it. Besides he was hungry and the food was good. Soon Sally was getting on with her own chores and ignoring him. It seemed as if this was a regular happening for her husband to bring in some waif or stray.

'You can take a wash outside by the boathouse, boy, if you want to,' said Charlie. 'The fishing smacks will be in shortly.' He stood looking out to sea. 'You can come down with me to see what the catch is like. Perhaps you will get news of your ship.'

When he had eaten his fill and refreshed himself with a wash and brush-up, Fred felt completely restored. He then walked down to the shore with Charlie who chattered cheerily all the way. He informed Fred that he owned half a share of one of the fishing boats with a friend.

Soon they were at the quayside where the fishing fleet had come in. The noise was terrific as the fishermen hurled the fish up onto the quayside in baskets at the same time as the traders were shouting and bartering for the fresh catch.

By eleven o'clock, the bearded fishermen in their navy blue pullovers and peaked caps had finished haggling with the traders and their boats were all washed down ready for the next fishing trip. Now they were all back in the Forester's consuming large jars of ale and still arguing about the price of the fish and the capabilities of particular boats. Charlie, a great host, shouted out to each and every one and his hearty peels of laughter echoed around his homely room. Fred found the atmosphere warm and exciting, so different to his reception on the island the night before.

At three o'clock the fishermen all drifted home to sleep until the evening when it would all start again.

Charlie had taken a shine to Fred. 'Fred, me lad,' he said, 'give me a hand to clean up, it'll save bothering my Sally. Now, I knows a man who might give you a job, so hang around a bit. You'll get some money in your pocket which will help you save enough to get you passage home.'

The warmth and generosity from these people overwhelmed Fred. He felt very happy as he stayed around helping Charlie with various jobs. He ate a good supper and slept well in the boathouse at night.

The next morning, as he helped Charlie clean out the bar, he said, 'You've not been to sea long, have you, lad? You don't seem the type somehow.'

'It was my first voyage,' said Fred, a little sheepishly.

'Oh well, that's not everything,' said Charlie. 'I've done my stint of long voyages but you can't beat a regular job. By the way, what's your surname?'

Fred looked a little shifty as he replied. 'It's Fred Smith. I was born in Australia and that's where I'm trying to get back to.'

'Get a bit of regular work, lad,' said Charlie, 'it will help you save enough to get you to France. The big Australian tea clippers put into berth there and it won't be hard for you to get a job aboard one. You're not in a hurry, are you?'

'No,' said Fred, 'my time is my own.'

'Good,' said Charlie. 'We'll go up to the Hotel Royal. I know they need help there 'cause it's the off-season and they just needs a sort of all-round helper.'

Fred spruced himself up a little and, accompanied

by Charlie, went to the big hotel situated on the seafront. The job going was for a porter, dishwasher and groom, an off-season position until the hotel workers returned in the spring.

Fred was given the job and a small attic room high up overlooking the sea. There were a few perks, plus tips, but he had to work a month before he got a very meagre wage.

Good-natured Fred accepted his lot and it was not long before he had become popular. He enjoyed his job more or less and he felt free. No one asked him where he came from. It was an absolutely new life far away from gentlemen of vice and the dark alleys of London. He had landed on a soft spot and was quite content. He spent his leisure hours at the Forester's Inn where he was always welcome and everyone now called him Smithy.

Charlie and Fred became very good friends and soon Fred asked Charlie about his name, and whether he was related to the Duke of Duquin Beauclair?

Charlie was very eager to explain to Fred about his heritage. He pointed to the coat of arms over the fireplace. 'Those are the arms of the Duquins,' he said with more than a hint of pride. 'They came here from France, aristocrats escaping the French Revolution. There's a darned lot of us on this island now, my father and four brothers. They are all married to Guernsey women and we get together at weddings and funerals. Most of Guernsey's inhabitants are, in fact, of Norman descent.'

One day, Charlie took Fred over the heath and

pointed to the hotel on the cliff. 'You see that big house over there, the hotel?' asked Charlie.

Fred nodded.

'That's where my ancestors used to live,' said Charlie. Now he did not try to hide the pride in his voice.

As Fred gazed up at the big old house, with its mullioned windows and tall chimneys, his thoughts were on Charlie Dukes, his own father. There had to be a connection somewhere, he thought.

The two men sat high up on the hill looking down at the grand landscape before them, the huge yellow rock with the little waves which swept its base as if trying to climb up it. Around the bay there was a group of little cottages, little whitewashed fishermen's cottages gleaming in the sun. They looked like match-boxes from this height.

'When my great grandfather came out here to live,' said Charlie, 'he was known as the Count but he dropped the title and became a farmer. He grew orchids and fuchsias in great greenhouses.'

'What has happened to it all now?' enquired Fred.

'Well, when the old man died, his eldest son, my great uncle, took over. He had married an Englishwoman who hated the place and would not stay on the island, so they left to live in England. He lost all his money there and he had to rent out the land here to small farmers. Finally he came back when my grandmother deserted him and he lived in the big house until his death. His son, my cousin, was also called Charlie.

'For a long time we thought Charlie had drowned at sea and that the title had passed to another cousin. But then I gather they traced Charlie to Australia, where he seemed to have a wife and three sons. Charlie died out there in some unfortunate circumstances, I believe, so presumably one of the sons is the current duke.'

The older man smiled. 'I'm proud of my roots but this title business is all nonsense to me. I like to work hard for what I have. I don't want money and riches falling into my lap for nothing. And generally we are a modest lot. We married local women and settled down to farming and fishing. The girl I married, Sally, came from Coba Bay. That's her folks' cottage right ahead. Her family still live there, real fishing folk, they are. My brother had five children. Sally and I are only sad that we never managed to have a family. It's our one regret.'

Fred sat in silent thought. That, then, was the link! The other Charlie Dukes had been Fred's own father! His heart was racing as he wondered what to do or say. Should he declare himself to be a relative of this man? No, not yet, he decided. It was best not to rock the boat.

Charlie heaved his great hulk up from the grass. 'We'd better get back to Sally,' he said. 'I've got to open the bar tonight, and you're on duty, I believe.'

Slowly the two men made their way down the great slopes towards the village. Below them, sitting by a rock pool with her skirt hitched high and her feet in the cool water, sat the girl from the baker's shop in town.

'Oh my! What have we here?' said Charlie. 'Pull down your skirt, Rachel! You're a big girl now.'

With a quick giggle the girl looked up at them. Fred froze. It was the lovely vision from the baker's shop, her lovely black hair blowing in the wind.

'What you doing up here, Charlie?' she asked.

'Just bringing my friend to see the sights.'

Rachel looked at Fred and as her lips curled up in the wide smile, his heart suddenly started to beat quickly. He wanted to reach out and touch the beautiful thick mane of black hair which hung to her waist, over the flowery summer dress which clung to her figure.

'This is Sally's younger sister, Rachel,' said Charlie. 'She lives in the village.'

Fred was feeling rather embarrassed as the girl stared at him. She had recognized him and now there was suspicion in her eyes.

'This is Fred Smith,' Charlie said, introducing him to her. 'He's working at the Royal. He's from England.' He was trying hard to break the ice. 'Why don't you come down for Sunday tea? Sally will be pleased to see you.'

'I might,' said Rachel, staring at Fred and showing the fascinating dimples which appeared on each side of her cheeks. Fred knew then that she was hooked. He just knew that some day she would belong to him even if he had to wait for ever.

Charlie gave the girl a hand up out of the pool. She spun around on her toes and skipped away down the path calling out as she went, 'Bye Charlie.'

Charlie turned to Fred and muttered, 'I've heard she's a little bugger. It'll take a strong man to tame her.'

Fred nodded thoughtfully. He was ready and willing to take on that challenge, he thought.

The days following, Fred spent most of his free time waiting outside the baker's shop and offering to escort Rachel home or to walk with her to get the tram for home.

Rachel responded haughtily. 'I am not free,' she insisted. 'I am spoken for.'

'Who is this fellow?' Fred demanded, disturbed by the jealousy that flowed through him.

'He is a soldier up at the fort,' Rachel answered coyly, 'and we have been walking out for quite a time.'

'I don't believe you,' said Fred, holding on to her arm fiercely.

'Well, it is not your business,' she said, pulling away abruptly and striding away.

Fred ran after her and held her. 'Rachel, I love you and want to marry you.' It was madness but he felt he had no choice but to tell her of the feeling that gripped him.

'Well, I do not love you,' she retorted defiantly.

Fred was cast down by her rejection, and felt even worse a few days later when he saw Rachel walking with her soldier boy by the fort. He felt that he wanted to kill him.

Fred told his tale of woe to Charlie who was annoyed by what he heard. For it was not the done thing for a respectable island girl to mix with soldiers at the fort. On these matters the fishing folk were very strict. They were mostly Chapel people and were very careful with their young girls. To be seen walking with a soldier was not for the bright young girls of Coba Bay. Concern for young Rachel prompted Charlie and Sally to go down to see the old folk, Sally's and Rachel's parents.

Later Charlie told Fred, 'I spoke for you to her parents, Smithy, and they like you. So don't lose heart, lad.'

'What is the good? She hates me,' said Fred dismally.

Charlie gave him a hearty thump on his back. 'Cheer up, matey, the cock always gets the hen no matter how she keeps running.'

Rachel was made to stay home away from the town. She no longer worked in the baker's shop and she did not come to Sally's either.

On Sunday when Fred had his day off, he would sit high up on the hill watching the fishermen's cottages for a sight of Rachel. He saw her once picking flowers in the garden and another time hanging out the washing on the line, but he did not have the courage to call on her.

One day he could not believe his luck as Rachel came up the path towards the fort, a black-and-white sheep dog trotting at her heels. She looked unhappy and her lovely eyes were red from weeping. Fred went forward to greet her and stood in her path so that she could not pass.

'Oh, it is you, Smithy,' she said petulantly. 'What do you want?'

'You, darling,' returned Fred, holding out his arms to her.

'Now, you stop that,' she said crossly. Then she was silent and stared at him for a while.

'What is wrong?' asked Fred. 'You have been weeping.'

'Oh!' she exclaimed. 'I am so unhappy. My soldier boy has gone to India. I may never see him again.'

'Oh, I am very sorry,' said Fred. He did not sound very sincere and inside he felt elated. Guiding her to a sheltered spot beside a craggy rock, Fred pulled her down to sit beside him on the grass. 'Hush, darling,' he whispered, 'don't cry.' He soothed her and put his arms around her. Then when he started to kiss her, Rachel did not object.

'I have been so miserable,' she sobbed. 'I really love him, you know.'

'Yes, darling, I know,' lied Fred, petting her.

'Oh Fred, you are so comical,' she said. 'You do make me laugh.'

Fred moved closer and closer. Here was the lovely girl he had waited for. He was not about to let her go now. He rolled her over gently and kissed her. She did not seem to object and was even generous with her kisses, but when Fred went a step too far she sat up.

'Oh no, Smithy,' she scolded. 'You behave yourself.' Suddenly she was being prim again.

'Do you still hate me, Rachel?' he asked.

'No, of course I don't,' she laughed. And the dimples appeared as she smiled at him. He knew then that he had got her.

* * *

So began that passionate love affair of Rachel and Fred. She was his and soon Fred was the happiest lad on the island. All the family were delighted, for they were all fond of Smithy and certainly preferred him to any soldier at the fort.

This lovely girl was his! Whenever they met his lips met hers and she did not protest. When they first made love, Rachel flew into a fiery temper but Fred held her close getting satisfaction from her raging passion. The sex act was not new to her, he was sure of that, but he did not care. This lovely girl was his very own now, she belonged to him. There had been all kinds of women in Fred's young life but never one he had wanted as much as he did Rachel.

Rachel was inclined to be a dreamer. 'When I am turned eighteen,' she would say, 'I am going to France or even to England. I will go into service. I could not bear to spend the rest of my life cooped up on this island.'

'I don't know why,' said Fred, 'it is so beautiful.'

'Oh, it is all right for you,' she replied scornfully. 'I have lived here all of my life, with the smell of fish and washing the dirty stale clothes. I need more than that. I would like to wear nice dresses and be clean.'

'You look perfect to me,' said Fred.

Looking in admiration at her lovely slim white neck and high bosom, Fred smiled. 'Now, my little dove, you belong to Smithy. And where he goes, so shall you.'

'Where are you going to go, Smithy? she asked with a laugh.

'Nowhere. I have got a steady job now. I am a regular porter at the Royal and I like this place. It is wild and free, away from the bustling outside world, and that appeals to me. And now I have got you, darling, so let's get married, shall we?'

Rachel was now very much in love with Fred, and she tried to control her own emotions as he caressed her. She knew that he was right. 'Oh well,' she said. 'At least I will not be marrying a fisherman, that's something.'

'That is right, darling, I am a hall porter and I do not stink of fish.' Fred's laugh was loud and hearty but Rachel did not smile. She did not have much of a sense of humour, which was a shame. 'Come,' said Fred. 'Let's go down and tell Sally and Charlie the good news first.'

They wandered down the hill to the Forester's Inn at St Peter Port. Charlie was in the bar. This was a place reserved for men. No woman ever entered this inner sanctum while the men were partaking of drink there, not even Sally.

Sally was, in fact, in the back room with a few fish-wives. She was always in the big kitchen with its huge brick oven where she baked bread and cooked vast joints of meat on Sundays for herself and neighbours. There were always bean jars in the fierce oven too. The bean jar was a special breakfast dish of the island. It consisted of a big earthenware jar full of beans, bacon and herbs, and any bits of left-overs, which would all be cooked in the oven after the bread had been baked. All the neighbours brought their own jars covered with brown paper to go into Sally's big oven and very often Rachel would help Sally get them in.

Rachel had first told Sally her good news in the confines of the kitchen and then Sally relayed it to Charlie. In no time at all, Fred had joined the men in a big celebration. He was popular with the menfolk as he went out in the boats and played football for the team on the village green.

Sally took off her apron. 'I'll come right down to Da's with you,' she said to her sister. 'Give me a hand with the jars and then we will go and tell Mama and Papa the news.'

That evening when the sun was setting like a great orange ball over the sea, the two couples – Sally and Charlie, Rachel and Fred – rode in the pony cart up to the old folk.

The men were very tipsy, which was not surprising considering the number of celebratory drinks they had drunk. The women chatted and laughed in the back seat. Fred, although a bit woozy, breathed in the refreshing salt air. He felt ecstatic. On this island he had found great happiness; this was where he would dig in his roots, the place his father had called home.

As Rachel had warned him, the cottage smelt of fish but it was perfectly clean. The big family fishing boat was beached on the slip-way at the bottom of the garden, the nets hanging out to dry on the walls. The old parents sat each side of a big wood fire.

Old Cedric was a descendant of the Vikings. He always wore a peak cap on the back of his head, and his long beard, which had once been blond, was now silver. He was snoring away peacefully, while Mama, her hair snow white, sat knitting long socks for the menfolk's sea boots.

'Don't get up, Mama,' cried Sally. 'We will make the tea. Now you know Fred, Rachel's young man. Well, today he proposed, so here we are to ask your permission.'

It was an orderly straightforward ritual. The old couple murmured in unison to Smithy and nodded their approval. 'Aye,' said the old fellow, rousing himself into a sitting position. 'Come here, Rachel, I hear my baby is going to be married, eh?'

'Oh, Pa,' said Rachel. 'He is not a Guernsey man. He is from England.'

Papa winked at Fred. 'Well, I have known a few good Englishmen in my time. Now, Fred, if you take my daughter, there will be no dowry, for we are only working-class.'

Fred gazed at the old man anxiously, not quite sure how to respond. But the old man put out his brown wrinkled hand and said: 'God bless you, boy.'

Fred was happy, as was everyone! Soon the nephews and the brothers arrived and the house was full of delighted people. Some were huge blond hefty men, descendants of the Viking chiefs who had first colonized the island.

They all gave Fred a hearty welcome and brought out jars of homemade wine. Everyone wished the happy couple well. That this close-knit community had accepted Fred and welcomed him was indeed a little miracle.

Rachel, as her sister Sally had done, was to leave the bay. Among the fishing folk this was indeed unusual but there were rumours that they were not sorry to see Rachel wed, since she had been a little wayward most of her youth.

'You know,' boasted Charlie, 'When Sally married me, a Duquin, she was considered to be marrying into high society.'

Fred grinned. Charlie's remark made him think of London and those silly debutantes who had so often been foisted on him. No debutantes for him! He had won his beautiful Rachel and was now very content with his lot.

Plans went ahead for Rachel's wedding. Fred bought her a diamond ring, which delighted her, and there was a lot of controversy as to whether the wedding would be held in the village chapel or the town church.

Fred did not care but Rachel insisted that she be married in the Parish church right on the front where all could see her. After all, was this not where her sister Sally had been married?

One day, to escape the family rows about wedding etiquette, Rachel took Fred sailing out into the wild bay in a little boat which she handled with great skill. Fred sat watching her and admiring her low-necked muslin blouse and cotton skirt. Her black hair was tied back out of the wind, and her feet were bare as she expertly handled the sail with her legs astride. Fred reached out and stroked her thigh and pressed her to drop anchor in a quiet bay so that they could make love. The rhythm of the boat matched the movement of their bodies and it was an experience neither of them would ever forget . . .

25

Married Bliss

Rachel and Fred's wedding was a great occasion, officiated by the parson of the Parish church at St Peter Port on a sunny Sunday in September. Rachel was dressed in virginal white with a Brussels' lace headdress and train borrowed from a cousin. She was attended by bridesmaids in brightly coloured dresses, all of whom carried bouquets of bud roses and sweetpeas. Rachel's bouquet was made up of delicately shaded orchids.

Fred was feeling slightly under the weather having spent his stag night at the Forester's Inn in the good Guernsey manner with Charlie and his fishermen friends. He would have felt worse but a good ducking in the sea had brought him round.

All the town's residents turned out for this big ceremony and there were many Duquins all dressed in their top hats and tails.

The sun shone on the grey granite walls of the church and the sound of wedding bells rang out over the sea. The town folk lined the cobbled streets to watch: it was indeed a smart wedding.

The reception was held at the Royal, for was not Fred the head porter? He was granted a few concessions! His wedding reception was very special. The table groaned under the weight of the feast and the booze consumed would have floated the navy. Fred began to worry about who was going to pay all the bills.

'Now don't worry, matey,' declared Charlie. 'We all chip in together for these sorts of affairs. That's the Guernsey way.'

As always poor old Maggie Owen turned up to get in the photograph. She was a drunk and a derelict, and well known in the harbour bars. Should there be a grand wedding, Maggie would always arrive in a faded old bridesmaid's frock and battered ornamental flowers in her grizzled hair. She would stand in front of the wedding group with her toothless grin, determined to be in that wedding photograph.

The extraordinary thing was that nobody minded. If you got married, you expected to get Maggie Owen in your wedding photograph. She was part of the Guernsey scene around the harbour.

The bride and groom stood to receive all the relations. It was a long, seemingly endless queue, for almost half the island was related to Charlie, the other half to Rachel's family.

Rachel and Fred settled into a little house in St Peter Port. It was just along the front, not far from Charlie's bar.

Fred was now head porter in a scarlet suit and a grey top hat. He was kept very busy as the Royal was slowly becoming a very popular tourist centre. Many people stayed there on their way to France.

Every evening Rachel would put on her best dress and go to meet Fred when he came off duty, and together they would go home to their little white house with its roses around the door. This house did not smell of fish, for Rachel's home was clean and neat. On Saturday nights they would go walking and on Sunday they would board a bus to ride out to Coba Bay to see Rachel's parents. Often wearing a new hat, Rachel looked very proud and was very sedate.

In early spring when the tide ran high, Rachel was well into her first pregnancy. One night, a gale had been blowing hard. 'I do worry about my Pa and brothers on a night like this,' she whispered.

That night as the baby kicked within her, she could not sleep. The wind howled about the little house and the spray from the shore crashed upon the window panes. Suddenly there was a knock on the door which woke Fred from his deep sleep. Fred opened the door to Find Charlie and Sally standing there all wrapped up in oilskins with the rain pouring down on them. They whispered to Fred in the hall.

'We are off to Coba,' they said. 'Pa's ship is in distress, so we must go to Mama. Don't tell Rachel.'

But Rachel was already out of bed and struggling into a warm cloak. 'I must go to Mama,' she said.

The others tried to persuade her to stay, telling her that it might upset her and the baby if she rode out on such a stormy night.

Rachel insisted, 'No, you stay, Fred, if you want to, but I am going to Mama.'

Wrapped up in heavy shawls and blankets, they went in the pony cart to Coba. Charlie drove through the night along the dark winding lanes battling with the high gale and as they came over the hill they saw a small pathetic group of women standing on the shore gazing out at the stormy sea. The bright lights of the rockets soared out into the night air, signifying a ship in distress and far out they could see the lifeboat that left St Peter Port battling with the huge waves in a brave effort to reach the small fishing boat stranded on the rocks.

Sally and Rachel took their place beside their mother and the three sister-in-law rallied around them. One little boy cuddled his sister close under a coat and all stood in a silent vigil pathetically looking out to the raging sea which threatened to engulf their loved ones.

Fred and Charlie went up to the fort to talk to the look-out high on the cliff edge. 'It is your father-in-law's boat, *La Belle Sal*,' he said. 'And they have signalled that the lifeboat is on its way.'

So there they all stood wet and cold and silent until the cold light of dawn came over the horizon. Then, finally, the lookout signalled that the lifeboat was coming back as they were unable to get up to the rocks. The sea was now empty, silent and lonely, there was no sign of *La Belle Sal*.

The little group returned to the cottage in silence. Sally started up the fire and they made pots of tea. Rachel's face was white as death, as she sat silently huddled by the fire. It was then that her labour pains began.

The neighbours came to say that the men from the village were out with their boats in search for the bodies. Slowly one by one, they were brought ashore: Cedric, his three handsome sons and one little grandson. The sea had taken its toll.

Rachel's mother sat silently by the fire, a shawl around her shoulders. Her face was white, her only movement came from her lips moving in prayer.

Then amid the sound of the weeping women, Rachel uttered a sharp cry. The women went to her and took her into the bedroom. Charlie turned to Fred. 'Come, Fred boy, there's nothing we can do. Leave it to the women now.'

In the big double bed where Rachel herself had been born, she gave birth prematurely to a lovely little baby boy. With her face still wet from crying for the loss of her fisherman father, Rachel insisted that this baby be called Cedric after her grandfather.

In 1914 the roses around Rachel's cottage bloomed better than ever before. She herself had matured and was more and more in love with Fred, who gave her warmth and security. Fred had done well for himself in the past four years. He had left the Royal and now managed a restaurant and bar further up the town. He was always full of ideas. He wanted to build a house and talked of a piece of land nearby where he could build a real modern bungalow. To this, Rachel really looked forward.

That spring there was much talk of war, and many more English soldiers had been sent out to man the

forts around the island. The big guns were recondi-
tioned and pointed out to sea. The news was that
Britain would go to war with Germany.

'If England goes to war, we will be up to our necks
in it,' muttered Charlie one night.

The fishermen argued that it was nothing to do
with them. They were an independent island. If
England and Germany went to war, it would not affect
them.

In August war was officially declared. The people in
Guernsey were not unduly worried then. The English
army moved out of Guernsey to France and the *Elvira*,
the boat that sailed between Guernsey and Southampton,
was commandeered as military transport. Everyone
went down to St Peter Port to watch the soldiers embark
as they took them away to serve in foreign lands.

Fred and Rachel went down to watch the soldiers
go, holding little Cedric by the hand. Cedric was very
excited but Sally and Charlie were doleful.

'They have taken away all the soldiers who were to
defend us if the Germans came,' they said.

The *Elvira* sailed away to the sound of 'God Save
the King', so Charlie and Fred went down and volunteered for the militia which had been formed to defend
the island. When they were sworn in and given a
uniform they were told that they would never have to
serve overseas. All they had to do was defend their
own island from any invading force. Yet within six
months, the Guernsey Light Infantry was declared a
regular army force. Fred was recruited but Charlie
was too old. Otherwise life was just the same in

Guernsey. The islanders watched the German Zeppelins going over to bomb England but so far no Germans had invaded their island.

Out in France, England was taking a beating. In the bay, ships were bombed and torpedoed. On many occasions, bodies floated to the Guernsey shore and were washed up on the rocks just below the castle.

While the battles continued in France, the Guernsey Light Infantry marched around the town on Sunday mornings with flags flying and bands playing. Everybody thought it a lot of fun, until suddenly, almost overnight, it was declared a regular wing of the British Army and recruited into service overseas.

Rachel could not believe it. Fred had given up his job to serve in the army to defend the island and now they were sending him to France to serve for England.

Although food was a little short, until that day, the war had not made a lot of difference to them. Now their men were being sent away.

Fred was not happy to be leaving. He was not at all patriotic and England was not really his country. Now he had to leave Rachel and his small son, and give up the life he had struggled so hard for. It rankled but nevertheless he was a good soldier. In no time at all he was promoted to sergeant.

Over the years he had kept a journal. Now he decided to leave it at home rather than take it with him. He wrapped it up in brown paper and put it in a drawer with his watch and a few photographs. The journal contained all the details of his life which Rachel and her family remained ignorant about.

With plenty of waving and cheering, Fred Smith, sergeant in the Light Infantry, sailed off to France with his fellows. Their women stood on the quayside to wave them goodbye.

'We will take care of Rachel and Cedric,' Charlie and Sally called out.

Dressed in his khaki uniform, Fred gave his cheery grin and left his lovely island. He took a last glimpse at that great rock as the transport ship sailed out to sea. He was confident that he would come back.

However, fate had rolled the dice against him. Out of nine hundred of that ill-trained infantry from Guernsey, six hundred lost their lives in France. Fred never came back to his lovely island but his heart remained with Rachel and his beloved son Cedric.

26

Onslow House

The sun shone very brightly on the green school playing fields in Sussex. It was a hot day in July and over the field could be seen the white-clad figures of the cricket players, all young girls of good families, brought up with silver spoons in their mouths. Here was the captain of the home team, her long red gold plait of hair flying out in the cool breeze, her well-structured limbs moving swiftly as she bowled accurately and fast. Fleur Beauclair was just eighteen years old. She had a personality that was as bright as her appearance. She was a tall, slim red-head with a wide charming smile. She looked just like her grandmother, the Dowager Duchess Daisy, in her youth.

The Dowager Duchess now sat watching the cricket match with a hint of boredom on her face.

'Bloody silly game for girls to play,' she muttered. 'They're likely to do each other damage, they are.'

Her face was red in the heat of the afternoon sun, mainly because she was wearing a magnificent but heavy hat. It was very wide at the brim and loaded with all kinds of artificial fruits – bunches of highly coloured cherries, dark red plums – mixed in with bunches of bright blue false forget-me-nots.

'Good enough to eat,' one man remarked as he stared through his eyeglass at Daisy's hat.

Grandma Daisy's hat caused quite a sensation, but that was to be expected! The Dowager Duchess was well known as a great character in that pre-war scene. Now she sat proudly as she watched her granddaughter display her talents on the cricket pitch.

It was the end of the term and the parents' Open Day. Beside Daisy sat a young girl of about sixteen years old. She was dressed in a snow-white dress with a frilled hem-line and two huge bows of ribbon in her dark wavy hair. Her full mouth was set in a sullen droop and heavy black lashes veiled her olive green eyes as she stared mournfully out across the green grass.

'Cheer yourself up, Charlotte, for Gawd's sake,' declared Daisy, giving the girl a poke with her parasol.

Charlotte raised a wan smile. 'I'm sorry, Grandma, I was just thinking of Mama and Rosa and wondering what will happen if England goes to war with Germany.'

'Stuff and nonsense!' declared Daisy. 'Why don't you stop worrying and make the most of this expensive school you are attending. Look at Fleur – see how popular she is, and how happy she is at school.'

The cricket was over. Fleur at that moment was being cheered by her classmates and obviously enjoyed every minute of it.

For a moment, Charlotte's green eyes flashed in anger. 'Well, Fleur is so popular because she is truly English. It makes a great deal of difference, I can assure you. Being German in these times is no joke.'

Daisy sighed deeply. She did feel sorry for this gloomy child, Rosa Feldman's niece. The child had been staying with her for some time now and she always seemed a little lonely. 'Go have your tea, dear, I'll be over later,' she told Charlotte very gently.

Obediently Charlotte went back to the white pavilion where afternoon tea was being served. Daisy sat quietly, reminiscing on the last part of her life and wondering what had happened to her son Fred. So many years had passed and she had never heard from him. Perhaps he was dead but somehow Daisy did not think so because Fred was a survivor, so much like her late husband. She wondered whether Fred had ever got married or if he had children. She did hope that perhaps Fred had a son to carry on this aristocratic line, for so far only one daughter, Fleur, had been produced. Daisy nowadays also had Fleur's half-sisters in her care. Emily and Deirdre were sweet little girls and had stayed with Daisy since that silly Vanessa, their mother, had married another soldier and gone off to India.

Poor old Jackie often got a bit fed up with noise in the house when it was full of children, but he just had to put up with it!

Daisy rose a little stiffly. Her legs had been playing up lately probably from too much horse-riding. She made her way into the pavilion where there was a colourful and noisy scene, with the chatting and laughter of the pupils and their parents, and huge bowls of fresh strawberries on the white tableclothed tables. There were piles of bread and butter and large home-baked cakes.

After tea the headmistress got up to give her usual speech. Her face was unusually white and strained. 'I do not want to spoil your tea, but it does look very possible that we shall be at war within a short time. If that happens the school will be evacuated from the coast. We shall, of course, be in touch with details of such an event. Now I wish you all a happy holiday. May God bless you all and see you safely home.'

Parents got up hustling their girls to go and collect their belongings.

Daisy said to her girls. 'Get your kit and we'll be off!' She watched the sturdy Charlotte set off to pack her bag and was close enough to see a girl go up to Charlotte and hiss: 'German! Hun!'

As she watched Charlotte pale and dash away, Daisy shook her head. 'Oh, dear,' she murmured, 'this is not going to be easy.'

Soon they were travelling on the London train in a first-class compartment. 'What am I going to do with all you kids?' Daisy complained. 'It's the height of the season and the racing calendar is full.'

Fleur giggled. 'Well, they will not have horse racing if there is a war on,' she said.

'Stuff and nonsense!' cried Daisy. 'What will they do with all them thoroughbreds? Let them eat their heads off?'

'I heard that in the Boer and the Crimean wars the army commandeered all the horses,' Fleur informed her.

Daisy looked quite put out. 'Now, Fleur, don't you josh me. You may have had a tip-top education and I have not, but I do know all there is to know about horseflesh. And you don't.'

'Oh, well, darling Grandmama,' teased Fleur, 'have it your own way. Some say that when the troops get short of meat, they eat the horses.'

Daisy reached over and gave her granddaughter a gentle whack with her parasol. 'Stop it, you naughty girl!' she said with the same wide grin.

While all this was going on, Charlotte sat as still as a statue looking dreamily out of the window. Her lovely eyes looked very sad. 'If there is a war we could go to school in Switzerland,' she said vaguely. 'I have friends who are at school there.'

Fleur shot her cousin a scornful look. 'Silly fool,' she said. 'No one goes anywhere when there is a war on.'

'Who said it would last long?' asked Daisy. 'I'm sure it will be over by Christmas.'

On their arrival in Onslow Square, the two young girls came out to greet them. They were Emily and Deirdre, Fleur's half-sisters, who were being educated at day-schools in London while their mother was in India. They lived with their Grandma Daisy. Even though she was not related to them by blood, she was happy to have charge of them.

The moment the party arrived, the little girls pounced on Charlotte and demanded that she go with them to the nursery and play with them.

Fleur was impatient with them and pushed them aside as they probed into her luggage. 'Don't touch!' she ordered. 'Don't you dare!'

Emily and Deirdre ignored their older sister and danced around Charlotte, who gave them an indulgent smile. Taking them by the hand, she took them off to the nursery.

The maid brought in a tray of tea and Fleur and her grandmother relaxed in the dark and heavily furnished drawing-room overlooked by portraits of Charlie Dukes' ancestors. There were beautiful flower arrangements in valuable vases and exotic Persian rugs thrown on the parquet floor. In a far corner a grand piano stood, draped with a colourful Spanish shawl. On the mahogany occasional tables, silver-framed photographs were placed, photographs mainly of the famous racehorses that Daisy loved. It was warm and cosy in Grandma's drawing-room and Fleur settled in happily. It was good to come home.

'Oh,' Fleur said, 'a war would be exciting, don't you think? Patrick is with his regiment up north. I expect he would go to France. But I don't suppose Duncan will get enrolled because his eyes are so bad.'

'Oh,' said Grandma, shaking her head disapprovingly. 'Surely you should stick to one nice young man. You seem to have a string of them.'

'That is much more fun, like racehorses, Grandma!' Fleur replied, nibbling on a dainty cucumber sandwich.

'Oh well, I don't suppose that any worse can happen to you than did to me at your age,' sighed Daisy.

'I bet you were a devil,' grinned Fleur.

'Oh, I had me moments,' sighed Daisy again.

* * *

As predicted, Germany declared war on France on the third of August and invaded Belgium that same day. Britain declared war on Germany the next day and what everyone had expected happened.

Daisy's world was not affected until the day when Fleur returned home saying that she was going to Guy's Hospital to train as a nurse.

Her grandmother was shocked.

'You can't!' Daisy cried. 'You are far too young! Why, the sight of all those wounded naked bodies at your age is quite shocking. And besides, it is very hard work, Fleur, and not for the likes of you.'

'Oh, what do you know?' returned Fleur haughtily. 'Duncan's sisters are there and both of the Warner girls work at St Thomas's. Anyway, it's too late. I have passed the interview, Grandmama, so will you please sign this paper for me?'

'Now, ducks,' cajoled Daisy, 'you should go with your education. I will get a tutor for you and then you can go on to university.'

Fleur's mouth was set in a hard line. 'If you do not sign for me, I will run away and try to get to France. The troops are already in action, and I can go with the Red Cross canteen if I want to. Really I would prefer to train as a nurse, and that is what I am going to do, Grandmama.'

'Oh, get on with it then,' said Daisy irritably, signing the papers. 'But don't complain when you find it too much.'

A jubilant Fleur went off the next week to Guy's Hospital to train as a wartime probationary nurse.

After her first week, she came home on her day off utterly exhausted. She did wonder about the wisdom of having joined but she would not give up. She hated the authority and the enforced protection, the cold grim corridors, the menial things she had to do for the poor sick people. She loathed the uniform of faded mauve-and-white striped dress with its stiffly starched apron and collar which nearly cut her throat. She could not bear the absurd little cap held in place on her head by an unreliable pin.

She was now a very tired girl who staggered around with full bedpans to empty and worked long hours until her legs felt as though they would drop off. Gone was the dream of glamour she had misguidedly associated with looking after the wounded soldiers. 'I am in the women's ward,' she told her grandmother. 'There are poor neglected women recovering from operations and accidents in the street. We have a demented woman whose husband was killed in France. My God, how she howled in the night! I am fed-up with it all. I feel sick and I cannot eat the food.'

Grandma was sipping tea from a pretty china teacup. 'Well, come home, then,' she said. 'Don't say I never warned you.'

'I won't!' declared Fleur defiantly. 'I will stick to it even if it bloody kills me.'

'Now, now, no bad language in my house,' said Daisy.

'Oh, shut up! You exasperate me,' cried Fleur, 'you are such a hypocrite.'

Daisy roared with laughter. 'Now, Fleur,' she

cackled, 'that's very nice!' She crossed the room and poured Fleur a glass of sherry to calm her down.

'Thank you so much, Grandmama,' said Fleur, taking the glass gratefully. 'You always cheer me up.'

Soon Daisy was also working for the war effort. She went out on recruiting campaigns, her voice ringing out across Trafalgar Square telling the young men that their country needed them. She also collected for the wounded and became very involved in every possible way.

The terrible war did not end at Christmas as everyone had hoped. It seemed to get more serious and to pull in more and more countries.

Sometimes Daisy would pay a visit to her daughter Petal in Regent's Street.

Since losing her lover Sam in the *Titanic*, Petal's bloom had faded in every way. She no longer entertained, her dress agency was run by a manager and Petal herself spent the day lolling apathetically about her fabulous apartment. The walls were painted gold and the windows draped with yellow taffeta, and the rooms were full of beautiful Georgian furniture. There were also long mirrors everywhere which Petal rarely looked at these days. She was nearly always dressed in black with long strings of pearls and lots of rings. This once glamorous leader of fashion had left that bright gaudy world, and now she just existed, staring solemnly out of the window at the London traffic.

It irritated Daisy to visit Petal. Her daughter had once been so smooth, so cultured, and so fêted by

Edwardian society. But now she sat, all alone, and it made Daisy furious. She herself was in the evening of her old age, and a strong survivor without any patience for those without the resolve to fight life. When she rang the bell of Petal's apartment, the pretty French maid answered the door. 'How is Madame, this morning, Babette?' Daisy asked.

'Not so bad, Madame,' replied Babette. 'She is resting.'

'Oh, she is always resting,' said Daisy impatiently. 'I know where to find her.'

Like a strong Atlantic wind, Daisy swept into Petal's boudoir and found her slouched in a chair by the window.

'Still lolling about, I see,' Daisy challenged.

'Hullo, mother,' replied Petal without interest. 'Now don't start as soon as you get here, will you? I have a sick headache.'

'Not enough fresh air, that's what's wrong with you,' said Daisy irritably. 'It's time you pulled yourself together.'

Petal turned her head away. 'Mother, I am quite happy doing what I want to do, so shut up.'

'A bright gal like you letting yourself go and a bloody war going on out there,' sniffed Daisy.

'Women are losing their husbands and sons every day and you do nothing but sit about. I am ashamed when my friends ask me about you.'

'Oh, that is your problem,' sneered Petal, lighting a cigarette in a long holder. She sat back and puffed out rings of smoke.

'That's a nasty dirty habit for a young woman,' said Daisy, who had never smoked.

'The boys in the trenches could do with those fags you puff into clouds.'

'Are you finished, Mother?' asked Petal coolly.

'No, I am not! I would like a cheque from you for the Red Cross parcels and then I will be on my way. Perhaps the next time I come you will get up off your backside and make me welcome.'

Petal gave her a bemused smile. She reached out to a side table for her cheque book and pen, and wrote out a cheque for a substantial amount. She handed it to her mother. 'Goodbye,' she said. 'See you next time.'

Daisy snatched the cheque and marched out, slamming the door very hard as she went.

As the door slammed Petal's mouth drooped at the corners and tears filled her eyes. But she did not cry; she still hurt too deeply.

In the second year of that world war the situation became pretty desperate. The Germans had swept through neutral Belgium, and the French army had been practically defeated. The British troops were entrenched, wallowing in mud and blood, while on the home front the British people tried to keep living as normally as they could in the circumstances. The Suffragettes gave up their fight for the vote to work for the war effort, and women were recruited to drive trams and buses while their men were out dying in the trenches.

During this time, Daisy turned her big house into a convalescent home for wounded soldiers. The family was pushed into one wing of the house while the rest was handed over for the soldiers. Jackie got involved in this project, too, and was pleased to have something to do. Daisy kept busy with her Red Cross work and her recruiting campaign. Fleur passed her exams as a probationer and came home to help her grandmother run the convalescent home. Now she was much happier. Not surprisingly, she won many admiring glances from the convalescing soldiers. When off duty, she still attended lots of parties. She was highly strung and was often badly affected by the deaths of her young men friends.

So many men had died and were still dying out in France. There was not a family in the land that had not been touched by death. Fleur at least always had her friend Duncan around to soothe and comfort her when she was low. He seemed to expect very little of her in return.

Young women went around distributing white feathers to the men not in the army. It was a cruel gesture, especially towards men like Duncan because he had tried very hard to get into the army but had failed the medical because of his poor eyesight. Unable to fight, Duncan Browne had got himself an administrative job at the Foreign Office. He was the last of Fleur's old friends and he adored her as he always had.

Daisy was not particularly fond of Duncan. 'I wish that bloody silly fellow would get out from under my feet,' she would complain. 'I am always knocking into him. I don't think he can see where he is going in spite of those thick specs.'

'Grandma, don't be so unkind,' protested Fleur. 'He comes to play cards and chess with the patients, and he is a great help to us.'

'Oh, if you say so,' returned Daisy. 'Why don't you marry that bloody fellow then? He's besotted with you, sitting around looking cow-eyed at you all day.'

Fleur sniffed and glared at her grandmother. 'It's none of your business, so please stay out of it,' she said crossly.

Daisy also complained about Fleur's tendency to drink a lot off duty and Fleur snapped again. 'Oh, shut up, Grandma. Surely a few glasses of wine won't hurt me. I have to work hard.'

'No, perhaps not, darling,' said Daisy with a smile. She did not like to nag Fleur but she felt it necessary to keep her on the straight and narrow. She changed the subject. 'I hear there is a new lot of injured coming in later today. I'll go down to meet the hospital train. The bloody Huns have used mustard gas, so they tell me. The poor devils will be blinded by it. This is certainly a wicked war.'

'That is terrible!' said Fleur. 'I'll come with you.'

Daisy and her granddaughter went to Victoria Station to meet the hospital train. A little knot of officials waited as the train rolled in. The stretcher bearers went forward to bring out the badly wounded, while Fleur, tall, slim and lovely in her nurse's uniform, wended her way along the platform with packets of cigarettes in her hand to give to those who could walk. Fleur paused and drew in her breath at the sight before her. An officer led a line of mud-spattered soldiers with bandages over their eyes. They all held on to each other in a long line. Guided along the platform, they coughed and wheezed and were unable to see anything. This miserable line of men staggered slowly passed her.

Fleur stood there with tears streaming down her pretty young face. These were young men in their prime perhaps totally blinded by the awful mustard gas.

'Oh, my God, how absolutely dreadful!' she sobbed.

A strong voice beside her made her start. 'Come on, gal, don't stand dreaming. There's lots of chaps on the stretchers who would like a fag while they are waiting to be moved.'

Fleur collected her wits and turned her attention to the long line of stretcher cases. Among them was a strong contingent of Australians.

They were in a group by themselves. Fleur noticed one in particular, a young man with golden curls above the blood-stained bandage. His uniform was caked with mud. He was an officer.

'Oh thanks, Ginger,' he whispered as Fleur lit a cigarette for him. Fleur winced. She hated to be called Ginger, but she wiped the dirt from around the youth's mouth and held a wet sponge to his perspiring head.

The ambulances had begun to move the injured men out to various hospitals.

In her bossy way, Daisy strode up and down with the nurses and doctors choosing the patients that she would take care of. As she passed Fleur she stopped to look at the young Aussie.

'Can I help that one?' she asked.

'Well, yes, he's just had a minor head injury,' said the doctor. 'But he is badly undernourished. That lot have been up the front line quite a time.'

'All right,' Daisy said. 'I'll look to him.' She motioned the stretcher-bearer to carry him to the ambulance.

The young Australian gave her a weak grin and then, in a hoarse voice, he said: 'Wotcha, Daisy!'

Daisy peered at him in astonishment.

'Hullo! Hullo! who's this?' she asked, staring closer at him. Then in her loud voice she called out, 'Well, I'll be blowed if it ain't young Alastair. Jackie will be so pleased to see you. How d'ya feel, mate?'

'Fine, just a little bushed,' croaked Alastair as the stretcher men bore him away.

'You know who that is, Fleur?' Daisy asked.

Fleur shook her head.

'Wal, that is Jackie's son by his Australian wife,' said Daisy. 'Jackie will be tickled pink.'

'Are they taking him home?' asked Fleur.

'You bet they are!' said Daisy. 'He is in my charge. Come on now Fleur, get on with it, we ain't finished yet.'

Late on into the night the two women worked, giving out cigarettes and comforting the badly wounded. Fleur was so like her grandmother – strong as an ox and able to work for hours at a time to give aid to the needy.

That night in the house in Onslow Square, the corridors were alive with wounded soldiers. Young men in blue uniforms hung around talking. Some were laughing, many were smoking. All were glad to be alive and made room for the needier men who had just arrived.

Fleur was off-duty at last and she took a bath in the big hip bath in her bedroom, then went out to get drunk with Duncan. This seemed to be the only way she could relax and cope with the horror of those days.

Daisy sat in an easy chair in her drawing-room with her feet up on a foot-stool. She looked weary but exceedingly cheerful. 'You'll never guess what happened today,' she said to Charlotte. 'We picked Jackie's son up at the station. I can't wait for Jackie to come home to tell him. Alastair's in number two ward. He looks very bright now, though he was a bloody mess when he got off the train. Now, are the girls asleep?'

Charlotte nodded. 'Yes, down in the cellar. There was a warning of Zeppelin raids in the newspaper tonight but the children like it down there in the cellar anyway. They think it's great fun.'

'Well, you might as well go down and help Sister Manners. She will tell you how Alastair is progressing. I think I'll have an early night,' said Daisy.

Charlotte flushed and looked sulky. She hated those grinning swearing men down in the cellar, but Daisy's word was law and she had to obey.

Alastair was in the small ward for officers only. He sat up and looked around at the other two fellows rolling about restlessly in their narrow white beds. Having slept in damp dug-outs for many weeks, the extraordinary comforts of a mattress and clean linen had to be got used to. He had been bathed and deloused and his head wound redressed. He was feeling much better and even hungry. He reached over and rang his bedside bell. He wanted some supper.

In response to his call there came a short dumpy girl in a dark frock. She also wore a big white apron, and had a mop of dark curly hair piled up on her head. A starched white bonnet perched precariously atop her dark curls.

'Did you want anything, sir?' she asked. She had a slightly guttural accent.

'Yes, me darling,' replied Alastair with a grin. 'I want me supper.'

'It will be ready in ten minutes,' she said precisely.

'Well, let me out of this cot and I'll find the little boy's room,' he said.

'You are not allowed out of bed, sir,' she said.

'Well, fetch a bloody bottle, then,' he shouted.

Charlotted replied very seriously: 'I am not allowed to give you a bottle, sir. I am only a helper. The nurse will do that.'

'Well, go and get her, nit-wit,' Alastair said. 'You don't want me to wet the bed, do you?'

Charlotte disappeared quickly to find Sister Manners. 'That dreadful fellow in the officer's ward,' she panted, 'he wants a bottle.'

'Oh, that's our Aussie. He's very sweet really.' The sister smiled as she bustled away towards the officers' room.

Well, thought Charlotte, so that loud-mouthed fellow was Jackie's son! She could hardly believe it. But her heart leaped a little as she thought of him again. He was so fair with such a mop of hair and beautiful skin . . . He was quite beautiful.

From a distance, Charlotte watched the nurse escort him down the corridor to the lavatory. His arm was around the nurse's shoulder, and he joked and smiled all the while. How tall he was, thought Charlotte. To someone with her small stature, Alastair looked like a giant of a man. Charlotte felt herself glowing inside. For the first time in her life, little Charlotte had fallen in love.

Two weeks later, Alastair had fully recovered. Now he joined the family for a celebration dinner before he returned to his unit. Everyone was there, including Duncan, and Daisy was delighted to have her family about her. She talked excitedly about her successful efforts to collect money for the wounded.

Jackie was so pleased and proud to have his son with him after all this time and to get news from home in Australia.

Charlotte looked a little flushed but was very quiet. She watched in agony as the lovely Fleur flirted with Alastair and his blue Celtic eyes shone with admiration every time he glanced at her exposed white shoulders.

Fleur, the exhibitionist, was having a very good time. 'After dinner, Duncan and I will take you to the Cheshire Cheese Club for a drink. Then you will meet some of the crows – is that all right, Grandmama?'

'Go where you please,' replied Daisy. 'I am in need of my bed. But do take Charlotte with you, it will be a nice change for her.'

'I would sooner not go,' said Charlotte quietly. 'I like to stay at home with the children in case we have a raid.'

Fleur looking quickly at her cousin. 'Oh, Charlotte is such a home bird,' she said slightly sneeringly. 'She is German-born, you know, and does not like us all very much.'

Tears came into Charlotte's eyes at these cruel words. She felt helpless.

'Now Fleur, behave yourself,' demanded Daisy. 'I'll have no such talk in my house, if you don't mind.'

'Well, it's true, isn't it?' insisted Fleur. 'Charlotte was born in Germany. She's German.'

Daisy began to get angry but because there were guests present she held her temper. 'It is no matter where you are born,' she said firmly. 'It is the family heritage that counts. So, you be a little bit kinder to your cousin while she is our guest.'

Fleur was flushed with wine. She could not stand the look of amusement on Alastair's fair face nor the look of embarrassment on Duncan's. She burst out angrily: 'She is *not* my cousin. She is a Jew.'

Charlotte got up from the table and suddenly cried out: 'I hate you, Fleur. I do not want to be related to you.' With a loud sob, she dashed from the room.

'Oh, you have really done it now, Fleur,' sighed Daisy. 'Go out if you are going and let's have some peace and quiet.' She slowly hauled her large bulk up from the table. 'Jackie, let's have a hand of whist, it will pass the evening away,' she said.

Jackie went like a lamb. He was always affectionate and quiet, always loyal to his Daisy.

Fleur dashed off to get a wrap; then quite jubilant and delighted to be escorted by two admirers, she went off to do the rounds in that wartime social whirl, flitting from one night club to another to end up at a party at the house of a friend called Pat Horner.

By midnight Duncan was very drunk. After staggering and stumbling about, he eventually lay down on a rug in Pat Horner's house and promptly fell into a deep drunken sleep. All around him the young men and women were dancing and laughing and behaving as though this were the last time they would all meet. In those dark days, such thoughts were not so far from reality.

In a deep chesterfield in the library, Fleur sat on Alastair's lap and twisted her long slim legs around his.

Alastair was feeling quite boozy and was very aware of Fleur's hot lips and her slim warm body. He sighed, 'Fleur, I hope you know what you are doing to me,' he said.

She smiled coyly and pressed herself closer. That stiff hot part of his body pressed against her thigh and excited her. She had blanket-bathed many young men, so their bodies held no secret for her. But this was different. She moved a long slim leg just to feel the rapturous heat of the male body, and as Alastair's lips caressed her shoulder and nibbled her ear, Fleur almost swooned with desire.

As his hand slid under the long silken skirt with its many folds of petticoats Fleur slipped off his lap and said sleepily: 'Oh no, Alastair, we mustn't go any further, you know. One doesn't.'

Alastair gave her a rough push. 'Oh, so you are only a tease,' he said angrily. 'Go and make a fool of old Duncan, not me. I am going back to the barracks. You can take yourself home.' His long lean figure rose from the easy chair and he stumbled out of the room.

Sulkily, Fleur sat on the floor for a while nibbling her finger nails. She was not used to being treated like that. 'Silly fool,' she thought, 'well, he's from the outback, what's to be expected?' She went to find Duncan and gave his prostrate body a push with the toe of her dainty pointed shoe. He did not move. 'Oh, stay there, then,' she sniffed, and impatiently signalled to a departing party of friends. 'Give me a ride to Onslow Square, will you?'

In her long silver dress and white fur coat, Fleur arrived home alone and stomped up the stairs to her bedroom. Lying awake in her bed, Daisy wondered who had upset her little madam.

All alone in her room, Charlotte also heard Fleur arrive home late. She pressed her tear-stained face into the pillow. Oh, how she hated Fleur! How she wished she were home with her beloved mother!

The voices she had heard earlier that evening were still ringing in her ears. An official had arrived at the door and spoken to Aunt Daisy.

'Intern her?' Charlotte had heard Daisy exclaim. 'Don't be a bloody fool, man, she is only a child, what harm can she do?'

'Well, she will be turning eighteen soon, your ladyship. I will try to stop it, but then I can do very little once she is of adult age. All German-born citizens are about to be interned for the duration of the hostilities.'

Charlotte gasped and rammed her fist into her mouth. Could her life really get worse than it already was? When would this misfortune end for her?

27

Rosa at the Russian Front

Rosa was sitting at breakfast opposite her sister Ursula. They were in an inn in a little village on the Russian border. Rosa grumbled continuously about the hard black bread which had been served to them and the coffee without cream. In good Yiddish she complained to the woman waiting table, who replied in Russian, a language that Rosa had long forgotten. She did not understand the words but she caught the scornful tone in the woman's voice and the hostility directed towards her and Ursula, probably because they were Jewish.

Ursula was a much calmer personality. She sat facing Rosa, sipping her tea and enjoying it. 'They do not understand you, Rosa,' she said. She was silent for a while and then she said. 'You know, I wish we were back home in Frankfurt. I hate this cold country. I am sorry I came now and I get the feeling that something is happening.'

'Well, it was your idea to visit our place of birth,' retorted Rosa. 'I can't help it if you didn't like it, can I? You should have listened to Zvia. She knew it was a bad idea.'

After their months in Germany, where Rosa became

acquainted with her sister Ursula, Zvia had decided that it was time to return to America. The trip with Rosa had brought both happiness and confusion to her and she felt that she needed to return home to reassess everything.

Zvia had discovered her roots, with the help of Rosa, but this discovery had not brought her peace of mind. She had to go home and start a new life for herself, an adult life, no longer a younger version of the formidable Rosa.

When she heard Rosa encouraging Ursula to find her family roots, Zvia felt uneasy. Life was just not as simple as the forthright Rosa would have everyone think. Searching for one's roots and beginnings could stir up feelings that you had to be able to handle. Zvia had had enough of Rosa's control. She had had enough of Europe. She was going home, and she was rather relieved to be going home alone.

A week before Rosa and Ursula set off for the Russian border, Zvia boarded a train for France and said goodbye.

Free from the demands of Rosa, Zvia suddenly felt alive for the first time. She returned to New York, met a man with whom she fell in love and within a year she was married and pregnant with her first child. She went on to have six children, creating her own family where she had thought she had none. Zvia was a happy woman at last.

Meanwhile, Rosa and Ursula were still arguing.

Oh, dear,' sighed Ursula. 'It was just a dirty old

ghetto, with no love, no kindness. Just poverty-stricken folk and filthy food in the markets.' She shivered and pulled her shawl around her. 'It was most depressing.'

'Well, we are at least on our way back home,' declared Rosa. 'I think you're right about something odd happening here. I am going to see if I can find out.'

Determinedly she rose and went in search of the hostel manager, while Ursula settled her wide soprano's body more securely into the hard chair and thought of her daughter Charlotte. She wondered how she was settling in England. She missed her letters; since she and Rosa had been travelling, there had been no letters exchanged. Yes, she was glad to be going home. This trip in search of their roots had been very disappointing, a mistake, in fact, and she would be so happy to get home to her warm cosy apartment and her friends.

Suddenly Rosa appeared. She was hurrying and was accompanied by a tall guard with a large fur hat on his head and a rifle slung over his shoulder.

Ursula's blue eyes widened with fear. Rosa had evidently got herself into more trouble! How typical!

The man was talking to them in Yiddish, in an urgent voice: 'Old women, go! Go now! The border will be closed and then you not go at all.'

'Oh, whatever is he saying, Rosa?' pleaded Ursula, her fat limbs all aquiver.

Rosa put an arm around her sister. 'Now, Ursula, don't get upset. It seems that we are having a war with Germany and they are closing the borders this very day. We must hurry. It is fifty miles to Riga. Come on now, get packed.'

For the rest of the day, the two women tried to find transport but everyone seemed to be going in the other direction. 'The Hun is coming!' the people cried as they set off across the fields, peasants trundling along pushing their little barrows piled high with their belongings, farmers driving herds of goats and cows along the road, all seeking shelter from the dreaded Hun.

'Oh dear, don't these people panic!' declared Rosa.

Ursula was not as calm as she had been earlier. She was close to panic herself. Her big round face was full of fear. Although she was eleven years younger than her sister, she was not so fit. Her pampered life as an opera star had made her a trifle obese, and then losing her dear husband last year had not improved her health. 'Oh mein Gott!' she cried, 'we will never get home. Oh, my poor Charlotte, what will happen to her?' Tears began to pour down her cheeks.

'Oh, cheer up,' said Rosa, 'we will be all right. But to be on the safe side, do speak English.'

Before nightfall they had found an old wagon driven by a farmer who had removed some of his stock to safety and was returning for the remainder. Rosa offered him a very large sum of money to take them to the border town.

They sat in the wagon looking miserable and wrapped in their expensive fur coats. The old driver, also huddled in furs, stopped every so often to take a swig from a bottle and he chatted to them in a combination of Yiddish and Russian. 'Don't know if you will be lucky,' he said. 'Border will be closed off by now.'

'Oh dear,' blubbered Ursula. 'What will happen to us?'

'If you got American passport,' he said, 'we might get through but we don't like the Hun. We have been invaded before, in Napoleon time, but they won't get through. It is the climate, beats them.'

'You could be right about that,' said Rosa abruptly hugging her fur coat tightly about her. 'It is absolutely freezing. I've never been so cold.'

At the border post they found themselves huddled close together with many other stranded travellers, all trying to get home: Germans, Poles, English and Americans. No one seemed to worry about them or even seemed to care.

All night the troops moved past the huddle of huts singing Russian songs, their boots crunching in the deep snow. An Englishman brought in the news that the Germans were at the border and fighting had begun. Now the boom of guns could be heard.

'Don't know if we will get through the German lines. They will send us back behind the Russian lines, I believe, possibly nearer to Petrograd where we will get some sort of diplomatic protection.'

This sounded a little more encouraging.

At midday army guards came in to examine people's papers and everyone was sent off in different directions. On examining Rosa's passport, the guard stared curiously at her. 'American?' he asked, then turning the page. 'But you were born in Russia. You stay.'

Poor Ursula shivering and shaking produced her papers.

'Hun,' he said. 'Born in Germany.'

'Not so,' cried Rosa, 'she is my sister.'

With the butt of his gun, Rosa was pushed back, then the guard urged Ursula towards a big wagon which contained more unhappy people with fear of the unknown on their faces.

'German Jews,' the Army Guard shouted, 'to prison camp.'

Rosa surged forward waving her arms. 'No, no,' she cried. 'We are Americans. That is my sister.'

Then gruffly the officer gave her a push forward this time. 'Well, go with her if you want to. He turned towards the wagon. 'Another Jewess for you,' he shouted to the guard who hustled her into the wagon.

Rosa held on to her weeping sister Ursula. She did not cry herself but that scene of misery and desolation swept over her, the freezing wind of the endless snow-covered lane, the prisoners huddled together in that old farm wagon which smelt of pigs. Rosa's knees buckled as she knelt to comfort Ursula. Real fear gripped her by the throat, but forever brave, she declared: 'Don't worry, folk, once we get into the town they will take care of you all. It will only be a matter of time and we will be released. They can do nothing to us, they dare not for we are on their side. England is fighting Germany.'

'But if you notice, we in here are all Jews. The

Russians never liked us even in peace time,' said one of the prisoners.

The cold was terrible. They were all numb, thirsty and hungry so the sight of the camp with its long line of wooden huts with smoke coming from the chimneys was a welcome relief. That night they slept in bunk beds recently vacated by the army. In the morning the men and women were separated and some were sent on to further camps.

Rosa clung to her sister. 'We are together,' she shouted to the brutal-looking bearded guards. They reminded her of the Cossacks of her youth who had ridden poor Grandpa down. She could still see the bloodied snow in her mind. How on earth was she going to get away from them? Meanwhile, she had to survive. She queued for their supper of soup and black bread. From the chatter of the other detainees she learned that the Germans were all along the front line and were pushing ahead all the time.

For one week they held out in this desolate camp until one morning the guards had all gone and the shells rattled over the roof tops. The Germans had broken through.

'It's all right, Ursula,' Rosa consoled her sister. 'They think that you are German-born, they will not hurt you, and I can take care of myself. I am going to demand to see the American Ambassador.'

Confidently they awaited the German Army's arrival. The soldiers came in that evening and stood the detainees all in a line to question them. The poor terrified women grovelled on the floor pleading for mercy but there was none.

'You are Russian enemy of the Imperial German Army,' declared a very upright officer. 'Women stay and work for army.'

Once more they were bundled off through the miles of wasteland, the guns thundering around them. Finally they arrived at a large farmhouse already occupied by German troops.

'Here you stay. Here you work,' they were told.

The group consisted of ten women and one teenage girl. 'I demand medical treatment and hot food,' cried Rosa. 'We demand diplomatic safety. I wish to appeal to the American Embassy.'

But the officer grinned and came closer to scrutinize her. 'You old woman,' he said. 'No good. Can you cook?'

'Oh yes,' burst out the terrified Ursula. 'We can cook good German food.'

'Good,' he said, 'you can cook for me.'

So it was to the farm kitchen that they were transported to cook for German officers.

In her forthright manner, Rosa decided to get on with the enemy. After all, the way to any man's heart was through his stomach, she thought. She organized the other women to clean up and serve the meals in comfort. She got on well with the young Russian who had been left behind the lines, and she tried to shut her eyes to the horrors young women suffered when the officers were drunk and raided the kitchen quarters seeking sex.

Ursula eked out a terrified existence. She hardly ate anything. She grew very thin and became extremely depressed. But she was always grateful to have her strong forthright older sister there to protect her.

From early in the war to the New Year all through that terrible Russian winter Rosa and her sister Ursula spent their time in the German military camp just behind the lines. The rumble of the guns and the long lines of dead and wounded which passed the camp were depressing sights.

They were not allowed to contact anyone, and they were more or less marooned in the captain's house where they cleaned and cooked and prepared the meals. The captain was a youngish officer of the old type, happy and generous, and always slightly drunk. But they were fed and warm and the other men did not bother them. Rosa frequently stated that she was an American and the war was nothing to do with her country, but all her papers had been confiscated so no one was interested.

The snow piled high all around the wide open country as the German Army dug in on the Russian borders. The young recruits suffered terribly in the cold and more than once a guard was found in the morning frozen to death at his post.

Yet Rosa was as tough as ever. Soon she discovered that her command of Yiddish and German came in useful and as her Russian slowly came back to her she was often asked to translate testaments made by the occasional peasant who was taken prisoner.

Ursula, however, pined constantly for her homeland.

Her condition seemed to deteriorate from day to day.

One day a new person was added to the captain's household, a young Slav girl called Sonia. She had fine chiselled features, strange greeny grey eyes and dark hair which she wound about her head. She spoke German and English. 'Me Sonia,' she told Rosa. 'Me captain's woman. He not bad.'

She was good to Ursula and took on her share of the chores along with her own.

It was almost spring when the young captain got posted elsewhere and a nasty old fellow took his place. This new man had an ugly scarred face and a huge thick body. He came to inspect his quarters and when he saw Ursula crouched in her usual spot next to the big stove in the centre of the kitchen, he poked her with his cane. 'What this?' he said in loud guttural German. 'Women! What they do here?'

Rosa had been kneading the long loaves of rye bread. She wiped her hands on her apron and said sharply: 'We work for the captain.'

The officer grunted and stared harder at Ursula. 'You Jewish? You born here?'

'I am from Deutschland,' replied Ursula timidly.

'What?' he roared. 'This woman is Jew. Why she not in prison camp?'

Rosa rushed forward to explain. 'She is my sister,' she cried.

The man swung round on her, his eyes blazing. 'Ah! so you Jew also? Guard!' he roared. 'Get this trash out of my kitchen! Send them to prison camp!'

Without more ado, Rosa and her sick sister were bundled into a lorry with only a few of their possessions. Sonia crept up behind the lorry and threw in their fur coats. 'Don't worry,' she whispered. 'I will find you. God bless you.'

Once more they set off across the snow-covered fields towards Riga, now ten miles away. There were many bodies lying stiff in the snow. Rosa held her weeping sister and cursed the Germans in her loud voice, insisting still that she was an American. But it made no difference, and her heart sank as they were driven through the dreaded empty no-man's land behind the German lines to the squalor and cruelty of a prison camp.

They were all women from all over the globe caught up in this big offensive. Some were nuns from France, some school-teachers from Berlin, some were women from the Turkish borders. All were lost and very far from home – all were Jews. Every day they were marched in parties off to the frozen fields and factories. Some days a few were herded into big railway wagons and those who went that way never came back.

Ursula became very ill and soon was unable to get up out of her narrow bunk bed. Rosa covered her with both their fur coats to keep her warm.

Ursula grew weaker and then, one very cold night, the soldiers carried out Ursula's body along with the two fur coats, which were never seen again.

Rosa was heart-broken. She had only recently discovered her sister and now she had lost her. She felt so alone. However, she did have one friend and that was the beautiful young Sonia who, as promised, had sought her out in the fields. Rosa had been digging in the frozen ground to find spring cabbages, when Sonia had appeared and slipped Rosa a piece of cooked chicken. Rosa stood behind a hedge to gnaw at it ravenously.

Sonia told Rosa that she had smiled sweetly at the guard and told him that she had come to get a cabbage for the captain's dinner. The soldier had joked in Russian and said that if she could find any worth eating she was welcome to them.

Still licking her lips from that tasty morsel of chicken, Rosa came out from behind the hedge.

Sonia whispered to Rosa. 'Soon Russians come. Then I will go home. I take you with me to Petrograd. Just be ready. Goodbye.'

Rosa's wan face lit up. 'Of course I'll be ready,' she said. 'Any place will be better than this.'

The next morning at dawn the attack came from over the hill – hordes of untrained soliders, the Russian peasants, driven on by mounted Cossacks to drive out the dreaded Hun. The Germans were caught by surprise and were forced to retreat rapidly. By nightfall hundreds of prisoners had been captured.

Rosa found herself pushed into a truck once more rattling its way through the roads of Russia. She felt a little bewildered but was reassured by the presence of that bright alert young miss, Sonia, who cuddled up to her affectionately.

'No worry,' said Sonia. 'I go with you to Petrograd, my home city. I did not like that other captain. He a very bad man.'

Rosa tried to smile but her lips drooped as if she had forgotten how to. 'Well now, where are we off to?' she asked.

'To Petrograd,' said Sonia brightly. 'When we get to river they will stay. Wait for barge to cross over, maybe they take them across or maybe shoot, I do not know. I will get through at post because I am born at that part. I will say you are my mother, so you be quiet, play part of foolish old woman and it will work.'

At the river the trucks halted. Prisoners were separated. Some were marched away, others were bid to sit and wait for the barge to cross the river. It was quite a sight – long lines of miserable wretches speaking a host of languages, all refugees of the war and driven from their farms and homes into this nomadic existence.

Sonia flirted brazenly with the young soldier guarding them. 'This is my mother,' she told him. 'She is very ill. You will see we get seat in boat?' she smiled broadly at him.

The soldier grinned and made a rude remark. Sonia understood. She put an old black kerchief about Rosa's head. 'Hunch your back,' she said, 'it will make you look much older.'

'What will they do with us?' asked Rosa.

'They will sort us out before we get a barge to Riga then those that are lucky and have nothing to hide will go on the train to Petrograd to work in the big factories, I suppose. Now you go to sleep, Rosa, it will pass the night away much quicker.'

With an army blanket wrapped around her, Rosa

lay looking up at the black sky and the myriad of silver stars, wondering how Zvia had fared and how little Charlotte was getting on in England. She thought about her family in various parts of the world and wondered how these events were affecting them now.

Rosa was nearly asleep when the young soldier crept quietly over to Sonia and pulled her by the hand but she noticed that Sonia went willingly, and that she placed her finger on her lips to hush Rosa and not to let anyone else know.

In the still light of the morning Rosa sat huddled around the big camp fired with all the other miserable wretches. Sonia was looking somewhat bedraggled but she still had a bright smile on her face when she came to sit beside Rosa and handed her half a cup of black coffee.

'I save some for you,' Sonia said. 'Warm it on the fire. We will be all right. We will get through this together.'

Rosa looked at her questioningly. What had Sonia done to get aid for her? She sighed and then gratefully sipped the half cup of coffee.

Sonia smiled. She seemed to read Rosa's thoughts. 'Oh, it was not so bad,' she said. 'Nice young man. I've had worse. Now it is easy, but only a favour for a favour, that is one lesson I learned.'

'Have you got parents and a home?' asked Rosa.

'I have,' declared Sonia, 'and soon you will see them.'

Rosa squeezed her hand. 'Whither thou goest, there go I,' she said quietly.

'Where is that from?' demanded Sonia. 'What does it mean?'

'It is from a bible story,' said Rosa.

'Oh no, no,' said Sonia shaking her head. 'I do not believe in religion. I only believe in equality for the Russian people. One day we all fight this oppression and then Russia will be free.'

Rosa stared at her in amazement and smiled. Amid all this sorrow she had met a real socialist, a girl after her own heart.

As Sonia had predicted, it was easy to get aboard the barge. Rosa bent her back and tried to look like a very old woman with a dark kerchief about her head. She muttered and mumbled to herself and spoke not one intelligent word.

Sonia waggled her wide hips and explained to the soldiers in her own dialect, for this was her part of Russia, that she and her mother had been visiting relatives and then got caught up on the border and been taken prisoner by the Germans. She wiped a tear from her eyes as she told them how badly they had been treated and she nodded appreciatively as she received sympathetic remarks about the Deutschlander bastards.

Sonia looked very pleased with herself as she settled herself and Rosa in a comfortable spot below deck to cross the river. Then they boarded a train into Petrograd where Rosa, almost sixty, was to spend the years of the war. After the war, when Revolution broke out, then she boarded a boat across the Black Sea and escaped to Palestine where she spent the rest of her days living in a settlement and helping to create a new nation out of the dry desert. She lived in a tent and picked oranges by day but she was happy and content living with other Jews who all had the same mission in life. Rosa was a woman who lived and died by her passion for a cause.

28

The Fruits of War

Every day, Daisy the Dowager Duchess rode around Hyde Park in her carriage collecting war news from the wives of the government men. With her outrageous hats, her wide friendly smile and her loud voice with its Australian twang, she was a well-known figure. She had had many battles over the months with the Home Office, about its attempts to intern her German-born charge, Charlotte. She had managed to pull enough strings to hold on to her up until now, but this phase of the war was becoming very desperate. People were no longer so sure that England would win and much was said about German atrocities, while refugees from Belgium flooded the land. There was a universal paranoid feeling about German spies and people acted accordingly. All German-owned shops were looted and anyone with a foreign name was likely to be victimized in some way. More importantly, the law on internees was tightened up. Charlotte was eighteen and could no longer be an exception. Daisy was finally powerless to prevent young Charlotte being whisked off to the Isle of Man to a huge internment camp there.

Sobbing and broken-hearted, Charlotte was put in a car with other internees. It was a terrible scene. The younger girls were crying and the servants were also all upset and arguing with each other about the point of doing this dreadful thing to dear Miss Charlotte.

Only the sweet-tempered Jackie showed any real sense. He put on his hat and said: 'I'll go to see she gets the train.'

Daisy ranted and raved and almost physically attacked the man from the Home Office. 'After all the work I have done for the war effort,' she shouted, 'this is damned disgraceful.'

'Madam,' said the man quietly, 'she will be all right. She is going with good recommendations from the Home Office. There is no need for alarm and she will probably get an administrative job in the camp.'

'Camp! Camp!' yelled Daisy. 'What is it? Lines of bloody tents on a wind-swept island? What sort of place is that for a well-brought-up girl?'

'It is not like that, madam,' the official tried to console Daisy. 'And possibly she will get released the moment all this scare dies down a bit.'

So Daisy was beaten by red tape. She felt exhausted by it. It was not often that she got beaten in an argument.

Only Fleur was able to calm her. She held her hand and said gently: 'Grandmama, do not get so upset or you will make yourself ill.'

Fleur herself was not sad for the weeping Charlotte. She just hated her for causing all this upset and upheaval in the family. The girls had never got on and the situation was not going to change easily.

* * *

Internment did not, in fact, prove as bad as Charlotte had thought it would be. The Isle of Man was a lovely place with long meadows full of wild flowers and big mountains which seemed to dominate the scene and the sandy coves. And the people were very pleasant.

The internees lived in wooden huts which had previously been country holiday homes. There were many, many Germans, some who had left Germany years before and spoke only English. There were German brass bands, German writers and many German families from the inner London immigration area of Whitechapel and the East End. The camp was lively and noisy and no one was bothered much. They were out of the war so the children played happily and went to school, and the housewives squabbled and complained about rations because they were idle and had nothing much to do. In fact, Charlotte gained a lot of freedom in this place that she had imagined to be a prison.

As promised, after a week or two, Charlotte landed a secretarial post in the administration office. This suited her very well. She was happy just to do her job to the best of her ability, not to have to conform with society, and to be away from Daisy's eagle eye and out of reach from that spiteful Fleur. She soon found that she was good at sorting out the problems that arose on the camp and could soothe over trivial squabbles with impressive ease.

In an odd way she felt more at home here in this camp than she ever had at Onslow Square. She could send on their way in fluent German or Yiddish the most difficult of people and not let the swearing or the bad jokes of the men worry her in the least. So, Charlotte quietly and easily became attached to this small island with its mixed community.

'Good gracious!' declared Daisy after reading a letter from Charlotte. 'The damned gel does not want me to get her released. Says that she likes it there! Well, I'll be blowed!' She puffed out her cheeks with indignation.

'She is with her own kind, Grandmama,' said Fleur sarcastically.

'Oh, shut up, Fleur!' snapped Daisy. 'What's wrong with you? Why don't you go for a walk like you used to instead of sitting mooning about here all day and out all night? You have begun to look very washed out.'

Fleur hung her head and did not reply. Her grandmother had touched a nerve. Her happy carefree life was being disturbed by the fact that Alastair was leaving London, having been posted up to Scotland.

'But why?' she had asked him. 'Your regiment is not going.'

'No,' said Alastair. 'I have warned you not to talk about it. It's very secret, just a few of us picked men are going on training to start a new regiment but that is all I can tell you.'

'Let us be married before you go,' begged Fleur. 'I will face Grandmama and you can get around Jackie, I know you can.'

Alastair stood before her looking tall and upright.

The sun shone in the window on his mop of red curls. 'I do not want to be married yet, Fleur,' he said. 'If I take this command and I am being promoted, I dare not be married.'

Fleur sniffed. 'Oh, so that is all you care about me. It is just army, army, army. You are obsessed with the army.'

Alastair put an arm about her and hugged her to him. 'Now, darling,' he said. 'I love you and I won't marry anyone else, but the way we are going, it might be better to part for a while or I'll be getting you pregnant.'

'Oh,' giggled Fleur, 'that would be marvellous and all those old fogies would have to approve just to avoid a family scandal.' Her tune had changed over the months!

'No, that's not for me. I am a man of honour and nearly being a bastard myself I don't wish to leave one behind, no matter how mighty your family is.'

When Fleur said goodbye to Alastair that evening she was quite exhausted. And she received another shock when she arrived home. There was Duncan waiting to greet her, dressed in full military uniform with every brass button shining and gaiters. He also had one pip and the letters W.D. on his shoulder.

'Oh, no, Duncan, you are joking! Have they really passed you fit at last?' she cried.

'Not exactly,' returned Duncan. Old Uncle William pulled some strings and now I have got a post at the War Office behind the scenes. Isn't it great?' His goofy teeth seemed to stick out more than ever with all the excitement of the moment and sweat gleamed on his brow.

Fleur looked at him sadly. He had been her best friend for many years. He was always around. Now she was going to miss him. 'Oh well, Duncan, I wish you well,' she said quietly.

'We are off to camp,' Duncan informed her. 'It's just a six-week course and I will be back, darling. What about a celebration tonight? I will round up some of the old crowd.'

'Is there anyone left?' said Fleur bitterly. 'I will go and get ready.'

That evening they celebrated, flitting from club to club gathering a party of friends, then on to the Savoy for an egg-and-bacon breakfast in spite of the rationing.

When Duncan took Fleur home at dawn, he said. 'It was a ripping good night, Fleur.'

She kissed him affectionately. 'It was nice to be out with you in uniform and not to have white feathers thrust at you.'

'Marry me, Fleur,' Duncan suddenly said with an urgency to his voice. 'Let us tell the folks now before I go.'

'Marry you? Don't be an idiot, Duncan. I do not love you,' declared Fleur standing back from him.

Duncan's mild blue eyes behind the thick specs looked very hurt. He replaced his cap and kissed her cheek. 'I will always be there when you need me, Fleur.'

Fleur felt as hard as nails as she confidently replied: 'Oh well, Duncan, someone will soon whip you up now that you are in uniform. You will get married, after all, it is only an office job. You won't get killed.'

Duncan was looking very forlorn.

'Oh, buck up!' snapped Fleur. 'I will miss you, I must agree, but I am in love with someone else so you might as well face it.'

'That Australian,' muttered a defeated Duncan. 'I wish you luck, Fleur.'

'Oh, good luck and goodbye, is it, and safe return?' Fleur said sarcastically.

'No, darling,' Duncan replied, kissing her hand courteously. 'I am sure I will win you one day, so I will wait.'

With Alastair on a secret mission in the Highlands of Scotland and Duncan in Reading in training school, her social life became pretty dull, but she took up her nursing more seriously at the general hospital and worked hard on the wards and eventually earned her Sister's cap.

Fleur's lovely red hair, fresh complexion and wide smile were welcome sights to the poor shattered soldiers lying in the wards. Fleur would talk with them saying: 'Now, you be good, otherwise I will ask my grandmother to come and chat with you and you will not like that.'

Dowager Duchess Daisy would visit them all anyway, to see the new patients and to write home to their folks when they passed on giving them a last wish and making sure that the padre conveyed their souls to Heaven. This was how she came to meet Bill Kennedy.

Bill had just come back from the Somme. He was so

badly injured that it was known that he would not live long. He was just twenty years old and a young recruit in the new tank regiment.

'Howdy, Bill, where are you from?' Daisy asked when she visited him for the first time. Bill smiled at her big red face under the flower-trimmed hat. He was still woozy from the anaesthetic since the other day when they had removed his legs.

Daisy knew from the nursing sister that he had been a six foot tall Irishman and did not want to go on without his legs. He was very down in the dumps, and the Dowager Duchess Daisy became a bright spot in his dark hours.

'I am from Ireland,' replied Bill.

'Shall I write to your mother for you?' asked Daisy.

Bill nodded. 'My folks live in a tiny hamlet outside of Cork. My father still works for the railway. His name is David Kennedy.'

'Wal now,' said Daisy, 'that's real nice. I ain't never been to Ireland but Jackie, me man, is an Irishman but we originally met in the East End and met up again out in the backwoods of Australia.'

Bill's blue eyes lit up. This was no old do-gooder to spout religion at him. This was a genuine good-natured person who had travelled widely. He brightened up.

After this, they met each day. And even though the condition of Bill's shrapnel-filled body worsened, he was as cheerful as he could be. His Irish blue eyes reminded Daisy so much of Jackie's as they brightened at her jovial comments and her passion for a bet on the horses.

On days when he was reasonably well, Bill told Daisy of his home and his seven brothers and sisters and how upset they had been when he ran away at nineteen to join the British Army. He told her of his favourite sister, Maggie, and about David his father, a strong man even in his old age, who had worked on the American railways.

Daisy told him tales of the bar she had run in the opal mining town, of the high blue mountains and the dry deserts that she had travelled with Dukey.

'My eldest brother is coming to see me,' Bill told Daisy one day. 'He is working at Woolwich Arsenal. He married a Cockney girl.'

'I would like to meet them,' Daisy said and meant it. 'Bye for now, till I come back tonight.'

When Daisy told Jackie about Bill, he was very interested. And he was keen to meet these young people from Ireland. He went with Daisy that evening to see Bill Kennedy. 'They must be family,' he said. 'For my mother was a Kennedy and came from West Cork. Also Alastair's mother, Julie, was a Kennedy. She was the one who was my mother's niece who went out to Australia with my mother when she went.'

'I'm sure you're right. He's more family,' said Daisy. 'If he gets well enough I'll bring him up to convalesce at the house. You and he might have a lot in common.'

But that night Bill took a turn for the worse and the nurse advised Daisy and Jackie not to tire him, to let him sleep.

The next day when Daisy visited Bill, there beside

his bed was a tall red-haired man who looked like Bill. He had tears in his eyes at the sight of his young brother.

Daisy introduced herself and then said: 'Now, now, you come and have a drink with me and my husband. Bill will be all right tomorrow, I'm sure.'

They sat in a hotel lounge drinking brandy. He told her that his name was Con Kennedy. He was in his late thirties, and was a quiet-spoken working-class man. He was poor but cleanly dressed. His brow was scarred and his hands were calloused. His shrewd blue eyes shed real tears for his young brother. The hospital sister had told him to stay around and he knew that could only mean one thing.

'Oh, I can't believe it,' wept Daisy. 'Bill was so bright yesterday.'

'Shrapnel has shifted to the heart and they can't operate any more on him,' said Con mournfully. 'He is our younger brother, the baby, and it will break mother's heart.'

Jackie patted him on the shoulder. 'Try to face it, boy, it is God's will.'

Con was getting a little emotional having had a few brandies. 'Here am I doing a civil job when I should be out there fighting the bloody Hun.'

Jackie ordered more brandies and tried to turn the conversation to home.

'Well, now, boy, it seems we might even be related. My mother was a Kennedy. She is quite old now but still hale and hearty and lives in Australia. This village you talk of, is it in Mallow?'

'No, it is near Bantry,' replied Con.

'Well, bedad, that's the next stop on the way to Killarny.'

'That's right, said Con, brightening up for the first time.

'What about your grandparents?' asked Jackie. 'Now don't tell me they were named Foley?'

'That's right. They went to the States in the time of famine. My mother went with them and married David Kennedy out there. But they did not stay long out there. In fact, I was born coming back in mid-Atlantic in 1876.'

'Well, now, there's a fascinating story, Jackie,' said Daisy. 'It brings back memories to us, doesn't it?'

'If your mother was Eli Lehane before marriage, it must be the same family who had a big farm called Inchalee before the English evicted them,' Jackie said.

Con's blue eyes opened wide in surprise. 'So you know the story too!' he exclaimed.

'Oh, quite well,' said Jackie with a smile. 'Because we come from the same family.' Jackie and Con grasped hands and drank a little more. 'Your father, David Kennedy, came from a very old Irish family. He was my mother's brother. You and I are first cousins,' Jackie informed him.

So, in spite of their sorrow they celebrated their new-found relationship. Soon Con was very drunk. 'I must go home to May,' he said finally. 'She will be worried about me.'

'Do you have a family, Con?' asked Daisy.

'Yes, I have three children and it is a worryin' time

with Zeppelin raids as well so I'll go home and come back in the morning.'

They put Con in a taxi and then went to see Fleur in her office. She told them that it would be a miracle if Bill Kennedy lasted out the night.

On the way home in the carriage, Daisy put her head on Jackie's shoulder and wept. They were closer that night than they had been for a long time.

'Oh, dear God,' Daisy cried, 'why does this war have to go on? The slaughter and the shortage of food are all too horrible. Won't it ever end?'

'Well, it might if the Americans come in with us. Let's face it, Daisy, we are on our last legs. Even the new tank regiment is not getting far. They say it's swimming in mud out there. I heard from Alastair that things are pretty bad. He is back on the front line and has command of this new regiment. One never knows from day to day,' he sighed.

Daisy cuddled up close. 'Come on, old man,' she said. 'We must cheer up, it's no good us giving in.'

The next morning Daisy and Jackie found Con at the hospital. Bill passed away that night. 'I want Bill's body sent home to Ireland,' he said. 'Mother will wish him to be buried at Kanturk with the rest of the family.'

'Well, what's the problem?' demanded Daisy. 'They seem to be making a lot of bother about it here.'

'Oh, it's something about expense and the dangers of transporting him over the sea with submarines lying out there.'

'They did what?' said Daisy in her indignant manner. 'Now, boy, you stay here and I'll sort this lot out.' And off she strode and she did not return until all arrangements had been made for Con to go home with his brother's body.

'I am eternally grateful to you, madam,' said Con.

''Tis nothing but what he is entitled to,' Jackie told him. 'Your brother gave his life for his country and he was a fine boy. Now Con, I want to be kept in touch with you and your family, seeing as you and I are related,' he added with much sincerity.

Daisy had bullied the Army and War Office into seeing that Bill Kennedy was properly transported home for a military funeral in his own village and that the expenses were paid for Con to accompany the coffin all the way home and arrange the funeral himself. Now, quite pleased with herself, Daisy sent a parcel of goodies to Con's wife, May, and then continued on with her own good works.

On their return to Onslow Square, Jackie and Daisy were greeted by another visitor. A tall, grave-looking young man in a long black habit and a stiff priest's collar.

'Who's that?' Daisy raised her lorgnette and squinted through them at this sandy-haired young man standing in the shadows in the big hall.

'Mean to say you don't recognize me, Mother?' The man spoke quietly, with a lilt in his tone. It was John, her youngest son.

With a cry of delight, Daisy rushed towards him. 'Well, I'll be . . .! If it ain't me baby son, after all these years!' Tears poured from her eyes as she wept profusely.

Jackie stepped forward to shake John's hand. 'Well, boy, it's been a long time.'

John smiled. 'It is so good to see you, too, and you are both looking so well.'

With arms linked, they went into the drawing room for coffee.

'What are you doing over here, boy? enquired Daisy. 'I thought you were hooked on all those heathens out there in New Zealand.'

John smiled slowly. His mother always amused him, for in spite of his sombre manner, there was some of Daisy in him. 'I came to join the army,' he told her.

'What for? You are a Catholic priest,' Daisy said.

'We are needed just as much, mother,' he said.

Daisy looked down sadly at her hands. Here was another son to the sacrifice. Charles was dead. Fred had disappeared and could be dead for all she knew. John was her last one.

John told them that he would be in England while he waited for his final papers to allow him to go to France with a non-combat unit.

The next day they went to visit Petal. She was still in a depressed state, lolling in the lounge chair near the window, and Daisy, as usual, nagged at her. 'How disgraceful to lie there without a care about what is going on out there in the world,' she said to her daughter.

Father John's grey eyes scrutinized Petal. Uncharacteristically, she got out of her chair and took his hand in welcome.

'Father John Duquin. That sounds very nice,' she said quietly.

John squeezed her hand affectionately. 'We are brother and sister but hardly acquainted. Perhaps we should get to know each other better.'

Petal smiled sadly but did not disagree. She just whispered, 'I have become a lonely woman since I lost Sam. I just don't care what goes on in the world outside.'

They had coffee while Daisy gossiped loudly about society's ills and her charity work for the wounded, and then collected another cheque from Petal. As Daisy and John got up to go, John whispered to Petal: 'I'll be back.'

Petal squeezed his hand in consent.

Daisy shouted loudly, 'It's time she got her backside out of that chair. There's plenty to be done out there, if the bloody Hun gets here he will make short work of all of us.'

The next day Father John left to stay at a monastery of his own order in the Midlands. As the Zeppelin raids became bad, Daisy decided to send her two small charges up North to stay with their other grandmother.

Daisy had begun to get worried about Fleur. She did not seem well lately and Daisy thought that perhaps she ought to have a holiday.

Fleur however refused. 'Oh, don't fuss Grandma, I am all right,' she had said.

Yet this was quite untrue. It was four weeks since Alastair left and she had missed her period. For on that last meeting they had gone further than ever before. She had kept her loss of virginity a deadly secret. She was proud of it but everyone else would have been shocked. Now she felt sick and not a little worried. She was a bit on edge, and had dark rings around her eyes. She also went about her duties in a furtive manner.

She wrote several letters to Alastair but he was on a secret mission and was unable to reply to a hoity-toity young miss. When no letters came back from him, Fleur began to panic.

The next two weeks were a nightmare. She could not imagine what she was going to do. Then, Duncan arrived dressed in his war regalia and looking very confident, having obtained a secretarial post which meant that he might not have to go overseas.

'Oh that is fine, Duncan,' said Fleur. 'I must say, you look very fit.'

'More than I can say for you, my lovely,' returned Duncan. 'You look positively bushed.'

'Oh, just a little tired,' replied Fleur, turning away.

'Why don't we get married?' cried Duncan. 'Think about it again. I will take good care of you, Fleur, you can go and live in the country with my parents while I am on active service.'

Fleur looked at him blankly for a moment and then, to his astonishment, said: 'Oh well, why not?' Duncan nearly fell off his chair. Then he looked wild with joy.

The next weeks were full of celebrations and both Daisy and the Browne parents were happy about this wedding. It was the wedding of the year and to the many grand families so devastated by the loss of their own young sons and fathers it was a bright spot and everyone took time off to attend.

One very surprising happening was the arrival of Madame de Petaal fantastically attired and clinging to the arm of a handsome priest, her half-brother. It was a talking point for weeks.

29

Charlotte Finds Her Love

After her wedding, Fleur had left London for the safety of Duncan's family house on the Welsh borders. The war had been going on for three years and still it continued its devastation. Food rationing was in force and long queues of poorly clad people stood outside the shops awaiting their ration of bread, meat or fruit and almost every night the German Zeppelins now came over London with only a search light or ack-ack guns or soldiers with rifles to deter them. Yet the true Londoner did not flee. They made the cellars as bomb proof as possible and stayed put. Cries of 'Take cover!' would be heard but often disregarded. People came out of pubs and houses and waved their fists and cursed those bloody Huns, and should a Zeppelin ever be brought down, the people danced, waved and cheered. For in that war most bombs fell into the Thames.

The troops were now 'dug in' out in France and there were so many casualties that all Londoners were affected. Their families were devastated. But no one ever thought for one moment that Britain would ever lose the war, not even Daisy, whose nursing home was always over-crowded, with one wing given over to the ordinary soldiers.

Only Jackie was lonely. He still lived in the mews flat and the stock exchange was so shaky that it was scarcely worth speculating any more. For him the fun had gone out of life.

Daisy was up to her neck in good works and had little time for Jackie. She was more concerned for Petal who had had a sudden change of heart and come out of her decline.

Visiting her apartment one morning, Daisy was confronted by Petal dressed in a long grey, severely styled dressed. Her hair was pushed up under a silk headdress, and she had a sweet serene smile on her face. She welcomed her mother with a kiss.

'What's all this?' asked Daisy suspiciously.

'Oh, do come in, Mother, and see who's here.'

Two men sat in the corner in close conversation. One was a sturdy good-looking young man with side whiskers and a little round skull cap on his head. 'Look, mother, Morris is home,' said Petal.

The other young man Daisy recognized, of course, since he was her own son, John, in his long cassock. 'Oh, John,' she said, 'so this is where you are. I haven't seen you for some time.'

John got to his feet and greeted his mother with a warm smile.

Then Morris embraced her. 'Hullo, Grandmama, it is lovely to see you looking so well.'

'Now, where did you spring from? Where have you been hiding for so long?' cried Daisy.

'My son is a full-blown rabbi,' said Petal proudly. 'He and John are staying with me now. They are waiting their call-up for the forces.'

'Oh, that's something,' sniffed Daisy. 'It's a bit of a dodgy business hiding in the church while men are fighting for their country.'

No one bothered to rise to this. They all knew that the argumentative old Duchess had a bark which was far worse than her bite.

Daisy sat herself down on the big chesterfield while Petal poured the tea.

'Wal,' said Daisy eventually. 'I am glad you are going to do your bit but when this war will end, God only knows.'

'Well, mother, we need parsons and rabbis as much as soldiers,' said Petal, 'if civilisation is to be kept going.'

Daisy raised her eyebrows quizzically. 'Since when did you get religious?' she enquired sharply.

'So, you did not notice my clothes, then, mother?' asked Petal with a slow smile.

'No, what is it supposed to be? Must say, you do look a bit brighter than you used to.'

'I belong to a new order,' said Petal. 'The Sisters of Charity.'

Daisy's mouth dropped open in astonishment. She stared at Petal in disbelief. 'A nun?' she gasped. 'I don't believe you!'

Father John rose to his feet in a graceful movement and came over to sit next to Daisy and Petal.

'Mother,' he said. 'I would like to explain. Petal has

given all her money to the Association for Blind Soldiers and is now in an open order. The Sisters of Charity have sworn to give their lives and possessions to the Church and work for the war wounded.'

'Well, I'll be blowed,' gasped Daisy. Then, after a moment's pause, she laughed. 'Jolly good luck, gel,' she cried. 'I really still can't believe it!'

'It is perfectly true, Grandma,' said Morris. 'It was John's influence that made Mother see the light, and I am very proud of her.'

'Well, so am I,' said Daisy getting up and giving Petal a hug. 'Now, by jingo, we are all in it. That Hun had better watch out.'

'I don't like to leave you, Mother,' said Petal, 'especially since I know how much you miss Fleur. But my apartment is being sold and I am going to live in Sussex, in a home for soldiers blinded in the war.'

'Oh, I'll get by,' Daisy assured her. 'Don't worry about me. Now, tonight it's dinner for us all at Onslow Square. I'll break the news to Jackie before then.'

Over an excellent meal that night, delivered by the hotel up the road as the cook had left and all servants were getting hard to find, Petal explained her conversion. It was, she said, her brother John who had made her see the light. 'At first it was a friendship,' she said, 'and then something a little deeper as John stayed frequently at home.'

John had said to her: 'Petal, I am so glad you are my sister for I have grown to love you very much but in no way will I break my vow to the church.'

Petal had stared at him with her lovely dreamy eyes.

'John,' she had said, 'you come to lighten my darkness. Now I will not let you out of my life.'

John had kissed her smooth hands and said: 'Well, join me in my life's work, Petal. That way we will be joined in God.' So began Petal's conversion.

Morris had been amazed. 'Why a Catholic, Mother? Why not a Jew?'

'I was never a Jewess, Morris,' replied Petal. 'When I married Maxwell, I made it quite clear that I would not adopt the Jewish faith.'

Morris was then told the story of Sam, who had been his real father and had not lived long enough to claim him for his son.

Morris had been moved but he made a joke of it. 'Well, that is a few millions lost,' he had said. 'Never mind, I don't need money. My work in life is for the Jewish race, and after the war it will be even harder for them.'

'Let us swear to stand together to work for humanity,' John had said and they had all linked hands, while Morris mumbled a prayer in Yiddish and John one in Latin, and Petal, with tears rolling down her cheeks, had just added 'Amen'.

At Onslow Square that night, everyone was feeling warm and loving, impressed by the moving story of Petal's conversion. Even Daisy had to admit that she was pleased to see her daughter revived and happy.

Petal had been living in Sussex for a while now. Morris had been away for some months with the Jewish Regiment and John was a padre to the British Army. There was at last talk of an Armistice.

Poor Alastair was wounded once more and this time very seriously. While commanding a tank regiment at the Somme, he had been badly burned and lost an eye.

Jackie went to visit him in hospital and was shocked to see his son's fine face so badly scarred. Yet Alastair was still in very bright spirits.

'Oh well, Dad, this has got me back to Blighty, at least,' he joked. 'How's everyone?'

'Fleur married Duncan,' said Jackie. 'You knew that, didn't you?'

'I did,' said Alastair. 'Fleur did not hesitate to send me a 'Dear John' letter. But I've forgotten her already. Besides,' he added with a sigh, 'the lovely Fleur would not look at me now.'

'Lovely is as lovely does,' said Jackie bitterly. He had never liked Fleur.

Soon the big strong Alastair was on his feet again. He was sent down to Sussex to Petal's home for blinded soldiers. There his good eye was cleared and the other socket taken care of. Soon he had been fitted with an artificial eye which gave him a quizzical look, but his sense of humour still shone through.

'Come home now, boy,' Jackie said when he went to collect him, 'and stay with me until this war is all over. Then we will go back home together to Australia.'

'No, I don't think so,' replied Alastair. 'I like the army and I think I will apply for non-combatant duties. This is the third time I've been wounded, so I should get a post.'

Jackie slapped him on the back. 'Good on ya, me boyo, don't give in.' But in his lonely heart Jackie was longing for the company of his son but, as usual, he did not complain.

That was how Alastair came to be at the Isle of Man in command of the refugee camp.

When the new Commander came to inspect the camp, Charlotte was standing by her desk in the administration office. The office was, as always, spick and span, for there were always regular checks by the military. To Charlotte this was quite a bore since she never knew just what they would find fault with and it was usually something pretty petty.

Charlotte had grown into a fine little woman. She was still short and sturdy but had lovely rosy cheeks, dark hair and wide sympathetic eyes. She was a little afraid to look in the direction of the new Commander when he arrived at the office surrounded by his staff. Like the last Commander, he was very tall and had a stiff military manner. He wore his peak cap pulled low on his forehead. She knew his name because she had seen it on the inspection list: Captain Alastair Murphy. And he had all those battle decorations . . .

Charlotte stood upright trying not to stare at his face too obviously. She noticed that it was scarred on one side and there was a fixed look about one of his eyes. But there was no doubt about it. Her heart skipped a beat. It was her fine Alastair.

Alastair was being very official, snapping orders to his staff officer and poking at this and that with his cane. As he marched out, he winked his one good eye in her direction. Charlotte, who seldom showed emotion, put her hands over her face and giggled out loud.

That afternoon she got out her battered old bike and rode out towards the cliffs where the military camp was situated. The sun was going down, like a great big orange ball over the sea, and the stormy waves dashed themselves on the granite rocks. Silhouetted against the horizon were the little gun turrets, but all was quiet and peaceful.

She waited patiently, as she knew she had to. The dark clouds had crossed the sky and mixed in with the gold when Alastair came, as she had known he would. He walked smartly, banging his swagger cane against his gaiters, but it was the crunching of the pebbles and the click of the cane that she heard first. She stood up to greet him.

He held her tight. 'Oh, little Charlotte, how great to see you again!'

Let us stand in the shadow of the rock,' whispered Charlotte. 'We are not supposed to come up here.'

Alastair grinned and took off his cap, exposing his poor scarred face to full view. 'You see what a mess they made of me,' he said. 'What do you think the grand Fleur Beauclair would say to that now?'

'Nothing, not if she truly loved you,' said Charlotte wistfully.

Alastair gently reached out and held her chin and kissed her softly on the lips. 'You were always a lovely little girl,' he said, 'but now you are a grand true-thinking woman. Let us be together. We are the discarded ones of this war, the kind they do not want.'

Charlotte snuggled close to him. 'Don't be so bitter. You will like it here. There is little trouble and the countryside is beautiful.'

'Will you help me live again, little Charlotte?' Alastair looked down at her from his great height. There was deep sincerity in that one very blue eye.

'Oh, I pray with all my heart that you will allow me to,' she said.

They walked along the cliff top, talking of the family back home. As it grew dark, he escorted her back to the refugee camp.

As they parted, he kissed her warmly. 'You know, Charlotte, I believe you will change my luck.' With a joyful laugh, he turned and set off for his barracks, swinging his swagger stick as he went.

Soon it became common knowledge in the camp that Charlotte was the commanding officer's woman. She was poked fun at, as fraternization was forbidden, but the refugees' loyalty was such that the camp dwellers kept her secret. And no one would ever openly acknowledge that they knew that Charlotte would cycle out to the Commanding Officer's isolated cottage along the shore, and not return to camp until dawn.

On Sundays Alastair and Charlotte could be seen pony trekking up the big mountain that dominated the island. Both would be dressed in old hand-knitted woollies and be as happy as the day was long. For out of the mess the war had made of their young lives had come true love. They lay in the sweet-smelling heather to tell each other of their thoughts and dreams. This was the secret island, the very place to dream. It was as if for them life stood still on this windswept island in the middle of the Irish Sea.

The great subject they had in common was their love of horses. He spoke of Australia and horses on the farm where he had been brought up, and of the grand horses his grandmother had bred there. After the war, he told her, he planned to buy some good stock from Ireland and take them back to Australia where they were short of good racehorses.

Charlotte would listen silently and a little wistfully. For when the war was over she had nothing and nobody. As far as she knew now, both her parents were dead and there was no place or country she could call home.

Alastair would see the tears in her eyes. He cuddled her close. 'When I take you home to Australia, I can just see how Grandma will learn to love you as I have.'

'Don't say it if you do not mean it, will you, Alastair?'

'Silly little Charlotte, of course I mean it. We will get married as soon as this lot is over and I'll take you home to the greatest land there ever was, and to Inchalee, the farm that my Grandma pioneered all alone. Now she owns the whole of the lovely green valley.'

'Will they let you marry me?' she asked. 'You know we are not supposed to associate because I am German-born.'

'Oh, that is all nonsense. When the war is over, everyone forgets.'

Lightly he dismissed her worries and together they roamed happily over the island. Love was young and very sweet and together the future held little fear for them.

Daisy still wrote regularly to Charlotte sending her pocket money and telling her all the family news, which she passed on to Alastair. 'Apparently Fleur has had a baby girl,' she said. 'I believe the Browne family were all furious,' she told him.

Suddenly Alastair looked sad.

'Oh,' said Charlotte, 'it was three weeks premature. I thought she married Duncan a bit quickly.' Charlotte added with a puzzled look on her face.

Alastair got up suddenly. His face was set in an angry expression. 'Shall we walk? I don't care to listen to family gossip.'

'Sorry, love,' Charlotte said. She had never seen him so disturbed but her sunny nature did not allow her to dwell on it. 'I can't help being bitchy,' she said. 'I hate Fleur and Fleur hates me.'

There was no comment from Alastair.

That night when she slept at his billet Alastair was excited. 'Come, little Charlotte, let us make a baby, a fine son to take home to Australia,' he said urgently.

'I will do anything for you, darling,' replied Charlotte, 'but do not let us spoil what we have, not until the war is over and we are safe.'

'Little one, you are always safe with me,' Alastair said, hugging Charlotte very tight.

In the spring it was rumoured that the war was won and by November the camp was celebrating the Armistice – soldiers and officers, refugees and staff all cavorted about the huge bonfire in a great celebration.

The lovers walked along the beach drunk and happy. Charlotte looked up at the bright star-studded sky. 'I shall miss you, my lovely island,' she said to the darkness.

Alastair mumbled drunkenly, 'Not when you have seen Australia, my love.'

30

Dolly

The excitement of the Armistice, the victory parades and peace parties kept Daisy very busy that year. She was still very active and not hardly showing her age. Her hair was still red and her figure good but often she was a little breathless and red-cheeked especially when in a temper.

Jackie had pleaded with her once more to come back to Australia with him now that the war was definitely over.

'How can I? I've too many commitments,' said Daisy. 'And I need to get my compensation from the government.'

'It will come, even if you are not here,' urged Jackie. 'Get an estate manager, he will do all the work.'

'Not on your nelly,' insisted Daisy. 'They're all rogues. Besides, what about our little girls, poor darlings? That silly Vanessa don't want them, lost another husband, she has, and now she is hanging on to her sick old mother up north.'

'It's not your responsibility, Daisy,' urged Jackie. 'The girls are old enough to go away to boarding school.'

'Oh no, they won't,' declared Daisy. 'I have got them a nanny. She seems a pretty nice gel. She's from some foreign island, but I understand she speaks very good English.'

Jackie sighed and retreated behind his newspaper. Daisy began to open her correspondence and forgot that Jackie was there.

'Well, I'll be buggered!' she exclaimed. 'It seems that our Charlotte has made off with your Alastair. They're gone on a cargo boat back to Australia.'

'I know,' said Jackie quietly, from behind his newspaper.

'Why didn't you tell me?' demanded Daisy irritably.

'Because you never listen to me, Daisy.'

'Don't listen? what do you mean?' she said querulously. 'I am by no means deaf so if you want to tell me anything just get on with it. Don't mutter and mumble apologetically.' Now she was getting aggressive. '*That* is when I don't listen.'

Jackie shot her a hurt look and deliberately folded his newspaper. 'I'm going for a walk in the park,' he said.

But as always, Daisy did not answer, for she was busy reading a thank-you letter from Con Kennedy who was now back home in London again, having buried his brother in Ireland last year. This was the first time she had heard from him.

'I write to thank you for your kindness and generosity to myself and my family,' he wrote. 'I am working on the tramways now and my wife has just had another child. We cannot forget how good you were. My poor brother would have never got back to his native land but for you. I wish to say that if in any way my humble self could return your kindness I'd be grateful to do so. Regards from me and my wife. We wish you well, Con Kennedy.'

Tears came into Daisy's eyes as she read this for while Con had been in Ireland she had visited his poor family in an obscure slum in the East End and taken them a food parcel. The over-crowded dwellings and bad conditions of the roads had been quite shocking. Oscar the butler had driven her there and had been quite concerned for her safety. 'Ma'am, I don't think you should come to this place,' he said.

'Wal, that is for me to decide,' said Daisy as she picked up her flowing skirts and marched down the rambling street. All around seemed to be hundreds of kids playing. Little did Oscar know that she had been born and bred not far from here, that it was here she first met her Jackie.

She stopped at a wide open street door, littered with ragged kids sitting on the step. A pert little girl with a dirty face looked up at her. 'Me Mum's gorn to work and me Da's gorn home to Ireland,' she said. 'Don't know when 'e's comin' back.'

Daisy looked down at this little girl with interest. She was a small child, and thin with sandy-coloured hair and a freckled face. She had large grey eyes and a turned-up nose. Although her voice was quite squeaky, it commanded attention.

'Who are you?' Daisy asked.

'I am Dolly,' the girl squeaked. 'I am ten and these are me brothers and sisters.'

Daisy looked at the bevvy of kids, all with pale faces

and runny noses. 'Oh dear, now this is a nice basket of goodies for your mother,' she said. 'Tell her that Daisy the Duchess brought them.' Then she fiddled in her bag and brought out two sovereigns. 'These are for you to buy something for yourself and your brothers and sisters.'

Dolly screwed up her funny little nose and stared suspiciously at the money. 'I'm not supposed to take money from strangers,' she said, wiping her finger across her wet nose.

Daisy found herself getting cross at Dolly's attitude. 'Are you the eldest, Dolly?' she asked.

''Course I am,' returned Dolly, a little amazed at the question.

'Well, you're responsible for the family in your parents' absence, I take it.'

'Yes,' said Dolly. 'I suppose so.'

'Well, now, you take this basket and these coins upstairs to where you live and put them on the table until your mother comes home.'

With a little sniff but without further argument, Dolly did as she was told.

Daisy watched the girl's thin little legs as they climbed up the bare wooden stairs to the room above where they all obviously lived. She looked kindly at the other children – two little boys and a pretty fair girl. 'Hullo,' she said, but they all got up and fled, leaving the baby yelling his head off.

Down came Dolly and stood with hands on hips calling out to her siblings in a shrill voice: 'Come back, you silly sods! Told yer not ter leave the baby, didn't I?'

The scene had been too overwhelming for Daisy, who turned on her heels and fled.

That had been the only time she had tried to contact that poor family. Now this morning, almost two years since she had seen Con, this letter from Jackie's own kinsman had arrived. She put the letter on the sideboard. 'I'll discuss it with Jackie later,' she muttered.

Daisy went off that morning to visit Fleur and her new baby in the newly acquired house in Hyde Park Gate. The white paint and the lack of comfortable furniture always depressed Daisy, who did not think much of Fleur's grand house. Least of all could she tolerate the nursery or the frosty-faced nanny in a navy blue dress who hung over her great-granddaughter and never even let her breathe on her charge. She was a lusty baby with a string of long names. Daisy put a finger out to this strapping babe with red curls, saying: 'Nan is here,' and the three-month-old baby held her finger tight in a strong grip.

The nanny hovered even closer and Daisy drew back. 'Oh wal,' she said. 'I don't suppose I'll get very close to her anyway.'

Fleur sighed and the nurse lifted up the baby and marched off, whereupon the baby let out a loud yell having taken a fancy to Great-grandma's brightly coloured hat.

'Got a good pair of lungs,' said Daisy with a wide grin.

Fleur looked rather pale and severe looking. She had changed a lot since she married. 'Oh, come,

Grandmama, let us go to lunch. I have a lot to talk to you about.'

At the impeccable lunch serve in the luxurious dining room, they relaxed a little. 'Have you heard the latest family news, Grandma?' asked Fleur.

'No,' said Daisy somewhat surprised. 'What have I been missing?'

'Well, you know that Duncan's job in the Home Office means that he handles most problems to do with refugees. He recently had a letter from Alastair.' The name was almost spat out.

Daisy raised her eyebrows and waited for what was to come. She knew her granddaughter very well.

'He had had the audacity to ask Duncan if he could help him get Charlotte free from that internment camp so they could get married. He has resigned his commission and wants to go back to Australia.' Fleur's lips twisted sarcastically and there was a hard look in her sky-blue eyes.

'Marry who?' Daisy squinted back at Fleur. Even though she did know this piece of news, she thought it better to keep quiet.

'That fast little German bitch that you fostered,' replied Fleur angrily.

'Well, now, that is good news,' cried Daisy looking delighted. 'Why wasn't I told?'

'I am telling you now!' declared Fleur impatiently.

'Where is the letter?' asked Daisy.

'The letter is Government property by right. Duncan should not really divulge the information but as it was a family matter he consulted me.'

'Wal! What is the problem?' enquired Daisy.

Fleur strode up and down the room like a restless cat. 'I am the problem,' she exclaimed. 'I have told him in no way will I consent to him helping either of them.'

'But why?' asked Daisy. She was astonished by Fleur's attitude.

Fleur snarled like a small dog, her eyes blazing. 'Because I hate the smarmy Jew bitch,' she cried with venom in her voice.

'Wal! I never knew you felt as badly as that about her,' replied Daisy. 'You had your squabbles as girls but that was only natural.'

'I hate her,' said Fleur, stamping her foot like a spoilt schoolgirl. 'And in no way will Duncan help her or Alastair. Not if I can prevent it.'

'Wal, that is very nice, I must say,' said Daisy. 'You are going up in the world, Fleur, and it would be a pity if you left friends and family behind, because that is what your attitude will bring you. I am going home. I can't say I feel very welcome here anyway.'

31

The Nanny

Like the rest of the Allies, Guernsey had celebrated the Armistice and the whole town had gone wild. Soon the survivors began to return from the prison camps and hospitals.

Rachel was a sad woman. Fred would come back no more. Everywhere Rachel went she carried in her pocket the fatal telegram which stated: 'Fred Smith. Missing, believed killed. France 1916.' For two long years she had waited for the sight and sound of that lively voice but now she knew she had to face it. Hers was to be a lonely life.

The Charterers of the Island had built a huge memorial in the square and as the sun shone over the sea she could see the name of Fred Smith outlined in fresh gold letters and she would point it out to young Cedric. 'That is your daddy's name,' she would say. 'He was a very brave soldier.'

Cedric was now seven years old and obsessed by the sea. He would go out in the fishing boat with his Uncle Charlie at every opportunity and could always be seen playing down by the harbour. He seemed also to prefer the company of Sally and Charlie to that of his sad mother, who was dressed in black and looked so morose all the time, sitting by the fire waiting for the husband who would never return. So in the ways that children have, Cedric found his own interest and occupation and that was among the fishing boats in St Peter Port harbour.

Rachel was aware of this and said one day, 'You know, Sal, Cedric does not seem to need me.'

'Nonsense!' declared Sally. 'He is just a happy lad who loves to be down by the boats.'

'Would you take care of him if I went away?'

'Where are you thinking of going?' asked the buxom, wide-eyed Sally.

'I would like to go to England and apply for a post as a nanny. I have always wanted to go into service. If I had not married Fred I would have gone away. I am twenty-five years old and though there is a shortage of men on this island, I doubt if I will marry again anyway.'

Sally consulted Charlie on the matter of the child and agreed. 'I think the best thing she can do is to get away from the island. Of course we will have the lad. He's a fine bonny lad and a born fisherman.'

Before Rachel left, she handed Sally a brown paper parcel. 'I do not want to but I would like you to give this to Cedric when he is old enough to read. Fred was writing a book about his life and kept it very secret. I have never opened this parcel.'

So Fred's journal with the secrets of his true identity was given over to Sally to take care of for Cedric.

Rachel sailed to England dressed in a blue serge suit and a straw boater hat. She looked very sweet standing on the deck of the ship looking back at the island. She had never been away from the island and was very apprehensive but something within her urged her on and in her purse she carried good references to her new employers whose address was Onslow Square. Unknown to Rachel, she was going to the home of her own mother-in-law, the Dowager Duchess Daisy. It was the strange arm of fate which was to draw them both into the same web of family life and which was then eventually to destroy our lovely bright Daisy.

It was a cold spring day in 1919 when Rachel, feeling a little queasy after her rough crossing from the island, got off the boat at Southampton and boarded the train for London.

When she stepped off the train in London, the noise terrified her: the loud rattle of the trams, the clatter on the cobbled station yard of the hoofs of the prancing horses and the crowds of people hurrying off the trains. It seemed like hell on earth to this demure little lady in a blue serge suit who had lived a secluded life on a quiet windswept island. With her heart beating wildly, she stood waiting for the person who was to meet her under the big station clock. As she held her little straw basket with her few belongings in it, her face was white and tense. She looked rooted to the spot until a tall man with a clean-shaven face approached her. He wore a dark suit and a bowler hat. Politely raising his voice, he asked in a exaggeratedly posh voice, 'Pardon me, but are you by any chance Mrs Smith?'

Rachel nodded demurely and looked trustingly up

into the kind eyes of Oscar the butler who had instructions to meet her at the appointed place. 'Yes, I am Rachel Smith,' she replied. 'You must be Oscar.'

With a slight bow, Oscar took Rachel's suitcase and, giving her a stiff little smile, he gently held her arm and escorted her to a waiting carriage. His hands were clean and soft; his gait was steady and sedate.

Rachel had never seen a real English butler and she was most impressed with this one.

'Onslow Square,' Oscar told the cabby. He helped Rachel in and he sat facing her in a stiff manner. Rachel felt quite awkward and decided to try and make conversation.

'Do you think I will like London?' she asked.

Oscar smiled his little smile again. It was less of a smile than a tightening of the mouth. 'I am quite sure you will,' he said. 'And you will certainly like Onslow Square. It is a very nice well-run house and, providing you are a good clean worker, you will do very well there.'

Oscar's open answer made Rachel feel a little less nervous than she had before.

Soon they reached the door of the house. When they alighted and entered the wide hall, the housekeeper, Mrs Morgan, greeted her. She was a fat motherly lady in a black dress. 'We will have some tea, m'dear,' she said. She had a strong Welsh accent. 'Then I will take you to meet your charges. Her Ladyship is away at the moment but she will probably see you tomorrow.'

After tea in the servants' quarters, Rachel was taken

to meet the children. They were two little blonde-haired girls neatly dressed in starched white frocks. They stared at Rachel with some apprehension but Rachel put out her hand and smiled sweetly as she said: 'Hullo, my dears.'

The little girls immediately smiled back. Soon they were skipping and prancing around her: 'Oh, my, you are pretty and you are not old,' said Deirdre. 'We were thinking you would be so old,' chimed in Emily.

That night they sat beside the warm nursery fire. The girls were dressed in their little flowered night dresses while Rachel cuddled them and told them a story about the fairies of the island of Sarnia, whence she came. With the warm glow of the fire on her cheek and the girls leaning against her breast, Rachel knew that she had found her place on earth.

In the morning she walked with the girls in the Square. It was one of those delightful London squares usually surrounded by iron railings and lots of little flower beds of daffodils and tulips. The railings had been removed during the war when iron had been in such short supply but the flowers were still there. Deirdre held Rachel's hand in a tight grip, while Emily skipped along in front of them, coming back every now and then to converse.

'Our Mama has gone up north to see her Mama, our grandmother,' she stated. 'We have not got a Papa because he got killed in the war.'

Rachel was now smartly dressed in her nanny's uniform – a grey dress, a little grey bonnet, and long grey cape. She bent down to tidy her charge's bonnet strings and kissed her on the cheek. 'Yes, darling, I also lost my Papa in the war.'

Emily put on a very grown-up face as she informed Rachel about the household in Onslow Square. 'And of course we live with our other grandmama. She loves to ride in Rotten Row.'

Rachel looked uneasy. She did not know whether to correct the child or not. She did not have the faintest idea what Rotten Row was or if the child was being rude. In the end she let it pass for she was determined to get on with these children and make them love her. Since the loss of her husband Fred she had felt empty inside. She also felt starved of affection from her son Cedric, who had always been with Charlie and Sally and who seemed naturally to prefer to be with Charlie, who was like a father to him.

Rachel hoped for nothing more than to be needed.

The next day she met Daisy, the Dowager Duchess, her employer.

In the morning a large red-haired woman burst into the nursery, picked up the girls and hugged them vigorously before handing them huge boxes of sweets. Then she turned and looked at Rachel with her shrewd eyes. A wealth of red hair was elaborately curled under a huge hat loaded with artificial fruit and flowers.

'Well, now,' Daisy said, looking the new nanny up and down. 'You're Rachel. Sit down, gel, don't stand on ceremony with me. I hear you're from some God-forsaken island. Well, that don't matter, I come from a God-forsaken country myself.'

Rachel's lips curled into a smile. She could hardly believe her ears.

Daisy sat down on a low nursery chair and the children climbed on to her ample lap. She kissed and cuddled them until her splendid hat was knocked sideways. Her wide mouth let out huge guffaws of laughter as she played. 'Now, you look after these babies, my gel,' she said, 'because they are all I've got left. Two fine sons I have lost already and the third spends most of his time shut away in a monastery. So these babies are all I've got to live for.

'You take no notice of no one else, gel, and if you've got anything to say, you come to me.'

Daisy put the girls down and, with some difficulty, hauled her shape from the low seat. Brushing down her rich velvet skirt, she said: 'I'll say goodbye then, I'm off, I have an engagement to keep but I'll see you again.' Kissing the girls on the forehead, she swept out of the nursery.

Rachel was slightly alarmed by Daisy's vibrant manner. She asked Mrs Morgan about her. 'Is she the mistress of the house?' Rachel asked.

'Bless you, no!' chuckled Mrs Morgan. 'No, that is the Dowager Duchess, her mother-in-law. The real Duchess is Lady Vanessa. She is never here but a sweeter, kinder lady you could not wish to meet. She has lost two husbands now fighting for their country, poor thing, and she is currently nursing her mother who is very sick. She is a lovely lady and we are all very fond of her. But the dowager . . .' Mrs Morgan picked up the china teapot to pour the tea and clicked her tongue contemptuously. 'She and that socialite daughter of hers, Petal, they, my dear, blows in with the wind, as you might say.'

This was all very puzzling to Rachel. For, despite remarks like that, she got the impression that the household was fond of Daisy, though no one took much notice of her. They were certainly strange people, these English. There was Daisy with all her elaborate finery, yet Mrs Morgan, the housekeeper, obviously felt she was superior to the Dowager. It was most odd.

Rachel became very happy at Onslow Square. She loved being with the children and adapted herself in this fine house and slowly from her mind receded the sad memories of Fred Smith and little Cedric far across the sea.

Amid the luxury and splendour of the great house in Onslow Square, Rachel clung to her charges. Their governess taught them lessons in the little schoolroom. They also had riding lessons in the park and tutors for dancing and deportment. Rachel's was a busy life but a lonely one too. For when the children were tucked up in bed and the winter gales howled around the chimney stacks, Rachel sat in her little attic room feeling very homesick for the people she had left behind. Every day she wrote long letters home to Guernsey, to Sally and Charlie and to her darling little boy, Cedric.

Meanwhile the hectic social life of London went on as life recovered from the Great War. The noise of the hansom cabs rattling around the Square taking people to the theatres and to parties was constant, and Rachel would read the society magazines which often portrayed the Dowager Daisy in a splendid costume chatting to the Prince of Wales at Ascot, for Daisy was still a fanatical racegoer. Rachel would also read about her at the huge banquets presided over by the Princess Alexandra and attended by ladies dressed in fabulous gowns.

It did not take too long for her to discover that she was not the only lonely person who lived in that house. There was a demure old gentleman with snow-white hair and a youngish face and bright blue eyes. He was always neatly dressed and he seemed to creep silently about the house and was always alone. It did not take long to discover from the other servants that this was Jack Murphy. Jackie, the man who gambled success-fully on the stock exchange and made pots of money which the illustrious Daisy spent. Jackie seemed not to fit into the high society life. He was always there await-ing Daisy's pleasure and when all high society became a tedious bore for her, Daisy would always creep back home to her Jackie, to find safety and security in those strong loving arms.

One evening Rachel was feeling particularly lonely and she decided to go down to the library to pour herself a glass of sherry from the decanter. As she entered the room, she soon discovered that she was not alone, for there was Jackie in a deep armchair with a bottle of brandy beside him.

'Oh, I beg your pardon,' Rachel began to back out of the room.

'That's all right, Nanny,' he said. 'Come and join me in a drink. There's no one in the house, so I am afraid that you and I are alone.'

So began the friendship of Rachel and Jackie, who met secretly in the library and often walked together in the park. When they spoke together it was of their own particular place where they had each lived, where their roots were the deepest.

Rachel spoke of Grand Rock, the huge rugged yellow rock which pushed out to sea from a little bay at Coba where she had been born. She spoke of the grandeur of the scenery as the heavy seas beat against the great rock and washed its feet, and of the silvery shine as the granite gleamed in the sunset. She spoke of the white sandy beach at evening tide, and the beauty of seeing the sun go down over her misty island.

Jackie in turn would gently hold her hand and tell of the high blue peaks of the mountains in Western Australia, and of the fine opals he had dug deep in the earth to find. He told her of having lived underground in a tunnel because the heat of the sun up on the land in the daytime was so unbearable. He told her of the deep silent bush where he had travelled from day to day without the sight of another human soul, and he described the bush, that rolling country of endless space.

Rachel would sit and listen silently as Jackie's blue eyes shone with boyish light remembering his youth. One day she asked a question she had wanted to ask him for a long time 'Why do you spend so much time in the house?'

Jackie replied immediately. 'There's nought outside that appeals to me,' he said.

'But the Dowager Duchess,' Rachel stammered. 'Are you parted? She is never home.'

'No, Rachel,' Jackie shook his head. 'We have never parted because we never married. Since Daisy lost her boys, she has had some sort of personality change. I have never been able to keep up with her in the social whirl out there, so I sit here and wait for the day when she will come and say, "Come on, let's go home to Australia." '

'You love her very much, then?' queried Rachel.

'Well, you could say that I've loved her all of my life but I just don't fit in with this London scene. This house isn't even ours. We just live here because it belongs to the family. But it's not my family,' he added, a little bitterly.

So Rachel became Jackie's friend. He took her on day trips on her days off to see the Tower of London and St Pauls Cathedral, and when she walked in the park with the girls, Jackie would always join them. In this way they established an affectionate relationship which was a secret to everyone else in that big house. And, although it was innocent, they both knew it could become much more serious if they were not careful.

Jackie began to get nervous and again approached Daisy about leaving. 'Let's go home, Daisy,' he said. 'You are not really happy here. You drink and gad about too much. We are both reaching an age when we should take life a bit more easily.'

Daisy scoffed. 'Don't be a fool,' she said. 'You might

be getting old but *I'm* not. And I don't intend to let myself go either. There's no way that you are going to get me back to that bloody outback.'

'Well, Daisy,' returned Jackie. 'I have warned you that you are overdoing it.'

Daisy began to weep. 'I have lost two fine sons,' she sobbed, 'and the third one is a priest. I will not leave my lovely grandchildren. It's here I belong and it's here I'm going to stay.'

'Oh, be sensible, Daisy,' said Jackie, trying desperately to be firm. 'Now, would it help if you and I married? Would you settle down then?'

'Now don't you be so daft!' snapped Daisy. 'What do we want to get married for at fifty-five? Why, we would be the laughing stock of society.'

'To hell with bloody society!' said Jackie, losing his temper. He shook his head and stomped out of the room.

A few weeks later, Jackie ostentatiously packed his bags. Daisy laughed at him. 'Oh, Jackie's off to the bloody Outback,' she mocked. 'He will come back,' she said. Then she went off to the Newmarket races.

In her attic room Rachel was also packing her bag, for she had received two weeks' notice from Vanessa, who had suddenly appeared to collect her children and take them up to Scotland, where she was about to remarry. No one needed Rachel any more. For nearly two years she had loved and guarded these girls and now they had gone off with just a friendly wave.

When Jackie first heard the news, he had said: 'Do

not weep, my darling, you can come with me. We will go back to Australia.'

At first Rachel had protested but then he said more. 'Come to Southampton and we will marry before we get on the boat. My mother is old and sick I would like to see her before she leaves this world. I would also like her to see you, for you are my ray of sunshine, my last hope of happiness.'

Jackie was so sweet and kind. Rachel was not sure if she actually loved him, but she had no regrets. She wrote to Sally telling her that she was going to be married again and going to live in Australia. She added a note to ask them to take care of Cedric until a time when she hoped he could come out to join them. That part had not been easy, but she had to burn her boats now.

So in April 1920, Jackie and Rachel stood hand in hand in the Registry Office in Southampton. They were about to bid farewell to England to sail on that three-month voyage to Australia.

Once the gold band was on her finger, Rachel lost her shyness and their love was mutual. She was no longer the timid nymph that Jackie had married but a nice-looking young woman whose silver-haired husband seemed to dote on her.

Three months later, the travel-weary couple arrived in Sydney to be greeted at the harbour by Jackie's younger brother, Shaun, who sadly informed them that their mother Rita had died the previous week.

Jackie knew that he should not be surprised but he was sad that he had missed seeing his mother by so little time. There were tears on his long dark lashes as Rachel squeezed his hand tightly, feeling his emotion.

As they travelled out to Melbourne and on to Inchalee, Shaun filled his brother in with what had been going on. 'There's a bit of a rumpus up there,' he said. 'It seems that Alastair was sure the farm would be his because he and that German wife of his have worked so hard to make it profitable and taken care of Mother in her old age. But no, she has left everything, lock, stock and barrel to you, Jackie.'

Jackie glanced away sadly. 'Oh, don't worry, Shaun,' he said. 'We will sort out these problems. We do not need the money.'

When the wide mountain range came into view with the softening sun setting behind it Jackie knew that he was well and truly home. There were his beloved rolling hills covered with white sheep. There were the cows lowing in the meadows and the spreading fields of waving golden corn.

'This whole valley is yours, Jackie,' said Shaun. 'Mother bought and had it cultivated. She had always dreamt of owning this valley and true to form, she achieved it.'

Soon they were standing beside Rita's grave. Jackie's eyes filled with tears again when he thought of his mother, that strong resilient woman who had pioneered this wild country in her own right without a man and had become one of the most respected people in the district.

'She was a strong powerful woman, our mother, Shaun,' said Jackie quietly. 'I spent little time with her but always in my mind I was influenced by her. It was here she dug in her roots deep into the earth and it's here I'll dig mine until the day I lie down there beside her.' He turned to his young wife and put his arm around her shoulders. 'This is our home, Rachel, and this I swear. We will settle and take care of our family on the land my pioneer mother worked to make fertile.'

Rachel smiled and rested her head on Jackie's shoulder. She was sorry not to meet Rita, as she had hoped, but she was extremely proud to be part of this brave family. She was a long way from home but she felt certain that she would be very happy here in Australia, particularly once her son Cedric could join her.

32

Con's Story

Daisy knew that Jackie had gone back to Australia because he told her what he was doing. She was not surprised, for she had known for a long time that he had been pining for his old home and had been longing to return. What she did not know was that he had gone there with Rachel, the young nanny.

Everyone else in the house and family seemed to know the truth but no one dared tell Daisy for fear of her reaction.

Daisy had always enjoyed spending and much of the family money had been used up. It concerned her quite a bit but that did not prevent her from fundraising for her charities, as she always had.

One day she visited Fleur in the hope of getting some donations. Daisy had recently become very interested in slum housing and health and would natter about it for hours. Fleur was still very fond of her grandmother but she often found her a little irritating. As she approached her thirties, Fleur had grown very beautiful. Tall and slim, she wore her lovely red golden hair in a chignon at the back of her slim neck. Her face was perfect but it was also extremely hard-looking. She moved gracefully like a gazelle with her

long legs and slim waist. Socially she was the acknowledged hostess of the times. Her husband, Duncan, was
very proud of her and of his two-year-old daughter, a
bonny baby called Camilla.

As Fleur looked at Grandma Daisy lolling in an
easy chair with her red-faced belligerent look, Fleur
sighed and wished that she had the courage to confront
Daisy on the mess she had made of her own life and
the embarrassment she was now to others.

'Grandma,' she said quietly, 'how about going to the
South of France? The weather is marvellous and lots
of older folk are settling out there. I think you would
love it.'

Daisy snorted. 'Where? France! Why, there's been a
bloody war out there. There are millions of graves and
people are starving hungry.'

'No, dear,' said Fleur patiently. 'Not down there,'
she said. 'The South of France is fine and the climate
is very good.'

'Bosh,' cried Daisy. 'Why should I go abroad? I've
got plenty to do here, clearing up the bloody mess the
war made.'

'Darling, there is little for you to do,' suggested
Fleur. 'Times are changing and it is time for you to
take life a little easy.'

'No, thank you,' returned Daisy. 'If I do go anywhere
I'll go and dig that bloody Jackie out of the bush. The
silly fool! He's too old to go tramping about in the
Outback.'

For a moment Fleur thought she ought to say something. But she did not. Instead, she bit her lip and

stared hard at her grandmother. Then she just got up. 'I have a big dinner tonight at the French Embassy,' she said. 'So I had better get some rest.'

'All right, I am going,' replied Daisy, rising slowly from her low seat. 'I know when I'm not welcome.'

She rammed her big hat pin more securely into her hat and flounced out of the house. She felt a little depressed and rather wished that she had not come.

Since Jackie had left, Daisy had moved into the mews flat. The servants, Oscar and Mrs Morgan, had left. The big house stood forlorn and empty, for Daisy was waiting for government funds to restore it to its former glory.

If Daisy wanted to go out anywhere, she ordered a hansom cab. Most wealthy people had these new-fangled cars but Daisy refused to ride in one. 'Good God, take my life in my hands?' she cried, when someone suggested she should get a Daimler and a chauffeur. 'And where do you think I would get the money from? Practically broke, I am, and that Jackie did not leave me a bean.'

A few days later, Daisy was sitting at her desk opening her mail. Most of the letters were bills or begging letters. Suddenly she spotted in a pile the letter from Con Kennedy which had come just before Jackie had left. She had completely forgotten to show it to him. Slowly she reread the letter and in her mind's eye she could see the dreary home and the brood of under-nourished children all in the charge of that perverse little girl Dolly.

She immediately wrote a note to Con Kennedy asking him to come and have tea with her some time soon. Then she continued with her post. There were appointments with the board of guardians who were supposed to care for the poor; the housing trust that was building flats for the poor; and with the voluntary assistants to the hospitals which were full of men still suffering from their war wounds and unable to cope with life.

Daisy felt desperately depressed. It was four years since the war was over, and her life seemed in ruins. Sadly she gazed at Jackie's brandy decanter and suddenly felt tempted to have a very large drink. She felt so alone and miserable. For a moment she hesitated but then she sighed and the urge had left her. But the sadness had not. Daisy lived in the limelight for so many years and now it was gone. It was a cold hard world; nothing would ever be the same any more. Daisy hated change. Perhaps she should go and find her Jackie once more, as she had done when she was young. She realized there and then that without his steadying influence, she was a lost soul.

The following week, Con Kennedy came to see her. He looked very shy with his cap in his hand. 'It is a pleasure to see you again,' said Daisy. 'I am in this pokey little flat waiting for the house to be put back in order. It's not very grand but it is warm and cosy, I suppose. I'll get the girl to bring some tea.'

''Tis foine,' said Con, looking around the walls at

Jackie's pictures of thoroughbreds and admiring the pipe racks. 'How is your husband, ma'am?' he asked.

'Wal, it is a long story, Con,' Daisy said, sitting down and stretching her legs. 'That little bugger went off back to Australia as soon as peace was declared. I've never heard hide nor hair of him since.'

'Oh, I am truly sorry, ma'am,' muttered Con.

'No need,' said Daisy. 'I am thinking of going back to Australia to rout him out! I am fed up with this country. We're going to have a Labour Government, so they tell me. I've been a Liberal all my life, and I don't fancy these Socialist fellows.'

Con smiled a little smile under his big ginger moustache. There was something very appealing about Daisy.

'Wal now,' said Daisy brightly as she poured the tea. 'Have a buttered scone and tell me how you have been these years since I saw you last.'

'As well as can be expected,' he said. 'I have a job and another son but me wife is not in good health. The war years pulled her down, but we are getting by.'

'I went to see your family,' said Daisy. 'It's not far from where I came from myself. I must say it was very run down the place you had. Still there, are you, son?'

'Unfortunately so,' Con sighed. 'But it is so hard to get other accommodation and it is very cheap. So we stay.'

'There is talk about clearing the slums,' said Daisy. 'But it's talk, talk, that's all they do. Look at me, even, poked in this mews flat while I wait for them to put my house back in shape. You would think that after all I did for the war effort they would get on with it. I am a little disillusioned with this country,' said Daisy. 'I am quite serious about clearing out.'

Con nodded sympathetically. 'A working man does not stand a chance. The wages are so low and the whole system seems to be in a muddle. It will come right, I hope.'

'Why don't you go home to Ireland if conditions are so bad here?' asked Daisy.

Con shook his head. 'It's even worse out there. There's no work at all and such troubles.'

'Troubles? What troubles?' Daisy asked. She rarely took an interest outside her own sphere.

'Well, young Ireland is seeking Home Rule and they will not forget the Black and Tans, not this generation nor the ones after that.'

'Black and Tans?' cried Daisy. 'Who or what are they?'

As Con related the story of his return to his home-land, Daisy listened with a mixture of horror and amazement.

When Con took his brother's body back to Ireland for burial, he sailed abroad the little mail boat which battled with the Irish Sea, with his brother's coffin secured in the hold.

Con, as he had told her, was the eldest son of his parents, Eli and David Kennedy. He was devoted to them but he had wanderlust and he had left Ireland to settle in England. Poverty and an early marriage had denied him the opportunity to return home. Now, after ten years, he was sailing back to see his family, to face his mother and return to her the body of her dead son. He would have wished to return in more happy circumstances but he had no choice. Now here he was approaching Cork Harbour where he knew the warmest of welcomes were awaiting him.

Many of them were there – his brothers and cousins and so many faces that Con had forgotten. When the greetings were over, the coffin was carried out on strong shoulders and loaded onto the hearse. Then they rode into the country to Banateer to the cottage beside the mountains where Eli and David awaited the return of their sons. In the small parlour, the coffin was placed on a trestle and covered with the green-and-gold flag of Ireland. The candles were lit and the priest arrived. The wake had begun. People came for miles around across the bogland to Bill's funeral.

Eli knelt throughout the night beside the coffin of her son. In her hands she clutched the white mother-of-pearl rosary which had once belonged to Grandma Foley and had travelled so many miles across the Atlantic and back from an Indian settlement. It was Eli's greatest treasure now as ever.

Eli was now a little thin figure with silver hair. At dawn her sons lifted her gently to her feet. 'Mother,' said Con. 'Take some rest. Bill will be buried at Kanturk today.'

Con had spent the night out in the barn with his brothers and their friends. They lay on the straw and talked of old times. Although Con had been away from

Ireland for ten years, the 'troubles' were not news to him but of late they had become worse.

'We must be ready for an attack,' said Dan. 'They might stay away as we are gathered tonight but knowing those bastards, they probably won't.'

''Tis the Black and Tans they talk of, Con,' explained Dan. ''Tis real bloody terror that we live in. They are all ex-convicts let out from British prison to persecute us in our own land while some of our boys are giving their lives out in France!'

'We hear very little about it back in London,' said Con, 'but I've heard rumours from the lads sometimes.'

His brother Hesty rolled up his trouser leg to reveal a wide red scar. 'Ripped me leg with a bullet, they did. They stood poor old Pa against the wall and shot bullets all around his head, and Maggie was knocked about by them. 'Twas only little Joe who saved her. They let her go when he went after them.'

'Dear God!' exclaimed Con holding his hand to his head. 'I never realized things had got that bad.'

'Ye haven't seen anything yet, me gossoon,' said another man. 'But we are ready for them.' He pushed away the straw to reveal to Con where the pistols were hidden.

With the dawn they were to bury Bill Kennedy. Strong shoulders carried the coffin along the country lanes to the church and all the villagers attended the mass. Then there was a slow procession to the small churchyard, with the priest leading the way to put Bill into the place where he belonged and where his great grandfather and all the family forebears of the Kennedys were laid to rest.

Many tears where shed for young Bill Kennedy. He had been a very popular boy. Some said how foolish he had been to volunteer so young but then so had many other village lads. The spirit of adventure that exists within every Irishman made them answer the call to fight for their country's freedom.

Eli stood with her daughter beside her. Beautiful young Maggie was still in her teens. The two women watched as the Kennedy boys carried the coffin on their broad shoulders.

The sun had risen over the mountain, painting its peak a myriad of colours as the long cortege went slowly down the country road. As they passed each cottage the mourners came out to join the throng. The women carried little posies of their finest flowers and wore their best black shawls draped over their heads. The long mass was held in the village church presided over by the priest who had baptized Bill as a baby. Then in silence the family and friends all stood around the graveside as they interred young soldier Bill into the soft moist land that he had loved.

As they stood with heads bent for that last prayer of farewell, a military lorry came down the road, packed with armed soldiers wearing khaki uniforms with black berets. At the sight of the funeral party they slowed down to watch. An urgent murmur passed around the mourners but suddenly the lorry started up once more and drove by. From the back the soldiers grinned and one put his hand to his lips and made a rude noise.

The faces of the brothers were set with angry expressions as the women knelt to pray for the soul of that dearly loved brother and son.

When it was all over, they went back to the cottage for tea. But tea was for the women; the men needed something stronger.

That night in Sullivan's bar, a discussion was held in whispering voices.

'We will get that bastard,' they said.

'He's a corporal. I know him and where to find him,' said Hesty.

'No! No!' said Danny, the eldest Foley brother. 'They know you too well, Hesty. We will draw lots for it. Two good men will go into town tonight.'

Con had watched amazed as a young boy jumped up and disappeared into the back room. When he returned, he held a bundle of long straws in his hands. Danny locked the bar. 'We will each draw a straw and those two who draw the short straws will be the ones to do it.'

Whiskey glasses were filled and a toast to Ireland was made in Gaelic. Then the straws were passed round. One man held the straws in his hand and the Foley cousin drew his pistol and stood guard beside the ancient bar in the low-ceilinged room smelling of tobacco and booze. There was a respectable silence as the ceremony proceeded.

'Not Con,' someone said. 'He has nought to do with it.'

One by one the men drew the straws. A youth not much past school age drew the first short straw. He gasped and waved his hands around jubilantly, so proud was he to be chosen.

Hesty drew the other short straw. 'Good,' he declared. 'I prayed that it would be mine. Let the lad off the hook. I'll go alone.'

'No,' said one of the big Foley cousins. ''Tis my family, too. I'll be with you, Hesty.'

The youth began to sulk and complain loudly in Gaelic, but the others filled him with whiskey till he shut up and then passed out.

Dan slid back the bolts of the bar door and let other customers enter. A fiddle was produced and a grand sing-song ended the evening as though there was nothing in the air.

Con felt sad and not much like celebrating. He was apprehensive for the rest of the family but soon the drink took its toll and he was walking home with the rest of them singing the old songs.

David and Eli stood by the cottage door to welcome them. Con put his arms around his mother as she hugged him. 'It is good to have you home again, my son, even in such sad circumstances.'

The mountain air and the call of the fresh green land persuaded Con to rise early and take a walk along the winding road along by the river Black Water. There shamrock grew in abundance in the moist meadows, the shimmering dew dripping off its leaves. A cock was crowing.

'The top of the morning to you,' said Con as he passed the big rooster yelling out its red-throated cry into the morning breeze. Con felt his heart lifting. It was good to be home, indeed.

One day soon he would bring the family out here. It would do the children so much good to get away from the dirty old London town. If only he could afford it.

He walked into the village and up the hill to the little church. All was peaceful and the doors of the church were wide open. Stepping into the shadowy porchway he saw Hesty kneeling in the front pew near the altar. His head was bowed in prayer. Tears rolled uncontrollably down his cheeks to fall on his mud-spattered and blood-stained clothes.

Without a word Con knelt beside him. Sorrow surrounded them, and there was silence as they looked up at the suffering face of Our Lord on the cross above them.

Hesty leaned over towards Con and whispered in a low voice: 'Do not hang about, don't wait here, Con. Just go home. Tell the family that the deed is done.'

Con felt as if the grey goose had walked over his grave. He shivered at the thought of murder being done.

Hesty raised his tear-stained face towards him. He looked anguished. 'Go, Con, I am waiting for Dan,' he said. 'We will go out over the mountains to join the corps so that they will not disturb the old folks. Goodbye and God bless.'

There was a noise from the vestry and the old priest waddled out in his robes to prepare the altar. Then the church bell began to ring. 'Go, Con,' urged Hesty. 'Danny's here. Pray God we meet again. God bless.'

He rose and walked weakly towards a small door at the side of the altar. As he went Con noticed that his hands were stained with blood.

Con stayed for the mass, which was attended by a few women and farm workers. When it was over and they came out of the church, a military lorry was at the door. As Con came out, a soldier stepped out in front of him holding him back with the butt of his rifle. 'Who are you?' he demanded.

'A visitor from England,' Con said quietly.

The soldier scrutinized him suspiciously and then went on inside the church to search for the two Kennedys. By now Dan and Hesty were well on their way to safety in the hills where their forefathers and cousins had sought refuge in the past and where their children would seek refuge in the future.

As Con walked back to his parents' home, all the small doors of the cottages opened. Folk were sitting out or standing about gossiping or waiting anxiously to see what the Black and Tans were about to do in retaliation for the murder of one of their kind. There was real fear in the air. Everyone had their eyes fixed on Con as he walked past and on the armed soldiers parading through the small village street.

No one cared for the British soldier who had been killed the night before. 'That's one bloody bastard less to worry us,' said one old man, splitting his chewing tobacco out on to the ground.

Full of sad thoughts, Con continued home in silence to Eli and David, who waited together outside their cottage. Roses entwined the doorway and the path was edged with summer flowers. Red roses also hemmed the little wooden porch where Eli and David, now old and grey, sat holding hands on a bench outside the front door. Eli was still clutching her rosary beads and the red-bearded David sat beside her in grim silence.

His buxom sister Maggie came out to greet him, her face red and tear-strained. 'They have been here, Con,' she whispered. 'But I handled them,' she added defiantly. 'They are now on their way out to Danny's farm.'

''Tis all clear, me darling,' said Con, embracing his young sister. 'I saw Hesty in the church. He and Danny are with the Foley boys and off to join the corps.'

'Oh dear,' sighed Maggie. 'Where will it all end?'

'God only knows,' said Con, 'but I have changed my mind about England since I've been home. Perhaps my family and I should all be over here.'

'Ah, don't be daft, Con,' said Maggie. 'You have a home and a family and a peaceful existence there. Thank God for that. Now it would be best if you and Joe left early tomorrow. The Black and Tans will leave the old folk in peace if they know there are no boys here.'

'Where is Joe?' asked Con.

'I made him hide out in the bog. He has overstayed his leave so I want you to make sure he goes back to the Navy. Otherwise he will land in trouble.'

At dusk Joe came home very drunk. He had been visiting old companions who had been very hospitable. He wore a blue jersey and a pair of old grey patched flannel pants, both of which were dusty and rumpled. His mop of red gold hair stuck out untidly on his head.

'Dear God,' said Eli. ''Tis a fine sight for Sunday evening. Go get cleaned up and back to the Navy, Joe.'

'No' goin',' slurred Joe. 'Bugger them Black and Tan bastards. Why should I fight for them?'

David's slow voice growled. 'Two wrongs don't make one right, my boy. You volunteered. Go home with Con and make your peace with the authorities.'

'Don't be a fool, Joe,' declared Maggie. 'They will come here and get you. Once you are named as a deserter that will still bring more trouble for Ma and Pa.'

Joe peered at them through bleary eyes. 'Well, I'm off to bed, first,' he said. 'I'll think about it tomorrow.'

The next morning, Con awoke to the sound of the blackbird and the hens clucking as Maggie threw corn to them out in the yard. A delicious smell of baking bread wafted up from the kitchen where Eli was busy preparing breakfast. Con dressed and eagerly went down to tuck in to that good breakfast of eggs and potato cake.

Elie was quiet and said little. She looked sad. Joe's sailor uniform, freshly pressed by Maggie, was hanging on the kitchen line.

Con's father, David, had gone down to the end of the meadow to feed the pigs. It was like an ordinary day. The whole domestic routine was followed as usual even though hearts had been broken and a family split.

'Now, Maggie,' said Eli. 'Rouse young Joe and make

him dress. He will leave with Con who will take good care of him.'

At last, with Joe freshly dressed in his clean uniform and Con with a bag of presents from Eli to the grandchildren, the two brothers set off down the road to walk the three miles to the railway station.

As they left, Con looked back at his parents waving from the cottage door and Maggie who raced down the path. His heart felt heavy. Something deep inside told him that he would never see them again. His chest tightened with concern for them and a powerful hatred for their persecutors.

Con and Joe reached Cork at midday. Their instructions were to go to the Woods' house in the coal quay until the boat for England sailed that evening.

Poor Mary Wood was now crippled with arthritis and did not leave her home any more but she was well taken care of by her unmarried daughters, Bluebell and Marion. They all made a great fuss of Con and Joe. A grand meal was laid on with good food and whiskey. Neighbours popped in and out but all the talk was about the troubles.

''T'will die down,' said Mary, still hale enough to voice her opinions. 'It's true we have been promised Home Rule when the war is over, and all my life there have been troubles. It's possible to live with it, if you keep your head down.'

'No, no,' declared Marion. 'We will have to fight! Much more blood will be shed before England lets go of Ireland.'

'Be Jasus,' cried Mary. 'I've a couple of rebellious

ones in me own family and their father was an English sergeant who gave his life for England.'

They all laughed and then the argument hotted up. Joe got up and said, 'I'll go around the corner for a drink.'

'Now Joe, I warn ye,' said Mary. 'In that uniform you might get trouble. It's very hot around here.'

'Oh, we can handle ourselves,' boasted Joe, putting his round sailor cap on his head. Con was reluctant to leave the women but he also felt that he must keep an eye on his brother, so he went with him to a seedy bar at the corner of the next street. It was full of working-class men – labourers from the coal yard and men from the bacon factory. As they entered, the jumble of conversation stopped.

'Evening to ye,' Con said politely but there was no response. The Kennedy brothers were strangers to the district and one was in a British uniform, so they were immediately viewed with suspicion.

Ignoring the atmosphere, Con and Joe had a few beers and talked of home affairs. But suddenly a big fellow pushed a fist into Joe's face. 'Get out of my way, you English bastard!' he shouted.

Quick-tempered Joe was at him in a flash. 'No man calls me a bastard!' he yelled.

The men grabbed each other by the throat and fought their way around the crowded bar. Joe lost his footing and went down and Con went to his aid. By then a crowd of tough men had joined in the fracas. The whole bar was in an uproar. Bottles and glasses flew about the room as everyone took sides.

Soon the soldiers appeared with rifles at the ready, only minutes before the Irish Constabulary in their red coats, who were no more popular then the English. The fight spread out into the street. Women joined in, screeching and throwing things, while children ran wildly among the fighting bodies as if it were a grand game. A flying bottle hit Con on the head and knocked him out.

Con woke up to find himself in the police cell. He was unable to remember what had happened or why he was there. There was no sign of Joe. 'Where's me brother?' he yelled through the bars.

One of the fellows in the cell with him shouted that the Red Caps had marched him off early that morning.

Oh dear, thought Con. Now Joe would be in real trouble with the Navy. And here was he stuck in a Cork police cell with two rebels who made no secret of their attitudes towards the British soldiers. One of the men was called Tommy Raleigh, an old timer who had survived the first rising. The other was a young lad called Mickey who was well versed with the rebel ways.

'They will let you go, Con,' Tommy told him. 'They can't hold you for long, they got nothing on you. They will soon find the truth about you coming to bury your brother, but they might keep you here for a bit. That's the way they have of showing who's boss in this country.'

'Ah, 'tis sure a distressed country. They are hanging men and women for the wearing o' the green.' That last sentence he sang in a strong clear voice.

'Shut up!' yelled the guard, banging on the door with the butt of his gun.

The men drew together closer and spoke on in whispers. 'We will be whisked off to Dublin jail shortly,' Tommy said.

''Tis plenty pals we have in there,' grinned Mickey.

'We need good men in England, Con, the fight is only just beginning. If we don't get freedom for our land when the war is finished, there are a lot of boys ready to fight for our cause.'

'Yes, so I heard,' said Con. 'But surely we don't want a civil war? Has not poor Ireland suffered enough? First the famine, then the mass emigration and now the Black and Tans?'

'Well, now's the time to end it all. England is low, she will come to terms.'

'I would not be so sure of that,' replied Con. 'I have lived there for ten years. It seems that the working man has nought to say or do with politics.'

'Oh, he will,' said Tommy confidently. 'We have some good leaders locked away in jail. Their time will soon come.'

The next day Tommy and Mickey were marched out singing, 'God bless Ireland'.

As they did so, the rest of the prisoners banged on their cell doors, raising hell, and yelling and cursing the Black and Tans.

Con was soon marched to the magistrate's court. As he sat in the dock, he could see Marion and Bluebell sitting in the gallery with very determined looks on their faces. They watched anxiously for the solicitor they had retained to do his job.

The solicitor stated that Con had left Ireland ten years ago and was just on a visit to bury his soldier brother. He pleaded for Con to be released to join his family left at home in England.

'The prisoner is a rebel,' said the Army officer prosecuting.

Bluebell could not contain herself. She leaped to her feet. 'Rebel!' she cried. 'In his own country? In these days we are born rebels while you tread us down!'

'Silence!' the judge shouted, banging his hammer on the bench. 'The defendant broke the peace. I sentence you to a twenty-pound fine or two months in jail.'

Marion paid the fine and she and her sister accompanied Con to the quayside to board a boat for home.

As the boat drew away from the dock, Con stood on deck looking back at the two sisters standing on the quayside. For all the horrors of Ireland, he was blessed with a loyal and steadfast family. For that, at least, he would be eternally grateful, he told Daisy as he drank his tea.

Daisy looked sad. 'Yes, family is the most important thing in the world,' she said as tears crept into her eyes. 'You have had a rough time but your family has looked after its members with such love.' She sighed heavily. 'Perhaps,' she said, reaching for a handkerchief, 'perhaps I have not valued my family quite enough. Or perhaps I have not shown what I really felt deep down enough to let them all know. I feel so lonely now. My Jackie has gone back to Australia, and I really do love him. I always have. I think I just took him for granted and he got fed up. Who can blame him? I feel estranged from my children, who have either left me or else grown to hate me. Even my own granddaughter despises me.'

Daisy's self-pity had taken over. Sensitive Con moved over to sit next to her and he put an arm around her. 'I think you should go back to Australia and find that old rogue Jackie again. He's a Kennedy, after all, so he can't be all bad,' he added, trying to sound jovial.

Daisy blew her nose noisily. 'Yes,' she said, 'I'm sure you're right. I shall plan to pack up things here in London and find my darling once again. It should not be so difficult this time around.

Con returned to his little slum street that evening feeling very thoughtful. As usual, his wife, Bernadette, gave him a hard time when he came in the door. She always accused him of loafing around and not helping enough. She had so many children that she could hardly cope, for Con did not help very much. Looking after children was for women. Bernadette was of Irish extraction but she was not fiercely patriotic. Her concerns were more personal. 'While children went hungry here,' she argued, 'the Irish were sheltering German submarines which sank our food ships. They're traitors, every bloody one of them,' she shouted one day, 'so don't you talk to me, Con Kennedy, about the poor afflicted Irish.'

As Bernadette yelled at him that evening, he felt sad. He noticed that his wife was losing her looks fast.

Her golden hair was fading and her teeth were beginning to decay. He barely listened to her haranguing. After a while, he quietly left to sit in the pub on the corner of the street where the locals returning from the war celebrated their freedom.

As her parents quarrelled, Dolly would sit and watch them with a pained look on her small round face. Would life ever get any better, she wondered. Or was she destined to live in such poverty and terrible conditions that no one could help be anything but bad-tempered? No, she decided, one day, she was going to get herself away from this way of life, and she knew that education and training was the only way to do it.

The problem was that Dolly did not like school one bit. She was always late, because she had to get the other kids to their school first, and she was never too clean. Every day she would find herself in trouble with one of the teachers because she had 'undertaker's nails', they said. The fact was that her nails contained black lead which she used to polish the grate after setting the fire, before going to school each morning. She would be forced by cruel Miss Paterson to stand beside the blackboard to hold up her hands and display all her dirty black nails to the rest of the class. The other children often, of course, laughed. But Dolly did not care. She just got her own back by making faces at the teacher behind her back and making the rest of the kids laugh. Then, as soon as break came, Dolly was off, just like a young pony set loose in the paddock, straight to old Mr Gregory's book shop.

Mr Gregory was an old man with bushy side whiskers. 'Wotcha cock, d'yer want a comic?' he would say, and sometimes he would hand her a second-hand book. ''Ere y'are, Doll,' he said. 'You 'ave this one. Nobody arahnd 'ere'll wanna read it.'

That kindly old man was Dolly's best friend in those early years. Clutching her precious book she would go back to the yard and sit amidst the coster barrows to read until her brothers and sisters came out of school.

Her mother irritated Dolly with her moaning and groaning but her dad was her hero. Everywhere he went, Dolly went too, if she could. She followed him to the big charity affairs in the West End, at King's Hall, where they collected money for the Sinn Fein movement and stood up and shouted: 'God save Ireland and God bless the Pope!'

Dolly did wonder why they never sang 'God save the King', as they did at school, but still she went along with it all and thoroughly enjoyed herself. Into all the Irish houses they went, Con to sit and drink with his compatriots, and Dolly would often kip down on sofas in strange houses if Dad had had too much to drink.

Whatever happened, Dolly was happy in her little faded cotton frock, wiping her runny nose on her bare arm. She was always there by Con's side ignored by the adults who were immersed in their seditious talk. But her bright little eyes and sharp ears took every bit of it in.

'You'll wear that child out traipsing about all the night with her,' Bernadette would say wearily.

'Now, now, leave Dolly be,' replied Con. 'She will come to no harm with me. You, Bernadette, 'tis you who should come visiting with me, but you are obstinate.'

'I go to work hard all the week,' Bernadette replied. 'I need rest at the weekend in my own home.' And so it was that they drifted further and further apart.

A crisis came when Con's younger brother, Joe Kennedy, came to live with them. He had just finished his term in the punishment cells and been released. He had no good references and, aged twenty-five, he was out of work, an embittered young man lounging on the street corner with the other out-of-work lads.

Out of his meagre wage from working on the trams, Con took care of his young brother while still sending five shillings regularly from his wages to his old folk back in Ireland.

It was Dolly's job to send this money as a postal order from the Post Office. She would seal it in the envelope and post it off to Ireland on behalf of her dear Daddy, who could do not wrong in her eyes. It had to be kept a dark secret from her mother, who disapproved of Con spending money on anyone except his own children. The arrival of Joe was the last straw for her. Whenever Joe was out, she would attack Con about the situation. 'How can we have another mouth to feed when we have hardly got enough food for our own family?' she would shout and stamp her feet.

Con would shake his head sadly. 'Joe is family,' he would reply. 'We must look after family when they are in trouble or not.' And that would be that, for Con was master in his own house.

What Con did not know was that his family was in even more trouble than he realised. Back home in Ireland, his mother Eli was lying dangerously ill from the terrible influenza that had been sweeping across Europe for the past few weeks.

The tiny cottage in Bannateer was still and quiet. Eli lay on the lumpy sofa in front of a fire which David kept stoking at regular intervals. Eli felt hot and she constantly threw off the blankets which David had placed over her, but her whole body shivered as though she were cold. Every now and then, David gently wiped the sweat from her brow with a damp cloth.

Eli was wheezing and finding it difficult to breathe. Her limbs ached and her head throbbed constantly. She felt like death and she knew that the chances were that she would not recover from this illness which had taken away her beloved daughter Maggie only a few days before. The night of Maggie's wake, Eli had felt the grip of this terrible influenza, too. Theirs was not the only family to be hit by the flu; there had been wakes in the neighbourhood every week for a month as normally fit young people were struck down.

Suddenly, Eli cried out. David rushed to her side and took her hand. 'I'm going to die, David,' she whispered. 'I can't hold on. I must see the priest before the end comes. Fetch him for me, my darling, will you?'

Tears were pouring down David's rugged face. In spite of his years he was a handsome man still. For a few moments he could not move. He could not believe that he was going to lose the love of his life.

Seeing him hesitate, Eli shook her head and smiled. 'We've had a good life together, David,' she whispered. Her voice was hoarse and faint. 'Remember America. Those years were hard but we came back to our beloved Ireland and the Lord brought our daughter Zvia home to us too. He brought us all together in the end . . .' She coughed painfully. 'The Lord will look after me and you now, too. We will be together again one day. We must accept His wishes.'

David lent over and kissed his wife gently on the forehead. 'I pray that you are wrong,' he said. 'I cannot bear the thought of ever losing you.' With that, he turned on his heels and went off to fetch the priest.

He returned with Father Patrick within half an hour. To his relief, Eli was still alive but very weak. Father Patrick stood over her and took her hand.

By the time the sun had gone down on that cold and hostile day, his darling Eli, with whom he had travelled so far, had faded away and died.

When Con heard the sad news from Ireland about his mother and his sister, Maggie, he was devastated. Worse was the fact that there was not enough money for both him and Joe to go home to see to the funeral. Con insisted that Joe must go.

So young Joe went home. Bernadette did not say so, but she was pleased to be free of him. But then a few days after Joe had left, the police came and raided Con's home. It seemed that Joe and some of his comrades had been involved in the escape from prison of the Sinn Fein leader, DeValera.

Dolly watched the police calmly and scornfully, her arms folded as they argued with Dad and pushed their way upstairs. Bernadette was hysterical and the little children crying. Neighbours yelled insults from out of their windows at the police.

The police could find no evidence against Joe, but they left the house in chaos. Bernadette had collapsed and Con looked utterly dejected. Only little Dolly seemed in control. 'Shall I wet the tay, Dad?' she asked.

Con nodded feebly. 'That's right, Dolly, make us a nice cup, there's a good girl.' He smiled, resting his head on his hands in a dejected way.

After that experience, Bernadette seemed to give up the struggle to survive. Her health had never been good and now it collapsed. Tired and grey in the face she seemed, literally, to fade away. An ambulance was called and it took her away to return no more.

Con sometimes took Dolly with him to visit Daisy who was now determined to make her way back to Australia. She would give Dolly sweets for the younger children and usually some little gift for Dolly herself, who stared at her silently and rarely thanked her. Dolly was a strange child, who made Daisy feel quite uncomfortable.

This particular Saturday when Con called with Dolly, they both had some news for each other.

'I'll be off to Australia in a week's time,' Daisy announced.

'I am sorry to hear it, ma'am. Australia is a long way from England, and Ireland.'

'Well, I've decided to set out. I've a pretty good idea where I'll find Jackie. He'll be at his mother's farm, so I am off next week to surprise him,' said Daisy.

'Well, ma'am,' said Con. 'I hope you find happiness once more out there,' said Con. 'I have also made a decision,' he said. 'As you know, my mother and sister recently died and Joe, my brother, fled to America. Now my father, who is losing his sight, has gone to live with my other sister. So the cottage is empty and the land is lying fallow. My sister-in-law suggested that I might like to return back home, take over the cottage and work on the farm with Hesty, who has now been released from Dublin Goal. Now that Bernadette has gone, there's not much here for me so I have begun to think it will be a good idea.'

'I'm not going,' said a voice from a dim corner.

'Now, be quiet, Dolly,' insisted her father. 'What I am doing is for your own good.'

'I am staying here to be a nurse when I am sixteen,' Dolly said, in a determined voice.

'Will you listen to her!' smiled Con. 'She is a big talker and so little a girl.'

'Might not be a bad idea,' returned Daisy. 'It would teach her discipline, I can assure you.'

'What! Me without Dolly?' queried Con. 'Oh no, I could never cope without Dolly. I have found it hard to get by without her mother but Dolly is my ray of sunshine. I can't part with her.'

'Well,' said Daisy, 'I don't think she will go with you, so you might have to give up the idea of Ireland.'

'Oh, whisht, Dolly don't mean what she says,' Con protested.

'Oh, yes I do,' piped up Dolly. 'I am going to be a nurse.'

'Wal,' said Daisy. 'It's a good idea. It's a clean tidy profession and she will have a place to live.'

'Now tell her, Dad,' ordered Dolly.

'Tell me what?' asked Daisy, a little confused.

As her father hesitated, Dolly got to her feet. 'All right, I'll tell her,' she said with a deep sign. She walked over and stood in front of Daisy. 'Well, seeing as you are my dad's good friend and a woman of importance, I asked him to get me a reference from you for my application to be a probationer nurse!'

Daisy smiled. She admired this saucy kid, though she would not admit it. 'You are too cheeky,' she said. 'You will have to learn to keep your place.'

'Oh well,' said Dolly with a shrug. 'Either you do or you don't. I'll find some other way to become a nurse but I won't go to live in Ireland.'

'She's awkward,' said Con apologetically as Dolly stuck her head in one of Daisy's racing books.

'I do admire her,' whispered Daisy. 'So much responsibility has been put on her at too early an age.'

Con looked sad. 'That's partly my fault. I loaded Bernadette with children and she could never cope. She left it all to Dolly.'

'Well, I will tell you what I'll do,' said Daisy going over to her desk. 'I'll write a reference for her and I'll also write to my granddaughter Fleur who is influential on the hospital board. When I go to Australia, I'll hand my chair to her, so when Dolly goes for her interview, Fleur will be there. I'm sure Dolly needs no more than a reference but it won't do any harm to have as much help as possible.'

'I can't thank you enough Daisy,' said Con. 'We have been good friends and I shall miss you.'

'Oh, I shall no doubt be coming back,' laughed Daisy. 'Perhaps I'll come and see you in that lovely old cottage by the Black Water you've told me about. Now, Con, take the opportunity for the sake of the other children and let Dolly alone. She is ready and willing to take on the world.'

The next week Daisy sailed for Australia. As she settled into her first-class cabin, she thought of the family she was leaving behind. She was sad to be leaving Fleur and little Camilla, but she would be back to visit them soon. But she was pleased with her most recent move to help Dolly. In a way, Dolly reminded Daisy of herself and she admired the girl's determination to pull herself out of the gutter. Yes, she had done a good turn and she knew that Dolly would probably make a success of her life. But most of all Daisy was pleased to have helped Dolly because she was essentially family – Jackie's family.

As these thoughts ran through her head, Daisy was suddenly overwhelmed by a surge of love for Jackie.

How could she have been so selfish for all these years? He was her sole support, her great love and he had never ceased loving her.

Daisy sipped her sherry and smiled. Yes, she thought, there is no doubt that when he went back to Australia he knew that Daisy would eventually follow him. He knew that he had to lure her away from British society life to reclaim his love. Daisy knew that he was waiting for her there on his mother's farm. And now she was going to meet him there in a few months' time.

33

The Final Step

When Daisy disembarked at Sydney Harbour, she was struck by how much the place had changed since the day she had arrived in Australia so many years before. She chuckled at the memory of herself as a young missionary protégée finding herself in Pearly's whore-house. How wild it all seemed then!

Now the place was gradually getting more civilised. Brick buildings were replacing the wooden shacks and the people walking about on the streets looked well dressed and generally healthy and well-to-do.

Daisy settled in to her hotel room and fell asleep early that night. Many months on board the ship had been all very wearing. She was beginning to feel her age. Occasionally she had painful twinges in her chest and back but she ignored them. She had always been a healthy person and she had no reason to think she would not remain so for the rest of her life. Tomorrow she would set out for Jackie's homestead. She reck-oned that it would take four days to get there if she could find a reliable driver to take her.

Just before she drifted into oblivion, she decided that she would write Jackie a letter to let him know that she was coming. She smiled as she thought of his face lighting up when he read it. It would be a good surprise for him, she thought, though it would be what he had been hoping for all along. He knew that in order to win her back properly he had to leave England. It was odd that he had not done so earlier.

They could enjoy their old age together, she and Jackie, in the country where they had found their love again so many years ago.

Three days later Jackie stood ashen-faced in the doorway of his house. In his trembling hands he held a piece of paper.

Rachel had just laid the table for breakfast, her lovely thick hair falling heavily over her shoulder as she placed the pots of jam and butter in the centre and neatly arranged the cutlery on the red-and-white checked tablecloth.

Her slim white hand rested on the swelling bump in front of her as she noticed the look on her husband's face.

'What is it? You look as though you've seen a ghost.' Her voice was high and frightened.

Jackie did not say a word. He shook his head forlornly and sat down at the table. He pushed the letter towards Rachel. 'I never believed she would leave,' he said flatly. 'I never believed she would come here.'

With wild, frightened eyes, Rachel read Daisy's letter. 'She's coming here? But what can we do? She doesn't even know about us . . .' Her voice trailed off into a whimper as she shook her head like a lost limb.

Jackie got up and put his protective arms around her. The difference in their ages was striking; with his white hair and moustache, Jackie could have been her father.

'Now don't you worry, my darling,' he said. 'We'll face this as we have to. You are a lawful wife and soon to be the mother of my child. It is a miracle that you have become pregnant and I thank the lord every day for it.

'I did love Daisy passionately for many many years, but she did not seem to reciprocate in the way I wanted her to and as the years went by she did not even seem to care about me that much either. I spent so much time in her shadow and leading a kind of non-life that coming back here, where I belong, has rejuvenated me. I may be sixty but I feel like a twenty-year-old.' He stroked Rachel's hair softly. 'You make me feel young again,' he said. 'You have given me back my life.'

Rachel smiled and cuddled up to him. 'Oh, how I love you, Jackie,' she whispered. 'I feel safest with you. Even though I am very frightened about seeing Daisy, I know that everything will be all right.'

Two hundred miles away Daisy was mopping her brow and complaining loudly. 'Oh, this bloody heat,' she grumbled. 'Give me an English summer any day.'

Tired and dusty and fed up to the teeth, her warm feelings towards Jackie were gradually being transformed into annoyance at his desertion of her. Why had he made her come all this way? How very selfish of him!

She was now travelling in an open buggy with only a piece of flapping cloth erected above her head to keep out the sun. The driver was an old man who chewed tobacco and occasionally coughed, barking out a loud hawking sound that echoed across the hot dry bush. They stopped for their own and the horses' refreshment at every chance they got but the watering holes were getting further and further apart.

The driver rarely said anything but occasionally he would mutter some curse about the drought that had been plaguing the farmers for several weeks now. What he was actually thinking about, but did not mention to his passenger, was the possibility of being held up by robbers. At the last place they had stopped, the woman had warned him that there had been several reports of people being held up at gunpoint and stripped of their belongings. She said that that area was not considered safe at all at the moment, after several years of relative peace.

'But you know, this kind of country attracts wild people,' the woman said, shaking her head. 'People think that because there are no houses for thousands of miles, then there aren't any laws either. They just go crazy and do just whatever they like.'

She indicated towards Daisy, who was sitting in the corner sipping a cup of iced tea, oblivious to the conversation on the other side of the room. 'Your passenger looks like a fine lady,' the woman said. 'She could attract some greedy looks, wearing clothes like those.'

The driver shrugged. 'I got my gun,' he said. 'I can take care of anybody,' he said, defiantly.

The truth was Daisy was paying him such a large fee to deliver her to her destination that he was prepared to risk anything to get her there! He was a good shot, after all. He had been a strong man in his youth and he prided himself on always getting his passengers to where they wanted to go.

Ahead of them there was a rundown and apparently deserted shack. They had passed several of these places along the way. The shacks were probably first built by hopeful couples dreaming of making a life for themselves and then finding that they had chosen an entirely unsuitable spot for anything other than a meagre living.

Daisy stared at this one, thinking about how the rotting wood and rusting corrugated iron represented the failed dreams of once optimistic young people. At what point had they acknowledged that they were fighting a losing battle? When had they had to admit that they had got it all wrong? How many failed crops had they had to endure before they could accept that they would never get it right?

Life was a long series of shattered hopes and dreams. It was a wonder that people were able to pick themselves up and continue again and again.

But you have to, Daisy told herself in an unusually reflective mood. You have to because the miracle is that more dreams come along. Even after disasters, the fear does not go away, but it eases and becomes tolerable and gradually you live again looking forward and not back. How else would she, Daisy, have withstood the deaths of her beloved Dukey, or her darling sons?

How else could she accept the coldness of her daughter Pearl and her granddaughter Fleur? She could because she could live in hope that everything would be all right in the end, just like in the fairy tales her sister had read her as a child. Everything was going to be all right for her in the end because she would be with Jackie, with whom she started life in that grubby little East End street where they had first met. They were destined to end their lives together, just as they had begun them together.

Sentimental tears came to her eyes as she imagined Jackie's face when he saw her in a day or so. They would hug each other and hold each other tight. Not much will need to be said.

Daisy's eyes suddenly caught a quick movement behind the old shack. The horses pulling the buggy shied violently as a dark figure on a horse emerged from the darkness inside.

'Whoa,' the driver called, trying to calm his spooked horses. He glanced at his rifle lying on the buggy floor at his feet. His hands were busy with the reins. Suddenly he felt afraid.

The horseman cantered out, waving a gun. 'Stop there!' he called, grabbing one of the horses and yanking it to a stop.

Daisy suddenly realized what was going on. She picked up her parasol and waved it threateningly at the man on the horse. 'Stay away,' she warned. 'Don't you meddle with us.'

The robber stared at her for a moment and then threw back his head and laughed. He had bad teeth and the gaps in his mouth made him look more evil than he probably was. Daisy was petrified with fear.

'Hand me your money!' the man ordered, pointing the gun at her. 'And don't bother, old man,' he added, moving the gun towards the driver. 'No funny business here. Do as you're told and you won't get hurt.'

In spite of his earlier bravado, the driver saw the sense in obeying. He gave up trying to reach his rifle and sat praying that he would get off lightly.

Daisy was furious. She stood up in the buggy, causing it to wobble precariously, and threw her parasol at the robber. 'How dare you!' she shrieked.

The robber's horse shied as the parasol hit it on the side of the head. The robber laughed again, a dry sadistic laugh which enraged Daisy even more. She opened the door of the buggy and began to climb down, her eyes blazing.

Suddenly the laughter died in the robber's throat as she saw the large, expensively dressed woman spin around, stop dead in her tracks and keel over. He felt utterly confused. He had not shot her. No one had shot anyone. But there she was, slumped in a heap on the dusty road. He stared at her in astonishment.

Daisy had had a heart attack.

The driver suddenly saw his chance. He lunged for his rifle and pointed it at the robber. 'Now, get away, cobber. You've killed her, you have!' he shouted, suddenly feeling courage return.

To his amazement the horseman looked frightened. Perhaps he had never seen a dead person before for in spite of his bad teeth, the robber was actually very young.

'Now, be off with you!' the driver shouted. 'You've done enough for today.' Now he felt like a father talking to his naughty son.

The horseman backed his horse away slowly. He did not take his eyes off the body lying on the ground until he spun his horse around. For the sake of bravado, he fired a few shots into the air and then galloped away into the hazy distance.

Once he had gone, the driver jumped down and rushed to Daisy. He knew what to do. He had once been shown by a doctor that if you push up and down on someone's chest sometimes they could be revived even when they seemed to be dead.

For a few minutes the man worked hard pressing his hands down on Daisy's chest and pushing as the doctor had shown him how. Miraculously it worked. Slowly Daisy seemed to be reviving. He could feel her heart beating again. The driver was a God-fearing man; now he was even more so. Now he had to get his passenger to where she was headed before she had another heart attack. Then he would get paid. If he did not, and just took her money anyway, his conscience would haunt him for the rest of his life.

No, he had to get her home as she had called it, and thus ensure that she was put into someone else's hands, or at least a decent funeral.

Tears were pouring down Jackie's face. As he became gripped by a vision of the cheeky little Cockney girl skipping in the street so many years before. 'I have been very lonely, it's true,' he said. 'But I want you to know that I have always loved you and always will.' He hesitated. 'It's just that Rachel suddenly offered me something different . . .'

A faint smile appeared on Daisy's lips. She nodded. 'I know,' she said, 'and I can see that you are to have a child of your own. That's something I never gave you.' She winced as a fresh pain shot across her shoulder.

Jackie placed an arm around her and kissed her grey hair. 'You never gave me a child but you gave me a hell of a lot of life,' he said. 'You are life itself.'

Daisy smiled ruefully. 'I am sorry for the way I have treated you at times,' she whispered. 'I love you, Jackie, I always have, and I am very glad that you are to have great happiness when I'm gone. It won't be long now,' she added softly.

Poor Jackie felt torn apart. His love for Daisy was immense, like a massive core inside him. He did not want her to leave him and yet he wanted to live his new life with Rachel as well. Only God could make the decision for him now.

The decision was made that night when Daisy had another heart attack and died in her sleep without a cry. The expression on her face in the morning seemed almost serene.

As Daisy's coffin was lowered into the grave under the gum trees, Jackie swallowed back his tears. He had decided to bury Daisy next to his mother. It seemed right that these two strong women should be side by side but the thought almost overwhelmed him.

Rachel stood next to him. She looked magnificent, so alive and blooming with pregnancy and health. And immensely relieved. She would not have wished Daisy's death upon her but it had solved the crisis that had dominated her life for a few terrible days and threatened to deprive her of the happiness she had found for herself.

Jackie shovelled the earth on to the top of the coffin. It fell in heavy lumps on the wood. One, two, three . . . He felt that he was preserving his memories of life with Daisy forever in that dark hole.

Glancing up, he smiled wanly at Rachel. She was his new life, and bringing forth new life that would unite them. He just hoped that he would live long enough to see this child grow to be an adult.

His thoughts turned back to Daisy. She had not had a bad life, in spite of all her misfortunes. And the reason for that was her amazing ability to enjoy herself whatever she was doing.

Her greatest sadness had been the death of her son Charles and the disappearance of Fred. They never discovered what happened to him. And what with John being a priest, the family had come to a standstill. It seemed so cruel having had three sons, that it should come to that.

Jackie sighed. He realized then that he was hoping that Rachel would give birth to a son to carry on ' own family line.

That evening, after the guests and family

Lena Kennedy

had left, Jackie and Rachel sat outside on the wooden porch of their home watching the reddening sky. Rachel rocked herself gently to and fro in the rocking chair that Jackie had made for her.

'What are you thinking?' asked Jackie, reaching over to take her slim hand.

Rachel smiled. 'I was thinking about Daisy and her three sons. And I was thinking of my son Cedric.' Her voice trembled as she spoke.

There was silence for a few moments. Then Jackie spoke, stroking the back of Rachel's hand as he did so. 'Would you like him to come and live here with us?' he asked. 'I know how much he means to you.'

Rachel looked up at him eagerly but then looked away. 'Oh, it's too far, and too long. He will have forgotten me by now. He probably thinks that my sister and her husband are his parents. I probably mean nothing to him. Or if I do, it will just be as someone who has abandoned him. He probably hates me for doing that.' Her voice rose in pitch as it turned into a sob.

Jackie shook his hand. 'Don't be silly, my darling,' he said. 'Cedric would understand that you had to leave to seek work and that you found happiness with me. Now that you are settled, with your own home why don't you write to your sister and suggest that he come out here to join you? I'm sure your sister has brought him well, but a boy should be with his mother.' He squeezed her hand. 'And I believe a mother should be with her boy.'

Rachel's face lighted up at the realization that it was

possible to have her son with her. That he might even want to be with her.

'I'll do it tomorrow,' she said, a broad smile spreading across her face. 'I'll write to my sister tomorrow and ask if Cedric would like to join us here.'

So it was that several months later a young fair-haired boy set off on a steamer on his way to join his mother and stepfather and new baby half-brother in Australia. In a large leather suitcase he had all his worldly possessions including a watch and photograph which had also belonged to the father he had never known.

Young Cedric Smith was unaware that he was heading for an Australian homestead where his grandmother lay buried under the gum trees. He was also unaware that one day he would learn that he was the holder of the grand title of the Duke of Beauclair, which had come down to him as the only surviving male descendant of Dukey, Daisy's husband. For lying in a wooden drawer in Guernsey was his father Fred's journal which he had kept most of his life. It would not be long before the truth about popular Fred 'Smith', who had won Guernsey's heart, became known.

And so we leave them all. Daisy's family had spread across the world like Eve's apples but some of the seeds were already returning to the places where they had been sown.

Do you wish this wasn't the end?

Join us at www.hodder.co.uk, or follow us on
Twitter @hodderbooks to be a part of our community
of people who love the very best in books and reading.

Whether you want to discover more about a book
or an author, watch trailers and interviews, have the
chance to win early limited editions, or simply browse
our expert readers' selection of the very best books,
we think you'll find what you're looking for.

And if you don't,
that's the place to tell us what's missing.

We love what we do, and we'd love you to be part of it.

www.hodder.co.uk

 @hodderbooks

HodderBooks

HodderBooks